Tempt the Stars

A CASSIE PALMER NOVEL

KAREN CHANCE

A SIGNET SELECT BOOK

SIGNET SELECT
Published by the Penguin Group
Penguin Group (USA) LLC, 375 Hudson Street,
New York, New York 10014

USA | Canada | UK | Ireland | Australia | New Zealand | India | South Africa | China
penguin.com
A Penguin Random House Company

First published by Signet Select, an imprint of New American Library,
a division of Penguin Group (USA) LLC

First Printing, October 2013

ISBN 978-0-451-41905-7

Printed in the United States of America
10 9 8 7 6 5 4 3

To the readers who helped this series make it all the way to book six! As a thank-you, please see my Web page, karenchance.com, for two novella-length stories written to accompany this book. They are prequels entitled "A Family Affair" and "Shadowland." Neither is required for understanding or enjoying this novel, but they're fun, they're free, and they give more insight into certain areas of Cassie's crazy world. Enjoy, and thank you for reading!

Chapter One

"You gots big."

The small voice came from the even smaller girl in the doorway. She was hard to see, shimmering in the night like the moonbeams falling through her, and over-written by the hazy, graffiti snarl of ghost trails weaving through the air. I felt some of the muscles in my neck unclench.

And then tense back up when a too-loud voice called from a nearby room, "Cassie?"

I refrained from jumping—just. Abrupt movements might scare her, and I couldn't afford that now. "Be right there," I said softly, smiling reassuringly at the ghost girl.

"What?" the voice asked, louder this time.

I looked behind me to see the wild white head of my partner in crime, Jonas Marsden, poking out of an office door. With the crazy hair and the pink cheeks and the Coke bottle glasses, he looked like Einstein on acid. But, despite appearances, he deserved his position as the de facto leader of the magical world. Jonas headed up the powerful Silver Circle, the largest organization of magic workers on earth.

But great mages are still human, and Jonas' ego wasn't taking the aging thing well. Like when he refused to put a hearing spell on himself because the rest of us just talked too softly. Unfortunately, the same couldn't be said for him.

"There's no need to whisper," he bellowed. "I assure you, the shield will hold."

"So you keep telling me." He was talking about the sound-deadening spell he'd cast to keep any noise we made from filtering out into the rest of the house. That was kind of important, since we were hovering on train-wreck territory here. Of course, that pretty much described my life lately.

My name is Cassie Palmer, and I'm the newly crowned Pythia, aka the world's chief seer. That sounds a lot more impressive than it is, since so far it's mostly involved giving taxi rides through time to strange people, in between almost getting killed. As I was currently a couple of decades back, trying to rob my old vampire master along with a guy who made eccentric look boring, today was pretty average.

But my nerves didn't think so.

Maybe that's why the spotted mirror over the fireplace showed me short blond curls that looked like I'd been running nervous fingers through them, a face pale enough to make my freckles stand out starkly, and wide, startled blue eyes. And a T-shirt that proclaimed *Good girls just never get caught*.

Let's hope so, I thought fervently.

Fortunately, as vampire courts went, this one was pretty lax, being run by a guy who had been the Renaissance equivalent of white trash. But Tony had one hard-and-fast rule: nobody missed dinner. I wasn't sure why, because vampires don't need to eat—food, anyway. And most don't, since any below master level, the gold standard for vamps, have nonworking taste buds.

Maybe it was tradition, something he'd done in life and still clung to in death. Or maybe he was being his usual asinine self and just wanted to enjoy his dinner in front of a bunch of people who mostly couldn't. Either way, it meant that Jonas and I should have an hour before anybody interrupted us.

Assuming the spell held, anyway.

Jonas didn't look too worried. "You could dance an Irish jig in here," he boasted, "in clogs, and no one would hear."

"No, but they might feel the reverberations—"

"In this?" He gestured around at the creaks of Revolution-era floorboards, the lash of rain against centuries-old windows, and the intermittent lightning that cracked the sky outside, sending shadows leaping across original plaster walls. Tony lived in a historic farmhouse in the Pennsylvania countryside, which was usually picture-postcard pretty.

This wasn't one of those times.

"Or scent us," I added.

"From across the house?" Jonas scoffed. "They're not superhuman."

I blinked. "Well, actually—"

"You give your vampires too much credit, Cassie," he told me severely. "In a contest between them and a good mage, always bet on the mage!"

Well, that's what I'm doing, I was going to point out. But I didn't because I wanted him to *shut up already*. I'm not usually twitchy, but then, I don't usually try to burglarize the booby-trapped office of a vampire mob boss, either. Not that I was doing that now. That was Jonas' thing. I was here for something else.

"Okay," I said, glancing nervously back at the girl.

Mercifully, she was still there, even a bit more substantial now. The old doll she dragged around by the hair had taken on a pinkish hue, and her dress, part of which disappeared through the floor, was now a pale shade of blue. I let out a breath I hadn't known I'd been holding.

The ghost's name was Laura and we'd played together as kids, back when I called this place home. Only I'd grown up and she . . . well, she never would.

It's one of the hard facts about ghosts: when you die, you pretty much stay the same way you were in life. Meaning if you're a one-armed man, you're going to be a one-armed ghost; it's just the way the energy manifests. Mostly, they learn to roll with it *Beetlejuice* style, throwing severed heads at unsuspecting tourists—the ghostly term for cemetery visitors—or trailing disemboweled intestines after them like a gory train.

Humor tends to take on a macabre bent after death.

But the downside is that, if you die at five years old, you stay five. You might learn new things, acquire new skills, even gain wisdom of a sort. But it's a kid's wisdom. You don't suddenly start thinking like an adult.

Even after more than a hundred years you don't.

That was a problem, since I needed information, and I needed it badly. Specifically, I needed to talk to my mother, who had once been Tony's guest, too. But who had died when I was younger than Laura appeared now.

Of course, visiting a dead woman should be easy enough for a time traveler, right? Only I never get easy. I'd spent the better part of a week looking for her, and come up with zilch. But I *had* to find her; a friend was in trouble and Mom was the only one who might know how to help him. And there was a damned good chance that Laura knew where she was.

But if I remembered right, getting her cooperation was likely to be tricky.

"Hey, Laura—" I began casually.

"What's he doing?" she asked, dragging her dolly over into the wedge of light coming out of the office.

"Nothing. It's fine," I whispered, trying to keep her out here, where we could talk in private.

So, of course, she went right on in.

I closed my eyes.

I've been able to talk to ghosts for as long as I can remember, far longer than I've been doing my current crazy job. But it's like with people—they talk to you only when they want to. Of course, they usually want to, since most ghosts are confined to a single place and don't get many visitors. Well, many who notice them, anyway. So if Jonas hadn't been here, I'd probably have been getting my ear chewed off.

But he was, and of the two of us, he was clearly the more interesting.

I accepted the inevitable and followed her inside.

Jonas must have done some dismantling, because nothing shot, stabbed, or grabbed me as I passed through the door. He looked pretty okay, too, if you ignored his habit of picking up random things and sticking them in the billowing mass he called hair. Or, in this case, on.

"He looks like Honeybun." Laura giggled. She was talking about my childhood pet rabbit, the one we'd basically shared since animals can sense ghosts a lot better than people can.

And she wasn't wrong.

"Did you find something?" Jonas asked, looking up from sorting through the mess on the desk. And sporting two outrageous tufts of white hair escaping from either side of an old fedora. It didn't match his outfit, and he hadn't had it on when we arrived. But I'd already discovered that trying to figure out Jonas only made my head hurt, so I mostly didn't.

"He's just fluffy."

"I beg your pardon?"

"Uh, no. Not yet," I told him, trying to surreptitiously shoo Laura back out the door.

She crawled under the desk instead.

"Done already?" Jonas asked, looking at me over the tops of his glasses as I crawled after her.

"Uh, yeah."

"Are you certain you didn't overlook anything? It's quite small, you know."

"Pretty sure."

What he wanted wasn't in the outer office. I knew that because I knew where it was, but I needed him to take a few minutes to find it. Minutes that I could use to pry some secrets out of Laura. But Jonas wasn't looking like he felt like giving them to me. For once, Jonas was looking focused.

"This is no time for games, Cassie," he said sternly, as Laura crawled through his legs.

"Couldn't agree more," I muttered, grabbing for her.

Only to have her go abruptly less substantial, and my hands to pass right on through. And grab Jonas' calf instead. "Is there a problem?" he asked dryly.

Yes, although the fading wasn't it. Laura's senses didn't work as well when she wasn't all there, so to speak, and she was curious enough to be back any second. The problem was worse than that.

The problem was that she thought I wanted to play.

"No, no, wait—oh, shit," I hissed as she blinked completely out of sight.

"What?" Jonas tensed, staring around. "What is it?"

Laura giggled and reappeared over by the threadbare plaid sofa, where Tony parked his guests so he could watch them squirm on the tough old springs. "Can't catch me!" she said, throwing out the usual challenge.

It had been fun when I was a child and didn't have anything better to do. It was less so now. "No, listen—"

"I *am* listening," Jonas said impatiently, as she disappeared again.

Damn it!

I crawled out from under the desk. "Cassie, what—"

"I'll be back in a second," I told him, through gritted teeth.

"Even for a Pythia, you're acting a bit crazed," he said mildly as I stomped out.

Not half as crazed as I was going to be if I didn't find a certain playful ghost, I thought grimly, staring around the outer room.

Nothing stared back, except for an old portrait on the wall, some glowering relative of the family that used to own this place before Tony decided he wanted it. It was limned with moonlight, like everything else in here, which was a problem. When faded, ghosts were little more than silver smudges, and damned hard to spot in a chiaroscuro of old furniture, stuffy portraits, and leaping shadows. Lightning flashed outside, making the whites of the painted eyes stand out creepily.

"No fair hiding," I called tensely.

But it looked like I was the only one who thought so.

This really wasn't going to be easy. And what else was new? I thought savagely. If there was one thing I'd learned in the last three months, it was that nothing ever was. It was like living in Murphy's Law.

Only no.

That would be a step up.

According to Murphy, if something can go wrong, it will. But that wouldn't work for my life. I needed a new rule. Cassie's rule. Something along the lines of "if something can't go wrong, because it is completely impossible for it to happen in the first place, it will somehow manage to go wrong anyway."

Case in point: most people would agree that having one's father killed by a vampire mob boss was kind of unlikely. And that having the soul of said father end up trapped in an enchanted paperweight, because the vampire was an asshole who wanted to gloat over his former servant for as long as possible, was just plain silly. Add in the fact that the fate of the world might now hinge on that paperweight and the spirit it held and the whole thing edged into the ludicrous. And if the magical community managed to lose said all-important paperweight, because said bastard of a vampire ran off to Faerie with it . . . well. I don't even know if they have a word for that.

But they need one. Because it happened anyway. Just like that, to me.

See the kind of thing I'm dealing with here?

But right now retrieving the paperweight of doom was Jonas' problem. He was the one trying to save a world. I wasn't that ambitious. I was just trying to save a friend.

And it wasn't going so great.

I gave up on subtlety and pulled the world's ugliest necklace out of my T-shirt.

A second later, a ghost appeared, like a genie from a bottle. Only this genie was wearing cowboy chic and looking pretty spooked. "No," he told me flatly. "No way, no how. Don't even *think* about—"

"I don't have a lot of time here," I whispered harshly. "And she can do this for hours. We had a game that lasted a whole week once."

"And that's my problem how?" he asked, glancing around nervously. "Damn, it's worse than I remembered. This whole place is dripping with ectoplasm."

"You know there's no such thing," I said impatiently. The ghost's name was Billy Joe, and despite being among the life-challenged himself, he didn't know crap about death. Maybe because he spent eternity watching cheesy old movies and driving me crazy.

We'd met when I was seventeen, and accidentally bought the necklace he haunted as a birthday gift for my governess. She'd ended up with some unhaunted hankies instead, and I got a nineteenth-century Irish gambler with a big mouth and a yellow streak. Some days, I still think she came out ahead.

"Oh, really?" Billy asked, his usual sarcasm overwritten by a tinge of panic. "Stop looking around like a human and check out Ghost Vision for a change!"

His tone gave it capitals when it was really just the way seers look at the world. Some people are double-jointed; we're double-sighted, with that second set of eyes the kind that focuses on the spirit world. I usually tried to tamp it down, since watching others tends to make it more likely that they're going to watch you back, and there's some scary stuff out there. But it didn't look like I was going to be finding Laura any other way.

"See what I mean?" Billy demanded, when I switched over. Only now, instead of a semitransparent cowboy in a ruffled shirt and a Stetson, he was a shining green column of vaguely cowboy-shaped smoke. And less distinct, instead of more as should have been the case, because he'd been right—the whole room glowed with the same eerie color.

It wasn't just that the farmhouse's previous owners had met a messy end. This place had started out as an Indian burial mound long before anybody ever built on it, and after that had been a battlefield in the Revolutionary War. And then there were the various rivals Tony had dragged back through the years, most of whom had ended up never leaving. And the vengeful spirits that had followed a few of the vamps home, wanting a little post-carnage payback. The final result was basically ghost central, with the glowing trails they left so thick on the floor and walls and ceiling that the whole room pulsed neon.

"You know the guys around here hate other ghosts," Billy said, whipping his head around at some sound I couldn't hear. "Like, really, really hate them!"

"This is supposed to be sacred ground," I pointed out. "The original owners didn't like the newbies, and they've been battling it out ever since."

"Yeah, well, they can battle it out without me," Billy said. "I'm done." And he started to disappear back into his necklace, which, since he haunted it, was neutral ground.

At least he did until I hauled him back out again.

"Laura won't hurt you," I said, wrestling him for control. "She's one of the sweetest ghosts I ever met. She just likes to play."

"Yeah, I bet. With my bones, if I had any!"

"She isn't like that!"

"Sure. 'Cause when the innocent little girl shows up in a horror flick, it's always a *good* thing!"

"This isn't a movie!" I told him, and wrenched the necklace back.

"Okay. Okay, sure. She's fine. She's wonderful. But what about the others?"

He had a point. The house was a war zone the humans never saw, as generations of spirits made and broke alliances, chased and occasionally cannibalized one another, and generally continued in death the battles they'd fought in life. And like in battles everywhere, the weak didn't survive for long.

"I don't want you to risk yourself," I told him honestly. "Just take a look around; see if she'll talk to you. You know what I need."

"Yeah, your head examined!" Billy snapped. "She's a *ghost*—it's not like she's going anywhere. You could find her in our own time, without the risk—"

"Don't you think I thought of that?" I hissed. "The house is empty in our time. Nobody trusts Tony's people—"

"Can't imagine why," Billy said sarcastically.

"—so they've been portioned out to other houses where they can be watched. Ever since he turned traitor, this place has stood empty. And without human energy to feed off of—"

"Ghosts go into hibernation mode," he finished for me.

He ought to know; he was as active as he was only because I let him draw energy from me. Other ghosts did the same, on a much smaller scale, from anybody intruding into their territory, because humans shed living energy all the time, like skin cells. That was why ghost sightings were usually reported in cemeteries or old houses. It wasn't just because their bodies often ended up there. It was because ghosts who originated elsewhere had a much harder time feeding enough to stay active.

"I can't find her at Tony's in our day," I told him. "And every time I try going back in time alone, I almost get caught. This may be my only chance." He looked like he wanted to argue, which Billy could do every bit as long as Laura could hide. But I didn't have time for that, either. "Billy, *please*. I don't know what else to do!"

He scowled. "That's not fair."

And it really wasn't. We sniped and argued and bitched at each other all the time, worse than an old married couple. And that was okay; that was standard in the families both of us had grown up in. But we didn't handle the softer emotions so well, because we hadn't encountered them too often.

Billy had been part of a raucous family of ten kids, and while I got the impression that his parents had been affectionate to a degree, there had been only so much to go around. And he'd often been lost in the shuffle. And as for me . . .

Well, growing up at Tony's had been a lot of things, but affectionate wasn't really one of them.

As a result, both of us preferred to stand aloof from the softer stuff, or to ignore it entirely. So yeah, teary-eyed pleading was kind of cheating. But I was desperate.

Billy made a disgusted sound after a minute and looked heavenward. Why, I don't know. He'd been actively avoiding it for something like a hundred and fifty years now. Then he took off without another word, but with an irritated flourish that let me know that I'd pay for this eventually.

That was okay. That was fine.

I'd worry about the fallout later.

Right now I just needed to *find her*.

"Come on," I wheedled, trying to sound calm and sweet. "I'm out of practice."

Nothing. Just a dark, echoing room, crossed and criss-crossed by ghost trails. So thick and so confusing that the Sight was no damned good at all.

"Damn it, Laura!"

And, finally, someone giggled.

It was hard to tell where it came from over the sound of the wind and rain, but patience had never been Laura's strong suit. A second later, there was an extra flutter next to the long sheers by a window. I lunged as she ran, too relieved to be careful, and slipped on a rug. And ended up falling straight through her.

"No fair fading!" I gasped, hitting hardwood.

She laughed, skipping merrily through the half-open door and into the hall as I scrambled to my feet. But she nodded. "No fading."

"No foolies?" I asked, following her. Because otherwise, it didn't count.

"No foolies," she agreed solemnly.

And then she stepped through a wall.

Technically that wasn't fading. It was also her patented get-out-of-jail-free card, since the child I had been couldn't follow. It was why she'd won, nine times out of ten, when we played this game. But I'd learned a few things since the last time, and a second later, I stepped through the wall after her.

Well, not exactly stepped. I shifted, moving spatially through the power of my office, just like I'd moved through time to get us here. It was a good trick, as Laura's face showed when I rematerialized a couple feet behind her. "How'd you do that?" she asked, eyes bright.

And then she took off again, vanishing through a bookcase.

I went after her, trying to remember the layout of these rooms as I ran. Because unlike Laura, I do not go incorporeal when I shift. I just pop out of one place and into another, and popping into the middle of a chair or a table wouldn't be fun. So my nerves were taking a beating even before I pelted across another room, shifted through a fireplace, barely missed skewering myself on a poker, and darted out into the hall—

And caught sight of Laura skipping straight through the middle of a couple of men headed this way.

Or no, I thought, suddenly frozen.

Not men.

At least, not anymore.

They were coming down a gorgeous old spiral staircase, one of the house's best features. It was made out of oak but had been burnished to a dark shine by the oil on thousands of hands over hundreds of years. But it didn't hold a candle to the vampires using it. Well, one of them, anyway.

Mircea Basarab, Tony's elegant master, would have probably made my heart race in plain old jeans. I say probably because I'd never seen him in anything so plebian, and tonight was no exception. A shimmering fall of midnight hair fell onto shoulders encased in a tuxedo so perfectly tailored he might have just stepped out of a photo shoot. The hair was actually mahogany brown, not black as it looked in the low light, but the broad shoulders, trim waist, and air of barely leashed power were no illusions.

Still, he looked a little out of place in a house where his host was lucky if he remembered to keep his tie out of the soup. Since Mircea never looked out of place anywhere, I assumed there was a reason he had decided to go all out. Probably the same one that had Tony forcing a family on a strict diet to sit through a feast every night.

For a second I wished I could have seen Tony, his three-hundred-plus pounds stuffed into a penguin suit, for once as supremely uncomfortable at one of his dinners as everyone else. But I wasn't going to. Because the vamp at Mircea's side, the one with the dark curly hair and the goatee and the deceptively kind brown eyes, wasn't Tony.

Shit, I thought viciously, and backed swiftly into the room I'd just run out of.

Which was absolutely the right thing to do.

At least it was until they followed me in.

In a panic, I shifted—also the right move, since there were no other doors out of there. But shifting in a split second in a panic isn't easy, and this time I didn't manage it. Or, rather, I didn't *completely* manage it.

Son of a bitch! I thought desperately, finding myself trapped in the fireplace as two high-level master vampires walked into the room.

Chapter Two

I tried shifting again but went nowhere, almost as if I was stuck. Which might have been because I was, I realized a second later. Half of my body was in the next room, having shifted back through the fireplace all nice and proper. But the other half . . .

The other half was still on this side of the wall, protruding through the blackened old bricks from just above the waist.

I twisted and turned desperately but went nowhere. And then I tried to shift again in a frenzy. But half a dozen attempts in quick succession only left me dizzy and with a serious desire to throw up. And no freer than I'd ever been.

A glance down at my waist showed that at least I hadn't been cut in two, like an inept magician's assistant, which is what I'd always assumed happened in these cases. Instead, an annoyed-looking bunch of bricks had puddled up around me in a working ring, like commuters jostling for space they weren't finding. And giving off the subtle grind of stone on stone in the process.

I freaked a little at that, because if it was audible to my ears, it probably sounded like an avalanche to the vamps. But when I looked up, only the fireplace screen was looking back at me. Literally, since it was one of those fake Tiffany things with a hundred colors and a bunch of bug-eyed insects all over it.

But there were no vamps, bug-eyed or otherwise. Amazingly, they hadn't noticed my struggles, any more than they had my heartbeat or my panicked breathing. Either the darkness in the big old fireplace or the tackiness of the screen had shielded me from sight. And I guessed the storm had covered any noise I made, or else I was still barely inside the sound shield Jonas had laid. He'd linked it into a section of the house wards, and I wasn't sure how far that extended.

Not that it mattered. Because sight and hearing aren't the only senses that are stronger for a vamp. And despite the temperature, I was sweating like a—

"It's the girl, isn't it?" the second vampire said abruptly.

I stopped struggling for a second, when it felt like even my heartbeat froze.

"Cassandra." Mircea nodded, handing his companion a drink. "She plays all over the house."

And then it started back up again.

Of course the house smelled like me, I thought dizzily. Of course it did. My younger self slept at the other end of the hall; why wouldn't it?

I swallowed and wondered, not for the first time, what the life expectancy was for Pythias.

Why didn't I think it was very high?

"No. I meant, that's why you're here," the other vamp said, dark eyes narrowed in suspicion.

That wasn't unusual. He could be as charming as any of his kind, but unlike with Mircea, it wasn't his job. His name was Kit Marlowe and he'd long ago transitioned from spying for Her Majesty, queen of England, to doing the same for another queen, this one in charge of the dreaded North American Vampire Senate.

Well, dreaded to most people, including most U.S. vamps because it served as their less-than-benevolent government. But for me, it didn't seem quite so scary anymore, maybe because I was dating one of the senators. The one who was currently looking with amused tolerance at Kit.

"What gave you that idea?"

"Don't be coy. I've seen you put less effort into charming countesses—"

"Who normally require little effort," Mircea murmured, sipping brandy.

"—than into that child. 'Why, isn't that a pretty painting, Cassie? However did you do it?'" Marlowe mimicked.

"The colors were quite nice," Mircea protested, lips quirking.

Kit didn't look so amused.

"What is your interest?" he asked bluntly.

"She's a charming child."

"She's a *seer*." Marlowe's eyes narrowed. "The real thing, by all accounts, but that is hardly enough to warrant camping out in the wilderness—"

"It is less than an hour to Philadelphia."

"The *wilderness*," Marlowe insisted, looking around disparagingly. "And in any case, if you wanted to see the blasted vamp, why not order him to your court? Why come here at all, much less for almost *a year*?"

"Ah. Is that what has your lady ordering you to check up on me?" Mircea asked, settling back into a dark red leather armchair. He still looked amused, although whether he actually was or not was anyone's guess.

His companion remained standing, and tensed up slightly. "I needed to ask you about a number of—"

"Now who's being coy?"

Marlowe dropped it. "Well, if she is curious, who can blame her? No one *does* this."

"Many masters visit their servants."

"Servants who live in Paris; servants who live in Rome. Not servants who live in the backwoods of Pennsylvania in a dump!" Marlowe gestured around, the small gold earring he wore in one ear flashing in a lightning burst. "What do you expect me to tell her?"

"That I am attending to family matters that do not concern her."

"Oh yes. Yes, that will go over well," Marlowe said sarcastically.

"It should. It's the truth."

"And you're not going to offer any further explanation, any more details," Marlowe said, prowling nearer to the fireplace.

"I don't see why she would expect them," Mircea commented as I started struggling again. "I am not a newborn who must be tended, and this has nothing to do with her."

"Nothing?" Marlowe spun, just before he reached me. And just before he would have gotten close enough for a good look over the screen.

I swallowed hard.

I was twenty-four.

And I was already too old for this.

"That is what I said."

Marlowe pounced. "Then the fact that her mother was Elizabeth O'Donnell, the Pythia's former heir, is irrelevant, is it?"

Mircea's head cocked, and his eyes narrowed slightly. "Now, I wonder. Is the mole in my family or Antonio's?"

"I don't need a mole," Marlowe said shortly, and drank scotch.

"Ah, a listening device, then. And yes, it would be simple enough here. Antonio's mages are not the best."

"They're shite," Marlowe said bluntly, "and that isn't the point. You have a line on a possible Pythia—"

"That's rather reaching, wouldn't you say?"

"No, I would not say! And you didn't tell us!"

Marlowe's tone was as accusatory as the words, but Mircea didn't look concerned. "As yet, there is nothing to tell. Cassandra's mother was heir to the Pythian throne at one time, yes, but she was removed—"

"But not for lack of ability! For consorting with that Roger Palmer character—"

"Whose capabilities are unknown."

"He worked for your servant. You ought to know them well enough!"

"Yet, nonetheless, I do not." Mircea's tone was calm, but then, it always was. More tellingly, his eyes stayed brown. Marlowe wasn't getting to him. "And as he and Elizabeth are now deceased, we may never do so. Leaving Cassandra's talents in question."

"Yet you decided to meet her anyway."

"Would you not have?"

"And to gain her trust."

"Only prudent."

Marlowe crossed his arms. And even though I could no longer see his face, the set of his shoulders told a story all on its own. "Only prudent, if you had told us. Only prudent if you hadn't shown, how shall we say, some persistent interest in the Pythian office before now."

I'd been trying to get a hand on the ring of jostling bricks, to force the damned things open. Only to have them slide through my fingers as my head abruptly jerked up. And then even more abruptly jerked down again, when I felt someone's hand on my butt.

That heart attack I'd been postponing for a few months now might have taken that moment to show up and say hi, except that the hand was not followed by a crushing blow or the sound of an alarm. But by a second hand on my other hip, and then by a sharp tug. My spine would have liquefied in relief, if it hadn't been busy being pulled out of my body.

It had to be Jonas; one of Tony's guys would have ripped me in two by now. Not that it didn't feel like he was trying. And worst of all, he was making it hard to concentrate on what the vamps were saying.

And I wanted to hear this.

"How many gifts," Marlowe asked, over the sound of

grinding rock, "have you given through the years? How many visits have you made?"

"Not enough, apparently." The tone was dry. "We remain as estranged from the seat of power as ever. If the consul would give up a bit of that stiff-necked pride and pay a visit herself, it might do more than any gift—"

"Do not take me for a fool, Mircea!" Marlowe said, striding forward and bending down, slapping his hands on both arms of Mircea's chair. "I've known you too long! You're the best ambassador among the senates. No one is questioning that. But you didn't go in your senate capacity, did you? You went alone, quietly, with no retinue and with no mention in the senate records. You went for *you*, not for us, and I want to know—"

"And what I want," Mircea said, his voice suddenly going flat, "is to know how you manage to run your department when all of your efforts appear to be occupied following me."

"What do you expect?" Marlowe demanded, but he backed off slightly. "You're her most powerful servant. Of course she is concerned at the thought of you allying yourself with a possible Pythia. It's the sort of move that could put you in an inviolable position." He hesitated, and then came out with it. "It's the sort of move that could allow you to make a bid to replace her."

"I have no such ambition," Mircea said, more evenly.

"And if you did?" Marlowe asked pointedly. "What would you say then?"

"If you have already made up your mind to doubt me, why ask?"

"To give you a chance to explain."

"Which I have done. You simply refuse to accept anything I say."

"Because it doesn't make sense! Do you really expect—"

I lost the thread of conversation again, because the stone around me suddenly heated up, and not like a rock on a sunny day. More like lava. Jonas gave a tremendous,

wrenching jerk, and it felt almost like the bricks liquefied for a split second—

And then suddenly hardened again, leaving me
trapped worse than before.

Way worse. Now my head and shoulders were sticking out, but my hands were stuck by my head like I'd
been thrown into the stocks, and my chest was com-
pressed to the point that it was hard to breathe. The
stones went back to their former grind a second later,
louder than ever, being right in my ear. And allowed me
to catch a breath only when the ones directly underneath my chest turned just so.

Which they did about half as much as I needed.

"Urk," I said, staring desperately at the sliver of Marlowe I could still see through the screen.

Hurry up, I thought, but not at Jonas. I could breathe,
sort of. I was okay. I was going to be okay. Probably. And
I wanted to hear—

"—control what you believe," Mircea was saying. "I
see many important people, including the leaders of
other senates—"

"And yet *every* Pythia," Marlowe said doggedly. "Before she was even crowned, in one case, receives a visit,
and not in an official capacity—"

"Official visits are cold and formal. I do my best work
in a more relaxed setting. I cannot charm anyone on behalf of the consul if I do not even know them."

"And yet these visits do not appear to be working,"
Marlowe pointed out.

"Do not appear to be working yet," Mircea said, finishing his drink. "Every Pythia is different—"

"Including the one you visited before joining the senate?"

Unlike Marlowe's other comments, it was said mildly,
almost diffidently, a rapier strike instead of a bludgeon.
And unlike the others, it landed. Mircea's eyes flashed
amber, bright enough to rival the lightning outside, and
Marlowe took a quick step back.

"You have been busy," Mircea hissed.

Marlowe blinked at him, as if he wasn't used to hearing that tone, either. But he recovered fast. "You have to admit, it looks suspicious—"

"It would not have, had you not gone looking for it!"

"It's my job to look for it. And I have a credible witness who saw you—"

"Paying a legitimate visit in broad daylight! Else you would have had no witness to worry you."

Marlowe blinked again at the implication. But then forged ahead anyway. "I wouldn't be worried if I knew why you were there. It could hardly have been on behalf of a consul you did not even know at the time."

"I never said it was."

"Then *why*?"

Yeah, I thought dizzily, why?

And then the stones started to heat up again.

No! I thought, kicking my legs, trying to get Jonas' attention. Not yet!

And got smacked on the butt for my efforts.

Son of a—

Another jerk, and this time, I was up to my neck. Which would have been an improvement, except that now I couldn't breathe at all. There was some agitated grasping going on in a way that would have been overly familiar if I hadn't been about to suffocate. And either the moon had just gone behind a cloud or the room was starting to dim.

That wasn't a great sign, and neither was the blood suddenly pounding in my ears, or the heart fluttering in my chest, or the damned moving bricks, which felt like they were trying to behead me. But the worst part was, I couldn't *hear*.

But it looked like Mircea had recovered, and was back to doing what he always did, soothing frazzled nerves, calming ruffled feathers, getting people to listen. And Marlowe was. The dark eyes were still sharp and still guarded, but his stance had relaxed somewhat, and the intelligent face was thoughtful. He looked like he might be buying it.

Whatever it was, I thought angrily as darkness flooded my vision, making it impossible even to lip read. Not that I could have concentrated enough with the rocks around my neck suddenly going nuclear. I'd have screamed in pain if I'd had the breath, or flailed around had my arms not been trapped like the rest of me. Only that wasn't true a second later, when strong hands grabbed me again, and pulled and yanked and *heaved*—

And thump.

And rattle and *crash*.

And *wheeeeeeeee*, loud enough to threaten my eardrums.

What the hell?

I pried my nose out of a dusty stretch of carpet and saw Jonas' grim face looking down at me for a second. And then he said something—harsh, guttural, frightening— and I decided that maybe I'd hit the floor too hard. Because it looked like the room suddenly came alive.

"Get up!" he barked as an armoire on the far wall threw itself across the room and slammed into the door.

And had a fist punched through it for its trouble.

A lamp hurled after it, barely missing my head as I was hauled to my feet, only to shatter against the impressive pile of furniture piling up at the opening. Another lamp lay splintered on the floor—the rattle and crash I'd heard earlier, I guessed—like maybe I'd kicked it when I came loose. But that still didn't explain—

"Isn't that a ward?" I yelled over the unearthly shriek as we ran through a connecting door into the next room, which was shifting and changing as much as the last one. And flinging its contents behind us.

"Yes," Jonas said abruptly, flattening us against the wall as a four-poster bed squeezed past.

"But . . . I thought . . . you took care of them," I gasped.

"I did!" Jonas said indignantly. "But when one is

forced to exert enough magic to level a small town, one tends to trip even the most inadequate of wards!"

"Sorry?"

Jonas didn't even bother responding to that. He just yanked me through the middle of two overstuffed armchairs that were muscling past and out into the hallway. Only to abruptly jerk me back again.

I didn't understand why until the furniture around us suddenly stopped trying to fit through the connecting door and launched itself at the one to the hall instead. We dodged out of the way and then joined the stream flowing out. Only to see a wall of heavy oak pieces, almost ceiling high, trying to bulldoze a path down the hall to the office.

Trying and failing.

Maybe because someone on the other side was quickly turning them to splinters.

We spun back around to see the same thing happening on the other end of the hall, alongside the fireplace room. Antique pieces and old bits of junk were working in a solid mass, twisting and dodging and trying to hold back massive blows from the other side, which nonetheless kept sending pieces flying back at us. A painting of a woman in nineteenth-century dress was getting batted around the surface of the pile, her comically open mouth looking like she was yelling for help as someone did his best to turn the mountain into a molehill.

And his best was pretty damned good.

The fat lady is singing, I thought numbly, right before Jonas grabbed me.

"What is happening?" he demanded, looking pissed that his impressive display of magic wasn't looking so impressive, after all. "Who is back there?"

"Mircea," I admitted, and Jonas cursed.

"A first-level master? You didn't tell me one of them would be here!"

"I didn't know. And . . . actually . . . it's two. Marlowe's with him," I admitted, glancing behind us. Mircea must have ended up on one side of the hall, when the first wave of animated furniture flooded the corridor, and Marlowe on the other. Which left us caught between the ultimate rock and a hard place, with two furniture dams barely holding back two master vamps and us stuck in the middle.

With nowhere to go.

"I suppose it is too much to hope that you can shift, just at the moment?" Jonas asked dryly.

I shook my head, and he scowled. But he didn't argue with me. He'd been the lover of the former Pythia, and he knew things about the job that most mages didn't. Like that the power of the office might be inexhaustible, but the Pythia herself wasn't. And that a shift, even a spatial one like to get us out to the road, required concentration.

Something that's a little difficult to manage after being almost choked to death.

Instead, he dropped my hand and raised both of his, mumbling a long string of something that made the hair on the back of my neck stand up and his already wild mane go positively electric. And all the doors to all the rooms between us and the furniture dams to slam open. And the contents start to stream out, like reinforcements going to the front lines.

"The instant you can, shift us out of here," he yelled, to be heard over the creak of wood and metal moving in ways the designers never intended, and the high-pitched shriek of the wards. "We'll have to come back for the other!"

"No . . . need," I gasped, trying to will air into my starved lungs.

"What?"

I reached up and yanked off the fedora, which was somehow still sticking to the crackling mass on his head, and fished something out. It was a smallish bronze sphere encased in glass, which glowed faintly when I touched it. "Spelled," I explained breathlessly. "You have to know . . . it's there . . . or it isn't."

Jonas' blue eyes moved from the paperweight to my face, going sharp and squinty along the way. "I assume there's a reason you didn't tell me about this before?"

I licked my lips. "Uh-huh."

"Pythias!" He threw his hands up in a manner that reminded me eerily of Agnes, my predecessor, who would probably have had some trick to get us out of this. But the most I could do was to slide down on my heels, put my arms over my head to cut the noise, and concentrate on recovering.

I only hoped I did it fast, because Jonas hadn't bought us much time. Two first-level masters redecorate quickly, and the rooms were already running out of things to shred. We needed to get out of here.

"Billy," I whispered. "The train is leaving the station."

I didn't get anything back, even though I knew he'd heard me. Billy didn't need ears to pick up on my call; whether he chose to answer it or not was another thing. But he'd sounded eager enough to leave before.

I started to try again, but Jonas grabbed my arm. "Change of plan. When you can shift, take us back to the office."

"What? Why?"

"We have the orb," he explained, less than helpfully. "Isn't that what you wanted?"

He looked exasperated. "Yes, but not to take it out of this time stream! The spirit it contains is the only thing keeping the world's protective barrier in place. To remove it would drop that protection, exactly as our enemy wants!"

"Then hide it somewhere. Someplace where Tony can't find it. Then we can look it up when we get back to our—"

Jonas shook his head. "We have no idea what Tony used it for between now and then."

"To hold down papers?"

"And what else?" Jonas asked severely. "We don't know; therefore we cannot risk removing a piece of a very delicate puzzle. We could inadvertently change history!"

I frowned. "If you're not going to take it and you're not going to hide it, then what are we doing here?"

"I needed to see it, to know what I'm looking for. 'Paperweight' could mean anything—"

"I described it to you!"

"—and to verify that the vampire Antonio had not lied about your father's fate merely to torture you."

Which he totally would have done, I realized. Tony and I had had what you might call a suboptimal relationship. "But he didn't."

"No. For once, it seems, he told the truth. Which means we must return this," Jonas said, shaking the paperweight at me, "lest Antonio realize its importance and alter his actions in the future. Then we may never find it!"

I said something unladylike, which he didn't hear because it was becoming impossible to hear anything. I felt like screaming right along with the wards, if I'd had the breath and if it would have done any good. But it wouldn't—just like using the last of my energy to shift us to the office, where we'd be trapped all over again, because I wasn't going to be doing this twice in close succession. Not the way I felt right now, and not carrying two. And that was assuming I could manage to do it at—

"Cass! Get ready to shift!" Billy's panicked voice cut through the din.

"In a minute," I said irritably, rubbing the back of my neck.

"Not in a minute! *Now*. Now, now, now, now, now, now, now!"

My head came up. "What is wrong with you?"

"You know how you said if I ran into problems to come back? Well, I'm coming back. And I got problems!"

"What kind of problems?"

"What kind you think?" he snapped. "I'm trying to lose 'em, but they know this place better than I do and I think they've finally found a reason to work together—"

"Wait." I glanced around. Narrow corridor; isolated part of the house; nobody around but us and a couple of more-or-less indestructible vampires. "Don't try to lose them."

"What?"

"Just get back here—now."

"You don't get it, Cass. When I said *problem*, I meant—"

"I got it. Just do it." I stood up.

"Cassandra?" Jonas was watching me narrowly. "What is it?"

"Um," I said brilliantly, since explaining this sort of thing usually didn't go well. But it didn't matter because I didn't have time anyway. A second later, a horrible wail cut through the air, making the shrieking wards sound like a melody in comparison.

I whipped my head around, but there was nothing to see. And Jonas didn't look like he'd noticed anything. Until the air suddenly became thick and cold and hard to breathe, and the hallway started to shake perceptibly, and the light fixtures overhead blew out, one after the other in a long line.

"Cassandra?" Jonas said, a little more forcefully this time.

"I think it's time for the midnight express," I said, hoping I hadn't just made a really big mistake.

"And what does that mean?" he demanded.

"It means choo-choo, motherfucker!" Billy screamed, swooping out of the ceiling. And right on his tail was a train, all right—of what looked like every damned ghost on the property.

Holy shit, I didn't say, because I was busy grabbing Jonas and throwing us at the nearest door, just before the unearthly wind slammed into the hallway like a tornado.

We crashed into the floor on the other side as it hit, boiling down the hall like a freight train of fury. Merely the wind of its passing was enough to rip light fixtures off the walls, to puff a week's worth of ashes out of the fireplace, and to send china figurines plummeting to their doom. Half a dozen books went flapping madly through the air over our heads, only to tangle in the wildly twisting drapes as I dragged myself back up.

Jonas lifted his head to stare at me. "What the—"

"Ghosts!" I told him, staggering for the door.

My ankle hurt, my lungs were still crying out for air, and my neck was on fire. But I didn't stick around to assess the damage. I didn't even wait until the storm was over. I stumbled out into the hall with Jonas on my heels, the two of us being buffeted here and there by late-arriving spirits.

And then I stopped for a second in awe.

Because there were no ghost trails here. The corridor in front of us was a solid rectangle of pulsing, angry green. There was no furniture dam anymore, either, just random bits of wood sticking out of the plaster like quills on a porcupine.

There was also no pissed-off vamp.

The one behind us was okay, judging by the renewed sounds of destruction battering the mound. But whoever had been on this end . . . well, I didn't know where he had ended up. But I didn't think it was a good idea to go looking for him.

Because the train was headed back this way.

"Run!" I screamed at Jonas, and sprang for the office door, just as the storm barreled back at us again, flinging a deadly cloud of debris ahead of it. He dove in behind me, damned spry for an old guy, as jagged shards of paneling whipped by outside like knives.

And then he slammed the door.

I stared at him incredulously. *"Ghosts, remember?"*

He looked a little shamefaced. "Right."

And then they were back.

We hadn't even made it into the inner office when Billy zoomed through the door, screeching something I couldn't understand because an infuriated tornado was right on his nonexistent heels. Something tore through the outer office as we dove into the inner one, upending filing cabinets and sending a blizzard of paperwork dancing madly through the air. Jonas leapt for the hat rack, I leapt for him, and Billy grabbed me around the neck, still babbling something.

"What?"

"You owe me, you *so* owe me!"

"Did you get it?"

"Yes, *I'm fine.* Thanks for asking!"

"Billy! Did. You. Get—"

"Yes, damn it, yes! I got it! I got it!"

"Thank you," I told him fervently.

And shifted.

Chapter Three

"Don't," I told Marco, a decade and a half later, when he opened the door to the Vegas hotel suite I called home. "Just . . . don't, okay?"

Marco is my chief bodyguard. He's about six foot five, maybe two hundred and fifty pounds, and built like a freight train. My legs aren't as big around as his arms, which might feel weird except that most *men's* aren't, either. He's a swarthy, hairy, foulmouthed, cigar-munching, example of machismo who is usually covered in weapons he doesn't need because he's also a master vampire.

Which is why it's annoying when he decides to play mother hen.

Not that that appeared to be happening tonight.

"Hadn't planned on it," Marco said, and yanked me inside.

"What's wrong with you?" I asked, because Marco was looking kind of freaked-out. That was worrying on someone who, I strongly suspected, had been assigned to lead my bodyguard because he was the oldest of Mircea's masters. He'd seen it all and he didn't rattle easy.

Although he was kind of looking rattled now.

"We got a problem," he told me grimly.

I shook my head, letting loose a little cloud of Tony's lousy housekeeping. "No."

"What does that mean?"

I'd have thought that was obvious since I was dragging in at two a.m., covered in soot, plaster, and sweat, with a bruised ring around my neck and an all-but-destroyed T-shirt. But apparently not. I edged around him, balancing a cup and a bag of heart-destroying pastries from the coffee shop downstairs, because it wasn't like I was going to live long enough to have to worry about cholesterol.

"It means I've had enough for one night. I'm tired; I'm going to bed. If there's a problem, it can wait until—"

I stopped, because I'd just noticed the living room. It would have been called sunken if it hadn't been on the twenty-second floor of the hotel. It was a tasteful medley of white and blue and yellow, since I'd had a say in redecorating after the last disaster hit. It was also usually deserted, the guards preferring to hang out in the lounge with the pool table and the beer fridge.

But that wasn't true tonight. Tonight, every guard on duty was either sitting in the little conversation area, smoking out on the tiny balcony, or gathered by the bar. It was like a party.

Or maybe a wake; the guys were looking pretty damned grim.

"Why's everybody out here?" I asked Marco, who had followed me down a short flight of stairs.

"'Cause of them in there," he said, hiking a thumb at the lounge. Which I'd just noticed was closed off, with the pocket doors shut tight. I'd never seen them that way; the guys preferred an open floor plan to better keep an eye on me.

But it looked like they felt they could do without an eye on whoever was inside.

"Who's 'them'? I don't have any appointments tonight." At least, I really hoped I didn't. The kind of guest

I got at two a.m. tended to be of the fanged variety, and not the fun kind. "Tell me it's not more senators," I said, because I really, really wasn't up to that.

"I wish."

I sighed and crossed my filthy arms. "Okay. Out with it."

But he didn't come out with it. "Where's Jonas? You're supposed to be with him."

I shrugged. "Home?" I'd dropped him off in the lobby before going for coffee. And it had been a while, since despite the fact that I looked like a war refugee, I'd still had to wait in line.

Vegas.

"Damn it!" Marco looked genuinely put out. No, that wasn't right. Marco looked almost—

The sliding doors opened and a small vamp sidled out, before slamming them dramatically shut behind him. "Refreshments!" he said shrilly.

"What?" Marco glowered at him.

"You heard me," the vamp said, wild-eyed. "They say if they have to wait any longer, that they deserve—"

"I'll tell you what they deserve," Marco said menacingly.

"—something to eat, but you know we don't have any food in the place and I don't know what—" The vamp stopped abruptly, staring at me.

Or, to be more precise, at my small white bakery bag.

"No," I said, trying to hide it behind me. But a second later, it was in his hand anyway.

The guy who had just crossed a room in an eyeblink was named Fred. He looked like an accountant when he stood still long enough—with wispy brown hair and a somewhat portly figure—which was fair, since that's what he had been before getting tapped for guard duty. I still hadn't found out who he'd had to piss off to get stuck with that.

I knew who he was managing to annoy tonight, though.

He saw my expression. "No, no, no!" he said, backing up, his big gray eyes going huge. And then the little weasel ran for it.

"Come back here!" I demanded, but Fred wasn't. Fred was a blur, clutching the bag I'd just stood in line twenty freaking minutes for, and heading for the kitchen.

Only to find me waiting on him when he arrived.

"What—how—shit!" He stared at me, hand over the heart that wasn't going to attack him, since it hadn't beaten in a few hundred years now. "You know I hate it when you do that!"

"Then give me back my stuff!"

"I . . . can't," he said, looking around desperately.

Marco had come in behind him, but he wasn't doing anything, just standing in front of the door with his massive arms crossed, waiting it out.

"Please," Fred said tragically when I grabbed for my property. And then, *"Please! Please! Gaaah! Gaaah!"*

I let go of the bag, because I honestly didn't know what the hell was wrong with him. "What the hell's wrong with him?" I asked Marco.

"He's afraid."

Fred didn't deny it.

"Of what?"

"Of them in there." The thumb hike was backward this time, over his shoulder. But it didn't help, since the shutters partitioning the kitchen from the lounge had been closed, like they were for the formal parties we never had.

"Who in there?"

Marco opened his mouth, but it was Fred who spoke. He was looking in the bag, and he didn't seem happy. Maybe because he'd squashed it in all the agitation, and a smear of red had bloomed like blood on one side.

He grabbed a plate and turned it upside down, dumping out the contents. And then he just stood there, staring at three sadly mushed pastries. "What are *those*?" he demanded.

"What do they look like?" I snapped. Damn it, most of the powdered sugar had come off, and that was the best part.

Big gray eyes lifted to meet mine, with the look of a man seeing his doom. "What did you *buy*?" he squeaked.

"What did you expect?"

"I don't know! They have all kinds of things down there—dainty tea cakes and tiny tarts and *pain au chocolate* and finger sandwiches and those cute little baby macaroons! *Why didn't you get the baby macaroons?*"

"I don't like macaroons."

He stared at me. "What do you mean you don't like macaroons? Everybody likes macaroons!"

"Well, I'm somebody and I don't," I said, reaching for the plate. And getting my hand slapped for my trouble.

"But . . . but I can't serve them *these*," he said, a little madly. "And room service takes forever and there's always a line downstairs and what am I supposed to *do*?"

"You're supposed to tell me what's going on before I strangle you," I said ominously.

But Fred was past that. Fred looked like he thought strangling would be a step up. He was hunched over the plate, his eyes darting around the kitchen's gleaming surfaces as if he thought a tea service and accompanying canapés were sure to appear somewhere.

"Oh God . . ." he said miserably when this did not happen.

I looked at Marco, expecting a little sanity. Only to find him regarding the plate, too. "Maybe you could . . . fluff 'em up," he said, apparently serious.

"Fluff 'em up? *Fluff 'em up?*" Fred hissed. "They're jelly doughnuts! There's nothing to fluff!"

"They're *my* doughnuts," I said, reaching for the plate again. And had it snatched away.

"Have an apple," Fred snarled, tossing me one from a bowl.

"If I'd wanted an apple, I wouldn't have bought doughnuts!"

"Well, that's too bad," he hissed, hunched over my dinner like Gollum with the ring. "Because I'm not going out there and telling a bunch of mumble—"

"What?"

"—that we don't have anything for them. I'm not, do you hear?"

Not really. "A bunch of what?" I asked, for clarification.

The darting eyes made a return, and his tone was barely audible. "Wumble," he said reverently.

"What?"

He looked up, a faintly annoyed frown creasing his forehead. "Wichel!"

"What's a wichel?"

Marco sighed. "Witches," he translated.

"Witches?" I frowned.

"Yes!" Fred said vehemently. "Witches! Witches! Wi—" He suddenly realized he'd been yelling, and bit off the word. And crouched down behind the kitchen table so, I suppose, Marco and I would be the better targets. "Witches," he whispered.

I put a hand to my head. I just wanted a doughnut. A sweet, squashy, jelly-filled reminder that there were good things in life, however much fate seemed determined to deprive me of them.

"What witches?" I finally asked.

"The coven kind," Marco said dourly. "They showed up almost an hour ago, demanding to see you."

"Did they have an appointment?"

Marco looked faintly uncomfortable. "No."

"Then why did you let them in?"

"'Cause they appeared on the balcony and let themselves in through the wards?" Fred asked, peeking over the table and prompting Marco to shoot him a look.

"Because one doesn't just tell a bunch of coven leaders to get lost!" Marco bit out.

"If they don't have an appointment, you do," I said grimly.

I wasn't trying to be inhospitable, but seriously, this shit had to stop. Morning, noon, and night, ever since my not-exactly-a-coronation, it had been the same thing: senate leaders, Circle leaders, Pack leaders, press-trying-to-pretend-to-be-leaders of something, anything, that would get them in, all showing up. To gawk at me. And in the case of the latter, to get the story of the century.

And the worst thing was, it wasn't even mine.

Yeah, I was the Pythia the vamps had pulled out of the woodwork a few months ago, who nobody knew anything about. And yes, that would have been front-page news in any situation. In any *other* situation.

But, suddenly, nobody cared that I had been brought up by Tony the Louse instead of being carefully nurtured at the Pythian Court. Nobody was bothered by the fact that I'd therefore received practically no training for the job I was supposed to be doing. They didn't even seem to care that an untutored vampire's protégée was occupying one of the most important positions in the magical world while said world was being consumed by a major war.

No.

They only cared about one thing.

They only cared about my mother.

You see, it wasn't my dad's soul that had put that paperweight at the top of Jonas' Christmas list. It was the fact that, shortly before he and Mom and their Buick were blown into a million pieces, my mother had done something that had linked her soul to his. So when Pop's spirit was captured in the magical snare Tony had devised, hers went along with it.

And hers was kind of a big deal.

Because hers belonged to a goddess.

Yeah, I know. It just gives the whole crazy mess that little extra touch of madness, doesn't it? I spent my childhood thinking that Tony had taken me in out of the goodness of his cold, slimy heart, after my parents were killed in a tragic accident, only to find out that he'd arranged the accident. One that had killed not only my father, but the creature the world had once known as Artemis.

Oh, she'd had other names, even before she started using the O'Donnell alias. All the gods had, skipping merrily around this new world they'd found, causing chaos and littering demigods about, while being worshipped under a hundred different titles. But she'd been Artemis in Greece, where she'd had an epiphany about just how much chaos the gods were causing during their sprees—and about how many humans were getting dead in the process.

She'd been Artemis when she grew a conscience.

At least, I assumed she had, although who knows? The gods were nothing if not capricious. Maybe she just woke up one day and decided to punk her fellow divine beings—by tossing their godly butts off the planet.

She did this, it turns out, by a spell sustained partly by—you guessed it—her own divine soul. It was the only thing powerful enough to cut off access to an entire world. And it had worked . . . sort of.

Meaning that it had worked at the time. And even later, after she started to decline from a lack of compatible magic on the planet she'd just stranded herself on—great idea there, Mom—it still had. The spell was now supported by the group Jonas currently led, an alliance of human mages known as the Silver Circle. So, presumably, even if it was somehow brought down, the mages should be able to recast it.

Assuming they had all the parts, that is.

Which, of course, is where the record scratched. Since Artemis' protection spell had been linked through her soul, that soul formed a vital part of the spell. Meaning that if it disappeared, the spell it was supporting went away, too.

And since the other gods hadn't been amused by her little come-to-Jesus moment or whatever the hell it had been, and *really* wanted back in, that was a problem.

Particularly when the other side in the war was only too willing to welcome them back with open arms. The whole mess had Jonas wanting to tear his crazy hair out.

What had me wanting to shred mine was that everybody assumed I could do something about all this.

Yeah, okay, at some point the goddess famous for virginity had decided to hook up with a human for some reason, and pop out baby me. But that did not automatically confer any special insight. I'd had to learn about the whole mess the hard way, like everyone else — by piecing clues together over the last several months, ever since the war made it obvious that the gods were getting serious about the reclaiming-their-playground thing. And I still didn't know much.

In fact, I probably knew less than most, since nobody seemed to think it important to actually tell me anything. I was just their ace in the hole, the quasi-divine chick they'd lucked into who was expected to pull something out of her ass every time a god or his little homicidal offspring showed up to wreak some more havoc. It was infuriating.

It was also terrifying.

Especially since, along with that lack of insight I'd gotten a big old goose egg in the divine equipment department. Sure, I had the power that came with my office, but all Pythias had had that. And most of them had known more about it than I did. But if there was some kind of demigod bonus I was supposed to get on the side, well, it had been lost in the mail. My maternal line notwithstanding, I was just Cassie.

And some days — most days — I was afraid that wasn't going to be nearly enough.

Like days when I was covered in bruises and my own blood, plus some two-decade-old spiderwebs I hadn't noticed until now. "Shit!" I said, running frantic hands through my hair and knocking off a couple of little brown things that scurried for cover. And didn't make it thanks to Marco's size-sixteen boot. "I need a drink," I told him honestly.

"Drinks!" Fred's head popped up. "That's right. We're going to need—"

"Don't even—" I warned as he grabbed the coffee cup I had stupidly set down on the kitchen counter.

"You couldn't get a large?" he snarled, playing keep-away. And then somehow my coffee ended up parsed out into three little demitasse cups, slapped on a tray along with the leaking doughnuts, and sped out the door, all in about the time it took to blink.

I started after it, but Marco didn't move out of the way. "Wait."

"I wait and I starve!"

"There are worse things."

"Like what?"

"Like having your dingle cursed off," Fred said, sidling back into the kitchen through the half inch of space left by Marco's bulk.

"What?"

"You know." He looked pointedly downward.

"They don't do that!"

"Like hell they don't! I've *seen* things, okay? And these aren't mages. They're not part of the Circle. They don't have rules—"

"They have rules, just ones decided by their covens," Marco argued.

"Yeah, rules like if someone pisses them off, they *can curse his ding*—"

"Would you man the hell up?" Marco snapped. And clapped a hand the size of a catcher's mitt over Fred's mouth. Fred's displeasure thereafter took the form of outraged grunts.

"I thought the covens were under the Circle's authority," I said, trying to remember all the info Jonas had been force feeding me lately.

"Not the most powerful ones. They never joined."

Marco shot a look over his shoulder. "I guess they figured they didn't need to."

Yeah. And if they'd just waltzed in here through the kinds of wards the Circle had on this place, I kind of agreed with them. But that still didn't make it okay.

"Why are they here?" I demanded.

"They wouldn't tell me," Marco said, effortlessly keeping Fred under wraps. And since, despite all evidence to the contrary, Fred was also a master-level vamp, that was actually kind of impressive. Or it would have been, had Marco not been simultaneously hiding from a few old ladies.

"You're intimidated," I accused.

He scowled. "Do you remember how old I am?"

"What does that mat—"

"It matters 'cause I didn't live this long by being stupid. Sometimes it's smart to be intimidated. Sometimes it's smart to look before you leap."

"I do that."

Fred suddenly stopped struggling, I guess so he and Marco could both send me the same look of stunned disbelief.

"I do!" I said again, and it was true. Mostly true. Okay, true when I had a chance to look, which wasn't often these days. But that wasn't the point.

"That isn't the point," I told him.

"Then what is?"

"That I'm sick of this, okay? I'm not their slave—or the Circle's or the vamps' or anybody else's. I'm not going to live like this—"

"It's your job."

"Bullshit." I glared at him, too tired and hungry and lacking in caffeine to bother with diplomacy, which was something else I sucked at anyway. "What do you think Agnes would have done if they'd broken in on her in the middle of the night?"

"I don't—"

"Well, I do!" I said, remembering my sweet-looking

predecessor, who had shot me in the ass the one and only time I'd tried it. "Agnes was a bitch, okay? But she *needed* to be a bitch. Because the people around her were all these big personalities with all this power and given half a chance they'd run roughshod over her. *And she knew it.* So she didn't put up with that. Not at any time, not for any reason, not from any of them! And as a result, they respected her. As a result, *they* were afraid of *her*, not the other way around."

Marco regarded me with a mixture of affection and exasperation and maybe a little bit of pity. But he didn't say anything. Fred, on the other hand, took the distraction of the moment to wiggle out of Marco's grasp. And he wasn't so subtle.

"Yeah, but you're not Agnes," he reminded me.

"I'm not Agnes *yet*," I hissed, and shifted.

Chapter Four

I went from light and noise and stress to someplace completely lacking two of those things. I didn't bother turning on a light. I could see well enough from the orange haze filtering in through a gap in a wall of curtains, and anyway, the view wasn't much.

The rooms that Dante's, my home on the Vegas Strip, reserves for its more budget-conscious guests are a little . . . Spartan. Ironically, that makes them less eye-wincing than the suites upstairs, which mostly conform to the hotel's over-the-top haunted house theme. But the designer had run short of money by the time he got this far, so the only affronts to taste were a few vintage horror movie posters and an ugly bedspread.

I hadn't been here for a while, and I wasn't sure why I was here now. Maybe because I didn't have the strength to go much farther. Or maybe because I didn't have anywhere else *to* go.

It was ironic; all of time was mine to explore—in theory, anyway—except for my own. In my own, I'd been living like a prisoner for weeks, with the few times I'd dared to venture outside the hotel not going well. And I didn't think I was likely to find anybody to go AWOL with again, since the last guy who had . . .

Well, he wasn't here anymore.

But his room was.

Although it was looking a little rough.

A river of glass crunched underfoot, glinting in the band of rusty light. A nightstand lay cracked in two, the ceramic lamp that had been on top pulverized almost into powder. A splatter of some potion had eaten right through to the studs on one wall, and still gave off a faint, noxious odor, despite a week of air-conditioning. And a large stain soiled the carpet by the window, looking black in the low light.

I stared at it, and everything came flooding back: the shock, the horror, the fury of the night when the obstinate son of a bitch who'd lived here had taken it upon himself to trade his life for mine. The week that had passed since hadn't dimmed the memory at all, or the emotion that went with it. If anything it was stronger than ever, the urge to grab him, to demand where he got the nerve, the *right*, to make that decision for me—

I stood there a minute, shaking, furious all over again but with no one to hit. Because he wasn't here. Just the room, cold and empty and generic without its larger-than-life occupant, the echoing silence broken only by my ragged breathing. I hugged my arms around myself and waited for my heartbeat to back off attack levels.

Only it didn't seem to be obliging.

I'd read once that there were five stages of grief: denial, anger, bargaining, depression, and acceptance. But that hadn't been my experience. There had been a little denial, yeah, when I first realized what had happened, but it hadn't lasted long. And afterward . . . well, let's just say that I'd entered phase two with a vengeance.

And that was where I'd stayed.

I supposed that was why my nails had sunk into my upper arms, hard enough to draw blood. I slowly pulled them out and carefully wiped my hands on my already filthy jeans. I wasn't going to do this now.

I was going to do this later.

I was going to do this once *I got him back*.

Although, so far, that wasn't going great.

It was another thing that should have been easy. Hell, I was a time traveler, wasn't I? Just go back and change a few things. Make a few adjustments. See to it that the good guys won. Simple, right?

Of course, I wasn't supposed to. In fact, it was pretty much exactly the kind of thing I was not supposed to do. Pythias guarded the timeline from alterations by others; we didn't change it ourselves.

Except, of course, when we did.

Agnes had, when she warned me that I was about to be assassinated. If she hadn't, I never would have met the maddening man known as John Pritkin in the first place, would never have needed him to save me, would never have royally screwed up his life in the process. He might have been better off if she'd minded her own business, but she hadn't and I'd lived. All because she'd changed one little thing . . .

But that was the problem. Agnes had been doing this kind of thing for decades. She'd known what to change and what to leave the heck alone. Not to mention that the night she bent a rule for me had been easy mode compared to the craziness a week ago. If I did go back, where did I make the cut? I'd lain awake at night for a week, trying to figure it out.

The obvious place was right here in this room. The fight that had left it looking even more trashed than usual had been because of me. Someone on the other side of the war had wanted a device Pritkin carried, one that would summon me to an impromptu execution the next time I tried to shift. They'd fought. Pritkin lost it, chased after it, and as a result, found me in the nick of time.

So, if I wanted to change things, the easiest way would be to warn him about what was coming.

And that would work great—*if* he took the hint. But Pritkin defined stubborn and was making headway on a new meaning for paranoid; he might well ignore a heads-up like the one Agnes had sent me. And even if he didn't and avoided following the would-be assassin to the battleground, that wouldn't work so well, either.

Since in that case I'd be dead.

So then where? In the middle of a fight that I'd barely won the first time? Because I just didn't see how that worked. The final battle had happened in a couple of minutes of frantic activity and gnawing terror. And, as usual, I'd survived by luck as much as skill. Any slight alteration might make things worse instead of better.

Not to mention the fact that, crazy as it had been, the duel I'd fought against another demigod had ended up being pretty damned useful. It had impressed the hell out of the six vampire senates, who had shortly thereafter decided that maybe they would join forces in the war, after all. If I avoided the battle, they might well avoid signing the treaty. And we needed that treaty.

Anyway, all of that was moot, because even if I found a way to save Pritkin, to not get myself killed in the process, and to not advertise that Pythias did alter time for their own purposes occasionally, what then? Because Pritkin would still be in a mess, and a bad one. And the fact that, for once, it had nothing to do with me didn't help at all.

I didn't want to rescue him just to put him back in the same tortured existence he'd been occupying for almost a century. I wanted to *save him*. For once, I wanted this power I'd never asked for, and which had been nothing but trouble from the moment I got it, to actually do its freaking job. And *help somebody*.

Somebody who deserved it.

I just wasn't sure how.

I sat down on the bed to wait out the mess upstairs. The room was quiet except for the faint sigh of the air-conditioning, and peaceful. Or it would have been if the gap in the drapes hadn't been illuminating a swath across one of the movie posters.

Not that it looked all that horrific at the moment. Someone had taken a Sharpie to it—some kid, I guessed, since I couldn't imagine the dour war mage I knew drawing a mustache and glasses on Bela Lugosi. But then, that wouldn't be the biggest surprise he'd handed me lately.

Sometimes I wondered if I'd known the man at all. I sure as hell didn't understand him. One minute he was being an absolute horse's ass, to the point that I just wanted to take him somewhere particularly nasty and *leave him there*, and then the next . . .

I felt my breath start to come faster, my hands to clench, and stupid tears to spring to my eyes. I dashed them away angrily. I'd said I wasn't going to do this anymore, and I damned well *wasn't*—

"Cass?"

"Ahhhh!" I leapt back, hitting the remaining nightstand with my already bruised butt, as Billy popped into existence through a flutter of playing cards.

The cards were mine. I hadn't even noticed that I'd been fingering them, but it wasn't a surprise. Kids have a favorite toy; Linus has his blanket; I have a greasy pack of tarot cards given to me by my old governess, which she'd had enchanted as a joke. And which were now all over the place and talking up a storm.

They had been spelled to tell your fortune on their own, and either by design or some flaw in the enchantment, they always tried to outdo one another. The result was seventy-eight tiny voices gradually getting louder and louder as each tried to talk over the rest. And ended up making a god-awful racket.

I started shoving them back into the pack, which was the only thing that kept them quiet, and simultaneously glared at Billy. "Don't do that!"

"Then don't run off without telling me. You're supposed to be sleeping."

Yeah. Like that had been going so great lately. "I had some unwelcome guests."

"So shift 'em out of there. Why'd you have to be the one to leave? It's your room!"

"And I don't want to have to redecorate it again. Like after three pissed-off witches finish trashing it."

"They wouldn't trash the Pythia's suite."

"Why not? They broke into it," I grumbled, managing to shove most of the cards back into place. Except for a few still chatting away somewhere. I threw the bedding around, trying to find the damned things. "It was easier for me to leave."

"But why come here?" Billy looked around and his nose wrinkled. "It smells like a combat zone."

"I don't care what it smells like."

"And it's probably booby-trapped all to hell."

I paused for a second, my hand halfway under the bed. I'd known Pritkin mainly in his role as my Circle-appointed bodyguard/personal trainer/drill sergeant, but he'd had other titles at times. Like war mage assassin.

"I don't think he does that anymore," I told Billy. Not since I'd popped in a few times unexpectedly.

"Maybe not. But what about somebody else? It looks like this place was ransacked."

"It always looks like that." Except for his weapons, Pritkin's idea of orderly living was roughly that of a fourteen-year-old boy.

"Yeah, but people gotta be wondering where he went off to," Billy pointed out. "He's a war mage, isn't he? Isn't anybody curious?"

"Everybody." I'd gotten asked about it daily by virtually everyone except Jonas, which was weird since Pritkin was technically his subordinate. But maybe Jonas felt that a guy like that could take care of himself. Or maybe it was like he'd told me: he didn't ask Pythias too many questions.

He so rarely liked the answers he got back.

"Then maybe you shouldn't be crawling around on the floor," Billy said pointedly.

"And maybe you should tell me what Laura said," I pointed out right back.

Billy gave up trying to reason with me, and parked his insubstantial rear a couple of inches above the ugly bedspread. "She said they're in the boathouse."

I grabbed the card that had ended up halfway under the bed, pulled it out, and stared at him. "My parents?"

He nodded.

I frowned. "What boathouse? Tony's farm is in the middle of the countryside. There isn't a lake for miles."

"Yeah, I mentioned that. Seems she was talking about some ramshackle cottage that used to be behind the house. Former owner stored his boat out there, and the name stuck. Until Tony had the place bulldozed to build a parking lot, anyway."

I nodded. Among other things, Tony had been in the loan shark business. And not all the items he repossessed when people failed to pay up were small enough to be stored in the house. Eventually, he'd had an area out back paved to accommodate the cars, trucks, and motor homes he kept until the mark came through or he sold them off. I hadn't gone out there much, since there wasn't anything to interest a kid — the repos were always kept locked.

"She said your folks didn't like the main house," Billy continued, "and Tony didn't like 'em in it — or their little friends."

"What friends?"

"Seems they attracted demons like nobody's business, and they were creeping out the vamps."

"Demons?" My dad had had some abilities with ghosts, which was where I got mine, I guessed. But I hadn't heard anything about demons before.

But then, he wasn't the only person out there, was he?

Billy nodded. "There were some incidents — poltergeist-type stuff, fires, one vamp got torched — "

"Who?"

"Manny," Billy said, referring to one of Tony's more

dim-witted vamps. "He recovered okay, but shortly after that, Mom and Pop got evicted."

"To the boathouse," I said, staring at the card in my hand without really seeing it.

"Yeah," Billy said, sounding suddenly annoyed. "And don't get that look."

"What look?"

"That I'm-gonna-go-ask-Mom-how-to-get-my-buddy-Pritkin-back look. It's not that easy!"

"Tell me about it." But that didn't matter, because if anyone knew how to get me out of this mess, it would be her.

Remember how I said the gods had different names in different places? Well, she'd been worshipped by the Norse as Hel, their goddess of death. Who, among other things, had been in charge of the regions that bore her name. And right now I really needed to know about those regions.

Because Pritkin had traded his life for mine, but not in the conventional sense. Of course not—when did he *ever* do the conventional thing? No, he'd had to get fancy with it.

By giving me energy when I was all but out, he'd saved my life. But he'd also broken a taboo that was the only thing allowing him to remain on earth. That had resulted in him being kidnapped by his bastard of a father, who had been waiting for something like a century for an excuse to put his only child back where he thought he belonged—on a throne in hell.

Or, more likely, in a bedroom, since Pritkin's father was Rosier, Lord of the Incubi. That made Pritkin a powerful half incubus who had been, in his father's warped view, playing about on earth long enough. It was time for him to take up his birthright and help the family by whoring himself out to the highest bidders.

The fact that that sort of existence would be worse than death to someone like Pritkin, who hated the demon half of himself and everything that went with it, was irrelevant to Rosier. He'd spent centuries trying to get a corporeal son to use as a bargaining chip, and he wasn't about to lose him now. And unlike Persephone, Pritkin wasn't even allowed visitation rights on earth.

Rosier had him and he planned on keeping him.

As if.

"Why are you looking like that?" Billy asked warily.

"Like what?"

"Like you're about to cut a bitch."

"I don't know what you're talking about," I said, and shoved the rest of the cards back into place.

"Okaaaaay. But before you run off for a family reunion, there's one other thing you might want to know."

"Such as?"

"Such as, if your parents were hoping for privacy in their cottage, they got it. Laura said nobody went out there—not even the other ghosts. Demons can feed off ghost energy even easier than human—there's no body to get through first, you know? And they weren't taking chances."

"So? I'm not a ghost."

"I said easier. Demons feed off humans just fine if they want to put in the effort, and there's a crap ton of them out there."

I frowned. "How many?"

"Laura didn't know. She never went there herself, not being stupid. But some of the vamps came back spooked as hell, telling stories about hearing what had to be hundreds of demons, seeing crazy lights, feeling space warp around them, the whole nine yards. They were scared shitless."

I frowned harder. "What kind of demons?"

"What difference does it make? The moral of the story is, if the scary-ass bastards at Tony's were afraid of that cottage, maybe you should be, too!"

"My *mother* is in there," I reminded him. And it wasn't like she couldn't handle demons. From what I understood of the old legends, she'd practically ruled them at one point.

"Yeah, sometimes," Billy said, sounding crabby. "But what if she's off somewhere when you pop in? And how exactly are you gonna do that when you don't know the layout of the place? You'll have to show up outside, where you can see where you're going, and that means getting through the woods to the front door. And then waiting for somebody to let you in—assuming somebody's home to start with. And that whole time, you'll be a sitting duck for a bunch of hungry demons. 'Cause you know as well as I do that you don't know how to fight 'em off—"

"Stop it."

"Okay, sure. I'll stop it. Just as soon as you tell me how you plan to get in."

I didn't say anything for a minute. "Jonas knows about demons."

"Yeah. And I'm sure he'll be thrilled about making another trip to Tony's right now. And even if so, he wouldn't be happy about helping you do something that could change your whole existence—"

"I'm just going to *talk*—"

"—and what excuse are you gonna give him for needing to see her, anyway? You can't tell him about the mage, 'cause that would tell him what Pritkin is. And you know how the Corps feels about demons—"

"I said stop it!" I told him savagely. I didn't need this. Another freaking roadblock in a week that had been full of nothing else. A week of trying to track Mom down, when she was busy avoiding anybody attempting to do just that. She'd had enemies of her own on her ass, and she'd turned evasion into an art form.

I'd finally bitten the bullet and realized that I was going to have to go back to Tony's, the only place I was sure I could find her. Only to discover—after tripping the wards and almost getting caught half a dozen times—

that she wasn't there, either. It had started to feel like she wasn't anywhere.

But then Jonas had shown up this afternoon, declaring that he simply had to be taken back in time right that moment. With his help, I'd avoided the wards—mostly—and Billy had pried the truth out of Laura. So now I discovered that I hadn't been able to find my folks at Tony's because they hadn't been there. They'd been in the cottage.

Which I now learned was surrounded by an army of freaking demons.

"Cass . . ."

"Don't." I said tightly. "Not now."

"Yes, now," Billy insisted. "Look, I helped, right? I tried—we both tried. But he's gone."

"He *isn't*."

"Yes, he is. And you can't bring him back by sheer force of will. Look, even if you got in there somehow, and even if she told you how to get into Rosier's court, what then?"

"Then I go *get* him," I said fiercely.

"Uh-huh." Billy looked at me, and he was solid enough that I could see the compassion in those hazel eyes. "Only you know that's not happening, right? Cass, don't take this the wrong way, but you couldn't even burglarize Tony's without help. And now you think you're just gonna waltz into hell—"

"Shut up."

"—and break Pritkin out? When Rosier is probably expecting something exactly like that from you? When he's *prepared*?"

"Billy! Shut up!"

"Not this time," he said flatly. "You need to hear this, and since nobody else knows what you've been up to, I'm the only one who can try to snap you out of it. Cass, it's *suicide*. Pritkin gave up everything to save you; think he would want you to throw your life away trying to get him back?"

I got up abruptly, because I couldn't stay still anymore. But it didn't shut Billy up. Of course it didn't. I'd never found anything that did.

"And even if, by some million-to-one chance, you were to get him out of there, what do you think would happen then?" he demanded. "It's not like anything would change. He broke his parole, or whatever you want to call it. Rosier would just drag him back—"

"We don't know that!"

"Yes, we do. Pritkin *told* you—"

"What he *knew*! But maybe he didn't know everything," I said, trying to pace and not being able to because of the damned glass. I kicked an arc of it out of the way and the shards flashed in the glow from outside for a moment, like licking flames.

"Oh. So you know more about hell than a guy who lived there."

"No, but maybe my mother does!" I rounded on him. "She lived there, too, if the old legends were right. And for centuries! If there's a loophole, she'll know it!"

"And if there isn't?"

"Then there isn't," I said, crossing my arms and glaring at him. "But until I hear that—from *her*—I'm not going to just give up. I can't, Billy—don't you *get* it?"

"Oh, I get it," he muttered. "I'm just not sure that you do."

"What does that mean?"

He shook his head. "Nothing. Just . . . nothing. But the fact remains, you can't get to her to ask."

I sat down on the bed, suddenly exhausted. It had been a long day at the end of a long week, and my chest hurt. I wanted to scream, to cry, to throw things, but I didn't have the energy. I wanted to black out and find Pritkin there when I woke up. I wanted . . .

God. Sometimes I didn't even know.

"Not tonight," I admitted, rubbing the back of my neck. If I hadn't felt up to dealing with a few nosy witches, I sure couldn't take whatever was guarding dear old Mom.

"Come back to the suite," Billy told me softly. "Before you give Marco a heart attack. Get some rest. Tomorrow . . . maybe things will look different."

In other words, tomorrow maybe I'd come to my senses.

"Yeah, maybe," I said, because I didn't want to argue anymore.

Billy nodded, and winked out, looking relieved. Which did exactly nothing to make me feel better. Despite the way he'd been sounding lately, Billy Joe wasn't the timid type. Billy Joe had been a high-stakes gambler in life, until he ended up in a sack at the bottom of the Mississippi for cheating the wrong guys. When Billy thought something was too risky . . .

Well, let's just say the odds weren't great.

And it wasn't like everything he'd said wasn't true. But so was something he hadn't bothered to mention. That if our positions were reversed, Pritkin would have come after me. Whether I'd liked it or not, whether I'd wanted him to risk it or not, he wouldn't have just left me there. It probably wouldn't even have crossed his mind. I knew that, with more certainty than I knew which direction the sun would rise tomorrow.

So how could I just leave him?

I curled up on his messy bed, and even after a week, the sheets still smelled good. Like soap and gunpowder and magic. I lay there, staring at the ceiling, and didn't cry. Because it was weak, and I couldn't afford to be weak.

And because you only cried for people who weren't coming back.

And that wasn't the case here, no matter how it looked. I had to get to him, had to get him away from his loathsome father, had to find a way to keep him. And for that, I had to get to my mother.

Somehow.

But it had been a week, and so far, I hadn't even managed that first step. I'd exhausted myself flipping around through time like a crazy woman. I'd been chased by guards through the old Pythian Court, almost gotten myself run over in London, been shot at by Tony's thugs. And for what? I was no closer to finding Pritkin than I'd been a week ago.

When he left me.

Chapter Five

"The Star . . ."

A soft chime woke me.

"The Star . . . The Star . . . The Star . . ."

A soft, annoying chime.

I groaned and rolled over, because it was too damned early, and the chime suddenly became more muffled. "The Star . . . The Star . . . The Star . . ."

I groaned again and sat up.

"The Star is universally considered to be the most beautiful card in the tarot," a smug voice informed me, from somewhere underneath my butt. "It is also one of the most fortunate, although not, perhaps, in the way that many people would prefer. The Star—"

I fumbled around, groggy and still half-asleep, and didn't find anything.

" —indicates that success is possible, but only in time and through great effort. The Star shines in the night sky, a beacon of light in a dark world, pulling the querent forward onto a heroic quest—"

I felt something stuck to the back of my leg. I peeled it off and brought it up to my bleary eyes. And saw a small rectangle with a night scene, a garden, and a naked chick with a jug.

" — worthy of an equally great reward," the little tarot card burbled at me. "Should the querent survive — "

"Survive?"

" — the undoubted dangers, snares, and, at times, mortal perils that lie in the way, the reward will be as sweet as the clear, cold water the lovely maiden pours into the pool reflecting the starlight. And if not — "

"What?" I croaked. "What if not?"

" — then one will have the knowledge that one fell in pursuit of an admirable goal," the card said, its small voice rising passionately. "The heavens shall sing praises of your bravery, as they do for the heroes for which the constellations are named, and your renown shall echo down the ages to — "

"Oh, shut up," I said viciously, fumbling around on the nightstand for the card pack. And not finding it. Great, I thought, and rolled off the bed.

But not mine.

I hit the floor, blinking at the god-awful coverlet that had half fallen off with me. Instead of tufted satin, it was one of the scratchy, cheapo kind the hotel reserved for rooms priced at less than a trip to Tahiti. And instead of a tasteful pale blue, it had a full-on Halloween theme in yellow, black, and gray, with a ghostly moon caged by the branches of a gaunt and lifeless tree.

Shit.

I must have accidentally fallen asleep in Pritkin's room, instead of dragging my weary butt back to my own bed. And wasn't *that* just going to get me blessed out by Marco? Of course, I was kind of surprised that it hadn't already, since I knew damned well the vamps kept a tracking spell on me. I'd had Pritkin take it off a few times, but it always ended up right back in place, usually within an hour or two. And since he'd been gone for a week, it was safe to assume that they knew exactly where —

I'd hauled myself to my feet, in preparation for getting my shit together, but tripped over something and went right back down again. Only this time I hit the carpet beside a pair of dirty boots. They were old, with massive soles and scratched leather uppers, at least what I could see through a coating of mud. It was so thick that the steel cap over the toes was barely visible.

Huh. That's weird, some tiny, more awake part of my brain commented. But it didn't explain why.

I sat up and frowned at them some more.

There was nothing particularly odd about them, except for the mud, which wasn't exactly common in Vegas. But they were the kind Pritkin wore, useful for caving in doors or bad guy's faces, and had been thrown in his usual haphazard fashion under the bed. Or beside it, but the dust ruffle had obscured most of them. Which maybe explained why I hadn't—

Okay, that was it. They weren't weird, but the fact that I hadn't noticed them last night was. Especially since I should have been able to smell them a couple of yards off. I wrinkled my nose at the locker room funk and pushed them to the side. And peered into the gloom beyond for the damned card pack, while a cheerful voice began to regale me with fun facts about the Star card.

That was bad, but if I didn't shut it up, it was going to segue into the possible meanings of the card in combination with others. And then into how it should be read in the different spreads. And if I remembered right, that would be followed by the whole history of the tarot, which could go on for literally hours before it finally wound down. And the way I felt, a migraine was going to explode my left eye long before then.

After a fruitless search, I surfaced, gasping from a combo of boot funk and dust bunnies, and started sorting through the jumbled bedclothes for the pack that simply had to be there somewhere. But I didn't see it. Maybe because it was hard to see anything in the wash of sunshine pouring in through the curtains.

I stopped and blinked at them.

The suddenly wide-open curtains.

The suddenly wide-open curtains that were being reflected in the mirror over the dresser.

And okay, no. That mirror had been in about a thousand pieces all over the floor last night. I mean, I couldn't be wrong about that, right? I'd stepped in the remains, and even kicked some when—

My brain came to a screeching halt as three things happened simultaneously. My eyes wandered over the view beyond the bed, which was noticeably lacking in broken glass, destroyed furniture, or ominous stains. My nose registered a complete dearth of potion residue. And my ears pricked up at a small, new sound.

A sound like the beep of a key card tripping an automatic lock.

My head jerked around to see the doorknob start to turn, and I tried to shift. But my fuzzy brain wasn't having it. Instead, it had gone into flight mode all right, but for some reason it had decided that the path to safety involved me trying to squash myself into the few inches of space under the bed. Only I couldn't because the damned boots were in the way. And by the time I shoved them aside, thrust the still-talking tarot card down my shirt, realized there was already something wedged in between my breasts, crammed the card into the top of a small, greasy package I found there, and started stuffing myself past the dust ruffle . . .

It was too late.

The door opened and someone came in, sneaker-clad feet quiet on the tiled floor of the entryway. They stopped abruptly, and there was no sound for a beat, then two. And then they crossed silently onto the carpet before pausing again, beside the bed.

Where they were currently being treated to the sight of my ass wriggling around in the air like Pooh Bear sticking out of Rabbit's house, because it hadn't made it under here with the rest of me.

For a moment, nothing was said.

Then a single finger pushed up the dust ruffle. And a

clear green eye peered underneath at me. I stared back
at it, and what little coherent thought I'd managed to
form went out the window.

"Is there . . . a problem?" a mild voice asked me.

I licked my lips, because, as usual for me, "problem"
didn't cover it. I opened my mouth to reply, and God
knows what I'd have said. Only, luckily, speech was one
of many things that didn't seem to be working right now.

Like motor control. Because the next moment, when
I was hauled out from under the bed and up to a pair of
so-familiar green eyes, I just hung there limply. And
stared.

At a face that was hard to look at.

Not that it was unattractive. There had been a time
when I'd thought so—the overlarge nose, the hard-as-
glass eyes, the I-couldn't-be-bothered-to-shave-today-
and-possibly-not-yesterday-either stubble didn't exactly
spell out movie-star good looks. But there was a lot
more to John Pritkin than looks, although even there I'd
started to come around recently. The strong, stubborn
jawline, the rock-hard body, and the flashes of humor
behind the taciturn expression—hell, even the rigid
blond spikes he called hair might not add up to handsome, but they added up to something.

Something that might have been disturbing if I hadn't
had plenty of other things to disturb me right now.

"What is it?" Pritkin demanded, fingers tightening on
my arms as his face suddenly swam in front of me.

I told myself to get a grip, but it wasn't working. To
suddenly have him just show up like that was . . . well, it
was what I guess most people felt when they saw a ghost.
It was startling and exhilarating and strangely terrifying . . .

And impossible, I realized, as the explanation
slammed into me.

This wasn't about Rosier growing a heart and sending
his son back where he belonged. Pritkin's expression
told me that much. I didn't know what look I might find

on his face if I ever caught up with him again, but I didn't think it would be mild concern mixed with a healthy dose of exasperation.

No. This was me, thinking, longing, dreaming . . . and shifting, while either asleep or as good as, back to a time where I knew I'd find him. Back to a time I was about to royally screw up if I didn't *get it together*.

"Cassie—" Pritkin was starting to look seriously worried, maybe because I was still hanging there lifelessly, staring at him like an idiot. Except for one hand, which had come up to gently touch his face. I jerked it back down, because yeah. Losing it.

I licked my lips again. "Um," I said, and stopped. I had nothing.

But something in my face must have reassured him anyway. Because he let go and sat on the edge of the bed, some of the concern draining out of his eyes. "We've discussed this," he said dryly.

"We . . . We have?"

"Yes. You can't merely shift down here because it's faster than taking the elevator. I keep dangerous substances—"

"I didn't touch the bookcase," I said quickly. The memory of the one and only time I had wasn't pleasant. Well, except for watching Rosier's smug face melt into a puddle of goo after having a few dozen vials of demon-fighting potion dumped on it. And after everything that had happened since, that was actually quite—

"Cassie?"

"Huh?"

"There are more dangers here than just the bookcase."

"Like what?"

"Like this," Pritkin said, reaching under the bed and pulling out one of his smelly boots. And then jerking something out of the interior. Something that was—

A thumb came down on top of what looked a lot like a grenade, except it was smooth and bluish steel in color, and had a sort of lever thing on top instead of a pin. A lever that had been halfway down when Pritkin noticed it. Which might have had something to do with the high-pitched whine it had been sending off.

And still was, I realized, as his eyes widened. He grabbed the other boot and turned it upside down. And then he grabbed me. "Where is it?"

"Where is what?"

"The potion grenade!"

"You have it," I said, looking in confusion at the object he'd just thrown onto the bed.

"No! The other one!"

"There's another one?"

"There's not supposed to be!"

"Well, I didn't bring one!" I said feverishly.

"Then what is—" His eyes suddenly fixed on the front of my tee. "There!"

And the next thing I knew, he was snatching up my shirt. And yanking something out of my bra. And flinging it away with a savage motion that I barely saw before he threw himself on top of me.

We hit the floor, and it hurt, because Pritkin is mostly muscle and he weighs a lot. And because my head clipped the edge of the nightstand on the way down. And because his shields snapped closed so hard and fast that they cut off an inch of my hair. Which promptly fell into my eyes.

But that didn't seem to matter so much if we were about to be blown to pieces by . . .

By a grenade that was taking its own sweet time, I thought, as seconds ticked by and nothing happened. Except for Pritkin's heart beating loud in my ear, because I was squashed underneath him, with my head squeezed between his chest and the floor. To the point that I couldn't . . . hardly . . .

"Air," I squawked, and Pritkin raised himself up slightly.

And as soon as he did, I realized what was making the objectionable whine.

"The Star is universally considered to be the most beautiful card in the tarot," a small voice said reproachfully, from above my head. Where it was protruding out of the elusive tarot deck. Which was now sticking out of an impact point on the wall. And squealing as seventy-eight cards simultaneously registered their disapproval at their rough treatment.

Pritkin lifted his head to stare at them. And then he looked back down at me. And then he crawled off a few feet and sat on the carpet, and put his head in his hands.

"Sorry," I said breathlessly, as the cards continued to mutter to themselves.

Pritkin didn't say anything.

That was okay. That was good. I needed a moment.

And a bath, I realized, as I lifted an arm to brush the fringe of severed hair out of my eyes. It wasn't only Pritkin's boots that were smelling up the place. I sat there, mortified, unable to believe I'd fallen asleep like this. "Is anything going to kill me if I use your bathroom?" I finally asked.

"Knowing you?" Pritkin's voice was muffled since he hadn't raised his head.

I frowned. "Is that a yes?"

A couple of fingers came up to massage his temple. "That is a no. Assuming you didn't bring anything deadly along with you."

"Just dirt," I said, realizing the extent of it. I was going to have a hard enough time explaining this without looking like I'd been spelunking in the Bat Cave. "I'm going to get a shower," I told him.

Pritkin didn't react to this, so I scampered off to the minuscule bath Dante's allowed its regular guests, which was about the size of my toilet cubbyhole upstairs.

Shit. *Upstairs.* Where the younger me was presumably hanging out and doing . . . well, whatever I'd been doing three weeks ago.

That was the first time Pritkin had taken me hiking on some god-awful mountain trail in the foothills of the

Rockies. The Corps, the official name for the war mage branch of the Circle, used it as a training ground. It had been a memorable experience, mainly because it had rained the night before, turning the whole mountain into a massive mud pit.

Pritkin had made me run the trail anyway.

Of course.

The only good thing was that I'd twisted an ankle near the end, when I fell over a tree root, and had milked it for three days off the hellish workouts. Judging by the state of his boots, this was the first of those days, since I didn't think he would leave them sitting around for long in that condition. Meaning that maybe Pritkin wouldn't be going upstairs, and I wasn't in as bad a mess as I'd originally thought.

Well, assuming I could come up with a reason for breaking into his room looking like a war refugee. The tee, what parts the bricks hadn't shredded, was streaked with soot, my jeans looked like I'd been auditioning for a role as a chimney sweep, and my hair—what I had left—was dirty and sleep-matted. Not to mention that I had that pale look I always got when I skipped meals.

A siren I wasn't.

I scowled at myself, wondering where that thought had come from. But it might not matter. For a guy who was so observant about other things, Pritkin never seemed to notice what I looked like.

Knuckles rapped on the door, loud enough to make me jump. "I'm going out."

I opened it a crack and stuck my head through, since the rest of me wasn't decent. "Why?" I asked, worried.

"To get some breakfast. What do you want?"

"How do you know I haven't eaten already?"

He just looked at me.

"Does it have to be healthy?"

The look did not change.

I sighed.

"I asked what you wanted," he reminded me. "I'll run it off you later."

"You already broke my foot!"

An eyebrow went north. "And yet you managed to get in there fast enough."

I decided that maybe I should just shut up now. "They have cheesy bacon biscuits down at the café, if it's before eleven."

Pritkin gave me an odd look. "It's seven thirty."

"Well . . . then they should have some."

He looked like he was going to say something else, but then stopped, eyes narrowing. *"Some?"*

"I want two."

"You'll get one."

"I didn't have dinner!"

"You ate with me," he said, frowning.

Crap.

"Oh. Yeah. Well, one, then," I said weakly, and slammed the door.

Chapter Six

I kept my back to it until I heard the door to the hall open and close, and then let out a trembling breath. God, I sucked at this. Which was why I ought to make up some excuse, leave him a note, and get the heck out of here before he returned.

So why was I getting into the shower instead?

Maybe because the active part of my brain had noticed something else it wasn't bothering to share with the rest of me. But it felt important. And maybe I'd figure it out once I'd been awake more than two minutes.

I let the hot water hit me right in the face, and I guess it helped. By the time I'd lathered up my hair, rinsed it off, decided the damage wasn't too bad, and washed a chimney's worth of soot down the drain, I'd also chased down that elusive thought. Which proved that my subconscious was smarter than I was.

I'd been thinking that I needed a demon expert to have any chance of reaching Mom. So it had brought me to one. In fact, it had brought me to *the* one, the guy who knew more about demons than everybody else in the Circle combined.

There was only one problem: Pritkin hated my shifts through time. He was absolutely of the opinion that, if we kept shifting around here and there, sooner or later we were going to mess up something that couldn't be fixed. He was so convinced that the first time I'd gone back in time to see my mother, when it had been about curiosity instead of abject need, I hadn't even thought about taking him along. I'd already known what his answer would be.

And considering how that had gone down—demigods crashing the party she was at, trying to kill her—it was probably just as well. Pritkin's reaction in cases of being shot at was to shoot back, and that wouldn't have worked on that particular foe. But demons . . . yeah, he knew all about them.

Half of the vials that were so precisely and uncharacteristically arranged in the racks on his bookcase were potions for fighting various varieties of hell-spawn, since that was what he'd done before hitching his star to my unlucky train. He'd probably forgotten more about demon fighting than the rest of the Corps had ever known. In fact, he might know as much about how I could break him out of his current predicament as Mom would, only I doubted he'd be willing to tell me.

Because Billy had been right—Pritkin wouldn't want me going after him. As badly as he hated his father, and as much as he might be hating his life right now, he wouldn't want me risking it. I was probably going to be in for a major ass-chewing whenever I found him. . . .

Only Billy had been right about that, too, I realized. I wasn't going to find him. Not without help.

I stepped out of the shower and into the hot air swirling around the bathroom. The mirror was all fogged up, and a swipe across it with my hand only changed that for a second. But a second was enough. It showed me a face still slightly round with baby fat, with heat-reddened cheeks, blond curls plastered to my head, a tip-tilted nose, and big, guileless blue eyes. Sopping wet, I looked about as dangerous as a stuffed rabbit. Sopping wet, I looked . . . well, like somebody who had no business going on some daring rescue.

I scowled, unconsciously imitating a certain war mage I knew. But while on him the expression was fierce, even terrifying, on me . . . mostly it made me look constipated. I sighed.

But unlike last night, when I'd been feeling helpless and battered and a lot like giving up, today my lack of badass credentials didn't seem so important. Because considering what I was up against, it wouldn't have mattered anyway. I could have been the biggest, baddest mage of them all, could have been a master-level vampire—hell, I could have had an army of both—and it wouldn't have made a difference.

Because I didn't see any of them just waltzing into hell, either.

In fact, I wasn't so sure that being me wasn't an asset right now. Because Billy might have been wrong about one thing—I didn't think Rosier was expecting me. Why would he be? Everyone else I knew underestimated me, and always had. Everybody else looked at me and saw the fluffy bunny in the mirror; well, almost everyone. But, despite his age, I didn't get the impression that Rosier had his son's insight, or much of anything else. And even Pritkin, when he wasn't running me up mountainsides or pushing me off cliffs, still sometimes acted like I was spun glass and might break.

But I hadn't broken.

I wouldn't break.

I didn't have that luxury.

And neither had Agnes. I looked in the mirror again, and decided that I didn't look any more delicate than she ever had. Maybe less, in fact. She'd been all of five foot two in her stocking feet, with a heart-shaped face and porcelain skin and a little-girl air about her that I was coming to believe she'd deliberately cultivated. So that people *would* underestimate her.

And then she shot them in the butt.

I let one finger run over the faint scar she'd given me, which thanks to a certain vampire's healing ability was far less prominent than it should have been. Just barely a dimple now, no big deal. But the thing was, I didn't think she'd been aiming for my butt at the time.

At the time, she'd been after a Guild member, one of a secret sect of crazies that wanted to alter time to their own ends, and she hadn't been playing around. She also hadn't had a problem going after him alone, without the war mage escort she'd been entitled to. She'd told me they often caused more problems than they solved by shooting everything in sight, and given what I'd seen in my brief acquaintanceship with the Corps, I had no reason to doubt her. But I thought most people chasing a dangerous dark mage would still have wanted one or two along, just in case.

Agnes hadn't even told them she was going.

So, yeah, if she'd started to lecture me about taking chances, I'd have had a few things to say right back. And then I'd have asked her what she'd have done in this situation. Only she probably wouldn't have told me because she'd refused to talk to me, in case I gave her some hint of the future that might cause her to mess it up.

But if she had been willing to talk . . . I think I knew what she'd have said. What she'd have done. Now I just had to figure out—

The bathroom door blew open before I could finish the thought, in a swirl of comparatively cold air. And before I could yelp, I found myself jerked out and slammed against the wall of the entryway. That left me facing the bathroom door, where clouds of steam were billowing out, like the place was on fire.

It was kind of appropriate, considering that they were framing the face of a livid half demon.

A second later, my hands hit the wall beside my head, which might have left me indecent, since they were clutching the bath towel I'd been in the process of wrapping around myself. Only I didn't let go. So the towel ended up being spread out as my hands were, forming a wet, clingy barrier in front of me.

Which, unless it was a lot more magical than it appeared, wasn't going to be enough.

Because Pritkin was looking pretty damned homicidal.

"They were out of cheesy biscuits?" my mouth said, because my mouth is an idiot.

"Who are you?" he demanded, getting in my face. "*What* are you?"

"What?" I said, staring up into furious green eyes.

"I'm not playing games," he warned, his voice low and flat and dead. "If the next words out of your mouth aren't a confession, they will be your last."

My brain froze up at that, because it had seen what Pritkin could do in a rage. But my mouth—my stupid, apparently unconnected-to-brain-matter mouth—began panicking. And running a mile a minute.

"Don't kill me! Don't kill me! It's me! You know it's me! It's like—God! Why would some crazed assassin come in here and *use your shower*? Do people *do* that? Especially when it needs cleaning that bad? I mean, you need to let housekeeping in here occasionally or stop brewing potions in there or something, because the creeping crud is going to kill you a long time before the bad guys have the chance and *don't slam me against the wall like that!* It hurts! I can explain, I promise, only I can'tifyoukillmeohGod!"

The last was in response to a couple of enchanted knives slipping out from inside Pritkin's old gray hoodie, the one he used on jogs because his battered leather trench would look a little weird. But he needed something to cover the arsenal of illegal and would-be-illegal-if-humans-knew-about-them weapons that went everywhere he did. These two rose on either side of his face, underscoring the fact that he didn't have to let me go in order to gut me, a thought that stopped even my mouth's inane babble. Maybe because it was too busy shrieking.

"Stop that!" he said as the slamming recommenced,

which of course only made me shriek harder. And try to shift away, only that didn't work because Pritkin was holding on to me. Which meant he came, too.

We ended up over by the window, something that didn't help my dignity, since my bare butt was now pressed firmly against the glass. Welcome to Vegas, I thought hysterically, wondering if I was flashing half the parking lot. And then wondering why I cared considering I was about to be killed by my own bodyguard.

Or maybe not.

Pritkin didn't let go, but the knives stayed on the other side of the room. Considering how fast they could remedy that situation, it didn't make me feel that much better. But potential death is better than imminent death, and I'd take it.

Only now it looked like I had some 'splaining to do.

"You just shifted us," he accused.

"Of course I did!" I said feverishly. "What was I supposed to do? Stay put and get skewered?"

"You're a Pythia."

I stared at him. *"Duh!"*

"Or some Pythian initiate pretending to be one!"

"Oh, for—Myra's *dead*," I reminded him. My rival for the Pythian power had tried to kill me, but had ended up shredded in my place. I hadn't done it, but I hadn't wasted a lot of tears over her memory, either.

"There are other initiates," Pritkin reminded me as he pressed closer, his eyes narrowed on my face.

I shivered. But not because of the words. But because my bare ass against the air-conditioned window had just caused me to break out in full-body goose bumps.

At least that's what I told myself.

I tried to move back, but there was nowhere to go. I was already flat against the damned window. And the sensation of slick cold on one side and hard heat on the other was . . . distracting.

Like those eyes on me, with an intensity that prickled over my skin, making me itchy and jumpy. Or like the heat of his body radiating through the wet towel, or the strong fingers digging into my skin, or the hot breath on my face. At least, I assumed that was why my breathing had sped up and my head had gone swimmy and I was suddenly oddly grateful that my hands were trapped beside my head.

Because they really wanted to run themselves through his hair.

Pritkin was saying something, something I should probably be paying attention to since he was looking a little . . . stressed. I suppose it was due to suspicion or anger or the kind of frustrated rage I seemed to call up in him sometimes. But it didn't look that way. Or, rather, it did to my brain, which was now wide awake. But to my body . . .

My body cheerfully informed me that he felt really good pressed against me like that, all hard muscles and smooth contours and ominous bulges. My body liked the air of barely leashed strength and caged mayhem he was giving off. My body thought he smelled really good, like heat and coffee and electricity.

My body was going to get me killed.

And okay, this was an unexpected complication. In a situation that was already complicated enough. But it wasn't exactly surprising.

Pritkin and I had been together a lot lately and he *was* half incubus. Hell, he was the son of their king, or whatever the creature's title was. It would have been odd if I *didn't* feel something occasionally. And that was without the memory of his last night on earth, when he'd given me energy the only way an incubus could.

I closed my eyes, but that only made it worse, shutting out distractions and allowing me to relive what I'd been trying really hard to forget. The familiar voice a sibilant whisper in my ear, the small of his back slick with sweat, the surprisingly soft hair brushing my body when he took control. And moved over me.

"Stop it," Pritkin grated, his voice somehow cutting

through the fog. But he didn't let go. I suppose he was afraid to, because a Pythia or one of her senior initiates could shift without him if there was no contact. But that left us stuck together, and that was becoming really, *really*—

Awesome, my body piped up enthusiastically.

"I told you, cut it out!" Pritkin said, sounding pissed.

"You first," I snarled, snapping my eyes open to glare at him, because he wasn't exactly helping.

Of course, neither did that.

He must have been jogging, probably his usual early morning ten-mile warm-up before coming to torture me. At least, I assumed that was why the rock-hard abs were outlined by a damp khaki T-shirt, the thin old sweatpants were clinging in all the right places, and the sleeves of the hoodie had been pushed to his elbows, showing the flexing muscles in his forearms. And then there were those hands and those eyes and that mouth . . .

I shivered again, a full-on shudder this time, and he cursed. But that didn't seem to matter. Because it had come out like a growl, and my body liked that, too. My hips shifted automatically, pressing us together, and I gave a little gasp because it felt so good.

And then gasped again when I was abruptly released.

It was fast enough that I almost lost my grip on the towel. I had to grab it in a hurry and then I just stayed there, breathing harder than technically necessary and still flat against the infernal window. Because he was too close to go anywhere without bumping up against him again.

And I didn't think that would be a great idea.

Pritkin had moved off a few paces, but he hadn't turned his back on the dangerous creature that had invaded his room and his life. So I was able to see the flush on his skin and the anger on his face. Anger that, for once, I completely didn't deserve.

"What the hell was that?" I demanded shrilly.

"My abilities are triggered by strong emotion," he said stiffly. "Whether mine or another's."

Incubus powers. No wonder I felt . . . like I felt. "No! I meant *that*," I said, waving the arm that wasn't busy keeping covered what little dignity I had left. "All the slamming and the knife waving and the . . . *that*. What is *wrong* with you?"

"Nothing." Accusatory green eyes met mine. "Other than the fact that the trace charm I have on you pinpoints your current location—five stories above our heads."

Damn. I should have thought of that. The vamps weren't the only ones who kept a tracking spell on me. Pritkin had his own to help him locate me in emergencies. But like all spells, it had to be renewed. And he hadn't been around to do that lately.

Meaning that the only spell in this time frame was on the other me.

And that meant—

"Oh, holy crap!" I grabbed him with my free hand. "Did you talk to her?"

"About you? No. I merely called—"

"You *called*?" I shook him. "What did you *say*?"

He scowled. "I inquired how she was, and satisfied myself that it was in fact her. You. Damn it! Who *are* you?"

"Who do you think?" I said, sitting down on the window ledge, suddenly weak-kneed with relief.

God, if he'd said anything, and if that had caused me to do anything differently . . . But he hadn't. He couldn't have. Proof of that was the fact that I was still here instead of having my bones scattered all over a field somewhere.

"You're from Cassandra's future, aren't you?" Pritkin demanded.

"Way to keep up," I said, pushing wet hair out of my eyes. I looked up to find him glowering at me, but I was too far gone to care. "Look, I need something—"

"Evidently."

"Don't get all British on me," I snapped as his accent

went clipped. That usually precipitated a hissy fit, but I was already having one and we didn't get to do that at the same time. "I need weapons. Against demons. A *lot* of demons."

"No."

I had been tucking in the towel, because I'd provided enough of a free show for whoever was down below as it was, so I wasn't sure I'd heard that right. "I beg your pardon?" I said nicely.

"You heard me." Pritkin was back to his default, steely-eyed look. And his voice had taken on some nuance again, with that faint lilt thing he did on the end of words sometimes. But that just meant he was less homicidal, not more helpful.

"I need weapons," I repeated. "Something easy to use. I don't know how to fight demons—"

"Which is why you aren't getting them," I was told flatly. "Angering a group of dangerous beings by shooting at them is hardly likely to improve your longev—"

"Shooting at them?" I perked up slightly. Because that would be good. Well, better than having to get close enough to dump a potion all over them, anyway.

"There is no reason to discuss weapons you are not going to be using," Pritkin said repressively.

I barely noticed because I was busy checking out his demon-fighting arsenal. I assumed that's what it was, given that most of his weapons were in a footlocker or taking up the space meant for clothes in his closet. But I figured that the demon fighting stuff would be together, because Pritkin was persnickety about his weapons if little else.

So I went to the bookshelf.

"What does this do?" I asked, reaching for one of the weird-looking guns arrayed on the wall above the racks of little vials. It had a maw at least twice the size of a .45, and looked like it should be used for shooting elephants. I bet it was heavy—

A hand clamped over my wrist, just before I had a chance to find out.

"Never. Touch. My. Weapons."

I scowled up at him; the hold was strong enough to hurt. "Ow."

He didn't apologize, and he didn't let go, although his grip softened a fraction. "You can't handle that gun."

"How do you know?"

"I've seen you shoot," he said sourly, taking it off the wall.

"You haven't seen me shoot that."

"And I'm not going to. What kind of demons?"

"What?"

"Demons. What kind are you facing?" Pritkin demanded.

"I don't know."

"You don't *know*?"

"My information wasn't that precise," I said, stung by the disbelief on his face. If he'd known what I'd had to go through to get that much . . . "I was just told that there's a lot of them. They're around this house and I . . . well, I need to get in."

"Where is the house?"

"Why do you need to know that?"

He looked at me, exasperated. "Different demon groups frequent different areas. They are often territorial, as your vampires used to be. Knowing where this house is could possibly tell us what you are facing, or at least narrow the field."

"Yeah," I said, because that made sense. "Only no."

Pritkin frowned. "What?"

I didn't say anything. It had just hit me that I *couldn't* say anything. Geography didn't matter because these demons weren't there for the usual reasons. They were there because Mom had summoned them—or whatever you did to call up an unholy army. I couldn't tell him where I was going, because he knew the location of Tony's farmhouse, and he was even less likely than Jonas to help me muck around with my own past. And of course, what I was planning to do was off-limits since no way would he go along with any plan to help me walk into hell.

Basically, I couldn't tell him anything.

"I can't tell you anything," I said, knowing how well that was likely to go over. "I wish I could, but I can't. I just need something that will get me through a forest of unknown demons and to the front door, long enough for someone to let me in. Do you have anything like that?"

Pritkin crossed his arms and glared at me. "Yes."

Chapter Seven

"I didn't mean you," I said viciously, when we materialized in the middle of a dark, foggy field a few minutes later.

Pritkin was too busy scanning the area Special Ops–style to bother answering. Just like he hadn't mentioned that he intended to grab me just as I started to shift. I should have figured it out when he suddenly got cooperative, but I'd been distracted trying to make the too-short emerald T-shirt he'd loaned me fit over my ass.

It wasn't working that great.

I pulled it down again, wishing that he was taller or that I had a coat. It was chilly, and the thin tee wasn't doing a lot to keep goose bumps from popping up. Or a couple of other things.

"Is it obvious that I'm not wearing a bra?" I asked nervously. I hadn't given a lot of thought to what I would wear when I went to visit my parents, but a thin old T-shirt with nothing underneath wasn't on the list.

"I . . . hadn't noticed," Pritkin told me.

I looked down at the offending mounds, which were straining the soft green cotton. And making a couple of points about my lack of underwear. "Do you think anyone else will?"

He glanced at me and then looked quickly away. "Well . . ."

"*Well* what?"

"They are a bit . . . jiggly."

"Jiggly?" I looked down in horror. I wasn't *jiggly*; I was too young to be jiggly. I bounced a little on my toes, and they moved, sure. But that was normal. Wasn't it? "They're not jiggly!"

"Perhaps it was a bad choice of word."

"You're damn right, it was!"

"I merely meant that they tend to sway a bit when you . . ."

"When I what?"

"Do anything, really."

I sighed and hunched over. "Does this help?"

Pritkin didn't say anything.

"Well?" I demanded.

"They're a little . . . large . . . to be easily concealed by—"

"They're not large!" I did not have large, jiggly boobs, damn it. I had nice, pert breasts. I'd always been proud of my breasts. I just didn't want to flash the parents, that was all. "They're the perfect size!"

"No arguments here."

I stared at him, because coming from any other guy that would have sounded flirtatious. But Pritkin didn't flirt. He did, however, pull off the hoodie he was still wearing and put it around me.

It was warm from his body and it smelled like him. And the fact that he was being an ass didn't stop me from clutching it for a second, and the hands that were trying to zip it up, not wanting to let him go. Stop it, I told myself harshly. I was going to get him back. I was going—

"Where are we?" he asked softly.

I just looked at him silently for a moment. And then said what had to be said. "I'm taking you back."

"No, you aren't."

"And how are you planning to stop me?" I looked pointedly down at his hands, which had tightened on the soft cotton of the hoodie. "By chaining me up? Because that doesn't work so well."

"No. By expecting you to use your brain. You said you need weapons—"

"And you have them. So hand 'em over!"

A lip quirked. "They are tools. *I* am the weapon. Without me they would do you little good."

"I'll take that chance!"

"No, you won't," he told me again, sounding certain. "You're smarter than that."

"If I was smarter, I'd have figured out some other way to do this!"

"Perhaps there is no other way."

"Perhaps I'm losing my mind," I muttered.

"It's not so bad, once you get used to it," he said, making me do a double take. Because Pritkin didn't do funny, either. "Can you at least give me the general layout?" he added, before I could comment. As if we'd settled something.

And I guess maybe we had, since I automatically replied, "There was a parking lo—no. That came later. There should be a bunch of trees, like a small wood."

Pritkin nodded at something behind me. "Those trees?"

I looked over my shoulder, and then turned around. The fog made sure I couldn't see too well. Not even Tony's house, which should be somewhere off to the right, assuming the gray lumps along the horizon were the trees in question. I couldn't tell for sure, since I didn't remember there being quite that many. And because my eyes weren't interested in trees.

They were looking for patrols, one of the ones Tony always had messing about, and which could be gliding silently through the fog toward us right now. Although, if memory served, they'd spent most nights under the covered driveway out front, smoking and gossiping, since who the hell broke into a vampire's stronghold anyway? Of course, Jonas and I had, but that would be years from now, after my parents were long dead. So even if it caused the patrols to be more vigilant afterward, it shouldn't affect—

"Cassie?"

"I don't know," I said, trying to focus on the maybe-trees when my eyes wanted to look for vamps. Not that they'd see them. That was the problem. You never saw them . . . until they wanted you to. "I should probably mention that there's a chance, um, that there might be somebody else around—"

"Somebody else?" Pritkin frowned. "You mean other than the demon army?"

"—so we should probably keep this quiet."

"How quiet?"

I cringed slightly. "Like too-low-for-vampire-ears quiet?"

The frown tipped over into a scowl. "How many vampires?" he asked grimly.

"That would depend on how loud . . ."

Pritkin swore—quietly—under his breath.

"Can you do a silence spell?" I asked hopefully.

"No." He started switching around some of the weapons in his holsters.

"But Jonas—"

Pritkin's head came up.

"I mean, he could, or he said he could, uh, rig something—"

"Yet you didn't bring him, did you?" Pritkin asked sweetly.

"He was . . . busy. . . ."

Pritkin shoved some more weapons into new holsters and muttered something that sounded like "smart man."

"But if Jonas could do it," I persisted. "You must be able—"

"It isn't the spell that's the issue," I was told shortly.

"Then what?"

"Magic is linked with human energy."

"So?"

"So human energy attracts demons!"

Well, shit.

Pritkin gestured at the lumps. "Are those the damned trees or not?"

I squinted. They looked a lot more ominous than the thin line I remembered, almost like a forest. But they were also the only ones in sight.

"Yes," I said. "I think so. Maybe?"

Pritkin muttered something else. He was doing that a lot tonight. "Let's go."

It was the right group of trees. I could tell as soon as we got close enough to see the spears of light shining through the branches. It wasn't moonlight—too bright and the wrong color—more like firelight or soft electric. But the mostly oaks with a scattering of white pine made it impossible to be sure, since I couldn't see the house.

And what I could see, I didn't like.

The weird lighting caused strange crisscrossing shadows to fall everywhere, turning the area under the trees into a half-lit maze. A foggy, half-lit maze, with the light beams sifting apart, like the eerie, otherworldly illumination UFOs gave off in the movies. I swallowed, suddenly really wishing for a Scully from *The X-Files*—some thoroughly prosaic presence to inform me that everything in life had a nice, comforting, scientific solution.

Of course, she'd gotten knocked up by some alien, hadn't she? So maybe it was just as well that my companion was more like Mulder. A coked-out Mulder with a lot of weapons, who knew that the monsters under the bed were real and would *gut* you.

Pritkin was certainly looking more than usually cautious. Or maybe he just didn't like fighting something he couldn't even name. Whatever the reason, he stopped at an outlying oak, standing like a vanguard a dozen yards in front of the rest, and pulled the weird, big-barreled gun I'd seen at Dante's.

"What is it?" I asked, suddenly tense. "What's wrong?"

"I don't sense anything."

"But . . . that's good, right?" I asked, watching him spin open the cylinder like an old-fashioned revolver.

"That's good if your information was wrong," he told me grimly, shoving some weird bullets from a leather case into place. They looked like tiny potion vials, with different-colored liquids sloshing against the transparent sides. I didn't know how something that looked so delicate would survive being fired from a gun, but then, I guessed they weren't actually made of glass. "How sure are you?"

"Pretty sure."

"Then it's not so good," Pritkin said dryly.

"Meaning?"

"One of two things. Either there are no demons in there . . ."

"Or?" I prompted, because he'd trailed off to scan the tree line again.

"Or we're dealing with something old enough and powerful enough to shield itself from detection—even in numbers."

I tried to fit my spine a little more snugly into the unyielding bark behind me. "So . . . that would be bad."

"Yes. Which is why you're staying here."

I started to say something and then bit my lip, because that had been in his don't-argue-with-me voice. Which I tended to pay attention to since it only got trotted out when the shit was already on its way to the fan. "You may need to leave fast," I pointed out, after a second. "I can get you out of there quicker than any weapon."

He clicked the gun shut. "Not if you're dead."

"If we stick together, I won't be. I'm telling you—"

I suddenly found myself jerked to within inches of a face with a tight jaw and hot green eyes. "No. You tell me nothing, not about this. *You do what I say.*"

"Damn it, Pritkin!"

The moonlight had washed all the color from his face, leaving it stark black and white. Uncompromising, like the hand on my arm, or the low timbre of his voice. "There are only two choices. You listen to me and we go forward; you refuse and we go back. You asked for my help; you do this my way. I haven't spent more than a century battling these creatures not to know exactly how dangerous they can be. Do you understand?"

Yeah, I understood fine. The problem was that he didn't. He thought he was protecting me, but if he ended up dead because I wasn't there to shift him away, we'd both be screwed. But I couldn't explain that, without explaining more than was safe for him to know right now.

"How much of a risk are you planning to take?" I whispered.

"No more than need be. I will find and draw off whatever is in there. When you see my signal, run for the house. Shift back here when you're done and I'll be waiting. But only move *when I signal you*. If I do not, you stay put."

"And if you don't come back?" I asked angrily.

"Then get out of here. Go back to your time—"

"The hell I will! I won't just leave—"

"Then I won't go."

And the infuriating man crossed his arms, leaned against the tree, and looked at me. Calmly. Pleasantly. Like he had all freaking night.

I glared back. "And here I thought you'd been getting better lately!"

"I've been indulging you."

"Indulg—" I tightened my lips on a torrent of words, none of which I could say. And not just because we needed to be quiet. Because for a second there I was actually rendered speechless.

Indulging me didn't involve treating me like a Parris Island recruit. It didn't involve questioning every order I ever gave. And it damned sure didn't involve trading his life for mine without even asking what I thought of the idea.

Or how I'd feel afterward.

Somehow, in all the crying I'd done over the man in the last week, I'd forgotten what an absolute *bastard* he could be.

Like when he calmly started to pick at a fingernail.

"Stop that!" I knocked his hand away.

He looked up, bemused.

"You . . . you'll get a hangnail," I snapped, because I couldn't say anything else.

"And that would ruin my evening."

I stood there for a moment, seriously considering just starting for the trees. He'd have to come along or watch me possibly get eaten by whatever was in there. Only, no. Any *other* man would have to.

Pritkin would knock me out with something in his arsenal, throw me over his shoulder, and cart me off God knew where. And that would be that. Except that I'd wake up tomorrow no closer to a solution than I was right now.

And I was getting damned tired of dead ends.

I crossed my own arms. "Fine."

"*Fine* what?"

"Fine, we'll do it your way." Like I had a choice.

Whatever his faults, Pritkin didn't gloat. "Wait for my signal," he reminded me. And then he was off, running hard for the tree line. Where, a second later, he disappeared.

And the minute he did, I was sure I'd made a mistake. It would be totally my luck to get the man killed while trying to save him. I peered around the trunk, my hands eating into the rough bark hard enough to send splinters under my fingernails.

Come on, I thought desperately, as the minutes clicked by. Come on, come on, come *on*.

But nothing happened. There was no sound, no movement, no anything. Just a soft breeze bringing the scent of rain and resin, and a hushed quiet making a mockery of my fears.

Until somebody started screaming.

I was running before I remembered the signal and then *fuck* the signal, because I'd never heard Pritkin scream. And I was desperately hoping I wasn't hearing it now. But it sounded human—if a human was being eaten by a bear or roasted over a fire or torn limb from limb or—

I shut my brain down before it shut me down, and put on an extra burst of speed. I should have just shifted, but I couldn't see clearly and anyway, it was too late now. The ground was growing uneven underfoot, the trees were closing in overhead, and I was slipping and sliding on a bunch of black-rotten leaves down an incline and through a wall of scratchy limbs. Before bursting out the other side and into—

What the fuck?

What looked like jerking red afterimages filled my vision, half blinding me, even though I hadn't been staring at any bright lights. Just like I wasn't out of breath, but the whole area pulsed in and out, like a marathoner's vision. It looked like a demon disco and felt like standing in the middle of a tumbling kaleidoscope, while that unearthly scream went on and on and—

Stopped as abruptly as it had begun.

It took the lights along with it, which would have been great. If it hadn't left me reeling in utter darkness, my heart pounding, my pulse racing, and my mind gibbering somewhere in terror. But as usual, my mouth was doing okay.

"Pritkin!" I called thickly. "Goddamnit, where—"

"Over here."

The voice was surprisingly calm. Or maybe my ears, which were still ringing from the howling, weren't able to discern subtleties. Like my legs didn't seem to be able to walk a straight line anymore. Not that they could have anyway with the slip-'n-slide going on under my feet. And my knees. And my butt as I stumbled and fell and recovered and then hit a particularly nasty patch of leaves and slid the rest of the way to the bottom.

Where Pritkin was kneeling in the muck, in the middle of a space with slightly fewer trees. The thicker cover around the sides formed a natural wall, which the misty drizzle would have faded to the same wet gray as everything else, if not for the otherworldly light show going on. But he seemed perfectly whole and unbothered.

At least he did until he looked up at me. And frowned. "What are you doing here?"

"I . . . what?" I asked unevenly, because the clearing was still spinning. And because that had been a damned stupid question.

"You were told to wait for the signal."

"You were screaming!"

"Which is usually a sign to stay away," he said, frown intensifying. "It also wasn't me."

"Then who—"

"Not who. What," he said, and tried to hand me something.

Since it strongly resembled a slime-covered snake, I shied back. "What the—"

"Didn't that vampire you lived with ever take you to a toy store?"

I stared. "What?"

"For a special occasion, a birthday . . . ?"

"Tony believed in getting presents, not giving them," I said, bending to peer at the creepy thing he held. It was long and black and lifeless, and still looked like either a short snake or a long slug. "Are you telling me that's a *toy*?"

"Was. The enchantment's played out."

Thank God.

"You mean that wasn't some kind of battle spell?" I demanded, gesturing around indignantly, and almost falling over in the process. Okay, that was getting old. "And what the hell's wrong with me?"

"A prank," Pritkin said, lips quirking in his version of

a smile. "The magical equivalent of a whoopee cushion. But instead of embarrassment, the visual component of the spell causes havoc with the optic nerves. It's best not to look at it."

Now he told me.

"Careful. There's likely more of them," he said as I started to take a step.

"How do you know?"

"They wouldn't be much use as an alarm, otherwise." He held up a finger with a slender cord draped over the top. He gave a gentle tug, and a long line of it rose from the muck, with a "snake" dangling down every six feet. It looked like a banner for an *Addams Family* birthday, with all the balloons predeflated.

"An alarm—okay, that's just stupid," I pointed out.

A blond eyebrow rose. "If it looks stupid but it works . . . then it's not stupid." He indicated a small silver thing near the top of the nearest snake. "Removing the cap sets them off. Luckily, I stepped on this one instead of tripping over the line and pulling out all the caps at once. That much noise would wake the dead."

"Wake the—oh, *crap*," I said, staring around.

"It's not a bad system," he commented, carefully laying the slimy thing back in the gunk. "Crude, but effective, and uses too little magic to be easily detectable. Of course, it presupposes an intruder would come through here. But given the thickness of the trees on either side, that's not too much of a stretch." He looked at me with narrowed green eyes. "The question is, why does someone with a demon army need a child's plaything for security?"

"That's a good question," I agreed, and tried to grab him.

But he was already on his feet and backing out of range. "Don't you think it's time you told me what's going on?"

"What's going on is that we're about to have company!" The demons around here might be deaf, but I knew some people who damned well weren't.

"Try again," Pritkin said. "I doubt there ever were any demons here."

"Screw demons!" I said, grabbing for him again. And again getting dodged. "Damn it, Pritkin! Tony's guys could have heard that from across the *state—*"

"Tony's?"

Shit.

Blond eyebrows came together. "The house we're looking for belongs to *your old guardian*?"

Shit, shit.

"I—no," I said lamely, trying to think up the lie I hadn't bothered with before. Which would have been easier if the damned forest wasn't still doing the cha-cha. I gave up. "Tony's place is over there." I gestured back toward the way we'd come. "But it's close enough to have heard all that, so we need to go!"

"Agreed," he said grimly, reaching for my hand. "And then we need to talk."

Only it didn't look like we were going to be doing either. His hand closed over mine, warm and real and steadying. But apparently not enough.

"What's wrong?" he asked, after a few seconds, when I just continued to stand there and look at him.

"It isn't working."

"You mean your Pythian power?"

"No, my singing ability," I snapped, trying again. And again went nowhere. Maybe because I couldn't concentrate with my brain sloshing around in my skull like this. "How long did you say these effects last?" I asked desperately.

"I didn't. And it depends on the person. Perhaps half an hour—"

"Half an *hour*?" I looked at him in horror. It might as well be the end of time.

And for us, it probably would be.

"I can only tell you what some of my colleagues said, after a visiting toddler turned one of these loose at Central. No one had shields up, and a few people were seen stumbling about for approximately that long—"

"Well, that's a problem, isn't it?" I said, trying for calm when I knew, *I knew*, we were screwed. Pritkin was good, but he was only one man and Tony could send dozens, many of them masters. And while they might not have magical party favors, they did have lots of things that went bang and crash and *blew people's heads off*. And we couldn't even shoot back, because we might get unlucky and kill one of them, and that would alter time and then—

"Perhaps no one heard," Pritkin said, not looking nearly concerned enough. "This many trees have a sound-deadening effect, and we are in a depression—"

"Yes, Pritkin! Because that's the kind of luck we get!" I said shrilly, because the calming thing wasn't working.

And that was before something started crashing through the trees across the clearing.

Chapter Eight

It wasn't a vampire. Not unless I was seriously misremembering, and Tony's stable had included someone the size of Sasquatch. But judging by Pritkin's expression, which had shifted over to his what-the-hell face, it also wasn't a demon.

It looked like maybe I'd been right at the start, I thought wildly. I should have brought Scully. Although I wasn't sure even she'd have been able to categorize *that*.

It emerged from the mist between the trunks and paused, as if looking for something. Maybe its head, because it didn't appear to have one. Unless you counted what looked like part of a croaker sack that somebody had stuffed and then crammed into the neck hole. Where it sat, wobbling around like a bobblehead under a floppy hat, staring at nothing because the eyes looked like they'd been Sharpie'd on.

It didn't make any more sense from the neck down. It was roughly the size and shape of a person, if the person was a barrel-chested linebacker on stilts. A lot of it was mismatched metal, and a lot of it was glass, the latter mostly a bunch of round containers set into indentations in what I guess was its armor. Most of those were sloshing with some silvery-blue substance, blending in with the mist, but a row of little gold ones crossed the front on a diagonal, like the potion bandolier Pritkin sometimes wore. But if they were potions, I didn't know how it was supposed to grab one.

Since it had what looked like gardening shears for hands.

For a moment, I just stared.

I knew I should probably be terrified, but I was having a hard time with it. Maybe because I was looking at something that any good horror movie producer would have fired his art department for. It looked like the Tin Man from *The Wizard of Oz* and Edward Scissorhands had had a baby. It looked like somebody had gone Dumpster-diving and built a robot out of the trash. It looked . . . well, it looked stupid.

"Homunculus," Pritkin breathed, without my having to ask.

Not that it helped.

"What?" I demanded, suddenly more angry than anything else. Because no, just no. The universe kept throwing these curveballs at me, and I was mostly going with it, but not when it came down to decapitated robots. I had principles. I had standards. I had—

A face full of muck when Pritkin suddenly shoved me back down.

Something flashed and something sizzled. And it looked like the Tin Man managed just fine with those shears of his, after all. Because when I looked up, I was seeing the world through more than a veil of mud. A bunch of glowing, golden strands had woven themselves around us, hovering maybe an arm's length away in a nice, neat circle. Like we were the catch of the day.

Which, okay, yeah.

"Pritkin . . ."

"When I tell you to run," he said calmly, never taking his eyes off the creature, "go for the trees. Don't stop and don't look back."

I didn't bother arguing, since I didn't see a way for

either of us to go anywhere. "And how do we lose the net?"

"Like this!" he said, and gave me a shove.

And suddenly, the net looked like another balloon, one that had just been pricked with a pin. I had maybe a second to realize that it had been caught on the outside of Pritkin's shields, and that by popping them, he'd bought us a couple of seconds to slide underneath the floaty wisps that were falling down on every side like a spiderweb. And then I was scrambling on my belly through the mud, and lurching to my feet and starting to run—

And realizing that he wasn't behind me.

I spun to see him fighting with the net, part of which had caught the back of his shirt. That wouldn't have been a big deal, but the other half had adhered to the ground, and it must have found a better hold than the slimy leaves. Because his best efforts were only stretching it, like bubble gum between a sidewalk and a shoe, and he wasn't going anywhere.

"Go!" he told me, furious, when I turned to help, maybe because the Tin Man had started lumbering down the slope, with the clumsy-cute gate of a toddler just learning to walk. A manic toddler armed with deadly blades and potion bombs.

Or maybe there was another reason, I thought, as the air rippled by my left ear. Something hit the muck in front of me, and something else failed to hit me between the eyes. Because I'd already rediscovered the ground.

I might not know how to deal with magic robots, but I understood bullet etiquette just fine.

Pritkin cursed and dove down beside me. "Now what?"

"I told you," I hissed, grabbing his lapel. "Tony's boys. Now lose the damned shirt!"

"Why didn't I think of that?" he snarled. And then "Don't touch it!" as I recognized the problem. A filmy strand had wrapped its way across the front of his clothes, as well. Which wouldn't have been an issue except for all the guns and belts and holsters he had holding said clothes to his body. And the fact that the strand appeared to have the tensile strength of solid steel.

"Take them off!" I told him, grabbing the front of his jeans. "Take everything off!"

"I'm trying!"

"Try harder!" I said as he jerked to the left, sliding us around in a half circle on the slimy ground, just before another potion bomb exploded where we'd been sitting. Fortunately, it hit a rock and flowed the other way, trapping maybe three yards' worth of leaves and making it look like a giant spider had been nesting in the area. And it was only going to get worse.

Pritkin must have thought the same, because he grabbed my hands, which had somehow gotten his belt off and were working on the bandolier, and shook me hard enough to rattle my teeth. "Get out of here!"

"Make me!" I snarled, and ripped the bandolier off, roughly enough to make him curse.

Too bad; he'd recover from some bruises. Unlike other things, I thought, glancing up to see that the toddler two-step covered ground pretty damned fast. And worse, the creature was rearing back to throw again, and we were running out of places to go.

I did what I should have done before and snatched one of the guns from Pritkin's belt. It looked like a .22, little and silver colored and unremarkable. It didn't look like it had any business fighting anything, much less demons. But maybe it would slow that thing down.

Only not if it was slammed to the ground first.

"What are you doing?" I demanded as Pritkin glared at me. "Shoot the damned thing!"

"Yes, shooting something made out of battle potions is a good plan," he snarled.

Only it looked like somebody else thought so. The words had barely left his mouth when something pinged off the Tin Man's shiny chest plate. And then something

else ripped off its hat. And then Pritkin cursed and
grabbed me.

"Run!"

"Where?"

"Anywhere!"

And I tried. But before I could move, three things
happened at once. A bunch of dark silhouettes shot out
of the tree line, the creature lobbed its potion, and Pritkin gave a massive jerk on what turned out to be the end
of the line of party favors.

And oh, shit.

If I'd thought the last trip to childhood bliss had been
hell, it was nothing compared to this one. I kind of wondered about magical parents who thought that giving
their kids an acid trip as a toy was a fun idea. But then, I
guess you weren't supposed to set off a case all at once.

It felt like my body was trying to turn inside out. It
felt like all my internal organs had turned to mush. It felt
like a fun-house mirror looks, with everything pulling
into weird, distorted shapes and patterns. I'd have been
sick if I still had a working stomach; I'd have screamed if
I could have remembered how.

As it was, I just lay in the muck and watched the vamps
stumble around, because it seemed to work on them, too.

The elegant, deadly horde had fallen out of stealth
mode like they'd hit a wall. And were currently in
wobbly-legged party mode, which was a lot less impressive. It would have been good times if the creature had
been stumbling around, too.

Unfortunately, the toys didn't seem to bother it at all.
Pritkin noticed, and slurred something drunkenly, but I
didn't hear most of it over the screaming toys and the
yelling vamps. But the next second he was free, and naked except for the ass-kicking boots. Which I hoped
were about to live up to their name. Because the latest
potion bomb hit down as he reached for the weapons
he'd shucked off, forcing him to jerk back empty-handed.

He didn't try again.

He snatched me up, got an arm around my waist, and we stumbled for the tree line.

And weirdly enough, the fact that neither of us could manage to walk in a straight line actually helped. Nets hit down in front of us, in back of us, and to either side, but not on us. Like maybe the creature couldn't figure out where we were going, either.

But while we might be drunkenly reeling all over the place, we were reeling fast. Pritkin put on an extra burst of speed as we approached the trees, and I was right there with him. We were almost to the thicker part of the woods now, where any net would tangle in the branches before it could land on us. Things were looking up—

Or they would have been. Except that this Tin Man must already have been to see the wizard. Because brainless he wasn't. Either that or his aim was suddenly terrible, spraying potion bombs in a rapid-fire line—at the trees right in front of us.

The result was a long, sticky, billowing web of holy shit, opening up practically in our faces.

For a second, I was sure I wouldn't be able to stop, since my legs were only taking orders about half the time. But either Pritkin was less affected by the spell, or ass-kicking boots have better traction than Keds. Because he managed to twist and wrench and flop us to the side, hitting the dirt inches away from the long line of netting.

A gust of wind made it billow out over our heads, and I yelped and hugged the ground, just as the Tin Man readied another shot.

One it never had a chance to take.

Tony's boys might be a lot of things, even lousy shots with the forest fun-housing around them and a moving target and not being able to focus their eyes. But they weren't quitters. Having a homicidal asshole for a boss tends to do that for you. They'd regrouped while we ran, and lousy shots or no, when you're spraying as many bullets around as they suddenly were, you're bound to hit something sooner or later.

"Bugger," Pritkin said, sounding almost casual. Because yeah. There was nothing we could do.

I didn't see the bullet that connected; everything was happening way too fast for that. But I sure saw the result. Everybody in three counties probably did, as the Tin Man detonated in a burst of searing white light and a mass of sizzling, smoking potion balls. I felt the wash of heat even halfway across the clearing, as a dozen separate eruptions burned through the forest all around us and lit up the air overhead, like unearthly comets.

One of them strobed Pritkin's face in blue-white flame as it tore overhead, close enough that I was surprised it didn't set his hair on fire. But not everything was so lucky. A second later, it slammed through the net and then into the tree line behind us. And I hit the dirt again, muck be damned, because I'd seen a few explosions in my time.

But I didn't see one now.

Instead, something shot back at us from the tree line, passing over our heads like a river of wood. Which I didn't understand until I noticed the flowing bark and bulging limbs and leaves the size of car tires spilling out of the forest behind us. And more swelling roots that were suddenly rushing everywhere, over and under the soil, trying desperately to support formerly petite-sized trees that were surging upward like two-hundred-year-old redwoods.

And you know, you'd think something like that would hold your attention. And it might have—if the rest of the comets hadn't taken that moment to discover gravity. They arced high above the treetops, brilliant, blue-white, and burning against the pinpricks of the stars for a long instant. And then they came hurtling back to the ground, silhouetting a bunch of seriously freaked-out vamps before disappearing with loud *whooshing* sounds into the wet and fertile soil.

Which promptly went nuclear.

Everywhere a comet hit down, it lit up the ground

like an X-ray for a couple of seconds, showing glimpses of gigantic things squirming around under there. I stared, because it looked like Cthulu had gotten lost and ended up napping beneath rural Pennsylvania. And he didn't seem happy about being disturbed.

He was no more unhappy than I was.

"Cassie! Come on!"

Pritkin practically dislocated my shoulder, not so much dragging as ripping me off the ground. But I didn't complain. Because trees were erupting from the dirt on all sides of us now, like a maze of wooden spears flying upward into the otherworldly sky. They would have been hard enough to avoid on their own, but as they shot up, a dark rain of mud and burning leaves and clods of earth was pelting back down, on us and on the mass of now desperate-to-flee vampires.

They had lost their undead cool and were running in all directions, including into each other. If the scene had had a sound track, it would have been full of kazoos. Instead, it was full of creaking wood, cursing vamps, burning leaves, and—

And the sound of a colossal tree ripping through the ground, right beneath our feet, throwing us in different directions.

"Pritkin!" I screamed, even before I hit the ground on my back, a ground that was bucking and tearing like an earthquake had hit it, and throwing me around like a drop of oil on a hot griddle.

My ears rang over the mad thud of my pulse. The ground heaved again and again and debris pattered down onto my head and shoulders. Dust caught in my eyelashes, making it hard to see, and dirt clogged the back of my throat, making it almost impossible to breathe. And then an arm grabbed my waist, wrenching me back and *up*.

And suddenly, I was flying through the trees at an insane speed, but not on foot.

For a couple of extremely disorienting seconds, I

didn't know what was happening—until I looked down. And then I still didn't. I saw a river of wood flowing underneath my butt, Pritkin's legs gripping it on either side of mine, and their owner holding on for dear life—to a steadily expanding root that was shooting out tiny feelers to tickle my face.

"What—" I yelped, in disbelief, because I was not riding a giant root like a goddamned motorcycle.

Only I was.

Somehow I totally was. Pritkin had snagged one of the crazy feelers this place was putting out, using it as a fast track out of here. A little too fast, I thought frantically, as trees raced by on either side, the smaller ones being shoved up and thrown aside as our wild ride threaded madly in between, seeking God knew what. And threatening to decapitate the two of us in the process.

"Duck!" Pritkin yelled; I don't know why. Since he simultaneously shoved my head down to the wood between my legs, to avoid the wood slashing by over my head as we tore through a particularly dense area.

Straight at the huge old oak looming up ahead.

I stared at it, openmouthed and horror-struck, because I knew this tree. Everyone at Tony's did. They called it the General. A leviathan of the forest, it had already been old when Washington and his mangy crew crossed the Delaware not far from here. It was ragged and timeworn now, with hoary old arms as thick as other trees' trunks and wearing a coating of gray-green moss. But it was solid as a damned mountain and almost as big. If a tree could look crotchety, it managed it. It clearly was not going anywhere.

Which meant we had to.

I felt Pritkin's arm tighten around me a fraction more, and then he tore us off the side and we were flying again. And this time without a safety net, if a massive, insane tree root can be called that. Only it was looking pretty good a second later, when we hit the ground without the benefit of Pritkin's shields.

I guess he'd been through a little too much to manage them just now. But that was okay. That was fine. Since a couple of seconds later, the irresistible force met the unyielding object and a wooden firework exploded through the forest.

It would have exploded through us, too, but by then, Pritkin had managed to get up a shield. Sort of. It was thin and wobbly and looked about as substantial as a soap bubble, and was likely to be as long-lived. But it was really, really appreciated, especially when a leg-sized sliver of oak came hurtling through the air, straight at us.

And the shield didn't break.

It did bend, though. Inward, to be precise, allowing me to watch as a column that wouldn't take my eye out because it would just cave in my whole head came closer, closer, closer, its ungodly inertia fighting Pritkin's faltering protection. Until I could barely see it anymore, because it was all of half an inch away from the end of my nose.

And then it fell over with a giant crash, smashing into the undergrowth hard enough to shake the ground beneath us. And to cover the sound of Pritkin's shield giving up the ghost a second later. I doubted I'd have heard the tiny pop anyway, next to all of the other crashes and explosions and trunks cracking in half that was still going on. And my heart, which sounded louder than all of them put together.

For a long moment, I just lay there.

I wanted to check on Pritkin, who was being uncharacteristically quiet. I wanted to get up and run screaming in a direction, any direction, that meant getting the hell out of here. I wanted to check out my body for damage, which was kind of feeling like it might add up to a lot right now.

I wanted to do a lot of things, but I didn't.

Because we were no longer alone.

Two more of the junky Tin Man clones crashed

through the trees as I lay there, trembling and helpless. One's glass bits were filled with evil, bubbling red, the other with an equally sinister green, and both were loaded down with more globules of the golden net spell. But before I had a chance to get worked up about it, not that I really felt able anymore, something else came through the trees.

Or, more accurately, someone.

Slashing through the undergrowth with a stick and a scowl was a long, horsey face under another floppy hat. The owner of the face stopped a yard off, taking in the burning forest, the flailing roots, the naked war mage and the screaming vamps. And me, sprawled over the partner I really hoped I hadn't just killed. For a long time, he didn't say anything. And then he sighed.

"Just like your mother," he told me. "You really know how to make an entrance."

Chapter Nine

The drizzle condensed into a driving rain on the way to the house, so conversation was kept to a minimum. Although I did protest when the massive red creature slung an unconscious Pritkin over one shoulder, like a sack of potatoes. And then again when Pritkin's head, now soaking wet and dripping, was allowed to bang against the creature's backside when it stood up.

"That thing will kill him!" I said, struggling to my feet.

But the man—our captor, Roger—didn't seem to care. I decided to go with Roger, since no way was I calling him Dad. And I had to call him something.

"He's a war mage. They're almost impossible to kill." He scowled. "Even on purpose."

He took off into the underbrush. And since Big Red followed, I had no choice but to go, too. Thankfully, we must have gone most of the distance on our crazy ride, because a few minutes later, our host shoved open a side door on a pretty, pale blue cottage.

And Big Red slammed Pritkin down on a table, hard enough to rattle the surrounding shelves.

"I thought you said you weren't trying to kill him!" I glared at Roger, who was shrugging out of his wet coat.

He shot me a disgruntled look. "Didn't look like you

needed the help." And then he disappeared up a flight of stairs.

I bent over Pritkin, my heart in my throat. One day, that famous hard head of his wasn't going to be hard enough. Maybe today, since it was oozing something all over the tabletop.

I couldn't tell what, because Roger hadn't turned on a light, and the room was mostly in shadow. A vague haze was filtering down the stairs, but it wasn't enough to see by. Until my fumbling hand finally found a light switch on the wall, and a small fixture over the table sprang to life.

And showed me a puddle of dirty water, not blood.

I sat down abruptly, feeling faint.

A quick check showed me a lot of cuts and scrapes on the too-still body, but nothing that looked life-threatening. I took off the hoodie and wrapped it around him to preserve whatever modesty either of us had left, and noticed that my hands were shaking. A moment later, the trembling had spread throughout my body, making even sitting up difficult.

I wasn't sure whether that was from worry about Pritkin, or from getting hit with a dozen or so little "toys" all at the same time, or from having an entire forest attack me. But my head suddenly seemed to think that it would feel better on my knees.

Like right now.

I flopped over, and then just stayed there, my body continuing its long-running demonstration on why I was not cut out for this crap.

For a few minutes, the only noise was my labored breathing and a clock ticking somewhere, annoyingly loud. And rain lashing the windows, because apparently I only visited Tony's in lousy weather. And something making a tiny *scrape, scrape, scrape* sound.

Something close.

My head jerked up, and my heart leapt back to what was starting to feel like its new home, just behind my tonsils. But all I saw was dark. Maybe because the main source of light was almost on top of me.

But nothing lunged at me out of the gloom, and my eyes slowly adjusted. And sent back images of a typical kitchen, circa the 1960s, which I guess was the last time anybody had bothered to update this place. Across a rectangular space was a lime trifecta of stove, fridge, and sink, a square window framed by white curtains, and a door leading into an adjacent room.

And a robot slumped on a chair, poking itself in the eye.

I froze.

It was the one with acid green potion bombs poking out of its chest like buboes on a plague victim. And while I wasn't clear on much right now, I was very, very clear on one thing: I did not want to find out what those bombs did. I was suddenly afraid to move, not knowing what it might view as a threat.

Minutes passed. The clock, a big wooden cuckoo by the door, continued to tick. The rain continued to beat against the windows. And the robot continued to scratch at its eye, only I couldn't figure out what it was—

Oh.

Like the Tin Man with his floppy garden sack, and Big Red, whose shoulders terminated in nothing but a small knob, this one didn't have a proper head. As if whoever had designed them had just lost interest above the collar. But somebody else had decided that wouldn't do, and had stuffed a white plastic bucket partly down the neck hole.

That might not have been so bad, since at least it had been formed into vaguely the right shape. And its cheerful, prosaic surface was less *Children of the Corn* than Tin Man's. But then somebody had had to go and ruin it.

By gluing a pair of false eyelashes to the front.

For a moment, I just stared.

They were thick and black and droopy, like two dispirited spiders, and one had slid halfway down what I guess you'd have to call the cheek, maybe because eye-lash glue was designed to stick to other eyelashes, not to shiny plastic. This seemed to bother the . . . whatever it was . . . which kept poking at it, trying to slide it back into place. But despite having nice, robotic-looking hands instead of gardening shears, it didn't appear to be making much progress.

I watched it for a while, blankly, a not-unpleasant white noise buzzing in my ears. And then I decided that maybe I just wouldn't think at all for a while. My brain obviously wasn't up to it, and zoning out was sounding really good right about

But of course not.

There was a heavy tread on the stairs, and then Roger burst back into the kitchen, with his usual frenetic en-ergy and a basin of water. "Dropping in like this," he was grumbling, as if he'd been talking to himself. "Could have gotten your damned fool self killed!"

"You're not exactly easy to find," I said, my voice sounding a little strange and a little breathy, like I was doing a bad Marilyn impression. I put my head down on the table.

That left me looking at him sideways, but it didn't help. He was scowling from this angle, too. "You might have called!"

"Called?"

"We're in the phone book!" he said, and slammed one down on the wood in front of me.

I blinked at it, cross-eyed. "Under what? Gods and demons?"

"The only demon is the one you brought with you," he said, transferring the scowl to Pritkin.

And okay, I thought. It looked like Mom was home. Because I didn't think her . . . lover? friend? pet? . . . was likely to have figured out what Pritkin was that fast. He'd barely laid eyes on the guy, and Pritkin looked like a human.

Well, usually. At the moment he looked more like a

corpse. I got up with the vague idea of doing something, only my legs vetoed that plan halfway through the motion, which left me stumbling awkwardly into the table.

It hurt. A lot. My knee came into painful contact with one of the table's sturdy legs, and the table won. I backed off, to the accompaniment of Roger cursing a string worthy of a war mage I knew.

"Sit down before you fall down!"

"Too late," I mumbled, but my butt somehow found the chair again anyway. He slammed the basin down on the tabletop and muttered some more, while cleaning off Pritkin like he was going to die of dirt or something. I kind of thought if that was the case, we'd both be goners, since we'd passed filthy a while ago. But on the plus side, I didn't look so improper anymore, being decently covered in mud.

Silver lining, I thought, and sprawled there, watching the robot try to fix its wonky eyelash.

It kind of looked like it had had a hard night.

I could relate.

"What is that?" I asked, after a few minutes.

Roger looked up from checking Pritkin for damage. "Is that what you came here to ask?"

"No."

"Then you don't need to know, do you?" he snapped, and slammed out.

I stared after him for a moment. And then I managed to get up and check on Pritkin, too, who was a good deal cleaner but no more conscious than he'd ever been. I felt my stomach fall, since my first-aid training hadn't included what to do for magical pranks or man-eating forests or attacks by supernatural robots.

I put a hand on his cheek, and his skin felt clammy. Or maybe it was just that it was chilly in here, too. His face turned into my palm, his breath warm on my skin, a gentle, reassuring caress.

Until it suddenly stopped.

I grabbed and shook him, which didn't make much of

a difference because I didn't have much strength. And then, about the time the room was starting to collapse in on me, and the light was graying out and I was contemplating a heart attack to go with my stroke, he gave a loud snort. Followed by what, even charitably, could only be called a snore.

I sat down abruptly, trying to decide between bursting into tears and passing out. But neither sounded all that great. So I finally settled for just listening to him breathe for a while.

And the man upstairs knock about angrily.

"I don't think he's happy to see me," I told Pritkin, who failed to have an opinion on the matter.

But somebody else did.

"Oh no, it's not like—" someone said, and then cut off with a little "eep."

I frowned. I was exhausted and freaked out and possibly edging up on crazy, but I wasn't quite there yet. And I was pretty sure that had come from the robot thing. And since it didn't have a mouth, that was . . .

Well, that was interesting.

I got up again.

The poking had suspiciously stopped, with the creature's hands lying demurely in its lap. A lap that I only just noticed was covered by a frilly half apron. It was green, too, with white gingham checks and an eyelet ruffle.

Nothing like color coordination, I thought, and edged closer.

The creature didn't move.

I stopped in front of it.

It just sat there.

I bent over and reached out a hand, which I admit was trembling a little. But that was probably a result of the evening's entertainment. Because whether due to the apron or the eyelashes or the fact that I was high as hell, I wasn't . . . actually . . .

"Oh, thank you!" someone said brightly as the eyelash slid back into place, and I snatched my hand back.

Someone else cursed, "Damn it, woman!"

"Well, what was I supposed to do?" the first voice asked. It was female, and she sounded peevish. "Anyway, it doesn't matter. She can obviously hear us."

"Yes, of course she can!" the man said. "That's the point!"

"Well, I wasn't going to be rude, what with her hurt and scared and nobody even getting the dear any dry clothes. . . . She could catch her death."

"Then she'd fit in here just fine," the male voice grumbled.

And okay. I might not be the world's greatest warrior. Or, you know, anywhere on the list. But there was one thing I did know. One thing I knew very . . . damned . . . well . . .

I bent closer. And in the shiny white surface of the bucket I saw the reflection of the light over the table, a blurry impression of an old pie safe, and the long rectangle serving as the stairwell. And a pair of big blue eyes, beaming back at me—from inside the plastic.

"Caught me," the woman said cheerily. "Look at you!"

I stood up, swaying a little, but managed to point a finger. "You. You're not a homun—humunk—whatever," I said accusingly. "You're a ghost."

A pleasant, lined face with a mop of gray hair popped up over top of the bucket, letting off a bit of green steam into the dark room. "Right in one," she said, apparently thrilled.

"No, she isn't!" the other voice crabbed. And an old gent in a blue uniform with swaying gold epaulettes poked partway out of the clock. "We're both. And the word is homunculus," he told me, officiously.

"It means 'little man' in Latin," the woman added. "Although I always thought that was awfully sexist. After all, I'm better at it than him." And she jerked a metal thumb at the male ghost.

"You are not!" His great gray sideburns quivered indignantly.

"Am, too," she said complaisantly. "That's why I get the good hands." She flexed one ostentatiously. And smiled at me. "He can't handle them."

"You can't even get an eyelash back on, woman!"

"I can so. I was trying to be subtle."

"Subtle? You're five hundred pounds and built like a tank!"

She rolled her eyes. "I bet you used to get all the girls."

I sat down again.

"What are you?" I asked, looking back and forth between the two of them. "If you're ghosts, why are you in . . . *that*?" I gestured at her metal hulk of a body.

She looked down. "It's not very pretty, is it?"

"It gets the job done," the old man told her severely.

"Well, yes, but . . ." She looked back up at me. "I wanted bosoms, you know."

"All right, that's enough," my host's irritated voice came from behind me.

I turned around slowly, because too-fast movements weren't working so well for me lately, and found him holding another pan of water. Or maybe the same one, only it had been washed out and a towel was draped over his arm. He thrust them at me, along with a bar of rose-scented soap.

"In case you want to clean up," he said stiffly.

I felt like pointing out that it would take more than a pan of water for that, like maybe a river. But I didn't. Because he hadn't had to bring it, and just getting my face clean would be nice.

Of course, I could have done that at the sink, just like he could have emptied the pan there. Maybe he was fastidious, and didn't want to wash off forest gunk in the same sink he prepared food over. But I was betting on another reason.

I deliberately didn't look at the stairs. "Thank you," I said, and sat at the table again.

"Your friend will be fine," he said, after a minute, without mentioning how he knew. "And once he is, you . . . well, you need to be going."

I ignored that, because I wasn't up to a fight right now. And because I wasn't going anywhere. I settled for washing my face while he stood around awkwardly.

I decided it was kind of nice not to be the one doing that, for a change.

There was a shiny silver kettle on the stove. I saw it when I was washing the back of my filthy neck. "I'd like some tea," I told him, because I would. And because it would stall for a while.

He looked like he was debating telling me he was out, or possibly to go to hell, but then the woman ghost spoke up. "Some of the peppermint, dear. It's wonderful for nerves."

"Don't help me," he snapped. But he went to make it.

My stomach rumbled, having never gotten dinner, however many hours ago that had been. "And there's some shortbread," she added. "I think it's in the—"

"I know where it is!"

"He's not usually like this," she confided as a bread box was opened and then slammed shut. "Just when he's nervous. I'm Daisy, by the way."

"Daisy." Daisy the ghost. Okay.

"Well, my real name was Gertrude, but I always hated it. Named after my grandmother, and I could never stand the woman. My husband called me Daisy, 'cause I loved them so." She smiled, a bit teary-eyed.

I looked from her to the . . . lieutenant? Colonel? Whatever. "Is . . . is he—"

"Good Lord, no," he said, mustache fluffing up in indignation.

"He should be so fortunate." She sniffed. "Ralph was my husband. He died in, oh, 1942, it was."

"Under enemy fire?" I guessed, considering the date.

"No." She looked surprised. "Under the six a.m. to Hoboken. He got drunk and went to sleep on the railroad tracks." She sighed. "He was not a bright man."

"All right, I mean it," Roger said, coming over with a tin of cookies. "Cut it out."

She rolled her eyes at him, too.

I took a cookie.

"Who are they?" I asked, gesturing at the robots again.

"Daisy has already introduced herself, I believe," he said sourly. "That's Sam."

"Servant, ma'am," the old gent muttered, and emerged the rest of the way out of the clock. He had a portly body covered by a starched blue uniform. "I left it outside," he told the man, I guess talking about Big Red. "Do y'want me to go back, see if I can salvage anything?"

"I don't know." My host looked at me. "Is there anything left?"

"Of the other one?" I guessed.

He nodded.

I thought about it. "The hat?"

He scowled. "No," he told the colonel, who muttered something and went over to give Pritkin the hairy eyeball.

"What did we destroy?" I asked, in between stuffing my face. The cookies were homemade. God, so good.

"Do they not feed you in your time?" my host demanded.

"Not often," I said honestly.

He joined the colonel in scowling at Pritkin.

"What was that thing?" I asked again as the kettle went off.

"My gardener," he told me, getting up to attend to it. "Your—my wife," he amended, glancing at Pritkin, "is fond of the woods. But there was not much left when we arrived. The former owners had cleared some land for farming and more to build the main house. And then Tony burnt a bunch of the rest in order to have an open field of fire, in case any of his enemies tried to sneak up on him."

That sounded like Tony.

"We managed to reverse much of the damage, but it requires upkeep to maintain. And more now," he said dryly, pulling down a couple of brightly colored pottery mugs.

"Then the potions . . ."

"Were fertilizer, yes."

"Some fertilizer!"

He frowned and slopped water in a teapot that matched the mugs. "It functions perfectly well in the correct amount. Maybe next time you should take a moment to find out what you're attacking!"

"We didn't attack anything," I said, remembered fear sharpening my voice. "Why did you tell it to target us? You had to have recognized me!"

"I wasn't there," he said, setting the teapot down on a tray, harder than necessary.

"Then you're telling me that creature did all that on its own?"

"That's the point of a homunculus—it has a will of its own. Too much sometimes." He shot a look at Daisy.

"I was just trying to trap you," she told me, looking sheepish.

"That was . . . wait." I took the mug I was offered, because my throat was full of cookie crumbs, and I could barely talk. But as soon as I gulped down some truly scalding tea, I put it down. "That was *you*?"

"Well, it wasn't me," the colonel said. "A good soldier knows when to act, and when to ask for instructions!"

"Too bad I'm not a soldier," Daisy huffed.

"As you continually demonstrate."

"And I wasn't expecting you," she told me, ignoring

him. "I was just doing a little pruning, tidying up and such, and then the alarms went off and practically scared me to—well, not death, but you know what I—"

"You lost your head!" the colonel accused.

"I don't have a head, old man, and neither do you!" she said snippily. "And I wasn't trying to hurt anybody, just to hold them until I could find out who they were. But then those horrid vampires arrived and blew me up. And by the time I came back here and got my other body and got back out there—"

"We were there, remember?" the colonel demanded.

"Then stop blaming me," she huffed.

"But you're a *ghost*," I said, stating the obvious. "And ghosts can't move things. Well, maybe a piece of paper, or a paper clip. But nothing like . . ." I gestured at the metal suit she was wearing, which was more intricate than the Tin Man outfit, almost like an old-fashioned diving suit. "No way you're lifting that."

"Well, no, of course not," she agreed. "I'm only directing it, dear."

"Then how—"

"Can we discuss why you're here?" Roger broke in.

"No," I said, and not just because I needed to stall until my mother joined the party. I'd thought I knew everything about ghosts, but this was a new one. "Are you telling me you just . . . made them new bodies?"

"I like to think of it as a whole body prosthesis," the colonel said.

I looked from him to Roger. "You—how does that work? Because I don't—"

He made an irritated sound. "Does it matter? It was an experiment, one that never quite panned out. But that's not—"

"What kind of experiment?" I looked around at the ungainly creatures. I could see a bit of Big Red outside, through a window by the door. Maybe because it was even larger than the green one and took up too much room, so had to be left in the drive like the family car. Only there was no such thing as a car for a ghost. "Who *does* this?"

"The Black Circle," Pritkin said harshly, from behind us.

Chapter Ten

Pritkin's voice was strong, but it looked like that was the only thing that was. He needed an arm underneath himself in order to sit up, and it was trembling slightly. Bruises had blossomed all along his rib cage, he had a good start on a black eye, and his skin tone was a grayish white that I didn't like at all. But he didn't appear to be interested in his health. He appeared to be interested in my father.

"You're Roger Palmer," he said flatly.

It wasn't a question. He'd had plenty of time to figure out who we were visiting, and no one had ever accused Pritkin of being slow. Including to anger, judging by his expression.

"Does he always state the obvious?" Roger asked me, pushing a fall of limp blond hair out of his face.

I didn't answer. I was too busy tensing up. I wasn't sure what happened when high-ranking light and dark mages met each other, but I didn't think it was likely to be fun. Even when one had no weapons, and the other . . . Well, at least he wasn't reaching for any.

Yet.

"This is what you've been working on for the Circle, isn't it?" Pritkin demanded, not helping matters.

"I'm retired," Roger said mildly, but failed to offer him any tea.

I passed over my mug. It didn't have milk, because I am a barbarian. But Pritkin took it anyway. He didn't drink it, though, being too busy staring Roger down. Which would have worked better if the man hadn't had his long nose stuck in the cookie tin.

"And yet you have at least three of these things, perhaps more!" Pritkin rasped. "For what purpose?"

"For whatever purpose I choose, war mage."

"For security," I said quickly, because Pritkin's pale face had just flushed purple. And because it was true.

I didn't need to be told that much. My parents had been hiding with Tony the bastard because, believe it or not, there were worse things out there. Like a bunch of leftover demigods from antiquity with long lives and longer grudges. The Spartoi had been the children of Ares, left behind when the gods were kicked off earth due to their mixed blood giving them a foothold here. They'd used it to do their father's bidding, which was to hunt down and destroy the person responsible for his exile.

My mother.

They'd failed, but not before giving it the old Olympus try. And right now Mom and her strange protector didn't realize that Tony the petty and rotund would one day be a lot more of a problem for them than any ancient half gods. All they knew was that her power had diminished considerably over the years, and that they needed a hideout no one would expect.

Roger was looking at me, as if he knew what I was thinking. Not too hard, since we'd battled the Spartoi together once. Well, sort of.

We'd mostly run away together.

"What kind of security?" Pritkin demanded. "If you're telling the truth, they're nothing but ghosts—"

"You think spirits are not powerful?" Roger asked archly. "You of all people should know better."

"And why would that be?" Pritkin asked silkily. There weren't too many people who could guess what he was, especially after half an hour's acquaintance. But Roger merely smirked at him.

Okay, this was going well. "I still don't get how you made them," I said quickly.

"The same way war mages make golems," Roger told me.

"They're nothing alike!" Pritkin said. And he should know. He'd had a golem once.

"Well, yes, there is the matter that your lot forces demons to power your constructs," Roger agreed. "While my associates do it of their own free will. But other than—"

"Golems are *controlled*—"

"A nicer word than enslaved."

"—so they are not free to wreak havoc—"

"Until they get loose and eat your face," Roger said dryly.

"—unlike that thing tonight! It might have killed us!"

"With what? She wasn't armed."

"It did a good enough job without—" Pritkin stopped. "She?"

"Her name's Daisy," I informed him.

Pritkin's mouth had been open for another retort, but at that he shut it. His eyes slid over to Roger and then back to me, as if he was trying to see the resemblance. I could feel my face heating; I didn't know why. I damned sure didn't see any myself.

Roger Palmer was a tall, lanky guy, a bit on the thin side, with a face, nose, and teeth that were all slightly too long. It gave him a horsey appearance, which wasn't helped by a shock of dishwater blond hair that liked to flop in his pale blue eyes. He was dressed in an old brown suit and a tan cardigan that had started to pill. He had on threadbare purple velvet slippers, since I guess the Wellies he'd worn to tromp through the forest had needed cleaning. He didn't look like a dangerous dark mage, despite that being the story I kept hearing. And he certainly didn't look like somebody who ought to be married to a goddess.

But then, I didn't look much like a Pythia, either, so looks could be deceiving. I just didn't know if they were in his case. I also didn't know if he was provoking Pritkin when he was already in a mood because he thought he could handle him, or if he merely didn't notice.

Judging by his reaction, I don't think Pritkin knew, either.

"But ghosts can't power anything," I repeated, before they started up again. "Most of them barely manage to take care of themselves—"

"Nonsense," Roger said. And for the first time, his face came alive. "Ghosts are amazing creatures, among the most versatile in existence. And powerful—"

"Powerful?" I repeated, because that hadn't been my experience. Sure, the ones at Tony's had wreaked some havoc, and I'd seen something similar on a few other occasions. But those were rare instances when a lot of ghosts found a reason to work together, usually in pursuit of their favorite sport—revenge—or of the power they needed so desperately. Without it, they ended up in a half existence, chained to whatever they were haunting and the tiny subsistence it afforded them until they finally faded altogether.

I'd often thought that was why so many eventually went mad. Eternity stops being a bonus when you're effectively a prisoner. And there were certainly enough crazed spirits out there.

But powerful?

"Oh yes," Roger insisted. "Take demons, for example. Everyone always talks about how strong they are, how difficult to control, how dangerous." He did little finger motions around the last word, as if mocking the idea of anybody being afraid of a lowly creature like a demon. "When if they only knew—ghosts are far more so."

"You're mad," Pritkin said, as if he'd finally come up with an explanation that satisfied him.

Roger sneered. "Oh yes, do let's trot out the hoary old stereotype—"

"Which you're currently doing your best to uphold."

"—of the mad necromancer—"

"Is that what you are?" I asked, feeling my stomach fall. Jonas had said as much, but I'd been hoping he was wrong.

Roger shot me an impatient look. "Despite what you may have been told, it isn't a bad word. It's merely a name for a magic worker who specializes in the dead—all sorts of dead. The only reason it has an evil connotation is that the Circle has gone out of its way to give it one."

"And because so many of the breed end up having to be locked away," Pritkin added.

"Yes, I always wondered about that," Roger said sweetly. "If we're so powerless, why bother?"

"It's not your power anyone questions, mage. It's your principles."

"Principles." Roger huffed out a laugh. "As if the Corps would know anything about them."

"As opposed to the Dark Circle, which has such a record for altruism."

"Yes, let's pretend those are the only two options."

"The Corps is the only option that keeps the magical community safe!" Pritkin said, flushing.

"From everything but itself."

"From those who would recklessly ignore the experience of centuries—"

"From those who resent the absurdity of stagnant magic that gets weaker every year—"

"—and attempt dangerous experiments that are almost certain to end in disaster!"

"—while our enemies get stronger! Yes! Cut off your nose to spite your face, war mage!" Roger snapped. "But don't doom the rest of us to go down with you. There are those who would prefer a fighting chance!" And the mug came crashing down.

Daisy and I jumped. The colonel's mustache twitched. Pritkin and Roger glared at each other. And I jumped in while I had the chance, since I might not get another.

"How are ghosts more powerful than demons?" I asked. Because if it was true, I really needed to have a chat with Billy Joe.

Roger sent me a glance, like he knew what I was doing. But after a moment, he answered anyway. "Well, for one thing, they're less vulnerable. Take the colonel. Do you see a control gem in his forehead?"

"He doesn't have a forehead," Daisy said, looking disapproving. "Doesn't even have a head—"

"I have a head, woman!" the colonel said indignantly.

"I meant on your new body."

"So did I! The whole point was to leave 'em empty above the neck so our own heads would have a place to go!"

"But nobody sees our heads," Daisy pointed out. "And they look so . . . odd."

"They're not the only thing odd around here."

"My point," Roger said, talking over them, "was that the colonel doesn't have to worry about someone erasing a spell on his forehead or pulling a scroll out of his mouth—"

"Which would be easy enough since it's usually open," Daisy put in.

"—or any of the other typical ways of immobilizing a construct like a golem. Because they're not constructs; they're just using them."

"Like driving a car," Daisy told me. "It gets totaled, but you walk away."

"Can't a demon walk away?" I asked.

"Yes, but it's not going to come back, then, is it?" Roger countered. "Once the golem—its prison, essentially—is destroyed, its sentence is over. And it doesn't usually waste any time getting out of there. Unless it decides to get . . . testy . . . with its former master. But either way, you've lost your servant."

Pritkin glowered at him, but he didn't refute it. Which I supposed meant Roger's account was pretty accurate. He enjoyed an argument even when he liked someone, and I didn't think he liked Roger.

"And then there's the way they feed," Roger continued, oblivious. "Ghosts and demons are both spirits, yes?"

"Well, some demons . . ."

"And they both gain strength by feeding off living energy."

I nodded.

"The difference is that demons can only hold so much. They're like humans that way, or vampires. They feed to satisfy their current needs, and to store up power for later. And, of course, with the elder demons, the amount they can hold can be very, very large. But even they have limits, although they don't like to admit it. Whereas ghosts . . ."

"What about ghosts?"

"They're eternal sponges: they never get full. You can feed them and feed them and feed them, and they just . . . soak it up."

Daisy nodded her substitute for a head, and the eyelash fell off again.

I frowned. "How do you know? No ghost has access to that kind of power." For most of the ghosts I'd known, the problem was finding enough energy to keep going, not in seeing how much they could store up.

"They do if someone provides it."

"But why would anyone—"

"You're making indestructible soldiers!" Pritkin accused.

I looked at him, faintly surprised, but not as much as Roger. Who seemed amazed that a magical jock could put two and two together. But he shook his head.

"Not indestructible. You discovered that much tonight. Not that that model was designed for combat, mind you, but any of them can be destroyed under the right circumstances. But that isn't really the issue."

"Then what is?"

Roger looked thoughtful. "I suppose the best analogy would be your Spitfires in the Second World War."

Judging by his confused expression, that didn't clear up much for Pritkin. It didn't for me, either, but I was a little distracted by the sick feeling that had opened up in the pit of my stomach. Because it wasn't the why of Roger's weird hobby that interested me.

It was the how.

"During World War Two, the Nazis planned to invade the British Isles," he told me. "But to do so, they first needed control of the skies, and that meant wiping out the RAF—that's the British Royal Air Force."

I nodded numbly.

"But the RAF held on, mainly because their airplanes, the Spitfires, were damned good little planes, and because their factories could churn them out in a seemingly endless supply. Every time a plane went down, there were two more waiting to replace it. There was just one problem."

"Factories couldn't churn out pilots, too," Pritkin said, narrowing his eyes at Daisy. Who was poking around in her apron for the lost lash.

"Exactly," Roger said. "The RAF kept running out of pilots, and couldn't train more fast enough to meet the demand. They only held out because of an influx of qualified personnel from abroad. And even then, it was a close thing. But imagine if you could train someone once, yet use him over and over. Imagine if, when one's vehicle was destroyed, one's body remained unharmed and could merely flit back and pick up another. And another after that, and another after that—"

"You'd never run out," I said, watching Pritkin. Who'd started out angry and was closing in on furious.

Roger nodded. "Think of it: an army of soldiers who can't die—they already did. Or be captured and forced to answer questions by their enemies. Or be prevented from returning to base. After all, what can trap a ghost?"

I could think of something, I didn't say, because Prit kin had reached apoplectic. Maybe he was thinking about the destruction such a force could wreak on the Corps. Or maybe it was Roger's attitude that bothered him. It was like he'd forgotten who his audience was and was happily holding forth on his favorite subject.

"Of course, there were problems," Roger told me. "Most annoyingly that the ghosts said the bodies didn't feel like theirs."

"I kept drifting up out of it," Daisy said. "And that was before I tried to move the thing!"

"And practice didn't help much," Roger added. "I finally realized that I had merely created a vehicle, when what they needed was a body. So I did some research and discovered that the binding spell for a golem has similarities to the way zombies are made, and once I understood that, well, things began popping."

"I'll say," Daisy put in.

"Of course, I still had to figure out an enchantment to lighten the weight of the bodies, so they weren't burning through power like a 747. And ghosts can't do magic. Therefore all their spells had to be transformed into a potion form that could be carried—"

"But you managed," I said, because obviously.

"Well more or less." He patted Daisy's massive thigh. "And unlike living soldiers, mine don't get tired. They can't be wounded. They don't need sleep. As long as there are bodies to house them and energy to supply them, they can go on and on and—"

He cut off because Pritkin had finally had enough. A wash of power suddenly filled the room, reminding me that Pritkin didn't need weapons. He was one. He was a war mage.

But then, so was Roger.

Pritkin launched himself off the table and into the air, with something in his hand I couldn't see but knew damned well he couldn't use. It's over, I wanted to yell. He can't hurt anyone! He's already dead!

But I never got the chance.

I was half out of my seat, hand outstretched and words forming on my lips, when Pritkin suddenly wasn't there anymore. But a second later, something hit the far wall with a crack. I looked over to see him peeling off the paint behind the table—and the plaster and the bricks—having been knocked across the room and partly through the wall by something that had moved so fast it had been only a blur.

And still was, because I was too busy running to look for it. I shoved a chair aside and knelt by the crumpled body, the one with an unexploded potion grenade falling out of one hand. Pritkin must have stayed conscious long enough to steal one off Big Red while being carried back, and shoved it down his boot.

And damn it! I should have thought of that. But I hadn't thought it necessary to frisk a naked man.

"That'll teach him not to bother with shields!" someone said, and I turned to see the creature itself standing in the doorway. The rain was blowing through a ghostly image of the colonel's head rising out of the neck and looking smug.

"It won't teach him anything if he's dead!"

"Would you prefer your father dead, girl?" the colonel demanded.

I picked up the golden grenade and threw it at him. "He was going to trap him—not kill him!"

The colonel dodged back out the door, avoiding the sticky strands that hit the jamb and spread over the opening, like a giant web. "Well, how was I to know that?" he demanded, glaring at me through a gap. "And what good would trappin' him do? This isn't your time!"

"It might force him to tell the truth! How many of you does the Black Circle have? Where are they keeping you—"

"I should have anticipated that," Roger said testily, coming over. He glanced at the colonel. "Next time, allow me to ask for assistance before you intervene."

"He's a war mage. You wouldn't have had time to ask," the colonel protested—to no one, because no one was listening to him anymore.

"Do something!" I told Roger, who had knelt beside Pritkin and was checking for a pulse for the second time that night.

He looked up at Big Red. "Flashlight."

The giant snagged one out of a tool belt with one of the hooks it used for hands, and pushed it through a gap in the net. From the look of what else was hanging around its waist, it was plain that Red's primary use wasn't gardening. He could have hit Pritkin with something far worse than the flat of his hand, although that might have been enough.

Roger retrieved the flashlight and pried up Pritkin's left eyelid, careful not to move the head. "Normal dilation," he told me, after a second. "And his heartbeat is strong. He should be all right, but we won't know for certain until he comes around."

"*If* he comes around!"

"You worry too much. He's half demon—"

"He's half human, too!"

"Well, what would you have me do?" he asked impatiently. "I'm not a doctor and he isn't a vampire. I can manipulate dead flesh any way you like, but I don't have power over the living."

Maybe not, but I knew someone who did.

He caught my arm as I jumped up. "She isn't there. She—"

"Like hell she isn't!" I broke away and ran for the stairs.

Chapter Eleven

There was only one flight, which let out onto a small hallway. There were two doors on either side, with the first opening onto a junk room, piled high with old furniture, and the next onto a tiny bath. But the door across the hall led to a bedroom, with a big brass bed, a window cracked enough to toss the sheers around, and an old-fashioned wardrobe. And another door—

Leading to a nursery.

There was no one in it except for a baby in a crib, who had somehow slept through the storm outside and the fight downstairs. But who woke up when I slammed in the door. Woke up and started screaming.

"All right, that's enough," Roger said, coming in behind me.

For a second, I wasn't sure if he was talking to me or to her.

Not that I guess it mattered.

He hurried past and picked up a small thing in a yellow onesie, with a mop of downy blond curls and a scrunched-up face. "Your mother is in the forest," he told me, feeling frantically around in his jacket for something. "Dealing with the mess you two made before it consumes half the state!"

I didn't say anything. He finally came up with a pacifier that he stuck in the wide-open mouth that was emitting all the noise. That worked for a couple of pulls, until she promptly spat it out. He sighed.

"I always wonder about babies who can be fooled by those things," he said, jiggling her up and down. "She—you—never is. A few pulls and when nothing comes out . . ." He shrugged and put her head on his shoulder, doing the please-shut-up baby dance all parents seem to know.

I sat down.

There was a rocker underneath my butt, but I'm not sure I'd known that. Right then I wasn't sure I knew anything. I was looking at a concerned father gently tending his fussy child, the dim moonlight from outside flooding in a small window to halo their blond heads, one straight as a pin, the other a mass of curls. And nothing made sense.

"You killed hundreds of people," I said numbly.

He looked up. "What?"

"Ghosts don't work for free. All that power . . ."

"What power?"

"To fuel your army. It had to come from somewhere."

He frowned. "Are we back to that again?"

I stared at him, wishing he looked like the picture I carried around in my head. The crazed mage shooting at me and Agnes in a dank dungeon; the manic, stumbling idiot, barely staying ahead of the Spartoi on a desperate flight through London; the sarcastic, angry man downstairs. Any of them would make this easier.

Instead, I got a frazzled-looking guy with spit-up on his shoulder. I got a hand desperately clutching a diapered bottom, with the please-don't-let-her-need-changing-while-her-mother-is-out look of men everywhere. I got a ridiculously goofy grin when he realized she was dry.

I didn't get easy.

"What did you offer your legions?" I said, deliberately making it harsh.

"My what?" He looked confused for a moment, maybe because he'd started trying to fish a bottle out of a dorm-type fridge stuck under a table while also holding a squirmy baby.

"The ones you were telling Pritkin about!"

He finally snared the bottle. "The war mage, you mean? We never got around to introductions."

"Yes! The one your creature almost killed! You told him—"

"What he wanted to hear," he said, sticking the bottle on the table. And then muttering something and waving a hand at it. And then trying to test it on a wrist, but that's a little hard with an infant drooling on your shoulder. "Here," he told me, pushing her at me.

I shied back, but he just thrust her at me again.

I took her.

She didn't look like me. She didn't look like anything in that distinctive way of babies and half-baked loaves of bread. Until she got bored staring at the pocket on Pritkin's shirt, and a familiar pair of baby blues met mine.

They didn't appear impressed.

"Son of a—" Roger cursed.

I looked up to find him with a red welt on his wrist, courtesy of the now steamy hot and curdled contents of the bottle. I waited while he fished out another, tried whatever spell he was using again, and finally managed to get the temperature right. "I don't usually do this," he explained. "I'm not, that is, I drop things, and her mother said—"

"Your. Legions," I repeated, because I had to. I had to know.

"Oh, for—" He broke off, looking like he wished he could still stop my mouth with a pacifier. "My legions consist of an ex-marine who died in the Spanish-American War and a bag lady who expired under the Forty-fourth Street Bridge! And I never drained anybody to keep them. It's quite the contrary—they usually end up draining me!"

He took the baby back, popped the bottle in her mouth, and glared at me.

"But . . . you made an army for the Black Circle. You just said—"

He shrugged. "I've always been good at telling tales. And your war mage . . . well, he deserved a few bad moments. He gave me enough tonight!"

"Are you trying to tell me that wasn't true? That you just made it all up?" I didn't believe it for a second. The evidence to the contrary had just thrown Pritkin halfway through a wall.

He looked at me impatiently. "The theory is sound enough, but in practice—it's like I told you. It was a *failed* experiment."

"It looked pretty successful to me!"

"Well, of course. It was designed to." He held the bottle under his chin and pulled over an ottoman, I guess so he wouldn't drop me, and plunked down.

"Designed to do what?"

"To fool the Black Circle." He saw my expression and made a disgusted sound. "Look, it doesn't work, all right? But the Circle didn't know that because no one had ever tried it. The demonologists who could create a proper binding spell couldn't see ghosts, and you can't bind what you can't even tell is there! And the necromancers who specialize in ghosts can't do a binding."

"Daisy said otherwise," I reminded him.

He rolled his eyes in unconscious imitation. "Do you know how zombies are made?" he demanded, putting the baby on his shoulder and patting her back. "They're not like ghosts. They have no souls. So a necromancer must send a tiny bit of his own to animate his creation."

"So?"

"So it's not like you can spare that much! That's why you don't see zombie armies roaming about, despite

what the movies would have you believe. A necromancer can only direct two, maybe three at a time with any
success. Any others he tries to raise will be on autopilot—
the lights are on but nobody's home, all right? And as
such, they're sitting ducks. Useless."

"I still don't see—"

The baby interrupted me with an astonishingly loud
burp. We both looked at her, me with shock, him with
satisfaction. He wiped her chin and popped the bottle
back in her mouth.

"I told you, I modified the binding spell used on
golems with the spell we use for making zombies. And it
worked, more or less. But you know how it is with
magic—it always bites you on the ass somehow. And in
this particular case, I found that the new spell was limited in the same way the zombie spell is—I could only
bind two or three 'bodies' at a time. I couldn't make an
army if I tried!"

I scanned his face, wanting to believe him. His blue
eyes looked guileless, and he sounded completely convincing. But then, he had downstairs, too.

Roger scowled, I guess because I was taking too long.
"Think, girl! Why do you think nobody's used ghosts as
a weapon before? I'm not a genius and nothing's new
under the sun. Somebody probably tried at some point,
then gave up in disgust and went back to zombies! They
may be disgusting, but at least they're reliable."

"Yet you've done it, at least with two—"

"Yes, two. And you wouldn't believe the merry hell
they give me, either. I mean, think about the logistics of
it for a minute. *If* you could find enough independent-
minded spirits, who weren't obsessing over revenge
twenty-four-seven, and *if* you could somehow find
enough energy to feed them, and *if* you could convince
them to support your cause . . . well, then you might
have a force to be reckoned with. But do you know what
the odds are on that?"

He was right, I realized. And if I hadn't been so busy

worrying about him and Pritkin going for each other's throats, I might have realized it on my own. Billy Joe was just one ghost and he gave me a fit. I couldn't imagine controlling an army, or even managing to recruit it to begin with. No wonder nobody had ever done it. It would be like trying to herd cats.

"Obsessive, chattering cats," Roger agreed, because I guess I'd spoken that last out loud.

"But Jonas—the head of the Silver Circle—told me your ghost army was watching the Circle's every move."

Roger laughed. "Did he, now?"

"You're telling me that wasn't true, either?"

"Of course it wasn't true. I don't like the Silver Circle, but the Black's even worse. I wasn't about to help them, but they kept insisting. They'd gotten the idea that I had several hundred ghosts lying about, which I suppose they thought was a waste since they were feeding them! So I made sure that rumors reached the Silver Circle to make them extra paranoid and give me an excuse for not catching much."

I stared at him. He sounded so blasé about it, like lying to the two most powerful magical organizations on earth was no big thing. "And your army—"

"When people hear the term 'army' paired with anything, they tend to give it respect. Ask Tony."

"You lied to him, too." It wasn't a question.

"Well, we couldn't stay at the house," he said peevishly, looking a bit annoyed. Like he'd expected me to ooh and aah over his accomplishments. I was impressed all right—that he'd lasted as long as he had. I was also coming around to Pritkin's point of view—there was a damned good possibility Daddy was nuts.

"Why couldn't you stay at the house?" I asked, not sure I wanted to know.

"Your mother outright refused. I told you, she prefers the woods, and anyway, she didn't like Tony."

Imagine that.

"And in any case, the bastard bunch of ghosts they

have over there kept trying to savage Sam and Daisy! I had to get us out."

"So you faked the demon attack so Tony would exile you to the cottage," I said, because of course he had.

"Fire spell. You know how vamps are."

"—and then you booby-trapped the forest—"

"Well, we had to grow it first."

"—and built those things so nobody would come out to spy on you."

"I'm less worried about the spying than the dying," he said dryly. "If the damned Spartoi show up, I need something better than Tony's lot to buy us time. Something even a god won't expect. And I still had the specs for the homunculi from when I was with the Black Circle, so . . ." He shrugged.

I sat there. I had about a thousand questions I wanted—needed—to ask, and this might be my only chance. Because if Mom was anything like Agnes, she wasn't going to be happy to see me. I knew that, knew I needed to seize the opportunity while it was here, but I was having a hard time with it.

"You . . . you lied about everything," I said, trying to wrap my brain around the idea of this completely ordinary guy somehow convincing everyone—the Black and Silver Circles, Agnes, a master vampire, *everyone*—that he was a force to be reckoned with. When all he had were some junky robots and a couple of smart-mouthed ghosts.

"I prefer to think of it as creative problem-solving," he told me stiffly.

"And you got away with it," I said wonderingly. Because that was probably the most difficult part to accept.

"You sound surprised."

"I'm flabbergasted," I told him honestly. He smirked. "You should have been dead *years* ago."

The smirk faded. "Thanks," he said sourly, switching the baby over to the other shoulder, since that one had been sufficiently drooled on. "But maybe one day you'll learn, people are gullible. Often they'll just believe what you tell them, if you sound confident enough—and if it's something they like. They want to believe, so they do half the work for you."

"But . . . but the *Black Circle*," I said, trying to impress on him the type of people he had been dealing with, since apparently he still didn't get it.

"The maxim holds true for crooks as much as anyone else," he told me. "Maybe more so. They get so used to everyone being too scared to try to con them that they just assume you must be telling the truth."

I just sat there and looked at him some more. "And that army you kept promising? Wouldn't they expect to see it, sooner or later?"

"Well, yes," he said, more quietly, because the baby had fallen back asleep. "That's why we had the falling out. They demanded results and I . . . well, I stalled for as long as I could, pointing out that ghost recruitment is a little more difficult than the usual kind. And then I had to build the prototype, and then work out the kinks, and then demonstrate it—they were happy that day, at least. But eventually they demanded to see more, and of course two was all I had."

"But why make any at all?" I said angrily, because none of this made any sense. "What were you even *doing* there?"

He frowned at me, maybe because I'd managed to wake the baby up, and stood to rock her. "I was there for the power, of course. I told them I couldn't recruit ghosts without it, or support an army on my own. If they wanted results, they had to pony up. And they did." He grinned. "Oh yes, they did. For years, I all but drained them dry—"

"For *what*?" I demanded, wanting at least one true thing in this house of lies he'd built. "Why risk your life for power you didn't even need?"

He started to answer but then looked up. And his whole face changed. For an instant, he was almost handsome. He was looking at something behind me, in the doorway, and I knew even before I turned around what it was.

Or, rather, I knew who.

"I found a war mage bleeding onto the linoleum," my mother said, coming in and taking the baby.

"Bleeding?" I jumped up.

"Healing was one of my gifts once," she told me. "I have not completely lost the skill."

"Is he awake?" I didn't doubt her, but I wanted to see that scowl for myself.

"He will be soon." She glanced at her husband. "Will you watch him?"

"Of course."

"Without further incident?"

He rolled his eyes but looked a little guilty. He left. Leaving me with a goddess I didn't know, and a mother I'd barely met.

For a long moment, I didn't say anything. She was as beautiful as I remembered, and nothing like the legends said. She was a warrior—I knew that, and not just because of some old, probably half-mangled stories. But because I'd seen it with my own eyes. She'd turned a Spartoi to dust, trapped another in a time loop, run a third down in the nineteenth-century version of a chariot. And then, with a little help from me, she'd dumped most of the rest in time, stranding them forever in the fall of history, with no way to stop.

But she didn't look it. Her beautiful spill of coppery bronze hair was curling in damp ringlets down her back, her soft white dress was wet and dirty around the hem, as if she'd had on a coat that had ended just a little short. And her beautiful face was serene as she soothed her child.

She smelled like lilacs, I thought blankly, the familiar scent circling my head like a caress. I remembered . . . from childhood . . . it was almost the only thing that I—

"Cassandra."

Violet-blue eyes met mine. They were calm, like her voice. But suddenly, I wasn't. Suddenly, I could barely breathe and my chest hurt.

"Cassie," I whispered. "Most people . . . they call me—"

A soft hand cupped my cheek. I froze, not because the touch was unwanted. But because I suddenly wanted to turn into it, to hide my face, to tell her a hundred different things that I couldn't seem to get past the swelling in my throat. I wanted—

"You should not have come."

It was like a kick in the gut, even though I'd been expecting it. "I . . . I know," I said, swallowing. "Agnes said . . . she didn't want to see me, either. She said it let her guess too much, just the fact that I . . . I mean, she said not to come back. And I didn't. But she couldn't have helped me with this anyway. I needed to see you . . . to ask—"

"I know why you've come."

"You do?" It brought me up short.

"I am not what I was, Cassandra. But I am not human."

No, but I was. It hung in the air, unspoken, but palpable. I wasn't what she was. I couldn't see myself in her at all. I never had. I was a lot more like the bumbling guy downstairs, the one who dropped babies—hey, maybe that was what was wrong with me—the one who picked fights he couldn't win, the one who stubbornly insisted on doing things his own way. It had gotten him killed.

I wondered what it would get me.

"I am glad to have seen you." Her hand was soft, gentle on my cheek for another moment, before falling away. "You should go."

I stared up at her, angry tears obscuring the sight of her holding the now calm baby, and wondered why she'd had me at all. Why she'd bothered. Did goddesses get knocked up, too? Hard to believe it had been on purpose, when she clearly could do without me now. Well, too bad. I was here and I was staying here, until I got what I'd come for. I'd gotten precious little in the way of preparation for this crazy life from either of my parents. But *I would have this*.

She turned away to put the baby in the crib. "You're as stubborn as your father."

"Then you know I won't just leave."

"You would do well to reconsider."

"Like he should have reconsidered, that night in London?" It came out before I could stop it, but I wasn't sorry. A human—a bumbling, clumsy, ham-fisted human—had saved her that night, from a group of creatures who made the gods shudder. It hadn't been pretty and it sure as hell hadn't been elegant, but it had worked.

Sometimes we mere mortals could surprise you.

"If he hadn't been there, I would have died," she agreed, tucking in the child. "But his life . . . might have been very different."

"And mine would have been nonexistent. So forgive me for being glad he was stubborn!"

She glanced at me. "You even sound like him."

Her voice had been fond, almost indulgent. It seemed impossible that she should have cared for someone so . . . not divine. I'd mostly been assuming that she'd been using him in some way. But it had sounded . . .

"How did you two meet?" I asked, because I'd always wondered.

She didn't answer. She also didn't sit down, so I couldn't, either. Maybe that's why this felt less like a visit, or even an audience, and more like a bum's rush to the door.

Fine, I thought, angrily. But I was going to ask anyway. She could ignore me, but I was going to ask what I damned well liked.

"It wasn't that night," I said defiantly.

She still didn't sit, but she leaned against the crib. She looked tired, I thought, and then I pushed it away. Goddesses didn't get tired . . . did they?

She smiled slightly. "We met when Agnes brought him back across more than three centuries. From a cellar in London, if you recall."

I remembered Agnes taking the furious mage he'd been away, but I hadn't thought she'd planned to keep him. "Why didn't she turn him over to the Circle?"

"The Circle has no facilities for dealing with time travelers, however inept. Such is the responsibility of the Pythian Court. She brought him to London, and shortly thereafter, I met him—in jail."

"And fell in love with an inept, time-traveling jail-bird?"

It came out before I could stop it, but she didn't seem offended. "No one knew he was inept at the time. I was designated to take him food, since he was presumed to be a dangerous dark mage and I could shift away on a second's notice. Instead, I stayed. And we talked."

"About what?" I couldn't imagine two people who had less in common.

"The past, the future . . . a hatred of fate, of rules, of suffocating order."

"I thought order was a good thing."

"It depends on whose."

I blinked. That had sounded grim. "I don't understand."

The lightning flashed outside, making her hair glow flame-red for an instant. "You do. You are the child of chaos, Cassie, of turmoil and mayhem and wild uncertainty. Your very existence is proof . . ."

"Of what?" I asked, when she trailed off.

"That hope cannot be chained. That fate can be undone!"

I blinked again. She'd said it fervently, passionately, which was just as well. Because, otherwise, it might have sounded less like prophecy from the lips of a goddess . . . and more like the cheap babble some so-called clairvoyants used in a reading when they didn't know what to say.

Or when they were trying to change the subject.

She smiled again, as if reading my mind. "You wish to rescue this demon, then?"

I nodded.

"Why?"

"I—what?"

"It is a simple question, is it not? You are proposing to risk much for him."

"He would do it for me."

"Would he? They are self-serving creatures, demons—"

"You could say the same about humans—or gods."

An eyebrow rose. "Perhaps. But we are not talking of them. But of a creature who is struggling against his very nature. Sooner or later, he will give in to it. Perhaps it is best if it is among his own kind."

"They aren't his kind! They're—" I thought about the demons I knew, from the mostly benign to the frankly terrifying. None of which reminded me in the slightest of the man downstairs. "He's human."

"He is part human. It is his other half about which he has yet to learn."

"I don't think he wants to learn about it," I said dryly. Pritkin had been pretty clear on that point.

"That is not his choice. We are who we are. All of us are governed by that, to some degree."

"And all of us choose to what degree—except him. The choice was made for him. He was *taken*—"

"From you."

"Yes."

"And you resent it."

"Yes!"

"Because he is yours."

"Y—" I stopped, suddenly confused. Until I remembered: the gods had always taken humans as their servants, or playthings, or whatever, without a second's thought. Before her epiphany, Mother probably had, too. But I wasn't a god, and that wasn't what had happened here. "No. He's his own person—"

"Then should he not decide this for himself?"

"You don't understand. He wasn't given a chance—"

"But he was. To save you and be damned, or to let you die. He chose the former."

"No! He—that wasn't a choice! It was forced on him by . . . by his father, by circumstance, by—"

"By fate?"

"Yes—I guess."

"And you wish now to remake his fate."

"If you want to put it like—"

"Be sure," she said, suddenly urgent. "Fate has many strings, Cassie, and when we pluck another's, our own often resonates."

Okay, I was beginning to think that maybe I wasn't keeping up with this conversation. I was also starting to understand the problem people used to have with oracles. "In English?" I said hopefully.

"When you change someone else's fate, it often changes your own."

"For the better?" I asked, already knowing what the answer was going to be.

"There is no way to know. That is the essence of chaos, of stepping off a cliff, not knowing what you will find at the bottom."

Yeah, only I knew what I usually found. "I think I like order better," I muttered.

"Indeed?" She arched a slim eyebrow. "Then leave him to his fate, and go back to yours."

"No."

"Then you choose chaos."

"All right, fine, I choose chaos!" I said passionately. "Just tell me what I need to know!"

Chapter Twelve

I rematerialized a few minutes later in my favorite se-
cluded corner of the hotel's lobby. It gave me a wall on
two sides, and a fat faux stalactite blocked most of the
view ahead. A stalactite I quickly had to grab on to the
side of to keep from falling on my butt.

Okay, I thought, as the room whirled madly around
my head.

Okay, I thought, as colors ran together and a wind-
tunnel-like effect roared in my ears and the whole thing
gave Roger's toys a run for their money.

Okay, I thought, as my stomach joined in and my
brain decided screw it and I fell on my butt anyway.

Okay.

There was a slight chance I needed a day off.

I let myself fall backward, since I was doing it anyway.
And then lay there, watching the girders in the gloom
high above my head wave around in ways girders weren't
supposed to. That was fairly entertaining, but I had to
close my eyes after a while, because it was starting to
make me sick.

And I was sick enough.

In hindsight, I probably should have hung around after dropping Pritkin off, and given myself a break before

the next time shift. Which, judging by the way I felt, I'd been doing a little too often lately. But he had started to come out of the groggy phase, and I'd wanted to avoid a conversation I wasn't prepared for, so I'd skipped out.

Not my best move, I decided, as the whirling thing got worse.

After a bit, I turned my head to the side, because if I passed out and threw up at the same time, I didn't want to choke. But I didn't pass out. And nothing came up, maybe because I didn't have enough in my stomach to bother with.

Skipping meals had its perks, I decided, and wondered if anybody would care if I just slept here.

The carpet smelled like shoes and cigarette butts.

I decided I could live with it and rolled over, trying to find a comfy spot.

And instead found myself nose-to-toes with a pair of shiny, shiny Ferragamos.

"I knew it," someone said bitterly.

It took a moment, but my eyes finally focused on the handsome face of a very pissed off vampire. Fortunately, it wasn't Marco. Or Mircea. Or anyone else I might have had to think up a good story for, because I wasn't up to that yet.

"I've been waiting," the vamp told me grimly. "I have a thousand other things to do, but I knew, I *knew*, you'd show up at the worst possible moment. And look. Faith confirmed."

"You don't have any faith," I slurred as my eyes tried to uncross.

The whirl of colors and sounds and music behind the vampire's legs slowly coalesced into a picture of the Underworld, if the Underworld sold tacky tees and fruity drinks and had people wandering around in tuxes.

Wait.

Tuxes?

"Oh, I have faith," the vampire said, dark eyes snapping. They went well with the tuxedo that was currently highlighting his Spanish good looks. "I have faith you're going to ruin my life!"

His name was Casanova. Yes, *the* Casanova, or so he claimed, although he wasn't and never had been. But the incubus possessing him had previously possessed the famous Latin lover, and the vampire community isn't immune to celebrity worship. So "Casanova" had adopted the name and the lifestyle along with the spirit, which meant that he was more accustomed to lying around in silken sheets than doing any actual work.

It had surprised me, then, that he'd taken to his first real job with a vengeance, although that might explain why he was glaring at me. Once again, I was sullying his hotel with my presence. Considering what the place usually looked like, that thought would have made me smile, if I wasn't too damned tired.

And if tonight wasn't the exception that proved the rule.

Dante's hotel and casino was by turns tasteless and vulgar and gaudy and cheesy, but it wasn't cheap. Nothing on a prime piece of the Vegas Strip was. But just because its guests were paying through the nose to poke more hard-earned cash into the casino's gaping maw didn't mean they dressed up. Despite what the movies would have you believe, standard Vegas evening attire was a T-shirt and shorts, except for the winter, when it might occasionally stretch to a hoodie and jeans.

But not tonight. Tonight, the stalactites and stalagmites and steam-shooting geysers in the overthemed lobby were being obscured—by the beautiful people. I'd never seen so many glittery dresses and sharp suits and sleek hairstyles around here at one time before.

And was that a string quartet?

"Are we having a party?" I asked, propping myself up on one arm.

"*We* aren't having anything," he said, snatching the glass of champagne a passing waitress had just bestowed on me. "And if I did believe in a Divine Being, he would have to be the biggest sadist since the marquis himself to have saddled me with you!"

"Okay, cut it out," I said, making a face—at the glass, because the one sip I'd managed to get had been foul. "I just got back. And if that's what you're serving the guests, you'd better be prepared for some lawsuits."

"They aren't guests; they're staff. And I'm not paying for champagne when the cameras can't tell the difference!"

"What cameras?"

"The cameras you don't need to be concerned about. Now twitch your nose or whatever it is you do and get out of here! And do it fast, before anyone sees you. There are bums credit-hustling the slots who look better than you!"

For once, he appeared genuinely offended.

I looked down.

And okay, I'd looked better.

The hoodie Pritkin had loaned me had largely protected my upper body during the melee. But my legs had been exposed and were covered in scratches and bug bites and dried mud and something I finally identified as patches of resinous tree gunk. My once white Keds were black, there was a layer of grime under my fingernails, and I thought it just as well that I hadn't seen my face in a mirror lately.

But it felt scratchy, too.

I picked a pine needle out of my hair and tried for dignified. "I told you, I just got back. And I'm not going up to the room until I get something to eat."

"I'll have something sent up!"

"Yeah, right. In two hours, and I'll be asleep by then."

"I'll tell them to hurry."

"They never hurry." Fred had been right about one thing—room service around here sucked. "I'm just going to run through the taco line—"

"That's all the way over on the drag!"

"So?"

"Oh, for—wait here," he told me, pointing to the floor in front of my filthy shoes. And then he stabbed the air a few more times for emphasis. "Right. Here. Do you understand?"

"I like them with guacamole and red sauce, but no lettuce," I told him, and sat down against the base of the fake rock again.

He was back in a second, but not with food. But with a large potted fern in a bronze bucket, like the ones that framed the check-in desk. I don't know what ferns had to do with the ambience, but Dante's didn't worry about little inconsistencies like that. Or about the fact that even hell wouldn't have had that carpet.

"Right. Here," he repeated, slamming the fern down. And then he was gone again.

I pushed fronds out of my face, since he'd set the thing directly in front of me, and checked out the party/convention/random assembly of beautiful people that was happening. I didn't know if Casanova was trying to attract a more well-heeled group by parading his off-duty employees in Gucci, or if there was something else going on. And, after a minute, I decided I didn't care.

I leaned my head back against the stalactite and closed my eyes. The room felt like it was spinning faster this way, but oddly, it made my stomach feel better. Which, of course, just meant that my brain woke up.

It started crowding me with thoughts of all the things I could have asked tonight, instead of just sitting around chatting with Roger's ghosts. But I'd been a little high and more than a little freaked-out, and they'd been hard to ignore. And then with Mother—

Damn. My mother. I swallowed, and then I banged my head a few times against the rock, because it deserved it.

I don't know what I'd expected her to do. Welcome me with open arms? Shower me with kisses? Tell me she'd missed me?

And yes, I realized. Some part of me *had* expected

that, or it wouldn't have hurt so much. Some stupid part, because of course she hadn't missed me. She'd never had the chance. She hadn't spent decades wondering, searching, dreaming. . . .

And she'd given me what I asked for. Well, more or less. And it had been nothing like I'd expected.

Not the information itself so much—after a week of contemplating breaking into hell, I'd been prepared for almost anything. But the fact that she hadn't laughed at me, or told me I was crazy, or shot me in the butt . . . She'd just . . . told me.

She'd given me what I needed to get up to some next-level shit without much of an argument at all. So, either she was seriously overestimating me, or . . . or maybe I actually had a shot at this? Maybe she saw something in me I didn't? Maybe . . .

Maybe she thought the best way to get rid of me was to give me what I wanted and let me figure out for myself that it was nuts.

I didn't know. I had this weird feeling that I knew less about my parents now than I had before. I sure *understood* less.

Like my father. I supposed the truth—if I'd even gotten the truth—was better than the rumors I'd heard, but it was no less bizarre. What was an ancient goddess doing with the magical version of a con man? And what had he been doing with the Black Circle?

He'd needed power, he said. But for what? Because a couple of ghosts couldn't possibly use that much, even if they were going around playing Iron Man. So what was he using it for?

It couldn't have been to help Mother. She'd been weak, yes. She'd needed magic, yes. But not the human variety. That was why the old legends spoke of the gods visiting earth, but living somewhere else—Asgard, Vanaheim, Olympus—whatever you wanted to call it. Because they couldn't feed off human magic. I didn't know if it was incompatible with theirs, or wasn't strong enough or what. But they would get weak if they stayed here very long.

It was why Mother had ended up losing most of her power after trapping herself here. And why she'd finally gone to the Pythian Court after avoiding it all those centuries. Apollo, god of prophecy, had gifted the oracles of Delphi with some of his own power, back when they'd been good little worshippers, and it was still going strong. I guess the trickle the Pythias used was negligible compared to the amount needed by a hungry god.

But Mom hadn't gotten to feast for long. Going to court had allowed her enemies to locate her, and she'd had to expend most of the power she'd gained fighting them off. So she'd ended up sitting in Tony's guest cottage with Dad, who was avoiding the Black Circle, who presumably wanted to do violent things to him. And waiting . . .

For what? Until tonight, I'd never really thought about it. I'd just assumed they were in hiding. That's what you did when bad people were after you. But now that I'd met them, that didn't make much sense, at least not as a long-term plan.

The Spartoi were relentless. She had to know they'd find her eventually, and as soon as they did, it was game over. Her power was all but gone, Tony's guys wouldn't fight for her, and even if they did, the Spartoi would make mincemeat out of them in about a minute flat. And having fought them both, I doubted Roger's crazy inventions would do much better. And even if I counted the forest as part of her defenses—and having been through it, I saw no reason why I *shouldn't*—well, Pritkin and I had survived it. A bunch of ancient demigods were hardly likely to do worse.

So, yeah, everything I'd seen had looked like a stopgap, something to buy my parents a little bit of time.

But to do *what?*

"Here!" I was jolted out of a half sleep, half reverie by somebody thrusting something under my nose. Something that looked divine, I realized, as I managed to push a silver serving tray far enough away to focus on the contents.

"That's not tacos," I said sleepily.

"No, it's better," Casanova snapped. "Now get back up to your room before somebody sees you!"

I would have snapped back, but I was feeling tender toward the guy who had just brought me a tray of luscious-looking hors d'oeuvres. It held equal parts gorgeous salmon, juicy sausages, fat shrimp wrapped in bacon, and hearty meatballs. My stomach woke up and started grumbling plaintively. Suddenly, I was starving.

A phone rang and Casanova snatched it out of his jacket. "Of course you do," he told it viciously. "I can't take five minutes . . . all right, all right. I'm coming!"

He thrust the platter at me and was gone, with that liquid speed vampires use when they aren't messing about. And I didn't waste any time, either. I grabbed a salmon sliver sitting on top of an artfully piped swirl of herbed cheese, which in turn was resting on a slice of fresh cucumber—

Which would remain fresh forever, I realized a second later.

Because it was made out of plastic.

I managed to spit the thing out before I choked on it, and then just sat there, looking at the slimy thing in my palm. And wondering how my life had come to this. I threw it down, wiped my hand on my filthy top, and picked up a rubbery shrimp—that appeared to be made out of real rubber. And then a sausage with a beautiful sear that had come out of a spray-paint bottle. And then—

"No," I said, increasingly desperate, pawing through the whole tray. But it was all the same. They were fake. They were all fake.

Casanova had just given me a tray of plastic food.

It looked like one of the sample trays the restaurants used out front as an enticement. It seemed that the employees not only weren't getting real champagne, but weren't getting fed, either. And neither was I.

"Son of a bitch!" I sat there, disbelieving and furious and utterly, utterly ravenous. For another second, before I was on my feet and pushing palm fronds around.

The place was packed. If possible, even more beautiful types had squashed into the already stuffed-with-tourists lobby since the last time I looked. There was no way to shift without being seen, and I didn't feel up to it anyway.

Maybe I did look like a bag lady, but this was supposed to be hell. If they could have satyrs serving in the bar upstairs and incubi manning the salon and cocktail waitresses in devil ears wandering around, a random street person shouldn't shock anybody. And if it did, that was just too bad. The universe might hate Casanova, but it was conspiring to starve me.

And I had had enough.

I was taking back control of my life, or at least my dinner.

I was heading out.

Or, you know, skulking behind the check-in desk, because I didn't want to get tossed out on my ear.

Fortunately, nobody was checking in at the moment. I got a couple of glances from the staff, but most of them knew me by now, and crawling behind the desk was one of the least strange things they'd seen me do. Nobody tried to stop me, and I scuttled from there to a service corridor, through the back of an ice cream shop and out into the lobby again. Right where the hellscape gave way to an Old West ghost town, if the Old West had featured plastic cactuses and neon cocktail signs and overpriced boutiques.

And a fiberglass donkey cart with a flashing taco sign.

I could have sworn a heavenly chorus started singing, if that hadn't been really unlikely around here. I lurched forward, drawn by the siren call of seared meat and habanero sauce, my mouth watering and my eyes glazed. And ran right into the front of a starched dress shirt.

"You thin' I don't know you by now?" Casanova demanded, his Castilian lisp showing up along with what looked like a full-on snit.

"Oh, for the love of   get out of my way!" I told him, trying to muscle past.

But I didn't have much muscle left, and Casanova, despite acting like a little bitch half the time, was a master vampire. I didn't go anywhere. Goddamnit!

"You are not ruining this for me," he told me menacingly.

"I'm just trying to get in the freaking taco line! I don't even know what 'this' is!"

"This is my attempt to save a failing business," he hissed, grabbing me by the arm and jerking me behind a couple of fake hay bales. "I am about to be on television, coast-to-coast coverage, in prime time!"

"For what?"

"For that!" Casanova said, gesturing at a big-toothed guy with a lapel mike who had just emerged into a cleared area in front of the lobby. He and the dozen black-shirted guys he had running interference were blocking most people's access to the elevators around the corner, but nobody seemed to mind. They were too busy watching him as he grinned at a professional-looking video camera.

"Fiends," he told it suddenly, with every appearance of relish. "Ogres. Giants. Freaks of all kinds. If you don't believe in monsters, you're part of a tiny minority. Throughout history, almost every culture on earth has believed. Even odder, they have all believed in the same monsters.

"Take zombies for instance: 'I shall raise up the dead and they shall eat the living . . . I shall make the dead outnumber the living.' Where do you think that quote comes from? Stephen King? *Night of the Living Dead*? No. It's from an ancient Babylonian epic that was written five thousand years ago. It's one of the oldest written works in the world. Zombies . . . have a pedigree."

"What is this?" I asked, feeling my stomach drop for a totally new reason. "How did the press get in here?"

"I invited them," Casanova said shortly.

"What?" I looked up at him in disbelief.

"Do you have any idea how hard it is," he asked fervently, "to make a profit when half your rooms and most of your staff have been appropriated by the damned senate?"

The "damned senate" was the vampire senate, which had lost its usual hangout in an earlier attack in the war. They'd temporarily moved in here, since the casino was owned by one of their own, being part of Mircea's extensive portfolio. So far, that had gone better than I'd expected, what with a bunch of senior masters and their entourages crowding up the place. But that could easily change—like tonight, for instance.

"Are you *insane*?" I hissed. "You know what's upstairs. What on earth could possibly have made this seem like a good idea?"

"I'm looking at her."

"What?"

"Oh, how quickly they forget!" he said, sneering. "Or do you perhaps vaguely recall all but destroying my hotel a little over a month ago?"

"Which time?" I asked uneasily. Because, okay, there'd been a few incidents.

"But zombies are newcomers compared to Weres," the announcer told us. "There are cave drawings from fourteen thousand years ago depicting humans with animal faces, or transforming into beasts of all kinds. From Europe come tales of the most famous Weres of all: werewolves. But did you know, in Central America there are stories of were-jaguars? In central Asia, of were-bears?"

"The huge battle?" Casanova whispered, spitting mad. "The one I'm still making repairs for?"

"Oh." That one. "What about it?"

"Well, word got out, didn't it? Containment isn't so easy when you have giant magical melees taking place in the air over the damned roof! We did the best we could, but ever since, there have been rumors. They finally became so insistent that the senate decided it would be easier to have the *Hogwash* people come in—"

"What people?"

"You must have seen them," he said impatiently. "With the little horns and the squeals and the—oh, never mind! The point is, their shtick is debunking urban legends and the like. If they come here and don't find anything—"

"And if they *do*?"

"Then there's everybody's perennial favorite, the vampire," the announcer intoned. "How far do they date back? Let's put it this way: there are shards of ancient Persian pottery depicting blood-sucking creatures. That predates all written records, folks."

"Then we make a few mental adjustments, erase some footage, whatever it takes!" Casanova said. "But in the end, they'll go off satisfied and, more important, I will have had an hour-long, prime-time advertisement for free and you are not going to mess that up for me!"

"I'm not doing anything," I said angrily. "What is your problem?"

"Oh, please! Don't think I don't know why those bitches are here!"

"What are you talking about?"

I didn't get an answer, because a guy in a security uniform ran up, looking freaked. Since most of the security detail around the casino were vamps, and vamps who had seen some shit, it didn't make me too happy. And for once, Casanova and I appeared to be on the same wavelength.

"What?" he demanded, before the guard even stopped.

"Sir, it's getting worse. We can't contain—"

"Then call for backup! They're *filming*!"

"Sir, we *have* called for backup. We have every guard on duty either in place or on the way, but we aren't, that is, we don't—"

"Don't give me that," Casanova snarled. "There's only three! Sit on them if you have to!"

"Sir, I don't think you under—"

"All right, you're going to have to hold it down," we were told, by a guy in a black tee with a pink pig on the front. "We're picking you up on the mikes."

"So sorry," Casanova whispered ingratiatingly, and jerked me back against the wall.

"And as for demons, well, they've been mentioned in almost every holy book going," the announcer said. "Along with plenty of secular texts. Take the incubus, for example. A spirit who supposedly visits people in their sleep, for, er, carnal relations. That idea goes back to Mesopotamia at the beginning of written history, at least forty-five hundred years."

Casanova turned on his vamp again. "They'll be through with the intro in another minute. Just hold on until—" A chicken flew past his face. "What the—what was that?"

"Sir, that's what I've been trying to tell you," the vampire said tightly. "We don't *have* a minute."

"But now all these legends, fables, myths, and—yes—monsters, have been brought together in one place, for your entertainment," the announcer said, throwing out an arm, "in the Vegas attraction everyone's talking about! Dante's, where it's rumored, unexplainable things happen on a regular—"

Another chicken flew by, this time in front of the man's face. "What's that? What's going on?" he demanded, breaking character.

"I do believe you missed one," a woman's voice rang out, sounding amused.

"What?"

"In your litany of supernatural creatures. You forgot the most important of all."

"Forgot who?" the guy asked, looking confused.

But not as much as when a whole flock of panicked birds suddenly descended onto the crowd, screeching and clucking and causing people to duck and squeal. Or when one of them suddenly morphed midflight into a naked vampire. Who hit the floor with a thud and a shriek: "Witches!"

He scrambled up and took off, bare butt flashing the camera, but I doubt anybody noticed. Because pandemonium had just broken loose. Chickens, sheep, and a flock of—yes—pigs were running and soaring and squawking and squealing everywhere, people were screaming and ducking, and something or somebody crashed into the taco stand. Which tipped over, scattering sweet-smelling meat and shredded cheese and my last chance at dinner everywhere.

And I finally reached tilt.

"Stop! It!" I screamed, at the top of my voice, unable to take any more.

And, just like that, it did.

It stopped.

Not something. Everything. Including a rogue head of lettuce, caught midbounce.

I looked at it for a moment. And then at the taco guy, who had been about to hand somebody a couple of huge white paper bags. I licked my lips. And then I walked over and tugged the bags out of his frozen fingers.

I'd feel bad about it later. Right now all I felt was hunger. I clutched my ill-gotten meal to my chest and stepped over the river of grease. And a fallen tourist. And a hovering bird. And then I rounded the corner—

To find that the time bubble I'd inadvertently created didn't extend out quite this far. A potted fern's fronds rustled slightly in the breeze from an air conditioner vent. A chicken caught inside a security guard's uniform stopped struggling to stare at me out of the neck hole. And a trio of women by one of the elevators exchanged glances.

The elevator dinged and the doors opened. I got on. One of the women started to say something, but I held up a hand. It had taco sauce on it. "Next time," I rasped, "try calling."

"Calling?"

"I'm in the book," I told her savagely.

And then the doors shut and I was gone.

Chapter Thirteen

So good. Oh God, so freaking—

There was a knock on the door. I looked up from the feast that was spread out on my bedspread, and glared at it. But, apparently, my mood did not communicate itself through the foam-core, because a moment later, the door opened.

A vampire looked in.

I hid my food as best I could, and snarled at him.

He backed up slightly, hands raised. "Jeez. I mean . . . Jeez," he said, gray eyes wide.

"Go. Away," I warned, and shoved another nacho in my face.

"Yeah, uh, yeah. Only Marco said to ask you—" He broke off, looking at something. "Hey, is that mole—"

"Get out!" And he suddenly disappeared.

Not left, *disappeared*.

I panicked for a second, but then I saw him, not mentally the way I had when I'd shifted someone once before, but running in a panic past the open door. For a second, I wondered if I'd actually shifted him at all. Vamps could move fast enough to make it *look*—

But no. The power drain hit a second later, forcing out a groan. Damn, I felt like crap.

No big surprise. The real shock was that I wasn't dead. Almost constant time shifts for a week, barely pausing for food and sleep before going out again, stopping time—a massive power drain right there—and then shifting somebody . . . no wonder he hadn't gone but a few feet. I was surprised he'd gone anywhere at all. And now I felt nauseated.

I drank margarita out of a classy foam cup and told my stomach to deal with it. A moment later, another vamp appeared in the doorway.

This one was smarter. This one didn't come in. This one just looked at me, all crossed arms and big-brotherly disapproval, although whether at my appearance, at my eating in bed, or at my scaring poor Fred, I didn't know.

"Is it safe to come in?" he asked, after a minute.

"Are you going to eat my food?"

Marco lifted a bushy black eyebrow. "Is that from the heartburn shack downstairs?"

"Yeah."

"Then it's sacred, I assure you."

"Then you can come in," I said, as if I had a choice. Marco went wherever he damned well pleased.

At the moment, he was pleased to occupy one of the delicate little princess chairs the designer had chosen to grace my bedroom. They always looked like they were going to crack under the strain, but somehow they never did.

"You were gone a long time," he finally said.

"I fell asleep."

"In a pine grove?" He picked something out of my hair.

Damn it, I thought I'd got them all.

"That was after I woke up."

He looked at me. I looked back. And then I ate another nacho.

He sighed. "You've been acting weird all week."

"I thought I always act weird, according to you."

"Weirder, then." He contemplated my scratched,

dirty, and habanero-splattered self. "Is there something you want to tell me?"

And suddenly, there was. There really, really was. I didn't know if he was doing the vampire thing and manipulating my emotions, but I doubted it. Marco didn't usually go in for that kind of stuff. It's why we'd developed a sort of bond over the weeks we'd both been trapped here.

I knew that Marco didn't like babysitting any more than I liked being babysat. But it was his job to guard me and my job to be guarded, at least in the current everybody-wants-to-kill-me era. And we both did our jobs. It was to Marco's credit that he did his with a little bit of grace, and made this place as welcoming for me as any gilded cage stuffed full of vampires could be.

Maybe that's why I had a sudden, insane urge to spill my guts. I wanted to tell him exactly what I'd been doing. I'd wanted to tell *somebody* all week. The pressure, the fear, the gnawing, gut-churning anxiety, had all been building until I'd started to feel like I wanted to scream.

And look how that had turned out, I thought grimly.

"No," I said, and chewed chocolate-covered chicken.

"You sure?" he asked, and looked pointedly at my T-shirt.

And crap. I didn't know what other weird smells the filthy thing held after mopping up half the forest, but it didn't matter. Vamps aren't herbivores. They aren't designed to differentiate between types of florae, even whacked out, god-induced florae. They're designed to find prey. Like the guy I'd just been rolling around a forest with.

I loaded up a nacho, and didn't answer.

Marco had never asked me where Pritkin was. But some of the other guys had hinted around, and some smart aleck had left a copy of one of the more scandalous rags on the kitchen counter. The one with a grainy pic of Pritkin and me making out on the boss' front lawn.

It had been taken at what was supposed to be my

coronation, after the Spartoi attacked me. We'd fought, and I'd won, a fact that continued to amaze me. But winning didn't ensure survival, and I almost hadn't. The picture had been of Pritkin donating the energy to me that I needed to live, basically giving me the incubus version of mouth to mouth. Only it hadn't looked that way.

And the fact that I'd been butt-naked at the time hadn't helped.

Maybe Marco thought the same as some of the others, that Pritkin was lying low to stay out of Mircea's way. I didn't know because we'd never talked about it. And we'd never talked about it because he'd never asked.

He didn't this time, either.

He just reached over and appropriated the massive nacho I'd been absentmindedly building, swallowing the guac and meat and cheese and refried beans and sour cream and salsa-laden pile all in one bite. And then said mildly, "'Cause you know who'll be asking next."

"The senate?"

Marco gave me an odd look. "In a way."

Crap, crap, crap.

"I thought Mircea was in New York." He was always in New York these days. Well, except for when he was in Vegas, or at his court in Washington State, or at one of half a dozen spots in between. I understood the need to avoid putting all your eggs in one basket in war time, so it made sense that the senate would spread out their power base. But this was getting ridiculous. I was surprised he didn't have whiplash.

"He don't need to be here to be here," Marco said. "If you get my drift."

"Yeah." That was one of the perks of being a master vamp: what his family saw, Mircea saw. But, unlike everybody else around here, I didn't have the ability to mindspeak, and I wasn't planning on picking up my phone. In fact, I might just jerk it out of the wall. Mircea my friend/lover/protector/occasional-partner-in-crime would have been welcome. Mircea the senator . . . not so much. Not until I finished my current errand, anyway.

He might own a casino themed like hell, but I had a pretty good idea what his view on my visiting the real thing would be.

Marco sighed again and looked over my spread. "When did they get mole'?"

"Last week," I told him, and handed it over. I had plenty left.

We ate in companionable silence for a while. Marco was one of those guys who didn't feel the need to talk all the time. I'd asked him about it once, and he'd said he spent years learning to block out the incessant chitchat from other family members that went on in his head. You'd think that vampire mental skills would be used only for important stuff, but apparently not. According to him, they gossiped all the time, and it almost drove him crazy before he learned how to filter. And now he didn't appreciate the verbal kind taking its place.

That was okay. I liked the quiet, too. Especially when the alternative was a lot of questions I couldn't answer.

Not that I wouldn't have liked to try. Marco had big shoulders, and it would have been a relief to dump some of this on them. But it wouldn't be fair, and anyway there was nothing he could do. Except tell Mircea what was going on, not because he was a fink, but because that was what vampire servants did. He'd basically just reminded me of that fact, since he was a decent guy. But I hadn't needed the hint.

I knew I couldn't tell anyone anything.

It was one of the hardest things about this job. And, I suspected, why a lot of Pythias developed reputations for being a little . . . odd. How could you not be when you knew things nobody else knew, things that nobody else could be *allowed* to know, and when you didn't even have anybody you could vent to once in a while about the absurdity of visiting dead parents or stopping time or *going to hell* . . . ?

It was driving me crazy, and I'd only had the job a few months. How had Agnes done it? And for decades?

Of course, she hadn't exactly been the poster child for normal. And that was despite having Jonas to help her. And while I doubted she'd told him everything, or even most things, I knew they'd talked. He wouldn't have been able to train me otherwise.

And suddenly, stupidly, I felt a sharp stab of jealousy for a dead woman.

And okaaaay. That was enough for one day.

I scraped the last of the guac out of the little plastic cup. "I'm think I'm gonna turn in," I told Marco. "What was it you wanted to ask me?"

The dark head tilted inquiringly.

"Fred said there was something?" I prompted.

He grinned. "Oh yeah. I wanted to know what you did to those witches."

"Why?" I asked warily.

"'Cause they just called asking for an appointment tomorrow."

"Um."

Dark eyes narrowed. "Is there a problem?"

"Better make it the day after. I'm . . . planning to sleep in."

He still didn't ask. "Get a bath," he told me, tapping the side of his nose.

And then he ruined it by stealing the rest of my nachos.

Bastard.

I was washing out the damned T-shirt when I got a text message. I grabbed my phone off the nightstand before it vibrated off the edge and saw a big black question mark staring at me. I stared back at it for a moment, and then texted *2moro*.

I waited to make sure it went through.

Shit.

Yeah. It went through.

I left the tee to soak and got my weary butt in the

shower. After washing an acre of Tony's back forty down the drain, I leaned my head against the water-slick tile, wrapped a hand around my neck, and tried to relax. It didn't work. I was tired, really, bone-achingly tired, to the point that I was surprised I didn't just fall asleep right there.

But I wasn't tired enough.

Not to relax, not to forget, not to just let it all go for a while and stop the whirlwind in my head. Lately, it had felt like one of those carnival games with the big spinning wheel and the barkers telling you to pay your money and take your chances. Only with my wheel, there was no point. Since every damned segment just held another problem.

And the space the little clicker landed on this time was labeled Mircea.

God, Mircea. No wonder Marco was being nice to me. He probably figured I was in for it already.

I kind of figured that, too. Vampires think differently than humans about a lot of things, but I didn't think seeing your girlfriend making out with another guy on your lawn was one of them. Not when it had been caught by some of the cameras on-site to record my big moment, which had ended up being different than expected.

Not that that had stopped them from broadcasting it to the whole freaking world.

I'd been expecting to hear about that—it was one reason the breakneck pace of the last week hadn't bothered me. I preferred being somewhere else. But sooner or later, Mircea and I were going to have to talk, and wasn't that going to be fun? When I couldn't even tell him what had been going on, because that would out Pritkin as part incubus? And that so-sharp intellect wouldn't take long to put two and two together, not when there'd only ever been one incubus-human hybrid in all history.

I wondered which would bother Mircea more, me making out with a war mage or with the guy the world remembered as Merlin?

Of course, I wasn't the only one with secrets. Like that whole thing with the Pythias I'd half overheard. What the hell did Mircea want with a Pythia so badly?

I knew what the senate wanted: having the Pythia in their corner gave them power in the supernatural community to rival that of the mages, something they'd never really had. And it didn't hurt their efforts in the war, either. But this hadn't been about the senate, had it? This had been about Mircea personally.

So what had he wanted?

Maybe it was only what I already knew—his brother Radu had been imprisoned by the Inquisition and tortured into madness. Going back in time to save him had been almost the first thing Mircea asked of me once we met again as adults. And it was certain that he loved his brother. He talked about him all the time. . . .

But he didn't talk about that. He didn't talk about the centuries-long campaign he'd waged to save him. I could understand not telling me before I did what he wanted, in case I figured out that changing time was usually a major no-no for Pythias. But he hadn't said anything afterward, either. And after he had Radu back, what was the harm in telling me?

Maybe it just hadn't come up. But that was the thing with Mircea—a lot of things just never came up. And whenever I tried to ask about anything beyond the superficial, the conversation got sidetracked fast. Real fast.

So what didn't he want me to know?

Maybe it was nothing, just the old habit of someone who had learned long ago to keep things to himself. But I wasn't a rival master. And we were dating. We should be talking more than this—shouldn't we?

I didn't know. It wasn't like I'd had a boyfriend before. Thanks to growing up at Tony's, it wasn't like I'd had any relationship that could, strictly speaking, be called normal. And Mircea could talk circles around ages-old vamps; he probably wouldn't even have to break a sweat to keep me in the dark.

But was he?

My brain didn't know, but my gut . . . my gut had other ideas. It had, for instance, vetoed the idea that I ask Rafe, Tony's old court painter and my childhood friend, about my parents. It would have been easier than running Laura down—a lot easier. And alone among Tony's old court, Rafe wouldn't lie to me.

But then, he wouldn't be able to lie to Mircea, either, if he was asked point-blank what I was up to. So I'd gone with Laura, even if maybe I hadn't had to. Even if maybe these doubts were all in my head. Even if . . .

For the tenth time I told myself to stop this and just wind down already. I had a full day tomorrow. I needed to clear my head. I needed some sleep. I needed—

Hell, I knew what I needed.

I also knew I wasn't going to get it.

It was one of the problems of living with creatures with supernatural senses. They were with me *all the time.* Even when they weren't right by my side, they might as well have been. And it wasn't just their noses I had to worry about. Vampire hearing meant every breath was noted, every word, every sigh—

My fingers curled against the warm, wet tile, but it didn't help. I needed some alone time. I needed some *space.* The most I'd been by myself lately had been that short time in Pritkin's room, and then I'd mostly been asleep. Not that it mattered, since a war zone wasn't conducive to certain things, although if I'd thought about it, I might have been desperate enough . . .

I glanced at the shower door, which was all fogged up. That and the heavy fall of warm water made it feel almost like I was somewhere else. I could close my eyes and imagine a waterfall or a rain forest or . . . or a *shower* with no vampires around. I wasn't real picky right now.

I stood there for a moment, wondering how a person got to the point where she actually had to have an internal debate over whether or not to masturbate. I felt a half-hysterical giggle rise to my lips at the sheer absurdity of it, which, of course, I also had to swallow back down. The great Pythia, demigoddess and heir to the throne of Artemis . . .

Couldn't even get herself off.

Only I could. I absolutely could. It felt like I wanted it so badly, was so close to the edge, that I might not have to do that much at all. I could just let my hand smooth over my breasts, slide over my stomach, and then just follow the trails of water a little . . . bit . . . lower. . . .

And feel the sudden shock of hands on my body, a tongue sliding up my naked spine.

I should have jumped; I almost did jump. But I knew that tongue. I knew those hands. I knew . . . oh *God*.

The palms were warm, in defiance of the legend. The fingers were roughened by calluses formed hundreds of years ago, in wars most people had forgotten. And the touch . . . was masterful.

That's what five hundred years of experience does for you, I thought wildly, as a water-slick body pressed against mine.

I didn't turn around. I didn't move. I hadn't expected to see Mircea tonight, had been psyching myself up for even a *phone call*, and now . . .

I wanted to speak, to tell him I was sorry, to tell him it hadn't been how it looked. But my throat had closed up, and nothing came out. Except a groan, as wet, naked skin slid against me, with an almost electric frisson.

Mircea didn't say anything, either, not in words. But I knew the tense and flex of that lean body, and it didn't need words. The hands that had been gentle a moment before gripped my hips, fingers digging into my naked flesh. And pulled me roughly back against him, abruptly enough to wrest another gasp from my lips.

Or maybe that was the image that flashed across my vision, of a powerful body standing under the spray, one arm braced against the wall, tight jaw beaded with water, and eyes half-lidded as he . . . pleasured himself?

It didn't make sense, any more than the fact that the

tiles he was leaning against were a different color from mine. Or that the shower he was standing in was configured in a different direction, making my brain hurt. But I didn't have time to process it, because the visuals were a little . . . overwhelming.

Wet dark hair streaming over his shoulders, free as few ever saw it. Chest running with rivulets, stomach and buttocks tight with effort, biceps hard and bunching on the arm that he was braced with, and the one he was using to hold himself. Only hold wasn't the right word.

He was pulling out of the cage of his palm in long, slow strokes and then surging in hard, letting me feel the power behind each thrust. There was none of the butterfly touch he often used with me, which I'd mistaken for his preference. But which I now realized was the result of a vampire overcompensating for the fragility of a human, so afraid he might hurt her that he was overgentle, overcautious.

He wasn't being cautious now. And it was beautiful, he was beautiful, in his casual brutality. Someone who couldn't hurt himself and knew he couldn't, pushing his limits, reaching for a climax that—

Suddenly included me?

Those incredible eyes closed, sharp teeth buried in his lower lip, and a frown of intense concentration came over his face. A hand pushed my wet curls to the side, the tongue found the indentations on my neck he'd left there as a mark of his possession. And something like an electric shock reverberated through me. Hands slid over my body, furling my nipples, tightening my skin, even before an unmistakable thickness slid against me.

It was hard and hot and unbelievably heavy. Mircea wasn't small, even soft, and like this he was both eyewidening and somewhat terrifying. At least normally. But right now there was none of that. Just this, just gasping breath and raw need and pulsing, unfulfilled ache, and I was actually going to explode, to come apart at the seams, to go completely insane if he didn't—

"Oh God. *Yes.*" That's what I'd wanted, what I'd needed, not my own touch but his, the feel of him as I wrapped my legs around his waist—

And almost fell off. My back was against wet, slippery tile, my front was against soapy, slippery vampire, and any moment now, I was going to land in an undignified heap. And given my experience, probably on my butt. But then Mircea slid strong hands underneath my thighs, boosting me up, bracing me with his body as he pushed into me—

Carefully, as he hadn't been just moments ago. He was slowing down, being cautious, holding back. And I didn't want that.

"No," I gasped, even as he held me, so, so carefully. Like I was china, like I might break. When I wanted to break; I wanted to *feel.* "Not like that. Like before."

"I'll hurt you."

"You won't."

But Mircea was being stubborn. "My fantasy, my rules," he told me, shifting position, getting that last half inch . . . just there. . . .

"That's cheating," I gasped. "And it's my fantasy."

A dark eyebrow quirked, causing a miniature cascade down one sculpted cheek. "Forgive me, *dulceaţă*, but I believe this is *my* fantasy, which would explain why you are being difficult."

"You like it when I'm difficult?"

"I like you any way," he murmured into my ear, dark, wet hair falling around me as he sped up—

But not enough.

Long, thick strokes were more maddening than satisfying, and I'd about had it. "Damn it!" I tongued his earlobe. "Do what I tell you!"

He slowed down even further, a long, sensual glide. "Make me."

I bit down on that tantalizing bit of flesh, and felt him vibrate against me. Oh, he'd liked that, had he? "Harder," I ordered.

"*That* is cheating," he muttered, but the pace sped noticeably up.

I bit his neck next, right at the spot where hard shoulder met strong throat, and he barked out a laugh. "Now I know I'm dreaming."

It bled a little, but the water washed it away. I bit higher next time, closer to the point where he'd left his mark on my own neck, and felt him suddenly go rigid against me. And then shove me into the wall and *take* me, with a reckless abandon that left me breathless and aching and gasping and—

"Cassie?"

I did jump that time, and gave a shriek, almost falling on my ass. Because that hadn't been Mircea's voice. It took a disorienting second of clinging to the soap dish to process the fact that a) those had been Marco's deep tones, b) they were outside the shower, c) there was no one in here except for me, and d) I might possibly be going crazy, but that wasn't exactly news.

"Are you all right?" Marco demanded.

I didn't answer. I wasn't sure I could. I was panting like a freight train and my eyes were crossing as I struggled to suppress a really inappropriate orgasm. What the *hell*?

"Cassie?"

I swallowed, staring at the fogged-up door, where the light from the bedroom was mostly blocked by Marco's Roman profile. He was looking at the wall, despite the fact that even vampire eyes couldn't have seen much in here, because he knew how I was. They all knew how I was about bodily modesty, which was stupid considering how much of the time I ended up naked, but there you go.

But he wouldn't be outside for long, if I didn't manage an answer. Preserving what was left of my modesty wasn't his job; keeping me alive was. And I'd almost died in the bath once before, because people hadn't wanted to disturb me, although how I would manage to kill myself in a shower was debatable. But let's face it, if anybody could . . .

"Cassie." And okay, that had the "you have exactly three seconds to respond before I charge in and save you, so if you don't want saving, you better damned well speak up" tone. And since I was still sprawled against the wall, body tight and shuddering, I decided that might not be a great plan.

"I . . . yes. Yes."

"Are you sure?" He didn't sound convinced, and I couldn't blame him. My voice had been a broken croak.

I cleared my throat and tried again. "Yes, I—I'm fine."

"Okay. It's just you've been in there awhile."

Yeah, I guessed so. My fingertips were going pruney, and I felt more than a little waterlogged. Along with really, really confused.

I swallowed. "I was just about to get out."

"All right."

"Marco . . . you . . . haven't heard from Mircea tonight, have you?"

"No, it's a little early for him to check in. There's a time difference between here and New York, you know."

"Yeah. I know."

"I'll tell him you're fine if he calls. Get some sleep, Cassie."

"I'll do that," I said, staring at my empty shower.

After all, tomorrow was going to be hell.

Chapter Fourteen

Hell, it turned out, looked a lot like Vegas.

Not the neon, glitz-and-twinkly-kind. More the arid-sand-littered-with-desperate-people kind, but still. There was a vague sort of familiarity to it. I wondered why a certain green-eyed demon had never mentioned it.

Of course, he hadn't mentioned much, I thought angrily, just as the guy at my side went sprawling.

There was nothing to have caused it that I could see, except for his own dusty pair of Pradas, but he hit hard nonetheless. I stopped abruptly and went into a crouch, afraid we'd just tripped some ward or other his senses had missed. But I guess not. Because a second later, he flipped over, sand clinging to one side of an elegant profile, and stared at the pale blue sphere I'd decided to call the sky. And cursed inventively.

I took a swig from the too-warm water in my canteen and waited it out. "Do you want to ride the camel thing?" I asked when the tirade finally tapered off.

The only answer was another spate of cursing.

"Guess not," I said, and passed the canteen to the third member of our trio, who finished it off in one hearty swallow.

"Did you just drink *all* the water?" Casanova demanded, struggling to sit up. Only to have the beast's ratty tail smack him in the face.

I'd have had some smart-aleck response to that. Something about Casanova being a vampire and not really needing water. Or about the likelihood of his spilling it, considering his current lack of grace. Or about the fact that we'd gone to a lot of trouble to find someone willing to sell us one of the camel things just so he could ride instead of staggering through the dust like a drunken frat boy.

But Caleb just looked down at him impassively. He did impassive well, along with big, black, bald, and intimidating. In fact, I hadn't seen anything Caleb didn't do well, except for putting up with Casanova's histrionics. I guess war mages were made of sterner stuff. At least, war mages willing to go into hell to rescue a buddy were. But even Caleb's patience was starting to wear thin.

As a dusty boot to Casanova's couture-clad posterior made plain. "Get up."

Brown eyes that were currently neither rich, nor mellow, nor enticing glared up at him from under a fall of silky dark hair. "If you'd release this infernal spell, I wouldn't be on the ground to begin with!"

"A hobble spell doesn't keep you from walking," Caleb said, crossing his arms.

"No, it keeps me from walking properly. Or running, which I might damned well need to do!"

"It wouldn't have been necessary if you'd volunteered."

"Oh, of course!" Casanova said, fighting with the voluminous robes that we'd bought off a fellow traveler to cover up his Armani. "Of course this is my fault! Of course it is. I can't imagine why I wouldn't volunteer to walk into hell!"

Caleb just continued to look at him. As one of Pritkin's oldest friends in the Corps, and the only other person besides Casanova who knew who he really was, he'd been a natural addition to the rescue posse. Casanova had been less so—a lot less—but we needed him. Or, more precisely, we needed the camouflage his body provided to our guide.

Said guide was looking at him in mild reproach at the moment. "I've told you—you aren't in any danger, Carlos," Rian said, using his birth name. I'd gotten the impression that she found his pretensions a bit trying. "A host is not responsible for the actions of his demon. If we are caught, I will tell them I forced you—"

"I *was* forced," he said viciously. "No one in his right mind would be here otherwise!"

Rian didn't comment. She did that a lot. It was probably why she and Casanova had managed to maintain their relationship for so long. Of course, the fact that she chose to manifest as a beautiful black-haired, vaguely Persian-looking woman, with huge dark eyes, honey-colored skin, and ruby red lips probably hadn't hurt.

And unlike her host, Rian had volunteered to help out. She'd known Pritkin a long time, from his days as a young man at his father's court, and she'd always been sympathetic to his situation. Which was lucky, since getting into said court was turning out to be more complicated than I'd thought.

Casanova, on the other hand, clearly felt that he was better suited for lounging around someone's boudoir than for slogging through hell. Not that he was slogging particularly well.

But he did finally drag his six feet of outraged litheness off the sand.

"How much farther?" he demanded.

Rian glanced at the sky. "Don't worry, I've timed it perfectly. We'll reach the city by nightfall. I'll need to merge with you at least an hour before that, or risk being detected."

"Yes, and we wouldn't want that," Casanova muttered.

"No, you wouldn't," she said seriously. "You're in no danger, Carlos. But if I am discovered, the master may well revoke my rights to any more time on earth. He feels it has been unfairly extended as it is."

"I don't see why," I said, grabbing the reins of the camel thing. It seemed to like Casanova. Or his hair, anyway. It kept trying to eat it.

"To avoid overfarming earth, the demon lords made an agreement," she reminded me. "Only a set number of each of our races is allowed on earth at one time. We have to take turns."

"But you're still on yours. Aren't you allowed three hosts?"

"Yes." She shot a sideways look at Casanova, who was reacting typically to the camel-slobber cowlick he'd just been graced with. "But I do not think anyone expected me to find an immortal for my last host. I should have been forced to return centuries ago."

"But, technically, you aren't breaking any rules."

"I am now," she said quietly as we merged back into the ragged line of similar groups all heading in the same direction.

I was actually grateful for them, since the "road" was invisible as far as I could see, just endless miles of reddish clay baked into giant cracked plates by the parching sun. Only an occasional dried-up twig of a tree poking out of one of the cracks broke the monotony, along with the scattered line of travelers, all going in more or less the same direction. Mother had neglected to mention that the main court of the incubi was a damned long way from the portal we'd passed through to get here.

Of course, that wouldn't normally have been a problem. Rian could shift into and out of the demon world the same way I could shift across the human. But the demon lords were paranoid of one another and closely guarded their main courts, and Rosier had just increased the security on his from tight to maniacal. So no shifting. She'd had to go through the incubus version of the TSA in order to get home, just like every other demon.

Luckily, our group didn't include any other demons. And as far as the guards at the gate had been concerned, that meant we basically counted as the in-flight meal. Of course, that begged the question of how, exactly, we were going to get out when our group *did* include another demon, and one on the top of the "no fly" list.

Damn, I hoped Mom had been right.

"Who are all these people?" Caleb asked, watching the passersby.

They weren't as interesting as I'd expected, at least what I could see. A lot of them were muffled up as much as we were, against the overhead glare and the intermittent gusts of wind that whipped fine sand into every available orifice. But they looked vaguely human, at least most of them, a bunch of tattered, hungry-looking types in dusty rags.

Or rather, those on foot like us were. But every once in a while, a clatter of hooves and a miniature dust cloud announced the passage of more prosperous-looking individuals, in fine, loose robes to protect them from the sun. I couldn't see much of them, either, since both men and women had veils hanging from turbans or other head coverings, probably to try to cut down on the amount of rose-colored dust they breathed in. But there were glimpses of bright-colored silks underneath their outer robes, and they rode in comfortable-looking carts.

Rian glanced around disinterestedly. "Servants, or those who would be so. Traders—the few who can be trusted. The people of this world returning home after journeys elsewhere . . ."

"People of this world?" Caleb looked confused.

"There are many hells," she told him. "It is merely a term for worlds in this dimension. Kazallu is one; earth is another."

"Bullshit. We do not live in hell!"

"Speak for yourself," Casanova said, limping from what turned out to be a rock in his shoe.

"*A* hell," Rian said, unperturbed. "When we found this one, eons ago, the people on it were . . . primitive, few in number, dying of disease, famine, war. We took control and helped them."

"Fed on them, you mean," Caleb interjected.

"To an extent. But they are not very . . . nutritious? They provide a subsistence, nothing more. That is why our time on earth is so prized. In a few years there, we amass power that would take centuries here."

"So we're cattle to you," Caleb said, as if she'd just confirmed something long suspected.

Rian shot him a flirtatious glance. "Prized cattle, surely."

"Oh, stop it," Casanova said irritably. "She's just teasing you," he added to Caleb, making me blink.

I looked at Rian, but her violet-dusted lids were lowered, the long lashes shading her high cheekbones. And then back at Casanova. And then I wondered how a predator didn't notice when he met a greater one.

But I didn't say anything, and neither did she, being busy pulling a veil across the bottom of her face and turning away slightly, as another vehicle approached ours.

This one was different, a sporty two-wheeler, almost like a chariot, and driven like one, too. I didn't have to ask who it belonged to; Rian's reaction was enough. The incubus-possessed driver hadn't bothered with an outer cloak like everyone else. Instead, he wore a fine, thin red silk robe embroidered with gold that flashed in the light as he all but ran us down, scattering us lesser beings to either side as he thundered past.

"Son of a—why couldn't we get one of those?" Casanova demanded.

"They're restricted to the Danim, those hosting an

incubus," Rian told him. "It would attract too much attention."

"And my bloody feet won't?"

"If it could cost you so much, why are you helping us?" Caleb asked her, eyes narrowed.

"Shouldn't you have asked that before we got here?" Casanova demanded.

"I'm asking now."

"The feud between John and his father is tearing the family apart," Rian told him. "Among other things, it is making the master look weak. Some have begun to say, if he cannot control his own son, perhaps he should not be the one to control the family—and that is dangerous."

"Who else would do it?"

"As at any court, ours has factions, senior demons and their followers, who constantly vie with each other for advantage. Rosier himself is usually above such squabbles, but John is his weak point and everyone knows it. And as with all who hold power, he has enemies."

"Imagine that," Casanova said poisonously. "And such a pleasant creature."

"He is better than those who would replace him," Rian said, more sharply.

"When you said this was tearing the family apart, does that mean some are taking Pritkin's side?" I asked hopefully. Because we could use more friends.

But of course not.

"No. No one understands his reluctance to feed. It is seen as proof of his humanness, his alienness. No incubus could go so long. . . ." She shuddered. "It is against our very nature, against everything we are."

"Then it sounds like everybody agrees with Rosier," I said sourly.

But she shook her head. "Almost no one does. Few understood his obsession with obtaining a half-human child, and even fewer can comprehend why he refuses to let that child live as he chooses. Yes, John could be an asset to the family if he would use his powers on our behalf. But if he will not . . ."

"Oh yes. The horror," Casanova said bitterly. "His father wants him to live in the lap of luxury, surrounded by beautiful women, and be treated like a prince. And all he has to do in return is sex up a few probably gorgeous demons. But what does he choose instead?"

"To live his own life," I said. "To not be prostituted out by his father to gain power for Rosier's ambitions. Which he doesn't have control over and which could be any damned—"

"Oh, please. We're all cogs in someone else's ambitions, whether we like it or not. That's life. If you're smart, instead of bucking the system, you get what you can out of it."

"Yeah, if you're a selfish son of a—"

"Don't even try that, little girl," Casanova snapped. "*I'm* selfish? What about your precious mage? We're at *war*, in case you didn't notice."

"That's the reason he's here," I said impatiently. "He saved me—"

"Yes, one person. And what about the rest of us?"

"What about you? What was Pritkin supposed to do—"

"He was supposed to realize that, if he would get his head out of his ass, bow that stubborn neck to his father, and ask nicely, maybe he could get us some allies worth a damn!"

"What are you talking about?"

"The demon lords," Casanova said severely. "The demon *council*. Do you have any idea how much power they have?"

"Carlos . . ." Rian said quietly.

"You want somebody to win this war for you, to do it fast?" Casanova demanded, ignoring her. "That's where you want to turn for help. But instead, what are we doing?" He flung out a hand. "We're doing our best to piss them off!"

"Carlos—" Rian said, a bit more urgently.

But Casanova was on a roll. "Let's look at the facts, shall we? The damned mage gets his back up, decides he doesn't want to be a demon. So he comes to earth, forgetting that you don't merely get to wave something like that away. You are what you are. Denying it is just a head game you play with yourself. But his head game resulted in a girl getting dead—"

"That's not fair!" I said, glaring at him.

"Of course it's fair. He may not have planned to kill her, but he drained her, didn't he? Yes, Rian told me," he said, at my outraged expression. "If I'm going to risk my neck getting him back, I deserved to know."

"Yes, but, Carlos—" she said.

"I'm not finished yet. So now he has a dead wife, courtesy of abilities he'd never bothered to learn anything about. So what does he do? Decide that perhaps his father had a point? Of course not. He goes insane and *tries to kill him*—"

"Rosier knew what she was planning to do," I said, furious.

The girl in question had been Pritkin's wife, and a low-level demon herself. But unlike him, she hadn't hated the demon world. She'd loved it, coveted it, wanted to be part of it more than anything. But she was barred from it because of her almost nonexistent power.

So she'd decided to augment that power—with some of Pritkin's. I don't know if that's why she'd gotten with him in the first place or if there had been genuine affection there, as well. But if there was affection, it hadn't been enough to stop her from initiating a power exchange on their wedding night, hoping to increase her own abilities and thereby her status in the demon world.

Unfortunately, it had backfired horrifically, and Pritkin hadn't been able to stop it. He'd never had sex with another demon before and didn't know the ritual she was using. And Rosier hadn't warned him, despite knowing her intentions ahead of time.

"We don't know what Rosier knew or didn't know," Casanova argued when I pointed that out. "She went to visit him before the wedding; who knows why? Perhaps she was attempting to get the two of them to reconcile. Perhaps she just wanted to meet her famous father-in-law. Perhaps a million other things. We don't know—and neither did he!"

"I think Pritkin knows his father a bit better than you do!"

"All right, say I give you that. Say Rosier knew ahead of time, or guessed, what the idiot girl was planning. Does that somehow obligate him to tell his estranged son—the son who said he wanted to know nothing of their world, the son who swore he wanted to live as a human—a damned thing?"

"Yes! If he wasn't a complete bastard—"

Casanova looked at me like I might be crazy. "*Demon lord?*"

"It was still a shitty thing to do."

"And striding into hell to kill him wasn't? How was that supposed to end well? And how is *this*?"

"Because this isn't about Rosier," I told him impatiently. "This is about the demon council. They're the ones who sentenced Pritkin to enslavement by his father for the attempted assassination. They're the ones who can reverse it."

"And why should they help you?" Casanova demanded nastily.

I took a deep breath, trying to keep my temper. Because he was an ass, but he was an ass with a point. If he was coming, he did deserve to know. And because we needed him.

Without Rian, we would never find Pritkin before Rosier's forces found us, and without Casanova, she would be spotted and identified before she could help us. She was supposed to be on earth, not here. And it wouldn't take anyone who had known her long to figure out why she'd suddenly decided to return home after avoiding it for a couple of hundred years now.

"You said it yourself," I reminded him. "We're at war. The council doesn't want the gods back any more than the rest of us—"

"And giving you one man is going to prevent that?"

"It's done a pretty good job so far!"

Casanova sneered. "It's done a pretty good job against exactly one god, who was already seriously weakened when he got here thanks to what he'd had to do to get through your mother's spell. And who underestimated you because"—he gestured up and down at me, and made a face—"he was overconfident and it got him dead. But I don't think the next ones will be!"

"All the more reason to give me what I want," I said, refusing to let him get to me. "It's a small enough request; it cost them nothing; it asks them to risk nothing. But the rewards could be substantial."

"Then why not ask them before we trooped in here?" he demanded.

"Because they can't go into another demon's realm! None of the council has the right to violate another lord's sovereignty. And none of them are going to try it and risk setting a precedent that might be used against them someday. But if we can get him out—"

"If being the operative word."

"—then they can tell Rosier it's for the common good." Or whatever they wanted to tell him; I didn't care. But Mother knew demons better than I did, and she thought they'd go for it—if we could get him out.

And we were going to. Somehow. But the city that shimmered into existence on the horizon, dim and distant and faintly blue, had me wishing we'd brought an extra canteen. Because my mouth had suddenly gone dry.

"We shouldn't fight among ourselves," Rian said, a little sharper than her usual tones. Maybe because she was looking at the city, too. "If this goes according to plan, it should be a simple enough procedure."

"And when does it ever?" Casanova groused.

Yeah. That's what I was afraid of.

Chapter Fifteen

As Rian had predicted, we reached the city at nightfall. And once again I felt it, the massive disconnect between everything I'd ever known and everything I was experiencing. It had been happening a lot lately, dating from the first time I'd shifted, going from a world of electricity and glass skyscrapers and the rule of law, to one filled with torchlight and stone castles and the rule of one man's caprice.

That had been a shock.

That had taken some adjustment.

This was worse.

The desert abruptly ended at a jagged cliff with an almost sheer drop-off down what looked like maybe a few thousand feet. A jumble of vehicles lay scattered around the entrance to a stone bridge way too narrow for my liking. It stretched over the precipice like a slender finger, too tight for anything but foot traffic. And on the other side, a triangular spar of land held a city so old and so massive it made human metropolises look like toys in comparison.

We lined up with everyone else, including their smaller animals and handcarts, and went across, while a wicked wind plucked at our clothes like hungry hands and howled a warning in our ears. It didn't help that the damned bridge was open on the sides, with just a flimsy railing between us and an epic free fall. Someone up ahead didn't keep hold of a fat barnyard bird, and had it torn out of her hands by the wind, to flutter out over the void for a second before dropping like a stone.

I didn't watch it fall.

"Is something wrong?" Rian asked me, in Casanova's voice. She'd merged with him a few miles out, making it harder to communicate, since they tended to talk over each other in the same body. But it was necessary. Inside a body, even her own people had trouble recognizing her. They could tell what she was, if they were paying attention, but not who.

At least, we really hoped they couldn't.

"This . . . isn't exactly what I expected," I confessed, staring down to where a river blazed gold with the last light of whatever passed for a sun, cutting a vivid scar across faceless red sand. There were some little black specks on it.

I realized with a jolt that they were boats.

"What did you expect?" She sounded curious.

"Something more like the Shadowland," I said, talking about the demon world where the council met and where Rosier had a small, secondary court for when it was in session. It wasn't like earth, but at least it was nice and compact, a small trade city in a twilit world, with everything and everyone close at hand.

It could have fit into the plaza we stumbled into on the bridge's other side.

Like the fortress that towered overhead, it was dull red and gleaming under the last of the day's sallow light. It was also jam-packed despite the size, and noisy, with people chatting, animals bellowing, bells on hems and bridles jangling, and our camel shaking off a wheelbarrow full of fine red dust all over us.

Most people started lining up to be allowed past the massive, studded gate maybe ten stories high, which appeared to be the only entrance through the main walls. But we shuffled off to the side with a few hundred others who apparently needed a break. Shaking sand out of our hair and clothes, we joined a queue for one of the shallow fountains on either side of the plaza.

A lot of the camel things, and a lot of the people, were drinking right out of the enormous basin, but we waited while Rian used vampire agility to grab us refills from higher up, where the first gush of water split the rust-colored rock.

"This . . . isn't good," Caleb rumbled in my ear.

And the understatement of the year award goes to, I thought, staring blankly around. But mostly up, up, up, at the nine walls within walls that made up the colossal fortress towering above us. It was so big it blocked out the last of the light, casting long shadows that bathed everything in smudged ochre.

"Rose red city half as old as time," Caleb murmured.

"What?"

"Just a quote about a city on earth once."

"I've never seen anything like that on earth."

"And you won't." For some reason, he didn't look as impressed as I was. "Human society is too fluid to have built up something like that. It would have been razed at some far earlier stage by a conqueror, or made obsolete by new technology. That must have taken thousands of years to build by a people stuck in one phase of existence and not allowed to move on."

"Maybe they don't want to move on."

Caleb shot me a look. "And maybe their overlords won't allow it, since it would make them harder to govern. Harder to control." His lip curled. "I'm beginning to understand why John hates this place."

He looked like he'd have said more, but Rian was back, thrusting overflowing canteens into our dusty hands. I drank some water, swirled it around my mouth, and spat it out, trying to get sand to stop cracking between my teeth. It didn't work.

"All right, *now* do you understand?" Casanova hissed. It was always easy to tell when he was talking; Rian's careful, measured voice and graceful movements gave way to wilder gestures and harsher tones.

At least they did when he was talking to me.

I didn't answer until we'd moved away from the crowd, closer to a small, built-up edge of stone, near the precipice. It was only about waist high, and the wind was something else, so I kept to the right side of the camel thing. But it didn't help; it felt like we might both go flying at any moment.

I squatted down, and that was a little better, mainly because I couldn't see the drop-off anymore.

"Now do I understand what?" I asked.

"Now do you understand how stupid this is?" Casanova demanded, squatting in front of me. "We need to get out of here before anyone recognizes us!"

"Recognizes?" I gestured around. "There's got to be two, three thousand people just on this damned platform."

"Yes, so with our luck, that should buy us about five minutes!"

"It's not the recognizing that's the problem," Caleb said, his eyes on the gate. "They're not checking everybody or even most people going in. It's the getting out."

"We're not going to get out. We're probably not even going to get in!" Casanova said, before Rian stopped his mouth with a canteen.

"We'll get out like we got in," I said, trying to reassure myself as much as them. "Mother said I should be able to open the gates between worlds, with or without the guard's approval. It was her greatest gift."

"Should be?" Casanova hissed, thrusting the canteen away. "You didn't *test it*?"

"How am I supposed to test it, Casanova?" I hissed back. "Demons tend to take a dim view of people breaking into their courts!"

"Dimmer than Rosier when we try to steal his heir and then can't get the hell out—"

The canteen was back.

"Mother said I could do it," I repeated, slowly enough to hopefully get through that thick skull of his. "'Should have' was my phrasing and it was . . . poorly chosen. I'm sorry."

I hoped an apology would calm him down, but of course not.

"If you're sorry, then get me out of here!" he spluttered, shoving the canteen away and spraying water all over me.

"I'm not leaving him here!"

"He's a demon lord! He can take care of himself! If he wants out, he'll find a way—"

"It's been six months, Carlos," Rian said, causing him to change octaves and facial expressions midway through a sentence. It gave him a weird, schizophrenic tic, but I didn't care. I was too busy trying to absorb what she was saying.

"Six *months*?"

"Time passes differently here," she reminded me. "That is why your power doesn't work. We are no longer in your time stream."

"But *six*—"

"That is one reason I agreed to come with you. Lord Rosier has waited a long time for this. He isn't going to lose his son again if he can help it."

"Is that why there are so many guards?" Caleb demanded.

"No." Rian glanced around, and for a second, I thought I saw her large, almond-shaped eyes sliding behind Casanova's. "I've never seen so many all at once. It's the only good sign."

"Good?" Casanova asked himself. "How is that—"

He abruptly stopped when several indigo-robed guards broke away from a nearby group and came in our direction. They were muffled up more than the tourists, just sharp dark eyes and arched black eyebrows showing between their turbans and the veils they'd tucked into the necks of their robes. Which didn't entirely obscure the no-nonsense curved swords at their sides.

I didn't say anything, either, as they came closer. Or move. Or even breathe. I tried to tell myself to act natural, but it wasn't working so great. And I wasn't the only one. Suddenly, the only movement in our small group was the wind whipping our robes around, and the camel thing chewing on Casanova's hair.

Until the guards passed by, and grabbed a couple of kids who had been playing on the rocky edge of the precipice. A frantic mother came up and retrieved them, already sobbing even before one of the men started telling her off. I swallowed sand and hung my head, and poured some of the water over my hot neck until they'd gone again.

"It is good," Rian said, clearing her throat. "For it shows that the master is worried. There are at least three times the usual number of guards on duty, perhaps more. Something that would not be the case if he didn't consider himself to be vulnerable."

"He thinks we can do it," I said, translating that.

"He thinks we'll be stupid enough to *try* to do it," Casanova corrected. "The guards are to make sure we don't succeed!"

I stared at the gate, which had a huge, old-fashioned portcullis at the top, its jagged teeth cast in some kind of black metal. The tips glinted dully in the light's last rays, as if they'd been dipped in blood. I glanced at Caleb, who was looking at them, too.

And unlike Casanova, he and I didn't have an out. Rosier had promised Pritkin recently not to attempt to assassinate me again, but I wasn't sure how that worked when I was the party on the offensive. But even if it did apply, it left a whole host of options wide-open—none of which I was likely to enjoy. And as for Caleb . . .

"If you want to go back, I'll understand," I told him quietly.

He pursed his lips slightly, and shot me a glance. It almost looked like he was trying to hold back a grin, except that Caleb didn't grin. It seemed to be against the war mage code or something. And because it would have been crazy under the circumstances.

"You going back?"

"No." It wasn't like this was going to get any easier later.

He stood up and stretched, corded muscles rippling under the thin material of the robes. "Guess I'll go when you do."

"Oh, for—God preserve me from brainless heroics!" Casanova snapped.

"Didn't think you believed in God."

"I believe in Satan," he said, pushing the camel thing away from his hair. "I ought to. I'm standing on his bloody doorstep!"

If Satan's doorstep was impressive, his atrium was breathtaking.

We passed through the gate into a chasm of a tunnel, the fading light from behind us washing along the ceiling like red water, too late in the day to really light our way, but too early for the lanterns that glinted in intervals overhead to be lit. I navigated by letting my fingertips trail over the rough, rocky surface of the nearest wall, which still held the heat of the day and probably would for hours considering the thickness of the stone. And felt some of that initial awe creep back.

Despite the air in here, which was pretty funky from too many bodies pressed too close together, and the constantly jostling crowd, and my seriously aching calf muscles, I still felt it—the weight of centuries pressing down like an extra atmosphere.

Caleb had been right; this place was old. Older than our pyramids, older than anything on earth. Maybe as old as this world itself, since there were chisel marks on the dark red stone, but no mortar lines that I could see. It was as if it had been carved instead of built. As if some giant had whittled away a mountain from the top down, leaving the pieces that fit his crazy blueprint and carrying away the rest.

It should have been impressive, and maybe if I was a tourist it would have been. As it was, it was more intimidating. I felt the knot in my stomach draw a little tighter, even before we stumbled out the other side a few minutes later.

Into something that looked a lot like a souk.

Shops lined streets going in all directions like spokes on a wheel. And selling everything from spices to live animals, bright metalware to gauzy clothing, pottery to vegetables, fish to leather goods, and wool to fresh-baked bread. Merchants called out offers to us new arrivals even as they tried to roll up the awnings over their shops, or light the lanterns strung like stars over the streets, or slap fresh meat onto grills, sending up mouth-watering aromas to tantalize our dust-covered taste buds. It was loud and raucous and crowded and strangely jolly, but Caleb didn't appear enthralled.

"Servants, my ass," he muttered.

It took me a moment to realize what he meant, because most of the people hanging around the gate, waiting for friends and family to come out, looked like a mix of those on the road. With one exception. A depressing number had what looked like slaves following along behind, thin men and women, and in some cases children, in bare feet and simple tunics, their arms reaching for packages and boxes or the reins of animals.

Most of the slaves didn't look native. Some of them didn't even look human. I was staring, probably rudely, at one with mottled blue skin and what looked like a few extra arms when Rian grabbed my sleeve.

Because yeah.

The guards were thick on the ground in here, too.

They were slightly less obvious, lounging by food stalls or interspersed with the crowd by the gate. But there were plenty of them, scanning the new arrivals with the watchfulness of cops and security forces everywhere. And they didn't look like they missed much.

But they missed us, thanks to Caleb.

He waved a hand, sending a jolt of something to goose the last in a line of camels a little ways in front of us. It gave a startled bleat and crashed into the next in line, and then the whole group, already tense from the dark tunnel they'd just been through, were bellowing and bucking and scattering in all directions. The frantic driver and his boy ran after them, yelling for help, which they reluctantly got from some of the merchants with vulnerable piles of fruit and veg.

They didn't get any from the guards.

But for a moment, everyone was watching the show instead of the line, and we slipped through.

"This way, quickly," Rian said, pulling us out of the crush around the gate and into the more anonymous crowd.

Or, at least, that's what it looked like she said. I couldn't hear a damned thing. To the sounds of people talking and cart wheels squeaking and animals bleating and merchants cursing and music blaring from every tavern on every street had just been added a blast of horns from the higher walls, heralding the arrival of night.

I grabbed Rian's arm, so I wouldn't lose her, and gave up on subtlety. Nobody could hear me in all this anyway. "Where are they keeping him?" I yelled, only to have her nod at the street directly ahead of us. And say something I couldn't make out, because I don't have vampire hearing.

But then, maybe I didn't need it.

Far above the smelly, raucous, lively streets was a long, low, elegant building of balconies and terraces and a few graceful towers. Patches of greenery interlaced the stone here and there, almost shocking in this landscape. What looked like fountains caught the last of the light in a few places. And while the place looked like it had also been carved out of the local stone, it must have come from a different strata. Because it was a pale, honey gold that shimmered against the darker layers all around, as if laced with gold dust.

If ever anything had screamed *palace*, that was it.

"It's not behind the highest wall," Caleb said, in my ear. As if he'd come to the same conclusion.

"So . . . that's good at least."

"Depends."

I turned to look at him. "On what?"

"On what's on those upper three levels."

They were dark, now that the local sun had set, set into the cliffs under an overhang of stone, with just a few stray lights gleaming here and there ominously. Like a heavy brow over glittering eyes. I felt myself start to tense up again, even without knowing why.

And then I got a reason when Caleb gave me a massive shove from behind.

I stumbled and then hit the ground, wrenching a wrist and skinning my hands in the process. But I didn't mind. Because a moment later, somebody in a swift-moving chariot tore through the souk—including the area where I'd just been standing. If I'd stayed where I was, I'd have been crushed under its wheels like the worldly belongings of one unfortunate immigrant.

The driver never even appeared to notice. I watched from the ground as he turned onto one of the spokelike streets radiating out from the hub formed by the gate, his bright green silk robe flapping as he whipped his chariot back and forth on a crazy course that seemed intent on doing the most damage possible. Until it hit the front of a shop and crashed inside, the camel creatures bucking and rearing and making enough noise to cut through even the noise of the crowd.

The driver jumped off, laughing, and disappeared into a tavern across the street, along with a girl in a skimpy outfit.

Leaving the merchant with the camel-filled shop to sort things out for himself.

And me to get hauled off the ground by an irate war mage.

"Thanks," I told him. "I didn't see—" I stopped, because Caleb wasn't looking real concerned over my skinned knees right now. Caleb was looking the way Pritkin had a few times back when we'd first met.

Right before he tried to kill me.

"What?" I said, looking around for another chariot. But the street was clear—at least of maniacal vehicles. People were washing back into the lane, including the immigrant's family scurrying to collect what remained of their belongings. Things were returning to what passed for normal around here.

But Caleb didn't look like he thought so.

"Notice anything?" he hissed.

"What are you—" I stopped because I had. I'd just noticed something. Not something added, but something missing.

Or somebody.

"Where," Caleb asked me through clenched teeth, "is that damned vampire?"

Chapter Sixteen

I scanned the crowd, but there was no sign of a mouthy vampire in a dusty Obi-Wan robe screeching about being almost run down. Or a calm, serene one under the control of a being probably used to the crazy drivers around here. There was no one at all but the thinning stream of people through the gate and the life around the shops getting back to normal.

I didn't understand. We'd been distracted for only a second. Where could she have gone so fast? And why would she just leave us in an alien city filled with guards who probably had our pictures taped to their dart-boards?

My mouth felt dry, so I swallowed. "I asked her where Pritkin was being kept. Maybe she went off to find out."

Caleb shot me a furious look. "And maybe she went off to win bonus points with her lord and master by ratting us out!"

I shook my head. "That's ridiculous. If she didn't want me going after Pritkin, all she had to do was stay in Vegas. I'd never have made it this far without her. I could have opened the gate, but not gotten past the guards. I needed an incubus for that—"

"And she made sure you got one!"

"Yes, so why help us if she just planned to turn us in?"

"Perhaps she thought she'd get more if we proved a credible threat," Caleb said, seething. "Telling her precious master what we have planned while we're still in Vegas might win her a point or two. But if she stops us when we're actually in his city, when we're less than a mile from our goal, she could expect him to be a lot more generous!"

"Not if she helped us get in to begin with!"

"She can say she was afraid if she didn't go along, we'd manage to find another way in, and she wouldn't be able to warn him since she wouldn't know what it was."

I tried to think of an objection to that—tried hard. Because if Rian had decided to rat us out, we were pretty much screwed. And that was especially true a moment later, when a rolling, metallic sound clattered across the souk, coming from the direction of the gate.

The door on this side was still open, and still coughing out straggling parties of new arrivals. But I had a really bad feeling that maybe that wasn't the case on the other side. It looked like they were rolling up the welcome mat for the night—with us inside.

"She timed it perfectly, all right," Caleb snarled, grabbing my hand and jerking me toward one of the side streets.

"Caleb, listen," I said, running along behind. "She's helped Pritkin before, more than once. She's even put herself in danger to help him. There's no reason to believe—"

"There's every reason! You heard her yourself. She's overdue to return, probably by a few hundred years. Maybe Rosier got tired of her little dodge and her helping his wayward son, and told her she had to make room for someone else. And maybe she decided to hell with that—and to hell with us!"

And damn it, that sounded horribly logical.

"Then why did Casanova spend all that time arguing with us?" I demanded. "He was trying to turn us back!"

"Maybe she told him to ham it up, to make sure we didn't suspect anything. Or maybe he really didn't know. He's a vamp, and they always look out for number one. And Mircea is his master. What kind of reception do you think he'll get when Mircea finds out he put you in danger?" He whirled on me suddenly. "Can he stop her from saying anything? Can he at least slow her down?"

"If she stays inside his body, maybe. I don't know. But she doesn't have to. She can come and go as she pleases, and I don't think he has any control over that." At least none that I'd ever seen.

Caleb used one of Pritkin's favorite swearwords. And then he used a few more. "Fucking demons. You can't trust them, not any of them. I *knew* better—"

I didn't bother pointing out that that was not exactly PC, because at the moment, I kind of agreed with it. "Fucking demons" sounded kind of like the phrase for the day.

Especially since I was about to run a bunch of them down.

"Where are we going?" I asked, ducking and dodging, and trying to avoid slamming into someone and putting a flashing arrow over our heads.

"Away. She'll be expecting us to stay put, to think we lost her in the crowd. She probably thought she'd be able to tell the guards right where to find us, while we wandered around, eating kebabs or some shit."

"So, what's the plan instead?"

"To find a place to hide!"

"Hide?" I grabbed his arm, pulling him into the shade of a balcony someone had forgotten to roll up. It wasn't much as a hiding place went, but at least it was off the street. "You know what the odds are of us avoiding them until morning?" I asked. "Or of making it back to the portal if we do?"

"You got a better idea?" he demanded. "Because I'm good—I'm real good—but I'm not going to be able to fight our way out of here!"

"Not on your own. But there's somebody else here who knows the place at least as well as Rian."

Caleb made a disgusted sound. "Casanova's her creature. He's also petrified of ruining that pretty face of his. Even if he didn't turn traitor, we can't rely on him to do a damned—"

"Not Casanova!" I said, because I pretty much agreed with that sentiment. *"Pritkin."*

Caleb looked at me like I'd finally tipped the scales, like I'd been hovering in his mind between eccentric and downright nuts, and he'd finally decided where the arrow pointed. "And just how," he said heavily, "do you expect us to reach him? The odds were bad enough before; any minute now, we'll have the whole city on our asses!"

"But the city will expect us to be hiding, if we figured it out, or hanging around the souk if we didn't. They won't expect us to be going after Pritkin."

"Yes, yes, that's probably true. *And there's a reason for that,*" Caleb hissed. And then he abruptly pulled up the hood on my robe.

"What—"

"Don't look behind you, but a bunch more guards just ran into the souk."

So much for any lingering faith I had in Rian. Goddamnit! If she had a neck, I'd wring it, I thought, glaring through the space under his arm at a bunch of guards who were pulling off veils and jerking robes apart and generally acting like none of the people had any damned rights at—

My thoughts screeched to a halt, just like something else had recently. Something else that was still poking out of a ruined shop front. Because around here, you were either a have or a have-not, and it looked like the haves could do whatever the hell they damned well pleased.

And nobody questioned it.

"Come on," I told Caleb. "I have an idea."

*   *   *

"You'd think we'd get more for a fine camel thing than that," I grumbled at Caleb, ten minutes later.

"Ever since the XP-38 came out, they're just not in demand."

"What?"

"You don't get cultural references, do you?"

I frowned. "I get them. You just have weird ones."

"That was from *Star Wars*. It wasn't weird."

"I've seen *Star Wars* and that wasn't in it."

"In the first movie, when they're in the desert?" he asked. "When they have to sell Luke's speeder?"

"Oh. You mean the old ones."

"The old ones? The *old* ones? You mean the only good—" He saw my expression. "Never mind. What did we need more money for?"

"So I could get an outfit like yours," I said, looking enviously at the rich green woolly fabric of his long, caftanlike garment. It was warm. It was attractive. It covered his ass.

"What's wrong with the one you have on?"

"Other than the fact that I look like a hooker?"

I tugged at the back of the tight pink panties I was wearing, but it didn't help. They were still at least two sizes too small and riding up my butt. But they'd been the closest thing the merchant we picked had that we could afford. And we hadn't had time to comparison shop.

Of course, it didn't matter if you were in a nice, all-encompassing robe like Caleb's. It was a little more problematic when it came to sexy slave girl attire, particularly when the only thing I had on besides the ass-baring panties was a pair of diaphanous, slit-up-to-heaven harem pants and a top that wasn't covering as much as my bra had. But it was the pants that were really bothering me for some reason.

"You look like *I Dream of Jeannie* without the ponytail," Caleb said, helping not at all.

"I think it looks like they copied it from a low-rent *Aladdin*," I snapped. "Along with everything else."

"If there was copying, I'd say it was the other way around," Caleb said, glancing a little longingly at the buildings we were passing. The people here might not have wood, but they'd used what they had to full advantage, carving lintels, columns, stairs, even elaborate grills over their windows, all out of the same red stone.

Caleb looked like he'd have liked a chance to explore a little. He looked like the proverbial kid in the candy store, only without any money. I felt kind of bad for him suddenly.

But I didn't think hanging around would be too healthy.

"What?" I asked.

"The incubi came from here to earth, right?" he asked.

I nodded.

"And this place came first. So I'd say the incubi brought bits of this culture to earth, not the other way around."

"Yeah, but why *these* bits?" I asked, still trying to dig one out of my ass.

Caleb just looked at me. "Really? You have to ask why incubi would encourage an outfit like that?"

I sighed. "It's just . . . once, you know? Just once, I'd like to go on a mission without my butt hanging out, or getting shot, or otherwise being an issue."

"Look at it this way," he said, handing me up to the back of the semiwrecked chariot we were about to steal. "Maybe the guards will be too busy staring at it to pay us any attention."

"Yeah. Maybe." Or maybe we were about to make Rosier's job really, really easy. But at least the shop owner wasn't trying to stop us, even though Caleb's outfit was striped and the other guy's had been plain, and even though his skin had been a different color, and even though I was a blonde and the driver had left with a brunette.

Of course, he was an incubus, so I supposed that last one could be explained.

But nobody was asking about the other stuff, either. Nobody was even looking directly at us, as if our glorious presence was too much for them to bear. In fact, Caleb got a little too close to a porter when he was fighting with the camel things, who had been contentedly grazing on the shopkeeper's wares all this time and were in no hurry to leave. And the man turned over his wheelbarrow, scattering packages everywhere, rather than brush up against the hem of Caleb's robes.

Damn it, I hadn't been here an hour and I already hated this place.

I really hoped I wasn't going to be a permanent resident.

"All right, then," Caleb said, gathering up the reins. And then he just stood there.

"All right, then," I agreed.

"All. Right," he said again, his lips pursing, as we continued to go nowhere.

"Is there a problem?" I asked, after a few seconds.

He shot me a glance. "You don't, uh, know how to drive one of these things, do you?"

I looked at him. "Do I know how to drive a chariot, Caleb? Is that what you're asking me?"

He sighed. "Yeah. Me, neither."

He fiddled with the reins some more, until one of the camel things turned around and gave him a withering look. Caleb glowered at it. "You know, they don't cover this in war mage training!"

"Do they cover stunning spells?"

"Yeah, why?"

"Because I think the owner wants his chariot back."

And I had to give it to Caleb. He might not be rivaling Ben-Hur anytime soon, but there was nothing wrong with his reflexes. He spun and thrust out a hand, and the pissed-off demon who had just lurched out of the bar went flying. Literally—the spell tore the guy off his feet and sent him sailing back at least five yards, crashing through the open front of the tavern and scattering chairs and tables and patrons everywhere.

And normally, that would have been that. Except for the fact that we weren't anywhere normal. So what happened instead was that a now super-pissed-off incubus rose out of its unconscious host and came for us, at about the same time that a dozen or so guards who'd been searching shops down the street realized they'd just hit the jackpot.

Well, this part's normal, I thought, and grabbed the reins. And Caleb started firing off spell after spell in what in a lesser mage might have looked like a panic. But war mages didn't panic. Or if they did, they made sure everyone in the vicinity was right there with them.

And there's nothing like the threat of imminent death to turn formerly meek people into a raging mob. A few fire spells setting half the street alight, a few pulse-types causing all the overhead lanterns to burst in a colorful rain, a few hammerlike percussion blows to wagons and piles of goods and tables outside eateries, and suddenly, the guards had more to worry about than us. Like being trampled as everyone on our end of the street, all couple hundred of them, suddenly decided they wanted to be somewhere else.

Everybody but His Assholeness, that is, who just kept coming.

But that was okay, because the fire had finally done what we couldn't and gotten the camels moving. Only they weren't just moving, they were *moving*, in a blind panic and with no more concern than their owner had shown for anybody else's person or property. I tried to steer them away from the people at least, but it was a little hard with so many running everywhere, and while also holding on for dear life. And Caleb couldn't help me, being busy trying to find out what in his arsenal worked on an incubus.

Not much, it looked like, and the demon was still coming and the state of the street didn't seem to bother him, because now he wasn't so much running after us as flying, and I didn't think we'd like what would happen when he caught up.

"My bag," I gasped at Caleb as we barreled through a gate, the incubus right on our heels and extra sparkly in the dimmer light of the brief tunnel.

"What bag?"

"That one!"

I bumped him with my hip, and the small tasseled piece of uselessness I'd bought to replace the pockets I'd lost with my robes shimmied. It was as tacky as, well, hell, but I'd had to have something, because I wasn't crazy enough to show up entirely unprepared.

And because I'd never given Pritkin back his little, silver demon-fighting gun.

"What does this do?" Caleb yelled, pulling it out.

"Shoot it and find out!"

I guess he agreed, because a second later he got off a perfect shot into the incubus' sparkly cloud formation. And a second after that, it broke apart into a bunch of smaller clouds, which hovered in the air for a moment, looking a lot less sparkly. And then flowed back together, both dimmer and smaller, but still moving fast.

In the other direction.

"Damn!" Caleb looked at it with bright eyes. "I gotta get me one of these!"

"Stop quoting and help me!" I yelled back, because the camels were demented and the streets weren't even close to level and the incubi weren't going to have to kill us in a minute, because we were going to capsize on our heads. "Take the reins!"

"I don't want the reins!"

"Damn it, why not? You can't be any worse than—"

"That's why not!"

I didn't have to wonder what he meant. A bolt of

something red and sizzling hit down beside us almost the moment the words were out of his mouth, causing the camels to rear and then swerve across to the other side of the street. All the way across. Suddenly, we were throwing sparks off the unyielding stone, having to duck baskets and rolled-up awnings and lunging through a pile of crockery, which was definitely going to be in the scratch and dent and shattered-to-bits bin tomorrow.

Of course, we might be, too.

Because in between trying to pull the damned creatures back into something like the middle of the street, and avoiding decapitation, and trying to miss the darting people, who luckily appeared to be used to horrifically bad driving, I saw security forces converging on us from all sides.

But not out of the gate ahead, where I guess the guards hadn't got the memo yet. Or maybe old training just died hard. They were so used to letting their lords and masters do whatever the hell they wanted that they just stood there with confused looks on their faces as we barreled past, despite having a dozen yelling guards right on our tail.

"How many gates is that?" Caleb asked, throwing a spell that caused the portcullis on our side to come crashing down as soon as we shot past it.

"Two!"

"Shit. And the outer wall makes three, and there's three above that damned palace. . . ."

"That leaves three."

"No, two. The palace is *on* the sixth level, not beyond it. We don't need to pass through the sixth gate."

Yeah, but we needed the fourth and fifth, and I didn't think we were going to get them. Because bells were suddenly clanging out a warning from higher up on the walls, and the guards were getting closer, and the warren of streets meant that we kept flashing by alleys on both sides, and more and more of those had red energy bolts coming out of them. At the rate we were going, I doubted we'd get one more.

Of course, I could be wrong.

A couple of guards stepped out in front of the next gate, arms stretched out in warning, too far away to worry about getting run down. But not too far to get blown off the street with a single spell. We shot through the gate, which they hadn't bothered to bring down, because of course we were going to stop when politely asked to do so.

Of course we were.

Our manners need work, I thought, and giggled. And wondered if I was going mad.

"One more," Caleb said, looking at me strangely.

"Yeah, maybe," I breathed, because suddenly I couldn't even see the palace anymore.

I stared around through frizzled blond hair, trying to figure out where, exactly, I'd taken a wrong turn, because I couldn't remember turning at all. But the streets up here were even worse than in the souk, a tangled mess of intersecting passages, like a bandit's dream, and anything but straight. And the palace, when I saw it at all, didn't seem to be getting any closer. Like a mirage, it gleamed in glimpses through buildings or at the end of alleys, shining mockingly as we scattered people and dodged lightning bolts and ran over every freaking thing—

And then plunged straight into a mass of guards.

They'd gathered in a small plaza, ahead of the last gate, which two of them appeared to be trying to bring down. But it looked like maybe these inner gates hadn't been shut in a very long time and weren't in the best repair, because they appeared to be having trouble. But they clearly didn't intend that we get any farther. A storm of red lightning tore through the air at us and then burst into a blinding halo just beyond our camels' noses as Caleb flung up a shield.

It kept us from being fried, but there were too many of them, and that shield wouldn't last long under this kind of pounding, and it looked like they'd finally gotten the gate moving and—

And *screw* it.

"Are you *crazy*?" Caleb said when I stopped trying to hold the half-crazed camels back and gave them a little smack on the butt with the reins instead.

I didn't answer, because I didn't have a good one, and because we'd just *jumped* ahead, hitting a dip in the street and sailing over, knocking several guards to the ground in the process and possibly running over a third. Although I didn't see how since I was pretty damned sure that both wheels had left the ground. And then we were hitting back down, hard enough to have me biting my cheek half in two as we flew through the last gate, the camels' noses almost straight out in front of their bodies, and me and Caleb ducking down to where ours were barely visible over the top of the chariot.

And I still felt those wicked spikes, miniature versions of the ones on the main gate outside, brush my curls as we passed.

I didn't care. I swallowed blood, too busy trying not to fall out on my ass to care about anything else. I didn't even try to steer anymore; it was virtually impossible at this speed anyway, and besides, the camels seemed to know where they were going. I just held on, the little leg brace on the side of the chariot digging into my thigh, my hands white-knuckled on the front, and Caleb cursing and camels screeching and bells clanging—

And the palace suddenly reappearing in front of us, up a long stretch of hill.

There was yet another gate in front of it, a flimsy-looking thing that seemed more ornamental than anything else, and a couple of white-robed guys with fancy gold belts who looked a lot prettier than the blue-robed fiends behind us. But judging by their expressions, they were also mostly there for looks.

I guess not too many people tried storming Rosier's palace.

Or if they did, these weren't the guys to stop them.

They took one disbelieving look at us, out-of-control camels and fleeing people and fiery spells just whaling on us now, as the guards converged into a single long line behind us. And then they jumped to either side as we burst through the gate, with shards of precious wood flying and several planters crashing and a swaying lantern overhead shattering.

And then we were in.

Chapter Seventeen

We didn't stop. There were more pretty, pretty guards coming down the sweeping front staircase and Caleb's shield had just given up the ghost. And judging by the pounding it had taken, it wasn't going back up anytime soon.

So we plowed through the middle of them, camels and all, straight up the stairs, and into a blur of brilliant colors and intricate patterns and gorgeous tile work. Servants in white and gold ringed an atrium with a long pool and fountains, serving a bunch of beautiful people. Who stopped eating long enough to stare at us party crashers in shock, one woman even having a canapé fall out of her lovely mouth.

And then Caleb had me by the hand and we were over the side of our messed-up vehicle and up another gorgeous set of stairs, not because we knew where we were going, but because the blue-robed guards couldn't be far behind.

"Which way?" Caleb asked as we burst onto the next floor, and almost got beaned by a guy in a skimpy outfit and a fancy tray.

I don't think it was on purpose; he looked like the servants downstairs, in flimsy gathered trousers and a gold sash. And once Caleb snatched the tray away from him, he just stood there quivering, his eyes huge. Until Caleb shoved him in the direction of the stairs and he went running, yelling something in a language I didn't know, but in the universal tone of "oh, shit!"

"Where?" Caleb said again, practically crushing my biceps.

"I don't know!"

"What do you mean—"

"That's what Rian was for!"

"Shit!"

And yeah. But then the noise from downstairs suddenly elevated, and we were out of time to debate it. "Run," I suggested.

It was seconded and carried, leading us to pound down the hall and up some more stairs, narrow back ones this time. It looked like they were only used by servants, which was fine—unless we got caught on them with no room to maneuver. But we didn't, because the guys chasing us were coming from behind, and the few people we saw going up made no effort to hinder us.

Which would have been great—if we knew where we were going.

"Look for guards!" Caleb told me as we passed a tiny landing leading to an expansive hallway. "He'll have some on his door!"

But there weren't any guards on any doors on that floor, or the next, or the one after that. I tried to tamp down my panic, but it wasn't working. This place hadn't looked so big from the souk, but up close was a different story. It would take hours to search it all, if Rian had even been telling the truth about Pritkin being here, which I wasn't placing any bets on right at the—

I crashed into Caleb, who had abruptly stopped, one foot on the next flight going up, in order to look at someone down the hall. Not a guard, although the guy was in blue. And not a servant, although he came staggering backward out of a room as if somebody hadn't liked the dinner entrée.

Or his face, I thought, as Casanova hit the wall and bounced off, only to meet a very familiar fist on the way back to his feet.

"Pritkin!" Caleb and I yelled together, and the irate blond who had just followed Casanova out the door looked up, and then did a double take, fist still clenched. And then clenched the other one as a scowl to beat all scowls spread over his face and took up residence there. He stared at me, and he looked *pissed.*

Only no, that didn't really cover it.

He looked like I'd felt when I woke up on that damp, burning hillside, only to find that he'd just given up the independence he'd worked so hard for, had suffered so much for, in trade for my life. When I realized that he'd just destroyed his future to save mine even though I hadn't asked, and would never have asked, him to. The same impotent, all-consuming, helpless fury was on his face that had been on mine that night and I was suddenly, viciously glad of it.

And then he jerked Casanova off the wall and dragged him inside and we ran after them and slammed the door. Which was stupid, because it wasn't like everybody didn't know where we'd gone, and I didn't think a flimsy piece of wood was going to hold them off for long. But it felt good to slam it, so good that I almost opened it and did it again.

I settled for glaring at Pritkin as he glared back, and dared him to say it. Dared him to tell me off for doing the *exact same thing* he'd done for me. Dared him to say *anything.*

"You broke my node!" Casanova screeched.

"You brought her here!" Pritkin said viciously, his eyes never leaving my face.

"Not willingly, you insufferable—"

"Where's Rian?" I demanded, cutting him off, but

staring at Pritkin. He looked different. The hair was longer, to the point it could actually be styled like a normal person's. He was shaved and his skin looked soft, with a slight shimmer to it like the people's downstairs. He was wearing some flowy, desert sheik caftan thing in a dark green that highlighted the breadth of his shoulders and brought out his eyes.

He looked terrible.

Pritkin's idea of a beauty regimen included soap and deodorant; I'd never even smelled cologne on him before. But I was smelling it now, something wild and seductive and—and wrong. Pritkin smelled like *sweat*. He smelled like burnt gunpowder. He smelled like nasty potion ingredients and too-strong coffee and those little licorice candies he snuck around to eat because he didn't want to set a bad example for my sweet tooth.

Only not now.

Now he smelled like this place.

Now he smelled like *nothing*.

"Where do you think?" Casanova said bitterly. "She told me we were coming here to look for John, but as soon as we arrived, she started asking after Rosier. When I demanded to know why, she left me and went to look for him on her own. And stupidly, I tried to warn—"

"I knew it was you," Pritkin told me, quietly furious. "Before he said a damned word. As soon as I heard the bells, I *knew*—"

I slapped him. Hard. It came out of nowhere, to the point that I didn't even realize I was going to do it until his head snapped back, until he was glaring at me over the imprint of my palm on his left cheek.

"I—we'll talk later," Casanova said, and slunk off somewhere.

"How's it feel?" I asked, voice low and shaking. And I wasn't talking about the slap.

"You—" Pritkin cut off and clamped his lips tight, as if he was afraid if he started he wouldn't know where to stop. Which was fine by me. My adrenaline was pumping,

my pulse was pounding, and anything he could throw—
just *any damned thing*—

Except that, I thought, as I was dragged against a
hard chest.

"You son of a *bitch*—" I began, only to have my voice
choked off by something caught in my throat. It wasn't
sentiment. It was too dark for that. I thought it might be
hate.

Yes, that was it. I *hated* him.

"Did you hear me?" Caleb barked, from across the
room.

"What?" I snapped. And finally looked up. And
blinked. Because a prison cell this wasn't.

Instead of the cramped, potion-filled, messy room in
Vegas, which even on a good day looked like it was in-
habited by a cross between a hyperactive toddler and
Rambo, this place was . . . beautiful. Graceful. Perfect.

It was huge, with couches and pillows and rugs scattered around, and a bed big enough for seven or eight
people. And maybe designed for it, considering where
we were. There were arched doorways on either end,
leading off to even more space, but the big story was the
balcony, which was easily as wide as the room and ran its
entire length.

Pierced bronze lanterns swayed softly on silken chains,
surrounded by geometrical halos. A breeze sent long
white curtains wafting languorously into the room, so
diaphanous the stars could be seen through them. Their
edges caressed diamond-shaped stones on the floor, in
every possible shade from honey to palest gold. I stared
at them, trying to wrap my head around the idea of Pritkin living in a palace instead of the middle of Dante's
tacky clutter, of him wearing fine, embroidered clothes
instead of old, scratched leather, of him inhabiting a
space as beautiful as it was alien, with nothing, not a
book, not a vial, not a picture, *nothing,* to remind him of
the world he'd lost.

As if it hadn't mattered. As if he hadn't even missed—

"Cassie!" Caleb said, more urgently this time. "Look at this."

I ran over to the balcony, which gave a pretty good view along the side of the cliff and over the sprawling city. But the twinkling lights didn't hold my attention nearly as well as what was coming down from above. So that's what's up there, I thought, watching a bunch of dark figures literally running down buildings and spars of rock above the palace. They weren't using the streets; they were leaping from roof to roof to outcropping as if making their own highway.

And every single one of them was headed straight for us.

"It looks like somebody called out the elite troops," Caleb said grimly. "What we're gonna do, we do now."

"Get her into the study," Pritkin said, coming up behind us. "Barricade yourselves inside. I can't call off the guards, but I can call my father—"

"We're not hiding; we're leaving," I said flatly.

"Not until I negotiate safe passage—"

"Your father isn't going to grant safe passage for you!"

"That is irrelevant—"

"Bull*shit.*"

"—as you knew quite well before you started this insanity! Damn it, Cassie! I thought you had more sense—"

"Have you met her?" Casanova asked, sticking his bloody nose onto the balcony.

And I lost it. I grabbed the front of Pritkin's gold-embroidered caftan—and since when did he wear a goddamned *caftan?*—and dragged him down to me. "I am going to say this one time. You are my servant. Sworn to my service until death. I never released you from that obligation. And if I want to come after you, I'll damned well come after you!"

Something shifted behind his eyes, something dangerous. "And I'll shut up and like it."

"Right now I don't give a *damn* whether you like it or

not. But I'm not leaving without you, so you may as well—"

The door blew open, and Caleb and Pritkin both flung out a hand. And whoever it was blew right back out again. The door clicked softly shut.

Pritkin glared at me for another second, and then transferred the look to Caleb. "The rugs," he snarled, and for a second, Caleb looked as confused as I was. And then—

"Aw, *hell* no!"

"You have a better idea?" Pritkin snapped, striding over and grabbing a big gold one that was anchoring a pleasant conversation area just inside the bedroom.

Caleb looked heavenward, but then apparently remembered where he was and gave up. And snatched up a red one from the balcony floor. And in the process sent one of the guards tumbling over the railing and into the night, who had just jumped down on top of it from the floor above.

Caleb grabbed Pritkin's arm as his buddy tossed what looked like an expensive rug after the demon. "My magic's weak here," he warned.

"That down in the souk was weak?" I asked, in disbelief.

Caleb glanced at me. "With the amount of power I let loose, the whole damned market should have been in flames. As it was, we barely made it here. And I don't know—"

"It'll have to be enough," Pritkin said grimly.

"Sure. Says the half demon."

"You're never going to let me live that down, are you?"

"After this?" Caleb rolled his eyes. And then he grabbed Casanova. "Are we taking this one?"

"Yes!" Casanova said heatedly. "I don't want to be here when Rosier finds out what you're doing!"

"What *we're* doing?"

"None of this is my fault!"

"Oh, you'll be here," Pritkin said grimly. But then he threw him over the balcony, too.

I was about to freak out, because that was a damned long way down, even for a vampire. But I didn't get a chance. Because I was next.

I didn't even have time to scream before my butt was bouncing on something firm but soft, not two yards under the balcony's lip. I didn't have time to see what it was before Pritkin landed beside me. And before we took off, in a blur of wind that had my eyes tearing up.

Or maybe that was the spell that flashed through the air right in front of my face, and set something on fire.

I turned back around, because that had come from above. And saw a bunch of guards hanging over the railing of the floor above Pritkin's, firing what looked like balls of pure lightning at us. They burned like it, too, I thought, smelling singed wool.

And realized that the something on fire was the something we were sitting on.

Something big and gold and—

And missing a corner when Pritkin pulled a knife and sliced off the burning bit of what had been a nice rug. No, not a rug, I thought blankly, gripping the suddenly very flimsy feeling sides. Now it was a flying—

Target, floating around over the city on a gentle wafting motion that was going to get us roasted any minute now. I stared across the void at Casanova, who was also clinging to the edge of his carpet with both hands, peering over the side with his ass in the air. And with an expression that somehow managed to combine pissed off and terrified.

And you know things are bad when you start agreeing with Casanova.

"They're still shooting at us!" I told Pritkin, who was crawling around, muttering something at the carpet.

"And this surprises you?"

"Yes! They have to know you're up here!"

"Obviously."

"But they could kill you!"

"That would be the idea."

"You're saying there are people here who want you dead?" A terse nod, but no information. Of course not. "Damn it, Pritkin! I don't understand—"

"No, you don't!" he said, turning on me savagely. "Which is why you shouldn't have come!"

"That's why you shouldn't have left!"

"I didn't have a choice!"

"Neither did I!"

"Get a room!" Casanova screeched as another spell flushed through the space between us. "And put these damned things into high gear or we are all going to *die*!"

"Layering spells isn't easy under the best of terms," Pritkin told him. "Which these are not!"

"What layering? Just move this thing!"

"Levitation spell—one," Caleb said, holding a finger in front of his face. "Keeping the damned carpet stiff and level—two." Another finger. "And now you want a propulsion spell, which is three, and which ain't happening."

Casanova stared from him to Pritkin and back again. "You mean, you threw us off the balcony and you didn't have a plan *for getting us down*?"

"Someone once said, if you're in a burning building, you jump out a window. You figure everything else out on the way to the ground."

"It's the ground I'm worried about!"

And I didn't blame him. A drop like that was one of the few things that could kill a master vampire. But it wasn't like we could go any lower. The red lightning balls seemed to have a range, and we had drifted too high for them to reach.

We'd also started moving forward a little, barely fast enough to ruffle my hair, although that would have been an improvement—if the guards hadn't just switched to other spells. These looked different, with long tails and a wider dispersion; I guess because they were harder to aim at this distance. But the result was a sky full of what looked a lot like fireworks, red and pink and yellow and orange, and would have been really beautiful . . .

If we hadn't been flying through the middle of them.

Casanova shrieked as another spell burned past, shedding yellow sparks that ate tiny holes in his robe before something Caleb muttered put them out. I was more worried about the shock waves from the explosions, which were rocking us every which way, like a boat on the high seas.

I'd just had the thought when another wave hit us, heavier than the rest, tipping the rug I was clinging to with both hands and a foot by at least thirty percent. I slid to the edge, and for a second, I stared straight down at a city full of deep blue shadows and orange lantern-light and exploding spells and streets full of people staring back at us. But I didn't scream.

Because there was one thing, at least, that I wasn't seeing.

"Why aren't the incubi coming after us?" I gasped as Pritkin grabbed me and the rug wobbled back into place. "They can reach us no matter how high we are!"

"Yeah, except that we shot one a few minutes ago," Caleb reminded me, the light from a passing bolt staining his face gold.

"With what?" Pritkin demanded.

Caleb held up the little silver gun I'd given him.

Which is when Pritkin started cursing.

"We didn't kill anybody," I said. "Which is more than they're trying to do to us!"

"There are many among the lords who would gladly see me dead," Pritkin said, reaching over and snatching his gun back. "But they aren't going to attack me—or those under my protection—right in front of my father. Unless you two give them a perfect reason by shooting at them!"

"It was only one," Caleb said diffidently.

"You're as bad as she is!"

"Why do they want you dead?" I demanded. "You're Rosier's heir—"

"And as such stand between them and power. I pushed everyone a step farther away from the throne the day I returned."

"But if they can't kill you in front of your father—"

"*They* can't. At least not openly, although half the guards around here are in the pay of one faction or another. But they're not the main—"

"Aughhh!" That was Casanova, bloodstained face lit up by a ruddy spell, giving him a truly hellish look. Not that he needed the help right now. "Am I the only sane one here? Am I the only one who realizes *this is not the time for a chat?* I don't care what you do or how you do it, but flying carpets are supposed to *fly!*"

"In the movies, maybe," Caleb said. "But in case you didn't notice, *this* is not in a movie. *That*"—he pointed at the glittering city, so far below us now—"is not CGI and *you* are going to get shoved off this rug if you don't shut up and let us think!"

Only that didn't seem to be going so well.

And that was before something rumbled the air around us like thunder. Only this place didn't look like it got a lot of thunder. And I didn't think thunder would put quite that expression on Pritkin's face.

"What is that?" Casanova asked, voice strained. Like he couldn't take any more bad news right now. Which was too bad, since that was the only kind we seemed to get.

"A demon prince in the seat of his power," Pritkin said tightly, as a massive sandstorm broke over the cliffs.

Chapter Eighteen

It dwarfed the city, making the considerable sprawl look like a child's toy in comparison. All along the horizon, as far as I could see in both directions, it came, a boiling mass of dirt and dust and outraged fury dozens of stories high. Casanova stared at it for a second, wild-eyed and disbelieving, like a man who had successfully dodged death for centuries seeing it come straight at him.

And then he started stripping.

He ripped off the dusty robes he'd worn all day even as the first gusts hit us and sent them billowing out all around him. He was fumbling and cursing and acting like a crazy man. But for once, I didn't think he was.

For once, I thought he had a damned good idea.

I grabbed Pritkin's pretty green caftan.

"Take it off!" I yelled, over the howl of the winds that were already almost on us, and for a miracle, he didn't argue.

Maybe he'd figured it out, too, or maybe the noise made discussion impossible. All I know is he skinned out of it, and thankfully, it was good, heavy wool, comfortable, but warm for those cold desert nights. And sturdy—I hoped.

I lashed one end of it around a corner of the rug and

reached for the other one—and realized we didn't have it thanks to the spell that had burned it away. There followed a mad scramble to get the robe untied and to crawl around to the other end of the rug and get it into place with Pritkin's help. He said something, but I couldn't hear him with the wind howling in my ears and the first flurries of dust scouring my face and panic making my hands fumble as badly as Casanova's, who I couldn't even see anymore.

But we got it tied, and the makeshift craft turned just before the storm hit. A furious blast of wind and sand slammed into us, with enough force to have launched us to the moon. Or across a city at insane speeds, like a bullet shot out of a gun.

A really, really unsteady gun. The jury-rigged "sail" bowing out in front of us was only tied at the bottom, meaning that Pritkin and I had to hold on to the top ends because we didn't have a mast. We also had to cling to the far side of the rug, so we didn't get launched over the top and end this whole thing real quick. But crazily enough, it worked, maybe because the spell keeping the rug level also seemed to stabilize it, leaving only one small problem.

The human body wasn't designed as sailboat rigging.

Really, really wasn't, I thought, glancing desperately over at Pritkin. He was holding his end of the rug in his teeth and fumbling with something he'd looped around one arm. But I couldn't tell what it was, or what he thought he was doing, because I was too busy feeling tendons stretch and ligaments pull and muscles shriek that this was not good, not good, *not good*—

And then I was bouncing onto the middle of the rug.

I panicked for an instant, thinking I'd just screwed us over, but we were still skipping ahead of the storm, and were as level as a jury-rigged vessel made out of scraps could be. Pritkin must have grabbed the piece I'd been holding, and was somehow managing to control both of them at once, because the sail was as full as ever. But I couldn't turn around to find out how, because I was half-blind from the sand and trying desperately to cling to a bucking magic carpet that wasn't nearly as fun as the legends would have you believe—

Until it suddenly evened out.

I twisted around, desperately hoping that Rosier had reconsidered, even knowing the odds on that. But over my shoulder was the same boiling mass of fury, just darker now as it swallowed the lights of the city we'd just left behind. But I barely noticed, because Pritkin was . . .

"No," I said, immediately rejecting what my eyes were telling me.

I blinked, and then I pushed a fluttering scarf out of my face and blinked again. But the scene didn't change. Pritkin was still leaning off the back edge of the rug, his feet were still anchored behind a rigid wrinkle in the cloth, and he was still arching back, to the point that he was lying almost flat. But now his forearms were looped around the ends of the long fabric sash he'd been wearing, which were tied securely around the top two corners of our sail.

Our wind-filled sail. That he was directing by pulling on one side of the makeshift rope or the other, or by turning his body this way and that. So, basically, he was—

"No!" I said again, because he was absolutely, positively not windsurfing in hell. It hurt my brain, my relatively sane-no-matter-what-Casanova-said brain, to even think the words, because things like this didn't happen.

Unless I really had gone nuts. An idea reinforced a second later, when Pritkin suddenly grinned—*grinned*—at me, and said something that the wind blew away. *"What?"*

"Why do these plans of yours always involve me getting naked?" he yelled, making me blink again. And then scowl, because damn it, brain, this was no time to lose it.

"You're not naked!" I yelled back, because it was

true, if not by much. He still had on a pair of silky gold
trousers, ruffling in the wind and looking ridiculous next
to the hard lines of his body.

And because what else do you say to a grinning,
windsurfing demon?

He said something that sounded like "disappointed?"
but wasn't because that would be absurd.

And then Caleb and Casanova dove by, just missing
the front of our crazy contraption, because they didn't
seem to have figured out Pritkin's modification. But with
vampire strength and Caleb's brawn, they seemed to be
doing okay just holding the ends of the sail, although
that gave them a lot less control than we had. But the
bucking, weaving, crazy course they were on didn't seem
to bother them.

At least, it didn't seem to bother Caleb. Who I finally
saw laughing and whooping and giving a good represen-
tation as to why war mages were viewed as being slightly
off by the rest of us. Like Casanova, who was upholding
the banner of sanity with a lot of horrified screeching.

I turned toward Pritkin, to point out that, see—that
was how a normal person reacted when being chased by
a giant storm of a demon lord through the skies of hell.
But I didn't, because he yelled something. Something
that sounded like "the gate."

And oh, *crap*.

I turned back around, flattened out, and stared underneath the rigid edge of our sail. And saw to my horror that in a few short minutes we'd managed to cover
almost as much ground as it had taken us hours to walk.
Which meant that the portal to this world was coming
up, and coming up fast.

It was already visible, the twin peaks of the canyon
where the doorway to Rosier's court originated, well
away from the city. So, I assumed, he'd have some warning if he was attacked. But I hadn't, and I didn't know for
sure that I could do this, and Casanova's outraged face

demanding why I hadn't tested Mother's theory was starting to sound a lot more like the voice of reason and—

"Shiiiit!" I yelled as the wind howled and the dust whirled and the guards around the portal saw us and hit the ground. And Casanova and Caleb screamed by again, and somehow snagged hold of the side of our carpet in the process, slinging us around in a huge arc. Because no one knew if the gate would stay open for anyone who wasn't with me.

Assuming it was going to open at all.

I couldn't tell if I was doing anything, because we spun back around, and then around again, still headed for possible oblivion, but in wild, whipping arcs that made concentration all but impossible. Or sight. Or anything that wasn't clinging to our crazy craft and screaming.

But vaguely, through the bands of golden-red sand I saw another swirl of colors, a bright azure twist that glowed from the inside. And that was all right, but I couldn't tell if the shield was covering the portal or not because it was mostly transparent even in good conditions and these *weren't good conditions.* But Pritkin, damn him, was doing his best to aim for it like I knew what I was doing when we'd conclusively proved that that was pretty much never the case, and suddenly Casanova and I were shrieking in unison but I didn't care because *oh God*—

And then we were through, tearing across a mad swirl of colors that usually made me dizzy but—too late—and then out into darkness.

But not that of Rosier's secondary court. That darkness was filled with sandstone and hushed servants and stately foreign elegance. This one was neon streaked, with flashing lights and peppy spend-more-money music and screaming slot machines. And a screaming guy, too, who we'd scooped up from the floor when Pritkin tried to course correct to keep us from plowing straight into

some butt-ugly carpet, and instead sent us careening
straight for a stalactite-littered ceiling.

Including an enormous one looming like a dagger directly in our path.

"Auggghhhh!" said the guy in the pink pig shirt.

"Auggghhhh!" said Casanova, straight in my ear, because he'd somehow ended up on our carpet.

Auggghhh, I didn't say, because he'd grabbed me
around the neck, trying to hold on, and was strangling
me in the process.

Which wasn't healthy but wasn't any worse than hitting the giant mass of fake rock that was about to skewer
all three of us—

Until Caleb sent a spell at the last second that burst
the thing into a cloud of plaster dust and a zillion flying
pieces.

And then I was just coughing and hacking and trying
to hold on. And simultaneously working to throw off
Casanova's death grip while also attempting to keep
pig-man from sliding off the rug ahead of me. Because
we were at least half a dozen stories up, careening
around a cavernous space like a . . .

Well, actually, there is nothing else quite like a speeding,
sand-filled flying carpet full of freaked-out passengers.

And then Pritkin finally managed to get it stopped,
pulling up hard and sending us falling back into him.
And then sprawling back onto the middle of the rug as
it flattened out, the spell that had felt so flimsy in hell
perking right up now that we were back. On earth?

I didn't understand, but the view through the carpet
fringe was unmistakably Dante's main drag, where the
theme was supposed to be ghost town, not Aladdin, but
nobody seemed to care. A crowd was gathering, and
staring up at us expectantly, like we were a better varia-
tion on the street performers who usually prowled
around trying to scare people. Only this time, it was the
other way around, judging by the way Casanova was still
shrieking.

I wasn't, for the same reason that I hadn't been yelling.

"Help," I choked, not able to get any air past the hundred and seventy pounds of vampire lying on my back. And as a result, a certain porcine T-shirt and the panicked guy wearing it were slowly sliding out of my hands—

Pritkin reached over and grabbed the guy, jerking him back onto the rug, right before he gave the crowd the spectacle they were hoping for. A bunch of Dante's security ran up underneath us, a moment too late, and then just stood there, staring upward like everyone else. Because their training stopped just short.

Until the boss crawled across me, dirty and naked except for a battered pair of tighty whities, and stuck his no-longer perfectly coiffed head over the edge. And screamed again. Only this time, it was actual words.

"Get me down, you cretins! Get me down, get me down, get me down!"

The guards started looking at one another, and then a bunch of them linked hands and looked back up at him. Hopefully. Which you had to kind of admire considering who their boss was.

I'd have thought he'd beaten that out of them years ago.

I guess Casanova did, too, because he started yelling some more, but I couldn't hear it. The wind had just picked up noticeably and blew the words away, like it was suddenly wafting my sweaty hair against my face. And since we were inside, that probably wasn't a great—

"John!" Caleb said urgently.

"I know."

"Get us down!"

"No time."

And there wasn't. A second later, a storm swept through the hotel like a cyclone on a prairie. The crowd screamed and ran for cover, a couple of tumbleweeds went spinning by, and we started wafting around again, our makeshift sail partially reinflating before Caleb could snatch it off.

I clung to the gently rotating rug, but it wasn't the fear of falling that had me worried. It wasn't even the storm, which we seemed to be in the eye of anyway. No, my fear was kind of occupied with the pair of elegant boots that were materializing on the carpet, as the storm swirled and spun and came together into the shape of a very pissed off demon lord.

Who grabbed for me almost before he'd finished consolidating, but I rolled to the side and he got pig-man instead.

Who he promptly dropped over the side.

"Oh my God!" I lunged for the edge of the rug, and got a split-second glimpse of a stunned-looking TV reporter sitting on a bunch of crossed vamp arms, until they unceremoniously dumped him on the floor. And then I was jerked up to meet a pair of furious green eyes.

"Try again," Rosier breathed.

"Drop her!" Pritkin snarled, pulling his knife and causing Rosier's eyes to briefly flick to him.

"Good plan," he said, and dangled me over the edge. "It was the woman!" he yelled, apparently at the storm. "She deceived him! Take her and do as you will!"

But the storm didn't seem impressed. If anything, it got louder and more ferocious, and new shapes started to coalesce out of the blowing sand. One landed on our rug, causing the whole thing to bounce and throwing me into Rosier.

Who promptly threw me off, only that turned out to be a good thing.

A flash of light seared my retinas as I fell back, and the piece of rug right beside my body went spinning off on its own trajectory, with Casanova clinging to it like a shipwrecked sailor to the last barrel left afloat.

For a second, I didn't realize what was happening, until Pritkin shoved me behind him. And lashed out with his knife, sending a hand and the curved sword it held spinning out over the void, neon running along the blade like blood until it hit one of the fake storefronts. And stuck there, quivering.

But not as much as I was when a now one-handed demon in black robes lunged for me. He was kicked viciously back onto Caleb's carpet by Pritkin, where two of his buddies had been about to launch themselves at us. But his added weight sent them flying before they were ready, one onto a nearby roof and one straight at us—

Where he landed on a sword held by . . . Rosier?

And judging by the vicious satisfaction on Rosier's face, I didn't think it had been a mistake.

"Call them off!" Pritkin yelled.

"I can't!" Rosier wrenched out the blade and kicked the body into the void. "They don't answer to me!"

"Then why did you bring them?" I demanded.

"I didn't bring them! I was trying to get my son away from them, before you managed to get him killed!" He glared at Pritkin. "What in the nine hells—"

"Cassie wouldn't leave without me! I was escorting her to safety!"

"And how's that working for you?" Rosier demanded as two more guards spun into existence—and were just as quickly dispatched.

"I thought we were going to the Shadowland," Pritkin said, looking at me.

"We were," I told him. "I thought . . . I must have shifted us—"

"You can't shift from my father's kingdom!"

"She didn't," Rosier snarled. "She linked the gates, mine and the one back to earth, bringing you straight back where she wanted you to be!"

"I couldn't have," I said hotly. "I wasn't even sure I knew how to open one—"

"We came through on your wake!"

Oh. "Then it was a mistake—"

"Some mistake!" Rosier hissed. "You just put my son under interdict!"

"I was restricted to Rosier's domain on the council's order," Pritkin explained. "The Shadowland is neutral ground; I could have accompanied you there. But here—"

"Here he's an outlaw, to be killed on sight!" Rosier panted, having just thrown another guard over the side.

"The council's order?" I repeated, getting a bad feeling suddenly. "But why would they want—"

"Because of *you*," Rosier spat, getting in my face. "He has his own past with them. They never liked him, but it wasn't until he allied with you that they began to *fear* him! A council-hating demon and a time-traveling, border-crossing menace? You could go back in history, destroy us all! Although you seem to be doing that well enough as it is!"

"I've told you before, I'm no threat to the council—"

"Yes, and it's so reassuring to have your word on that. Unfortunately, they'd prefer something a bit more certain—like my son's head!"

"Why not mine?"

"You're needed for the war effort," Rosier said bitterly. "He's expendable—"

"He's no such thing!"

"Tell them that."

"Summon them and I will!"

Rosier's eyes flashed neon, and if looks could kill . . . well, they would have saved him some trouble. "Yes, you'd like that, wouldn't you?" he snarled.

Pritkin cursed. "Do it! There's no choice!"

"You planned this," Rosier hissed. "You planned this all along. I know damned well she didn't come up with it on her own—"

Pritkin cursed again, although not as much as when the guards wised up, and four of them decided to attack us together. Four hit down onto our rug at the same time, landing between me and the two demon lords, and their combined weight sent me flying. Off and up and into the void, arms flailing and body desperately trying to shift—and failing.

And staring into Pritkin's panicked face as I started to fall, because it was a long, long way down.

Chapter Nineteen

Or it would have been if I hadn't fallen straight onto Casanova.

And that would have been great—if my added weight hadn't caused his bit of rug to dip a full story downward. And then to fly back up. And then to bounce back and forth between the two extremes, yo-yoing us past the battle that was now raging on both carpets.

"Ooooh," the crowd said, impressed at our acrobatics.

"Aaaaaah!" I said, grabbing Casanova around the neck, because I am not a member of Cirque du Soleil.

"Get off!" he snarled, because I don't think he'd planned the heroics. He'd been on hands and knees, peering over the edge of his unsteady perch as he tried to get his men re-formed into a safety net. But they were busy running around, trying to clear the crowd away from what they, at least, realized was not an act.

And therefore there was no one to catch either one of us.

Not that I was all that interested in getting down. The storm had dropped a few dozen more black-clad figures on the surrounding rooftops, too far away to reach the main battle, but only a few flights of stairs away from the floor. I assumed that was why Pritkin and Caleb were keeping the rugs in the air. Fighting on a tiny, unstable platform isn't fun.

But it beats getting mobbed by two dozen otherworldly soldiers all at the same time.

Especially these soldiers.

Between the dim light at Rosier's court and the flurry of activity around our escape, I hadn't gotten a good look at the elite, black-clad troops before. I was getting it now. One of the creatures' hoods slid back enough to show me his face—if he'd had one. Instead, a blank bronze faceplate gleamed under the lights, and my stomach abruptly started crowding my toes.

"Fuck," I said, with feeling.

"What?" Casanova's head whipped around. "What now?"

"That now," I said, pointing.

"What?"

"Allû."

"Allû?" For a second, he stared blankly at the nearest carpet, and then his face changed. "Fuck!"

And yeah, that about summed them up. The Allû were the council's personal guards, who were usually camped out in the Shadowland making life in hell a little more hellish for anybody who dared to cross their demonic masters. But occasionally they got sent on errands, like when the council really wanted somebody dead.

And they usually got their wish, since their freakish army couldn't actually die. I knew because I'd fought them before. Not that that experience was likely to help much at the moment, since it had mostly involved me getting killed over and over again. I'd been caught in a time loop and kept "resurrecting" whenever time reset itself, until I finally figured out a way to beat them.

Unfortunately, this time I didn't have a hundred chances to get it right.

"Take us closer!" I told Casanova, trying to grab the edge of Pritkin's rug as we headed back up again. But it was moving, too, as half a dozen men and creatures fought on top of it, and the fringe barely brushed my fingers.

Which was just as well, since an Allû fell off the rug a second later, burning from a fire spell and barely missing us on its way to slam into the floor far below. And then to get up, still burning. And to run to the nearest building to rejoin the fight.

A second later it burst back onto the roof, moving so fast that the oxygen made the flames lick up all the faster. Its outer robes were already mostly gone, with just a few flaming tatters still clinging to the metal underneath, which was now glowing red hot. Not that the Allû appeared to notice.

But Casanova did, the flames from the burning demon reflecting in his horrified eyes as he stared at me. "Are you *insane*? Shift us out of here!"

"I only have strength for maybe one shift, if I'm lucky," I told him. And that was assuming I could concentrate. But it was the only chance Pritkin had.

The good news was, the Allû didn't use spells. The bad news was, they didn't need them. They were freakishly strong, unbelievably fast, and impervious to pain since they didn't seem to actually have bodies in there. As far as I'd ever been able to tell, they were nothing more than animated suits of armor.

Which kind of limited attack strategy. The only way I'd found to get rid of them was to completely destroy that armor. As in shred it to bits with a submachine gun or blow it the hell up, or else they just kept coming back.

Or got bored and decided to start tossing those wicked blades around. Suddenly, the air was filled with shiny death, one of which Casanova grabbed as it passed over top of us. And used it to bat away several others that were tumbling our way because of our crazy course or plain bad luck.

But not because they were being aimed at us.

They were being aimed at Pritkin.

"Get me up there!" I told him, in a panic. Our tiny craft was still bouncing around, but it was well below the level of Pritkin's now. He and Rosier had just sent a bunch of their attackers flying, and the sudden lack of weight had caused them to shoot upward.

"I'm not a mage!" Casanova said furiously. "I don't know how to drive this thing!"

"Then think of something!"

"What do you expect me to do?" he demanded. "Jump? There's simply—" He caught sight of my expression. *"No."*

"You're a vampire. You'll live."

"It five floors down!"

"It's closer to four now—"

"That's four too many!"

"—and there's a wagon down there with hay—"

"It's fake! This whole place is fake!"

"You owe me!" I said, grabbing his arm. "You led me into a trap!"

"I led . . ." If possible, he looked even more outraged than usual. "You *kidnapped* me—"

"A trap that almost got me killed!"

"I didn't know what Rian was going to do!"

"So you say. But there's nothing but your word for it, is there? Help me now and I'll vouch for you with Mircea."

"You—*Dios!*" he spat. Followed by a lot of things in Spanish that probably weren't complimentary as we came as close to the floor as we were going to get.

And then he jumped. But I didn't get a chance to see how or where he landed. Because without his extra weight, the yo-yo effect became more like a slingshot.

The ride up was a terrifying blur, the jump from my perch onto Pritkin's rug was worse, and then I was screaming and Pritkin was cursing and Rosier was stabbing—a guard and not me, for a wonder—and I was shifting—

And going nowhere.

"Get him out of here!" Rosier growled, grabbing my arm. "Do it now!"

I stared at him, desperately trying over and over to do just that. But all I felt was the metaphysical equivalent of grinding gears. Hauling four people through three worlds had left me as dry as the sand that had finally tapered off, after depositing a few dozen more guards on the rooftops of the fake ghost town around us. Rosier must have managed to pick up every damned one off the hillside as he passed, and we couldn't fight them all.

A view he seemed to share. "If you've cost me my son, girl—"

"Stiff-necked pride did that years ago," Pritkin said, knocking his father's hand away. "Yours and mine. This is not her fight!"

"She's made it hers! She insists on making it hers!" Rosier snarled, and the hand was back, this time around my throat. A pair of green eyes, so like his son's but so different, burned into mine. "Shift him now!"

But I couldn't shift him, couldn't access my power at all, and there was no time for recovery. Because the Allû had decided that the knife-throwing act they were doing wasn't working, and had started throwing themselves instead. One flipped off a roof to the right, bounced off Caleb's rug, and then used the momentum to keep right on going, through the air and straight across the drag to a building on the other side.

And in his wake, he left a bloody line across Pritkin's stomach, where his sword would have gutted him if war mage reflexes were a little less sharp.

But that wouldn't help for long. More than a dozen guards were massing along the roofline, about to overwhelm us with numbers. And it was too late for anything but screaming as they jumped—

And went flying backward, like a bomb had been set off in front of them.

Pritkin's and Rosier's voices had risen together in a spell that not only saved us, but cleared the other rug, as well. Caleb had hit the carpet at the last second, and now stared up, looking both surprised and vastly relieved.

He'd been battling two of the creatures alone, and it hadn't been going great.

But then, neither was this. Because they'd be back. And I didn't think we'd last long with the air full of deadly blades kamikazied straight to their target by a bunch of immortal warriors.

And I guessed Rosier didn't, either.

Some of the Allû were still falling when he muttered something low and harsh and vicious, with enough power behind it to make the hairs on my neck stand up.

But that would have been fine; that would have been awesome.

If it had actually done anything.

"Was that supposed to *help*?" I asked as Rosier and Pritkin stared at each other blankly.

And then Rosier tried again, and this time, the power of his words prickled across my skin almost painfully. And kept right on prickling until Pritkin shot out a hand and grabbed his father's arm. "They aren't coming!"

"They have to," Rosier said, looking almost comically indignant. "I'm a member of the council!"

"The same one that's preventing you from shifting back to court?" Pritkin asked acidly.

"That's not them; it's *her*," Rosier said, gesturing at me. "She wants to force my hand—"

"Are you mad? She doesn't have that kind of power!"

"You know who her mother was! There's no telling what she's capable—"

"Face facts! The council would rather see you dead than risk their precious necks! They won't call off their guards until they've killed me—and anyone with me."

Pritkin's eyes focused on me with that last sentence, and I shook my head. Because I knew him. "No. No! I'm not leav—"

Which was as far as I got before he grabbed me and threw me off the rug—and into Caleb's arms.

"Pritkin! Damn it—"

"Listen to me! I need you to find Casanova. Tell him to have his men—"

But I didn't hear whatever he wanted Casanova to do. Because two very scary things happened at once. The crowd below gave a huge roar, like their favorite team had just scored a touchdown, and an almost solid sheet of scimitars came slicing through the air from the other side of the street.

I didn't even have time to scream before I was eating carpet, with Caleb's hand on my neck, holding me down. I saw Rosier pull a red-sheened blade out of his side, felt our carpet buck hard beneath me, heard Pritkin curse as he was jumped by the two guards who had just used us as a springboard. And then we were moving.

But not very fast. It looked like the spell was having problems, maybe because the Allû had practically hacked to pieces the platform it was trying to use. But despite the poor treatment, it didn't look like they wanted it going anywhere.

We, on the other hand, were another matter.

Something smashed into my side, and for the second time in less than thirty seconds, I felt myself flying.

And Caleb couldn't catch me this time.

Because he was right there with me.

But a second later, something *did* catch us, something I promptly fell off because it was the size of a smallish dish towel.

No, not a dish towel, I thought, as Caleb came rolling after me. I yelped and tried to make room for him on a carpet fragment the size of a single stair, only to fall again—onto another one. I looked up, and saw Pritkin hanging off the side of his carpet, Rosier and the Allû battling all around him, his hand outstretched and an intense frown of concentration on his face—

As he formed a staircase out of woolen fragments, in some case all of a foot wide.

And then Caleb fell into me again and we were roll-

ing and bouncing and falling down four "flights," with
pieces of rug managing to catch us every time I was convinced we were about to run out.

And then I hit something with my face that was a lot
harder than wool. And looked up to find Casanova staring down at me. And then snatching me up and flinging
me to the side.

Right before an Allû crashed into the space where I'd
been lying.

"Take it apart!" Casanova screamed, practically hysterical. And his men didn't waste any time. But they
were hotel security, not soldiers. They didn't carry gre-
nades or percussion bombs, and while somebody had
thought to break out the handguns, they weren't too useful against something with no internal organs.

I scrambled up and grabbed Casanova's arm. "Pritkin
wanted me to tell you something—"

Casanova swore. "I'd like to tell *him* something—"

"No, listen. I think it was about how to fight these
things! And he ought to know. He used to have a golem
once—remember? And they're not that different!"

"Well, what is it?"

"That's just it; I don't know! We have to get somebody back up there—"

Casanova said something that looked pretty profane,
but I couldn't hear it. Because the crowd was really getting into it now. They screamed in mock terror as bullets
riddled the fallen warrior, then yelled approval when it
got back up, the neon glow from a nearby storefront
streaming through the hundred or so holes in its body.

They were also pushing against the line of vamps Casanova had strung across the street, which would have
been okay. Since there was no way they were breaking
through that. But then the warrior sent a group of security who tried to rush him crashing back into their buddies, and opened up gaps that the crowd started to surge
through.

"Push them back, push them back, push them ba—"
Casanova was yelling, before he got backhanded, too.

I saw his men stare at him fearfully, unable to help
and control the crowd at the same time. I saw him sail
through the air and hit a wall. I grabbed a gun off a
nearby vamp and scrambled after him, because I *didn't*
see the Allü—

Until I was suddenly on my back again, with a blank
bronze face staring into mine.

Its weight was threatening to crush me, the jagged
edges the bullets had torn in its torso were stabbing me
like tiny knives, and the heat from several blackened
places on its armor was trying to scorch me. But I barely
noticed. Because that blank bronze faceplate was maybe
two inches from my nose, reflecting my own stunned
features back at me.

And, insanely, the only thing I could think of at that
moment was Daisy, peering at me out of the side of her
bucket, her eyelash drooping over one shiny cheek.

And the fact that that was a damned weird last
thought to have.

But then Caleb proved me wrong, jerking the bullet-
ridden body off me and sending it sliding over the
ground. Which wouldn't have helped much, except that
he slapped a shield over it before it could get back to its
feet. I scrambled after it, a half-formed thought ham-
mering at my brain, and found the creature lying on its
back like a bug caught in amber.

But not for long.

War mages are tough, and if the training Pritkin put
me through was anything to go on, they emphasize endur-
ance above everything. Because you can't channel magic
if you pass out from exhaustion. But Caleb had been
fighting all day, and part of that time had been somewhere
that required added effort. The strain was all over his face,
and I didn't think I was the only one who noticed.

There were no eyes, no mouth, nothing to form an

expression of any kind on that piece of burnished metal. Just blank determination as it pushed inexorably against the shield. So why did I get the definite impression of malice staring up at us?

These things might not feel pain, but they clearly felt something.

Like for the woman who had blown a bunch of them to pieces a couple of weeks ago.

Too bad I didn't have any of those weapons now. And the one I did have wasn't likely to do enough damage to matter. I didn't have *anything*—

My thoughts stopped, screeching to a halt at the sight of a small, diamond-shaped jewel glittering in the middle of a sea of bronze—what would have been the creature's forehead, if it had one. I hadn't noticed it before, because it was tiny, maybe half the size of my little fingernail, and reddish gold, almost the same shade as the metal surrounding it. It was virtually invisible at any distance. . . .

But I wasn't at a distance, and I saw it clearly.

Like I heard my father's voice saying, "Do you see a control gem in his forehead?"

Yeah, I thought dazedly, I kind of thought I did.

I also thought I knew what Pritkin had been trying to tell me.

Casanova came running up, and I grabbed him. "Do you have a gun?"

"Yes," he said sarcastically. "Of course. I keep it in my underwear!"

"Then get one!"

One of his vamps tossed him a Beretta, and he snagged it out of the air even while glaring at me. Vampire senses never ceased to amaze. At least, I really hoped this wasn't going to be the first time they let me down.

"I don't know what good you think this is going to do," he crabbed. "We've wasted a hundred rounds on that damned thing already—"

Caleb cut him off with a roar. "Casanova! Get her out of here!"

But it was too late.

The shield burst and we all went flying, and then landing, in the case of Casanova and me, a good five yards away and on our asses. It hurt, but not as much as it was about to. Only Caleb recovered almost as fast as the creature, tackling it around the knees as it went for me.

"Shoot the jewel!" I yelled, grabbing Casanova.

"What jewel? What are you—"

"Between its eyes! The one between its—"

"It doesn't have any eyes!" he screeched as the creature threw Caleb into the line of vamps and launched itself at us

And exploded into a bunch of bronze-colored junk when Casanova got off the shot of the century.

He looked even more surprised than I was, and his hands started to shake. But when I grabbed him and screamed, "Shoot the jewels, tell your men to shoot the—"

He did.

At least, I assumed he did; I don't hear vampire communication. But I saw it when vamps who had been standing around, worrying about crowd control, suddenly spun and started shooting every Allû in sight. And while humans might have had a problem with fast-moving targets smaller than M&M's half a football field away . . .

These weren't human.

For a second, I just sprawled there on my bruised butt. And watched as suits of armor exploded while leaping off buildings or standing on rooftops or getting thrown off the remains of two once-nice rugs by a couple of enraged demons. And despite the fact that everything hurt, and a migraine was pounding at my temples and I felt like I might possibly throw up, a slightly manic grin spread over my face.

And then the lights went out.

Chapter Twenty

The neon cactuses dancing on a bar sign opposite us abruptly went dark. The couple of dozen cell phone screens, which people had been holding up to record the show, went dead. The strings of Christmas lights draping the fake donkey winked out. And then all of it was replaced by a huge blue-black nothingness that tore at my mind.

And a presence that screamed of age. It was old, old, so very old; I could usually guess vampire ages, but this . . . I didn't have words for this. Or air, when its power slammed into me.

I struggled just to gasp in a breath, and didn't have to ask what was happening.

If this wasn't the demon council, it damned well ought to be.

A voice that spoke every language and none came from all directions at once. "You summoned us?"

"How kind of you to finally notice!" Rosier snarled as I climbed to my feet.

And then went back down again when what felt like an invisible fist tightened around my throat.

Rosier was saying something, something I couldn't hear over the vast ocean crashing into my ear canals.

I would have thought I was being strangled by a dis-embodied Allû, come to wreak vengeance, only they couldn't without bodies. And anyway, I knew that hand. I just didn't know what it was doing down here since the bastard of a demon lord it was attached to was on a carpet five stories up.

Pritkin was shouting something, but I couldn't tell if it was at me, at his homicidal father, or at whoever was speaking. All I could hear was the rushing of waves and the pounding of my heart, a slow, sluggish beat like I was about to pass out. But if I did, this would all have been for nothing. If I did, Pritkin would go back to his prison, if not face a worse fate for daring to leave it. If I did, the creatures who had sent their damned guards after him might find something else to finish the job, and remove a problem permanently.

So I didn't.

I didn't try to stand again, since that was about as likely as flying right now. I didn't even try to follow whatever was being said, because that clearly wasn't happening, either. I concentrated everything I had on just getting my damned tongue to quit lolling around my mouth and do something besides drool. To somehow form the words I'd dragged Pritkin across three worlds to say.

And I guess I managed, even though I couldn't hear my own voice. Because suddenly, the dark was eclipsed by a light, like a single star glowing in the distance. And then right in front of my face, blindingly bright and un-cannily beautiful this close, showering me with a prism of changing colors.

I stared into it, half-mesmerized, and would have had to fight an urge to reach out and touch it, if I had been able to move. As it was, I swallowed and tried again, un-sure if I'd spoken aloud, or only in my head. "Artemis . . . would address the council."

"The one you call Artemis is no more," the light in-formed me. "How would the dead speak to the living?"

I tried to answer, but the only thing that came out was a gagging wheeze. It felt like the horse that had been sitting on my chest had just been joined by an elephant. Rosier *really* didn't want me to speak, which only made me that much more determined.

"She gave me . . . a message," I gasped. "She said . . . there are things . . . you need to under—awk." My little speech was abruptly terminated when the elephant was joined by a couple of its buddies.

And okay, that was it. I couldn't talk anymore, couldn't even breathe. It felt like my chest had just been caved in.

Until the light moved forward and engulfed me, its shining rays blocking out the rest of the room, and the power that went with it.

"You . . . you're the council?" I gasped as the pressure abruptly eased.

"I am the Gatekeeper, child. I summon the council, if the need is sufficient. Tell me, why should I summon them for you?"

"To hear . . . my mother's message."

The light reflected on this for a moment as I struggled to reinflate my lungs. "Give it to me, and I will relay it to them."

And maybe it was me, but the nonvoice had taken on a sly note I really didn't like.

"She said . . . " I licked my lips and forced out the words. "She said . . . it would only work . . . if I play it in front of the full council."

"Play." The light fluctuated. "It is a recording?"

"Yes. Sort of." I wasn't really clear on that part, but this didn't seem the time to bring it up.

"From she whom you call Artemis . . . to us?"

"Yes. And it's about more than Pritkin . . . John . . . Emrys," I gasped, my oxygen-starved brain finally coming up with the name Rosier used for his son. "There are other things . . . you should know."

The light flickered again for a long moment, or maybe

that was me. I was starting to have trouble seeing now, too. I reached for my last reserves of strength, only to find that I didn't have any. This needed to be over. . . .

And then it was.

"We will hear what the Huntress would say to us," the light told me. "You will be summoned."

And then good old-fashioned electricity came rushing back, and a wave of furious clapping and whistling broke over me, and a couple of empty rugs spiraled out of the sky, their contents gone like the star, like the Allû, like the whole room as I fell into nothingness.

I woke up with a gasp, my hand on my throat, feeling like I was being choked. And that I was stuck in some twilit nothingness, waiting for a verdict that was so important, it meant everything, but that I couldn't control. Or even predict . . .

But I wasn't in dim light; I was in no light. And if anybody was here with me, they were being damned quiet about it. I stared around, panting, but as far as I could tell, nothing stared back. There was only velvety darkness, the soft shush of air-conditioning, and the familiar scent of the fabric softener the hotel used on my sheets.

I relaxed back against the bed with a relief so profound it made me dizzy.

Or maybe that was something else. It felt like the bed was slowly revolving beneath me, a faint, drifting feeling, like the lazy roll of the carpet before Rosier arrived. . . . Rosier.

And suddenly, everything came rushing back.

Pritkin, I breathed, and started up—

Which was when the lazy drift became a tidal wave threatening to sweep me off to some other shoreline altogether.

I lay back slowly, carefully. And the crashing waves gradually diminished to nauseating undulations. Which wasn't a great improvement, but at least I was conscious.

But lying there, trapped by my body, virtually helpless when I had about a thousand questions to ask —

I almost wished I was unconscious.

Because this was torture.

But, slowly, my eyes adjusted. Enough to see a strip of light leaking in under the door, some night-in-the-city faux dark sifting in through a minuscule gap in the blackout curtains over the windows, and the soft glow of my alarm clock, too dim to read. And a small rectangle gleaming on the nightstand, just below it . . .

And I found I could move, after all, because it was my phone.

My hands were shaking so much that I almost dropped it, and the light from the screen was blinding up close. But my fingers somehow found the right buttons. *U K?*

I hit SEND. And then I waited, feeling dizzy and sweaty and hopeful and sick. And keeping an eye on the door because the vamps usually knew when I'd woken up. Changes in my heart rate and breathing told them, even when I wasn't about to hyperventilate.

For a long moment, there was no response. And my breathing started to get ragged, which was stupid, because it wouldn't help. I told myself to calm down, that signs of distress were only going to get me noticed faster, that the last thing I needed was a bunch of questions I couldn't answer. . . .

But it wasn't working.

And then I got a text back, and felt my spine unknot slightly.

Until I read it.

Yes, now let me sleep.

Sure, Caleb, I thought viciously, jabbing in a response. *S P K? tel me w@ hapnd!*

There was no response for a long moment. My hand flexed and I had to almost physically restrain myself from throwing the phone at the wall. And then—

I am too old for this shit.

I stared at the little screen: *w@?!*

Stop doing that.

I took a deep breath. Caleb rarely used text speak, and he hated when I did. He was also a grammar Nazi, so I tried to be careful as I translated.

Is P. okay? What huppened?

H & r dis. tt C. P held. U sum.

I just stared at that bit of nonsense for a long moment, wondering if I was going crazy or if Caleb was. No wonder he hated text speak. He sucked at it.

In English?

I waited while Caleb typed. And typed. And typed. Was he *trying* to give me a heart attack?

He and Rosier disappeared. I talked to Casanova. He said P. is being held until the hearing. You'll be summoned.

I stared at that, but it still didn't make much sense.

Held where?

Where do you think?

Damn it, Caleb!

Well, what did you expect? That they were just going to leave him here?

YES! We went through all that, and they let R just TAKE him?

More interminable typing. I was beginning to think Caleb only used one finger. One that I was going to *break off . . .*

He doesn't have him. He's with the council. And before you freak out, Casanova said there are rules.

Rules? These are demons!

And he's part of their ruling class. And they have privileges, in case you didn't notice.

I flashed on the crazy chariot driver in the souk, and the way everyone had practically kowtowed while he ran them down. Yeah, I'd noticed. But Pritkin was half human, and his other half was incubus, and they didn't seem to get a lot of respect. The council sure hadn't seemed to mind the idea of losing Rosier.

Of course, that might just be good taste.

What privileges? I typed.

Like they can't kill him w/o a trial.

Great. That made my stomach feel so much better. *Wens it?*

What?

WHEN IS IT?

Don't yell at me. And I don't know. Casanova said it could be anything from hours to days.

How am I supposed to know when that is? I didn't subscribe to the *Hell Gazette.*

C. said you'll know. Now get some sleep. Or at least let me!

Yeah, right, I thought, and started typing in another message. But Caleb had the usual war mage stubbornness, either that or he'd turned off his phone. Because I didn't get anything back.

I lay there for a while, trying again. And again, and again, because I can be stubborn, too. But I finally gave up, panting, because even *texting* was exhausting me. So I just lay there, staring at the ceiling instead.

I didn't understand a goddamned thing. I'd spent a week, desperately trying everything I knew, in order to get to Pritkin. And when I finally did, what happened? He ended up right back where he started, only possibly even worse off. Because at least his father didn't want to kill him!

And the council shouldn't have, either. I'd expected to have to deal with Rosier; I'd anticipated problems with his court. But I hadn't thought much about the demon council, except as a sort of finish line. Because they shouldn't give a damn about any of this!

But there'd been plenty of evidence to the contrary downstairs. And it just seemed crazy to me. Why would the council send what had to be a large percentage of their own guards to watch over one little half demon? And an incubus to boot? You'd have thought Pritkin was Godzilla or something, by the way they were acting.

And okay, he'd tried to kill one of them once. But since the one in question had been Rosier, who they didn't appear too fond of anyway, I'd have thought a century would be enough time to get over that. His father obviously had.

And as far as his connection with me went, that was even more WTF. When had I ever done anything to the council? I'd even helped them out once, by assisting Pritkin to bring down some ancient demon that had its panties all in a twist. Admittedly, that had been mostly due to not wanting to get killed by said demon, but still. They had made out okay, too.

So what the hell was the deal?

Based on what Rosier had said, it seemed like they had somehow gotten it into their heads that Pritkin and I were making some elaborate plan to shift back in time and destroy them. Which was the biggest WTF of all, because since when did I go around changing time? I'd been doing my best to try to avoid it, despite some pretty severe temptation.

And if I *was* going to go on some time-traveling journey of vengeance, I'd be targeting the gods anyway. Not a bunch of demons I didn't even know. Assuming I had the power, which I didn't, which made this even crazier . . .

My head was spinning harder now, but I wasn't sure what to blame. It could be exhaustion. It could be the lack of food since breakfast, because I hadn't had time to eat any of the luscious-smelling sausages in the souk, even if I'd been willing to risk Rosier's Revenge. It could be the council being staffed by a bunch of paranoid nut jobs.

But I knew which I had my money on.

The waves finally reduced to a gentle lapping motion, and I decided I was tired of looking at the ceiling. I got up, carefully, and staggered over to the dresser. God, everything hurt. I messed about until I found some aspirin, then toted it off to the bathroom to get some water because no way was I up to running the gauntlet to the kitchen. Marco had been taking the I-see-nothing line lately, which had been really nice. But I thought even he might be a little curious about an epic battle taking place in the middle of the drag.

God, why did it have to happen here? Why did it always have to—

I stopped, blinking. And okay, maybe the bathroom had been a bad idea. Because it meant I got a glimpse in the mirror.

And one was enough. I looked away. And found myself staring at the massive bandage somebody had slapped over my stomach instead.

I stood there for a minute, trying to remember why my stomach deserved mummification.

And then it came back to me: the Allû, its nonface staring down at me while the jagged wounds in its body were punching matching holes in mine.

I had to lean against the sink suddenly, but not out of remembered fear. More out of a feeling of complete dissociation. Things like that didn't happen to normal people. Or even to the normal-if-you-squinted-and-ignored-a-few-things people, like I was.

Or like I'd been.

I looked at myself in the mirror again, even though I'd decided not to, and it didn't help.

Because I didn't look like me.

Of course, part of that was the aforementioned exhaustion, which had pinched my face and washed out my skin to the color of chalk. And the dirt, which was still mostly there, since nobody had wanted the hell once I woke up and found out I'd been bathed like a baby. For the same reason, I hadn't been stripped and popped into one of my pairs of shorty PJs. Leaving me looking like *I Dream of Jeannie* had gone on a two-day bender in bad company.

I smiled slightly, despite everything, and wondered what Caleb would say if he heard me describe him that way. Mr. So-Proper War Mage, who had laughed and whooped his way across the skies of hell like a madman. *"You're as crazy as she is,"* Pritkin had told him.

.And maybe he was. And maybe I was. Because the eyes in the mirror looked different tonight. Not in color or shape or anything I could put a finger on. Just different. Like maybe they'd seen things that had changed the mind behind them a little.

I fingered the fabric of the trousers, what there was of it, and realized that it wasn't silk. It wasn't from an insect or an animal I'd ever seen before. It wasn't from this *planet*. Like the dirt clinging to my temple.

I brushed it away, and it didn't feel any different under my fingertips.

But it was.

Three months. That's all it had been, since Agnes left me that heads-up on my computer, starting all of this. I wondered what that Cassie would think, what she'd say, if I told her what I'd seen today. If I described driving a chariot through—what had Caleb called it? A rose red city, half as old as time? Or riding a carpet high above an alien world, while spells exploded around me like fireworks. Or watching three moons rise in a deep blue twilight, under a canopy of stars I couldn't name . . .

Or being chased by a demon lord, or targeted by a bunch of bad-tempered guards, or almost eviscerated by a mass of vengeful golems.

I didn't have to guess; I knew what the old Cassie would have told me. In a word: *run.* Get out, get lost, go somewhere else, go somewhere safe. But that was the real trick, wasn't it? There was no place safe anymore. And once, quite recently, that thought would have terrified me.

It still did. Of course it did. It wasn't like I *enjoyed* getting chased or beaten up or almost killed. . . .

But there were things, about this new life . . . things I had sort of enjoyed. Or been in awe of. Or, like Caleb, wished I'd had longer to explore . . .

Or something. I frowned at my reflection and swallowed my pills. I didn't understand myself and I was starting to think in circles. I went back to bed.

It was soft and the room kept gently swirling underneath me, to the point that I closed my eyes, just to get it to stop. I'd get up in a minute. I'd go try to wring some more answers out of Casanova, like what a summons from the demon high council was supposed to look like. I'd get a bath, because I could certainly use one. I'd try to figure out what I was going to tell everyone about the whole thing on the drag. I'd . . . I'd . . .

Chapter Twenty-one

I woke up the second time to the most wonderful smell ever being wafted around under my nose.

"That's it," somebody said as I instinctively followed it. "Just a couple . . . more . . . there!"

And before I knew it, some bastard had plopped a pillow behind my back, preventing me from reattaching myself to my lovely soft bed. But since whoever it was also slid a tray full of bacon and flapjacks and maple syrup and OJ and coffee and fresh fruit and toast under my nose, I didn't complain too much. I also didn't answer, because I was already stuffing my face.

God, this one-meal-a-day thing had to go. But it was a hell of a meal. I was halfway through with it before I looked up, to see Fred eyeing my plate jealously.

"You know, I've never really seen the reason for pancakes and toast," he commented, sidling up next to the latter. "Not in the same meal, anyway. I mean, they're both basically bread—"

"My bread," I said, around a mouthful. And quickly slopped butter and strawberry jam all over the measly two pieces I'd been provided, because licking them would probably have been rude.

"There's more downstairs," Marco pointed out, earning him a grin. Had my back.

"Yeah, but I need 'em up here. You could have said you were ordering breakfast," Fred pointed out.

"I didn't whisper."

"But I was out on the balcony, making a call. I didn't hear—"

"Not my problem."

"—and who orders breakfast at seven p.m., anyway?"

"Seven p.m.?" I asked, confused. Because it sure felt like I'd slept longer than that.

"You've almost slept the clock around," Marco told me.

I stared at him a moment. And then—

"You're not going anywhere," he told me, which didn't impress. Unfortunately, he also had a hand on the shoulder I was trying to leverage out of bed, and I guess that did. Because I wasn't making any headway.

"I have to talk to Caleb, to Casanova—" I said, struggling. 'Cause despite the sleep, it didn't feel like I could shift.

"That war mage called a while ago—"

"What did he say?"

"—and I don't think Casanova wants to talk to you."

"Marco." I grabbed his shoulder in a grip that would have been painful on a human. Marco didn't even flinch. "What. Did. He. Say?"

"That you're not to worry, 'cause nothing's happened." Marco shot me a look. "Do I need to know what's supposed to be happening?"

"No. And stop stealing my food." That last was aimed at Fred, who appeared to have an appetite that would have done a trucker proud.

"It's not food; it's coffee," he said, shooting me a look. "And you have a whole pot."

"Not *now*," I pointed out, moving the purloined pot farther away from him. He rolled his eyes. And then he stole some of my cream. "Why are you here?" I demanded.

"I live here."

"Not in my bedroom!"

"Yeah, but the only alternative has witches in it."

I stopped eating. "What?"

"They showed up an hour ago—" Marco began.

"Well, send them away!"

He just looked at me. "They have an appointment. Remember?"

And I did. I suddenly, definitely remembered telling one of them to make an appointment. And *shit*.

"What do they want?"

"They haven't said."

"You didn't ask?"

He frowned. "I'm not your secretary. And they're not forthcoming."

"Marco!"

"Well, I asked," Fred said, his mouth full of something.

"And?"

He swallowed. "And they told me to mind my business. Only they weren't that nice. I think they're mad they had to wait."

I fell back onto the bed. For someone who had just had almost a day of sleep, I didn't feel rested. I felt achy and stiff, and sluggish from the five pounds of breakfast I'd just consumed. I so did not feel like dealing with three irate witches.

"It's your call," Marco said, and he sounded serious. Like if I said I wasn't up to it, he would march out there and tell them to get lost. If it was anyone else, I'd have assumed he was bluffing, but Marco had seen scarier things than a trio of pissed-off magic workers. I was afraid he'd actually do it.

And I didn't know the reverse spell for chicken.

"It's okay," I told him.

"You're sure?"

"Yeah. Just give me a couple minutes."

He nodded and they left me to finish eating, which I

did because I needed the energy, but I'd sort of lost my appetite. I felt a little better once I'd finished, though. Still tired and sore as hell, but less like a good gust of wind might blow me away. I faced up to it, put the tray on the bed, and swung my legs off the side.

And crap.

"What's wrong?"

I looked up to see that Fred had returned, maybe because there were no witches in my bedroom. Well, other than me, and I didn't count. "Trying to remember where Marco put the codeine," I told him truthfully.

"You can't have that stuff. Messes up your Pythia power. Remember?"

"That doesn't feel like it's on board right now, anyway. And I feel like death."

"No, you don't. Death doesn't hurt," he told me, and presented something on a small tray. "Well, you know. Not after the first bit."

"What's that?"

"What does it look like?"

"An Irish coffee," I said, perking up. And damn. It was like he'd read my mind.

"Better?" he asked, flopping on my bed.

I licked whipped cream off my nose. "Getting there."

And I was, with a warm tingle that didn't so much soothe away the aches as make me not care about them anymore. Until I peered into my closet. And realized that, in this case, the age-old lament was totally true.

"What now?" Fred asked as I just stood there, drinking and scowling.

"I don't have anything to wear."

"You got a whole closet full of stuff."

"Yeah. But not the *right* stuff."

"What difference does it make what you wear?" he asked. "We're talking about people who show up, uninvited, in the middle of the night and terrorize everybody. Why dress up for them?"

"They're not uninvited tonight," I pointed out. "And it's not for them."

"Who, then?"

"Me," I said grimly, flipping through the hangers. Like the perfect outfit was just going to magically appear.

But no. Magic gets me *into* trouble; it rarely gets me out. And this obviously wasn't one of those times.

"Meaning?"

"Meaning I'm tired, stressed, and my power is feeling wonky—"

"But you can't afford to look like it."

I turned, surprised, even though I shouldn't have been. Fred wasn't stupid. He was just . . . Fred.

Who was staring at something in my hand and scowling.

"What is that?" he asked, pointing at the hanger I was holding.

"A skirt," I said defensively. It was cute, a multicolored tie-dyed creation I'd bought from a street vendor, which swirled around my ankles whenever I wore it. And caused the vamps to make pained faces.

Fred didn't disappoint. "Put that back."

"Well, I don't have a lot of choices!" In fact, my closet had a serious identity crisis at the moment.

On the one side were my old clothes—T-shirts and jeans mostly, with a few pairs of shorts and sweats thrown in for variety. They were the kind of stuff I'd worn for years, and which had worked fine when my job was reading tarot cards at a nightclub or doing secretarial stuff at a travel agency where I never saw the public. They were comfortable and familiar and just the sight of them made me feel better.

Unfortunately, even I realized that they said Girl Who Dips Your Ice Cream at the Mall more than World's Chief Clairvoyant.

Of course, the other side wasn't any better. Not that it was bare; quite the contrary. There was hardly enough room to pack everything in, which explained why the rainbow spill of extravagant ball gowns had started to slum it with the 2-for-$10 tees.

It was doubly annoying, since I'd never worn any of them. Because who needs twenty ball gowns? No one, that's who. Least of all me, since I didn't get invited to those kinds of parties anyway.

Well, not usually.

And when I did, someone tried to kill me.

I put the skirt back and kept looking.

"Go with a power suit. They're mostly wearing power suits," Fred advised.

"I don't have any power suits."

"Why not?"

"Because my wardrobe keeps getting blown up!"

"Then wear something Pythia-like. What do they wear for official visit–type things?"

"Damned if I know." I'd seen Agnes in little-girl white, a retro-fifties cocktail dress, and an eighties standard evening gown. But if there was an official Pythia costume, I must have missed it.

"I bet it's something Grecian," Fred said. "You know, all flowy stuff and sandals like you see on those old statues. When they wear clothes, I mean."

I frowned. "I don't know. Delphi was a long time ago. They've probably modernized." Hell, even nuns didn't wear medieval habits anymore.

"Yeah, but does the average witch know that?" he asked shrewdly. "Besides, you should probably play up the whole goddess thing. For the intimidation factor."

"I'm not a goddess."

"But you're related to one."

I stopped thumbing through outfits but didn't turn around. This was the first time anybody had brought it up, at least in my hearing, since we all found out a week ago. I'd been too busy to really worry about it, but now I wondered. "Is that a problem?"

"You'd think it would be an asset, although they don't

seem to be real impressed so far. I mean, who breaks
into a goddess' penthouse, anyway?"

I finally turned around, and met gray eyes that looked
exactly the way they always did—vague. And staring approximately at my left ear. Fred had had terrible vision
before the change, which usually restored stuff like that.
But his eyes must have been really bad, because he was
still pretty myopic. He was the only vamp I knew who
wore glasses, although he did it on the sly.

"You can put them on, you know," I told him. "Nobody else is here."

"Yeah, but they could come in. Besides, I can see.
'Specially if you keep coming out with stuff like that tie-
dye. I mean, if it looks garish to *me*—"

"Fine. Just thought I'd offer." I stood there a minute.
"So, how are the guys taking it?"

"They don't know. At least, I don't think so. The ones
back home could have mentioned it, but they mostly
gossip about the master. And I don't think anybody's
seen me with glasses since I got here."

"No, I mean, about my, uh, lineage. How is everybody
taking it?"

"Oh, that." He shrugged. "I heard a couple say it
made sense. That no human woman could possibly get in
as much trouble as . . . uh, that is, they didn't seem too
bothered about it. If you know what I mean."

"I know what you mean." And I was suddenly, pro-
foundly grateful to be living with creatures hundreds of
years old, who took things in stride. Vampires were hard
to impress, but they were also hard to rattle. I felt my
spine relax a little as one fear evaporated, at least.

"Of course, they're a little worried that this makes
you more high-profile, so people are gonna start trying
to kill you more. But I told them, hey, remember last
time? I mean, if a bunch of other demigods couldn't take
you out, who are they gonna send? It'd have to be something really weird, something really unusual, something
really dangerous—"

"Like a trio of coven witches?"

Fred blinked. "Naw," he finally said. "There's only three of them. If they were gonna off you, they'd probably have sent more than that."

"Thanks," I said sourly. "That makes me feel a lot better."

"I'm here to help. Now, what are you gonna wear?"

"I don't know." I started looking through the dresses again, but they were hopeless, more ball-gown-y than goddess-y. And while I wanted to dress to impress, I didn't think looking like I was waiting on Prince Charming was the way to go.

"Those aren't gonna work," Fred agreed, slurping coffee. "But I bet Augustine has something."

"Augustine sent these," I pointed out, talking about the best—according to him, anyway—magical designer around. His boutique occupied the largest of the overpriced shops in the drag downstairs.

"Well, yeah. But he was just sending regular party stuff. I bet he has something that would work."

Augustine closed at six. And no way was I up to shifting back a couple of hours to try to catch the great man before he left.

"No problem," Fred said, suddenly businesslike. "What size do you wear?"

"Anywhere from a two to a six, depending on the outfit. But it doesn't matter. Augustine closes at—"

"Yeah, I know. What color you want?"

"White. But you can't get in, and he doesn't live around here. And by the time he could get back and open up, assuming he'd even do that for me—"

"Oh, he'd do it," Fred said cynically. "He might not like it, but he'd do it. Have you seen his sign lately?"

"What sign?"

"The one outside his shop. The one that says 'Couturier to the Pythia.' He left off the official part, but it's implied."

Well, that explained the gowns I kept getting. I should

have known Augustine wasn't being generous. He wasn't known for the softer emotions.

Or, you know, any.

"He's been making a mint off all the wealthy women who want to dress like you," Fred added.

I blinked at him. "Have they *seen* me?"

He laughed. "Point is, he's in no position to complain. We'll just take what we need, and let him know tomorrow. If he puts up a fuss, you can tell him to take his damned sign down."

"Yeah, but you aren't listening to me. We can't get in."

"Wanna bet?"

It took me a moment to realize what he was getting at. "No," I said sternly. "We can't."

"Fifty bucks? Or do you want to make it interesting?"

"It's interesting enough. Didn't you hear about those guys last week?"

"What guys?"

"Two teens with sticky fingers tried to rip off some T-shirts or something. So Augustine spelled them to actually get stuck."

Fred's forehead wrinkled. "To what?"

"To everything. He did some spell that made it like they were human Velcro. Only once something stuck, it didn't come off. One of the guys turned up at the end of the day, sobbing and freaked out, dragging a massive train of street trash, a folding chair, some kid's baby stroller . . . and a homeless person's grocery cart full of stuff."

"Well, that don't sound so—"

"*And* the homeless person, who was beating him over the head with a rolled-up newspaper." They'd been stuck together all day, since the guy had grabbed the kid's arm, begging for change.

"Oh. Well, yeah, that would kind of—"

"*And* he was the lucky one. They had to pry another guy off a taxi—after it went ten blocks!"

Fred's lips pursed. "Ten's not so bad if you're just riding along on the trunk or something."

"He was jogging along behind! He's just lucky it was a bad traffic day, and they weren't going too fast. . . ."

I trailed off, because Fred was no longer listening. He was staring at the wall instead, with unfocused eyes. "What's your shoe size?" he suddenly asked.

"An eight. Why?"

"No reason."

I narrowed my eyes at him. "Tell me you're not breaking in right now."

"Me? I'm just sitting here."

"And what about the others?" Fred was part of an unholy trio Mircea had gifted me a little over a week ago. At first, I'd thought he was just beefing up security after a couple of recent incidents. But lately, I'd begun to suspect that he might have had other reasons.

Selfish, selfish reasons.

"What others?" Fred asked, trying to look innocent, just as my door was flung open.

"Those others!" I said, pointing at the two guys who appeared in the doorway. Well, one guy, since I couldn't see the other under a mountain of clothes, although I knew he'd be there. "Damn it, Fred!"

But Fred wasn't listening to me. "Well?" he asked, turning around.

"I hate you," the mountain snarled.

And then started to stagger in the direction of my food-strewn bed, before everybody yelled, "No!"

The mountain cursed, and the handsome brunet vamp who sauntered in after it grinned, a quick flash of teeth in an olive face. "We got out clear," he told me. "Well, more or less."

"How much less?"

"We ran into a little ward. Or one of us did."

"Here. Put everything down on the chair," Fred said, coming over with an armchair from the window.

"You put it down!" the mountain snapped.

"What's the problem? Just drop them."

"I can't just drop them!"

"Why not?"

"You aren't stuck to them, are you?" I asked apprehensively.

A blue eye managed to glare at me through a gap in a layer of chiffon. "No! I'm stuck to me!" he said. And then raised both arms, causing a terribly expensive landslide onto my carpet.

My mouth fell open, but not because of the indignity to Augustine's work.

"Ooooooh," Fred said, looking impressed.

"Do something!" The mountain had resolved into a stressed-looking blond named Jules, who held out his hands. Or, I should say, his hand, since there was no longer any separation between the two. The fingers of one ran straight into those of the other, with no break in the smooth, pale skin. Leaving the thief stuck in handcuffs.

Made out of his own hands.

Chapter Twenty-two

"Where'd your fingernails go?" Fred asked, showing his bald spot as he bent to take a look. He seemed more curious than grossed out.

"How the hell should I know?" Jules screeched. "Just fix it!" And he thrust the creepy-looking finger cages out again—at me.

I managed not to shy back, but it was a close thing. Because Fred had been right; there were no little buffed ovals in sight. Just what looked like an extra joint where the fusion had taken place. And from the expression on Jules' face, he found that every bit as disturbing as I did.

But not as disturbing as suddenly having three sets of eyes on me, all at once. And all expectant, because the guys were new and hadn't picked up on a few things yet. Like the fact that I might be a clairvoyant, but I wasn't a witch.

Well, okay, yeah. Technically, I fell into that category, but only because every female magic user did. It was a catch-all term, like "wizard" was for guys, which said nothing about a person's level of ability, training, or specialty. Or in my case, whether I could even manage a basic spell.

Of course, I had the Pythian stuff, but that was only

useful for its own special brand of crazy. It could send me hurtling across time but it couldn't do a simple ward, or a glamourie to cover my freckles or help me cheat at cards. Which was why Billy always won.

According to Pritkin, I had a decent amount of the normal kind of magic, but it was all potential since I'd never learned how to use it. That was down to Tony the bastard, who had been afraid I might use anything I learned against him one day. And to my usual luck.

After running away from Tony, I'd ended up living with a null witch, one with the rare talent of being able to cancel out any magic done around her. That had been great for hiding from the bad guys, whose trace charms had slid over Tammy's house like water over glass. But it also meant that she couldn't do any magic herself, or teach it to me.

Then I went back to Tony's for three years, to try to set him up for what he'd done to my parents, so that was a wash. And then the second time I ran away, after my attempt at revenge went spectacularly wrong, I'd spent most of my time in the human world. Because it's a lot bigger than the sup community, giving me a bigger crowd to hide in.

It had worked—it had taken him another three years to find me, despite being *really* motivated. And in the meantime, I bet his boys had spent hundreds of hours checking all the places a young, untrained witch might go to rectify that little problem, and had found nothing. Because I hadn't gone to any of them.

That had been partly paranoia, and partly the old sour grapes thing. I'd done a good job of convincing myself I didn't want any part of the world I couldn't have anyway. But now it left me with a problem, and one I hadn't had a chance to remedy since having all the Pythian stuff dumped in my lap.

Not that any of that mattered to Jules, who was obviously close to tears.

His attitude wasn't a shock. Augustine's little joke

would have freaked out anybody, but it was especially cruel in Jules' case. His hands were as emblematic of the man as Marco's cigars or Fred's big gray eyes or Rico's one-liners. I'd wondered a few times if he was part Italian, as he had the same tendency to gesture when he talked. Or when he was arguing with the other vamps. Or when he was listening to music, following the notes with flutelike trills from those expressive fingers.

Fingers that, for once, were completely stiff and still.

And suddenly, I felt a genuine anger toward the smug shop owner. The other stuff had been sort of funny; this was just plain cruel. And he could damned well get his elegant ass out of bed and come and fix it.

"Get Augustine on the phone," I told Fred. "Tell him—"

"No!" Jules said, looking panicked. "No, you *can't*—"

He broke off abruptly. And whipped his head back and forth frantically. And then made a run for my bathroom, where we heard him clanging around while we stared at each other. And then finally went to take a look.

We found him in the shower.

He seemed to be trying to turn it on, only that didn't work so well with only elbows. *Help me,* he mouthed at Rico. Who sighed but obligingly went over and turned the knob. Water burst out of the wall at the same time that another burst—of noise—made me jump. Fred had hit the button for the radio, blasting Beyoncé's latest from every built-in speaker until it echoed off the tiled walls and rattled the towel bar.

And then Jules put his arms over my head and dragged me into the stall.

That wouldn't have been so bad, since I knew what he was doing. I'd done it myself a few times, trying to add to the ambient background noise of a loud casino and a louder Strip to confuse vampire hearing. But then the other two crowded in behind us.

And while it was a big shower, it wasn't *that* big.

But Jules didn't care what I thought. Jules was all about making his point. "You can't—promise me you won't call Augustine!" he whispered.

"Why not?" I demanded, trying to duck under his arms, since he couldn't very well let me go the usual way. But that didn't accomplish anything, since Rico was right on my ass. Resulting in me pushing Jules back into one of the shower levers—and I didn't have to ask which one.

The lukewarm stream suddenly jumped to the approximate temperature of lava.

A pain-filled gasp was all I got out before a hand clasped over my mouth. Rico's, I identified, from the nice gold bracelet around the elegant wrist. One I was going to make him *eat* if he didn't—

There was some rustling around. And then the temperature abruptly dropped back to bearable, leaving me only half-scalded. But no less furious. And no less mute, because the hand-over-my-mouth thing didn't change.

"Let her go," someone said as I started thrashing around.

It took a second for me to recognize the voice, because it held a surprising note of command. And because it was coming from the little guy squatting under the toiletry shelf, since he'd hit his head if he stood up. Fred scowled at Rico, and to my further surprise, Rico let me go and moved off a pace, giving me room to turn around and glare at him.

He didn't look too repentant, though, maybe because he wasn't exactly practiced with the expression. I doubted many women stayed mad at him for long, with his dark curls and his stubbly jaw and the six-pack visible under his rapidly dampening shirt. But it wouldn't have helped him with me—after dealing with Mircea for three months, it took more than a few muscles to fog my brain.

"And we're not calling Augustine because . . . ?" I demanded again.

"We *can't*," Jules said, going back into panic mode. "If we do the master is sure to find out!"

"So? It's not like he's going to assault Augustine—"

"Who cares about Augustine? I'm worried about me!"

I struggled back around to see what looked like genuine panic in those blue eyes. "Mircea doesn't go around assaulting his vampires, either," I pointed out. He didn't have to. Most of them acted like he was the second coming already.

"It's not so much assault that's the problem," Fred said, apparently in Zen mode, despite getting deluged by a waterfall from off the shelf.

"What, then?"

The three exchanged glances. At least, I guessed they did. I couldn't see Rico anymore, but Fred looked behind me and then at Jules. "I'm gonna tell her," he warned.

Nobody said anything.

"Tell me what?" I demanded.

"It's like . . ." Fred thought for a minute. "You know how the Brits used to send convicts to Australia?" he finally said.

I stared at him through the streams of muddy water cascading off my dirty bangs. *"What?"*

"You know, in the bad old days. When they needed to dump some troublemakers who hadn't done enough to hang but weren't good enough to keep around? How they'd load 'em up on ships and send 'em off to Oz?"

"No!"

"Australia is a bad example," Rico protested. "People died there. And before that there were hardship and pain and suffering—"

Fred raised an eyebrow. "And?"

Rico thought for a second. "Good point."

I shut my eyes and took a deep breath. And then opened them to glare at Fred. "Why are you telling me this?"

Gray eyes met mine with a hint of compassion. "Because you're Australia?"

I wanted to bang my head on the tiles, but I couldn't reach them. So I just stood there for a minute, wondering how much trouble I'd be in with Mircea if I killed three of his guys. If I was getting what they were saying, not all that much.

Rico huffed out a laugh. "I wish I could see her face."

"No," Fred told him. "You don't. But we don't have time for diplomacy."

"Just as well," Rico said, somehow managing to light a cigarette. "We all suck at it."

"So you're saying you screwed up and Mircea punished you by sending you to me?" I summarized.

"See?" Rico said. "I keep telling everyone she isn't really a dumb blonde."

I turned around, elbowing Jules in the gut in the process, and grabbed the cigarette out of Rico's mouth. And dropped it onto the soggy tiles, where it went out with a little hiss. "That was a compliment," he protested.

"The point is, we can't screw up again," Fred said quickly. "Or . . . well, I don't know what might happen. But I think it's safe to say that none of us wants to find out. But you know how Augustine is. The guy's touchy even on a good day—"

"They call it the artistic temperament," Rico said, sounding amused.

"Well, I call it being a dick," Fred said sourly. "But if he has to get out of bed, and come all the way up here, and reverse his hex or whatever, and then he sees the mess you guys left in the workroom—"

"You left a mess?" I asked Rico, squirming back to face him.

"You were in a hurry."

"I was—I didn't ask you to do a damned thing!"

"They're always telling us to be proactive," Jules said, sounding aggravated. "Back home, that is. A good servant knows what his master wants before his master does—"

"I'm not your master!" I told him, finally managing to duck under those encircling arms.

"Well, you're the closest thing I've got right now!" Jules said, using his wrists to shove a swath of wet blond hair out of his face. "And I went down there to take care of you. Now take care of me!"

I stared at him, feeling angry and waterlogged and pissed. But also strangely understanding. Because in two sentences, he'd just perfectly articulated the vampire code.

Real vampires were not the lone wolves of the movies, living out a solitary but sexy existence in a castle somewhere, pining for the love of a good woman. In fact, pretty much the opposite was true. If anything, they reminded me of ants, living in sprawling, social families, sometimes hundreds or even thousands strong, with each member slotted into a complex hierarchy that would have made most people's heads explode trying to comprehend it.

And all of those members—save one—were servants of varying ranks. Who were ordered around, controlled, and dictated to by those further up the ladder in ways that would have appalled most humans. But along with the restrictions came a strange sort of freedom most of those same humans would never know.

You might not make the rules, but you didn't have to deal with the fallout. You might not have the power, but you also didn't have the responsibility. Unless you were the head of your own household, everything was always somebody else's problem, somebody else's burden, whether said somebody had had anything to do with whatever mess you'd created or not. You might be disciplined, if you screwed up enough, but you'd never know the stress of having to deal with things all by yourself.

Because you would never *be* all by yourself.

And because the buck never stopped with you.

And right now that was sounding really attractive.

"It's all right," Fred said, after a minute. "He can wait."

Jules looked at him incredulously. And then at me. He didn't look like a guy who could wait.

"No!" he said, voice rising in alarm. "Fix it! Fix it *now*!"

And yeah. That's probably how I'd feel in his place. Like I wanted to rip my hands apart, or tear them off my body like the alien things they'd become. The only difference was Jules had vampire strength. He could do it. And sure, they'd eventually grow back, but not all scars heal. Like the memory of clawing off your own flesh, for instance.

"Okay," I told him, trapping his hands in mine. "Okay. Just . . . give me a second."

I closed my eyes again, not so much to think, because there was nothing to think about. But to avoid having to meet his. But it didn't help much since I could still see the afterimages of the hands I'd been staring at so intently.

And in the afterimage, they looked normal, handsome even, with fine bones and elegant lines. They were an artist's hands, an actor's hands. Not surprisingly, I guess, since that's what Jules had been once.

He'd been an aspiring Hollywood up-and-comer sometime in the early days of movies, when Mircea had met him and offered him a different kind of deal. Only it hadn't turned out as well as Jules had hoped. Maybe because, while he had talent, intellect, and drive, he was also hotheaded, blunt, and had a bad tendency to leap before he looked.

Like Rico had said, he was a terrible diplomat.

Which wouldn't have been so bad, but Mircea's family was all about diplomacy. So yeah, for a guy who didn't have much but his looks left, something like this would hurt. Which probably explained why his hands were suddenly trembling in mine.

Damn it! Pritkin could have handled this in a heartbeat, probably without even breaking a sweat. But thanks to Rosier, he wasn't here. And I couldn't very well call Jonas, who would find a bunch of coven witches in my living room and probably burst a gasket. Which would equally probably spark a retaliation, since the coven's leadership hadn't exactly impressed me with their restraint so far. And then both sides would call for help and then—

And then we'd all end the night clucking.

"Cassie?" Jules' voice came again, more timid this time. Like maybe the amount of time my examination was taking had started to worry him.

It had started to worry me, too, because I wasn't coming up with anything. Well, other than Roger's old mantra of fake it till you make it. Which might not help matters, but might keep Jules from running amok until I could find something that would.

"Yeah," I said thoughtfully, stroking the backs of his hands, and trying to channel every doctor I'd ever heard. "Yeah. I thought so."

"You thought *what*?"

"You shouldn't worry," I told him, opening my eyes and meeting his head-on. "This is no big deal."

"No big deal?" Jules sounded incredulous.

"Well, sure, it probably doesn't seem that way to you. But it's an easy spell. More a prank than anything else. The mages' kids sometime use it on each other for fun."

"For—" He broke off with a choked sound. "Mages are crazy."

"Tell me about it. Look, just take a load off and stay out of sight. I'll get rid of our guests as soon as I can, and we'll get you all fixed up. All right?"

He blinked at me through water-beaded lashes, sort of dazed, as if he'd been bracing for a death sentence. But then he nodded, looking a little calmer. And let Rico lead his sopping-wet form out of the shower.

Fred didn't follow. "Who you want me to call?"

I scowled at him. "How do you know I want you to call anybody?"

He just looked at me.

I sighed. "Central, the Corps' HQ. Ask for Caleb Carter."

"Who?"

"One of Pritkin's friends. You met him that night at the pizza place. Tell him what happened and ask him to get over here."

Fred sent me a look. "So I guess it's bad, huh?"

"I don't know. But Caleb will. And he knows how to keep his mouth shut."

"So does Pritkin," Fred pointed out. "Why not just call him?"

"He's . . . busy."

"Busy where? We haven't seen him all week. Some of the guys have been wondering—"

"I didn't think they'd miss a war mage."

"Miss might be a little much," he admitted. "But he's less of a pain than most, and he brings beer. So where'd he go again?"

"I sent him on an errand."

"Oh, jeez. Not back to Faerie? Didn't he almost get killed the last time?"

"He isn't—" I stopped myself. I wasn't getting caught up in this. The fewer lies I told, the better.

Unlike Roger, I wasn't that great with them.

"Look, just get Caleb, okay? Before Jules has a nervous breakdown." Or I did.

"Too late. He's Jules. He was born that way."

"Fred!"

"All right, all right. Relax. Have a bath." He looked me up and down, and then he smiled slightly. "Or, you know. Another one."

Chapter Twenty-three

I had the bath. And toweled my hair dry. And put on a T-shirt and jeans, because I was tired and fed up and had done all the pretending I was going to do for one night. Then I went on a witch hunt.

And found them in the lounge playing pool.

Well, two of them. The third was visible through the sliding doors to the living room, which were open again. Maybe because Marco had decided to turn on the charm. Or possibly to get himself a date; the jury was still out.

But he was talking to one of the witches, anyway, who I immediately christened Jasmine, because she looked like the Disney character. You know, if Jasmine had worn Armani and had her hair cut in a short, swingy style that framed her beautiful face. She was as lovely as a vamp, which might explain why Marco was chatting her up over by the bar. I couldn't tell if he was getting anywhere, because her sultry eyes were half-lidded, and the faint smile on her dark red lips could have been amusement or scorn.

But the other two witches were definitely veering toward amusement.

One was standing on a stool beside the pool table, cue in heavily beringed hands, lining up a shot. The stool

was needed because she was maybe four foot eight or
nine, if you didn't count a truly magnificent Afro, which
must have added an extra five inches. She was wearing a
green silk muumuu, had long nails painted a glittery
gold, and had on a bunch of matching gold chains that
clinked together as she took the shot. And sank the eight
ball, causing her companion to say a bad word.

The tiny witch cackled and got off her stool, reclaim-
ing a beer she'd left on a side table. Her opponent racked
up another game, since she'd just lost that one. It didn't
appear to faze her. I had the impression that there wasn't
a lot that did.

She was the one who had attempted to talk to me in
the lobby. I was kind of amazed that I'd just blown her
off now, since she was maybe six foot two in her hose
and easily six-four in the short-heeled black pumps she
was wearing. The pumps complemented the rest of the
look: hair short and gray, eyes piercing and steel-colored,
suit pin-striped and more serviceable than stylish. She
didn't look like a witch. She looked like an aging
Valkyrie. And more than a bit like Eugenie, my old governess, which probably explained why my stomach had
started to hurt.

Since they weren't paying me any attention anyway, I
went to the kitchen to find something to settle it down.
And instead found another witch. At least, I guessed so,
although it sort of messed up the Macbeth thing the trio
had going on. But I guess you couldn't stick to that stuff
all the time, especially if you thought you might need
backup.

Not that she looked likely to provide very much.

She was young, for one thing, maybe five or six years
younger than me. Or maybe even that was optimistic,
because while the body was that of an adult, she was
wearing a long white, high-necked gown that Eugenie
would have called "genteel" and I called a nineteenth-
century nightgown. It was one of the reasons I'd gone to
miniskirts and thigh-high boots as soon as I got away

from Tony's and acquired a paycheck: I'd spent my youth dressed like Wendy Darling.

Eugenie would have liked the girl's hairstyle, too, which was long and light brown and rippled down her back in a strangely familiar way. I could see it because she partly had her back to me, struggling with something on the counter. I recognized it about the same time I recognized her, or rather, who she reminded me of.

"Agnes?"

The brown head whipped around, but of course it wasn't her. I hadn't really thought so, since this chick was an inch or two taller than me, and Agnes had been a tiny little thing. But the overall look was similar, and her face was familiar, although I couldn't place it. She was also looking a little stressed, which had been Agnes' default, although it usually took more to get that expression on her face than a misbehaving coffeepot.

"It's one of those pod things," I told the girl helpfully.

She didn't say anything.

"You know, with the little cups?"

She obviously didn't know. Or maybe she didn't care. She had turned around, and was plastered against the sink, staring at me blankly out of a pale face and huge brown eyes. I decided there was a chance she didn't speak English.

"You need a pod," I repeated, slower, and sketched a pod shape with my fingers.

Nothing.

"Here," I told her, getting a box of coffee pods out of a cabinet and handing them to her. Or trying to. But she just stayed where she was, flat against the sink, hands gripping the counter and eyes big and freaked-out.

Only no, I realized, she didn't look freaked-out.

She looked terrified.

I whirled around, box of pods in hand, because you never knew around here. But no one was there. Not even one of the vamps, who tended to have an effect on sensitive-minded guests. But they were obviously traumatizing people elsewhere, because the doorway was empty.

I turned back around, but the horror-movie-victim pose hadn't changed, and it was starting to freak *me* out. I slid the pods onto the counter. I grabbed a beer out of the fridge. I backed slowly out of the door.

And ran into Marco, who was coming in. "Let's do this," he told me quietly. "I'm running out of jokes."

"You could always feed them."

A lip curled. "If we feed them, they'll stay longer."

"Not if the quality of the cuisine is anything like last time," the Valkyrie said, from across the room. "Or was that deliberate?"

She sank a ball.

Marco looked at me.

Enhanced hearing, I mouthed.

The wards are supposed to stop things like that, he mouthed back.

"And your wards are shit," the witch added, causing Marco to mutter something. "I heard that."

I sighed and walked over.

"At least most of them are," she amended, leaning on her stick and watching me. "There was a bastardized fey spell that gave us some trouble, mainly from us not expecting it."

"Woven with holly all around," the small witch added, in a singsong. "Shot through with sunlight and lightened by air, call on water, call on fire, call on wind—protect, protect, protect." She took a swig of her beer. "Three elements are a bitch."

"But we got past it," her companion added. "Mainly from your lot not maintaining it."

"The guy who usually does is out of town," I said evenly.

"Well, you need to get him back."

"Working on it." Although it would be easier to do that if they'd go away, so I could track down Casanova and find out what he knew about the council. But that didn't appear to be happening. And since I'd already pissed off the witches as much as I dared, it looked like I was going to have to practice my diplomacy for a while.

"You play?" the Valkyrie asked, racking up another game, even though they'd barely started the last one.

I looked over at the little witch, who grinned at me toothily. "I'll sit one out," she offered.

I shrugged. "Okay."

Marco looked surprised, probably because he'd never seen me play. Something about almost dying on a weekly basis took the fun out of it. "I used to work in a bar," I reminded him.

"Doing what?" the Valkyrie demanded.

"Bar-backing. Bartending sometimes, when somebody called in. Mostly reading tarot."

"The Pythia read tarot in a bar," the witch said, as if she thought I was lying to her.

"I wasn't Pythia then. And I like eating."

"You must have been quite the draw," she said dryly.

"Not really." I paused as she lined up the break, which she'd taken without bothering to flip me for it. "Most people didn't like what I had to tell them."

"And what was that?"

"The truth."

Her cue stuttered on the velvet, and she flubbed the break. She scowled at me, as if I'd done that deliberately. I fished the cue ball out of a corner pocket and tossed it to her. "Redo it."

She looked surprised that I was giving away my advantage. But I wasn't feeling real competitive right now. And I doubted they'd broken into my suite and trashed the lobby in order to play pool.

The witch racked 'em up and broke again, leaving herself a couple of easy shots to start with. She took one of them before looking up at me through a fringe of gray bangs. "Didn't expect to find you so polite."

"Why? Because I didn't talk to you after you broke in here?"

"No. But we have plenty of other reasons. Care to hear them?"

By the tone in her voice, I had a feeling I was going to anyway. "Sure." I walked over to the wall and chose a cue stick.

"You didn't invite us to the coronation, despite the fact that the damned Circle were there—in force." She sank her first shot with a savage little motion. "You haven't sent us the usual greetings or otherwise acknowledged our existence, despite having more than enough time to do so." She sank two balls with her second shot, clack-clack. "And you're living with a bunch of goddamned vampires!" She attempted a tough bank shot, and missed—barely.

She swore and moved off, and I took her place. Because no way was I giving her a second advantage after that. I took a moment to size up the table.

"Who I live with is my business," I said, chalking up. "And I didn't send you greetings because I didn't know I was supposed to." Or that you existed, I didn't add, because I decided it was barely possible that the head of a whole coven might have an ego. "As for the other, well, if it helps, I wasn't invited, either."

"Wasn't invited to what?" she demanded as I bent over the table.

"My coronation." I took the shot. It was an easy two ball in the side pocket. It went in—just. I was rusty.

"What do you mean, you weren't invited?" the witch repeated, as if I wasn't making sense. Which, okay. It hadn't made much sense to me at the time, either.

"The Circle and the senate got together and decided it was too dangerous for me to be there with all the death threats I've been getting," I explained. "So they moved the date up without telling me. I barely found out in time to make it."

"They moved the date?" She still looked confused.

"And when I did show up, they threw me out."

"Of what?"

I looked up from lining up my next shot, to find her frowning. "The building. Marlowe—that's Kit Marlowe—"

"I know who he is!"

"Well, then you know he can be pretty . . . persuasive. Not that he bothered that night. He just pushed me onto the back steps and slammed the door. They had some chick pretending to be me, and it would have been awkward if there were two of us running around."

The Valkyrie didn't say anything, but her lips tightened perceptibly.

"Then why not shift back in?" Afro asked, dark eyes dancing. Like she was expecting to hear about some serious shit going down. Too bad I was about to disappoint her.

"Because they had the damned thing warded. Some weird spell that parked the house in the middle of a ley line, basically taking it out of this world. It looked like it was there, but as far as my power was concerned, it wasn't. And I can't shift into nothing."

I sank the three ball easily, as her face fell.

"I'd have found a way to make them pay!" she declared, stamping the floor with a walking stick I hadn't noticed before, but which it didn't look like she needed. It was black and old and gnarly, but shined to a high gloss. Like the eyes that met mine defiantly.

"Too bad you weren't there, then," I said mildly. And sank the six as Jasmine wafted in, a highball in hand and Fred close behind her.

He was making weird faces and gestures at me, until he suddenly froze, one hand and one knee up, toes pigeoned and tongue lolling. He looked like he'd decided to join the Ministry of Silly Walks. He looked frankly demented. He looked like he was making fun of our guests, which was not likely to go down well.

And then he abruptly spun and ran out of the room, with the awkward gait and surprised look of a man who has a huge hand at the small of his back, helping him along. One look at Marco's face, and I decided that was probably not far from the truth. I sighed.

I didn't know what Fred's problem was, but I didn't try to follow. Because I had plenty of my own. Like the fact that all three witches were now looking at me judgmentally, especially the Valkyric.

"You let the bloody Circle and a bunch of vampires push you around like that?" she demanded.

And okay, I'd had about enough. I opened my mouth to point out a few salient facts, but I didn't get a chance. Because someone beat me to it.

"She killed a Spartoi!"

The voice had come from behind me, so I turned around. To see that the girl from the kitchen had decided to come shake in the doorway, instead of by the counter. Her face was still white, but there were two little spots of color high on her cheeks. She was either furious or about to pass out, and considering her actions so far, I knew which way I was betting.

"Move," I told Marco softly.

He looked at me, halfway through a sip of his whiskey sour. "What?"

"Go to the living room or something."

"Why?"

"Because I think you're scaring her."

He looked over at the girl and then back at me. "I'm just standing here."

Yeah, that was the problem. Some vamps managed to pass as human, if you squinted, even without a glamourie. But Marco wasn't one of them. It wasn't the looks so much, although two hundred and fifty pounds of predator is not easily disguised by a pink golf shirt, or the casual slouch he affected when standing so he didn't loom over people. But mainly, it was the 'tude. The guy could be smiling and he still looked like he could rip your throat out in less than a second.

It didn't help that it happened to be true.

He'd never worried me, possibly because I'd grown up with Alphonse, a Marco clone except not as good looking. But I'd learned early on that, despite the fiction, vampires weren't mindless predators and they didn't kill for no reason. And anyway, the smallest, most ineffectual one imaginable—Fred, for instance—could wreak just as much damage on a human as Marco, so what difference did looks make? But most people didn't see it that way, and in Marco's case especially, I'd seen grown men flatten themselves against a wall when he walked by, instinctively dropping into prey mode, hoping they wouldn't be noticed.

God only knew what effect he was having on a girl who apparently thought *I* was scary.

"Go on." I pushed on him, which of course was useless. "Get me a drink."

"You've got a drink."

"And now I want another one."

"You don't need another one. You had an Irish coffee earlier—"

I rolled my eyes. "Yeah, like Fred did more than wave the cork over the—"

"—and now you've got a beer. I don't want you yakking all over the place again."

"I never yak—" A bushy eyebrow went north. "Okay, one time. But that wasn't from a hangover."

"And this one isn't going to be, either." And he took my beer.

"Hey!"

"Is that coffee I smell?" he asked the girl, going over with a swagger and a grin, because despite all evidence to the contrary, Marco believed himself to be charming. And okay, sometimes he was, in his own big, hairy, swarthy, muscley way. But I didn't think she was likely to be impressed.

She wasn't, but not quite in the way I'd feared.

She shoved his outstretched hand away and pushed past, as if she barely even saw him. And maybe she didn't. Because her eyes were on the witches and I decided I might have been wrong earlier. They weren't afraid.

They were *pissed*.

"You . . . you dare . . ." she gasped.

"It's all right, Rhea," the Valkyrie said, looking uncomfortable.

"It is not all right! You weren't there—you didn't see! She saved us, she saved us *all*, and with nothing—and you *dare*—"

I didn't know what was going on, but the witches were going frowny, and the air was getting tense and things had been bad enough as they were. Marco must have thought the same, because he put an avuncular hand on the girl's shoulder. "Hey, why don't we—"

"Unhand me, vampire," she snarled, harsh enough to make him blink. And draw his hand back. And look at me.

"Cassie—"

"You know, I would like some of that coffee, after all," I said brightly, not really expecting it to work.

But it did.

The girl curtsied—yeah, that's what I said—deep and elegant and perfect. The kind Eugenie had always tried to teach me, but I'd never quite mastered. And then she withdrew, fading back through the swinging doors almost before I could blink.

Okay. That had gone . . . surprisingly well.

And then I turned back around to find the three witches still staring at me. And still unhappy. In fact, one was now actively glaring.

Take a guess which.

I sighed.

"Look, if it helps, I'm sorry, okay?" I told them. "I would have invited you to the party, if I'd known there was going to *be* a party, and I would have greeted you if I'd known you existed—"

"Knew we *existed*—" the Valkyrie spluttered.

Crap.

"And I'll make sure there are no more oversights where you're concerned," I added quickly. "Not that there's anything scheduled right now that I know of, but if and when I find out—"

"If?" The Valkyrie turned to look at her companions, spreading her hands. *"If?"*

"I'll make sure you get an invitation. Are we okay?"

"No!" she said severely. "Nothing about this is okay!"

I sighed again and leaned on my cue stick, wondering what the hell it was they wanted. And what it would take to get them to go away. And why my hand, which had reached for my beer, had come back empty.

Damn Marco.

"Would it help if I let you win?" I asked sourly. Because Jules wasn't the only one who had problems with this diplomacy thing.

The Valkyrie puffed up, but Jasmine intervened, her voice a cool river through the heated room. "It would help," she told me gently, "if you could tell us what your court is doing."

I looked back and forth between the three of them, thoroughly confused now. Like I'd been anything else all night. And then I said the words that I knew—I *knew*— I'd regret.

"What court?"

Chapter Twenty-four

That went over about as well as I'd thought it would. The Valkyrie blew up, the others started trying to talk her down, and then the fourth member of their party burst onto the scene again and things really got hot. I was tired and wanted my beer, so I started for the kitchen, only to be intercepted by Marco coming out of the living room.

I hadn't heard him leave, but then, that wasn't unusual. Vampires make little cat feet sound loud. "Hey, where did you put my—" I started, only to stop at the look on his face.

It was enough, but if I'd had any doubts, Caleb was right behind him.

"You need to see this," he told me grimly.

I was moving before he got all the words out.

Jules wasn't in the bedroom anymore. The living room sofa had been pushed against a wall, leaving a large cleared spot in front of the balcony doors. He was lying in it, on top of a sheet that must have been used to carry him in here.

I didn't have to ask why they'd wanted the sheet.

"What's wrong with him?" I whispered, feeling Caleb come up behind me.

"I don't know."

I whirled. "What do you mean, you don't know? Look at him!" I gestured at Jules, who was all but unrecognizable. His beautiful blond hair was the same, just curling a little in the damp from the shower. But as for the rest . . .

"I think I'm going to be sick," one of the vamps said, and sounded like he meant it.

"You've seen wounds before," Marco snapped.

"That's not a wound. That's . . . the opposite of a wound."

And he wasn't wrong. Instead of fissures opening up in Jules' body, like a knife or a bullet would have caused, he was . . . closing up. I didn't know what was going on inside him, but his face looked like a mask before anyone cut any holes in it. His ears were all but gone, melted back into his head. His nose and mouth were mere indentations in the paleness of his skin, which looked like it might have lost its pores, it was so unearthly smooth. And his eyes . . .

I shuddered and grabbed Marco's sleeve.

If Jules had been human, he'd have been dead by now, deprived of oxygen at the very least, since he no longer had openings to breathe through. And that was assuming worse changes weren't going on inside. But he wasn't human. Which was probably why that sightless face suddenly moved. And slowly, so very slowly, turned.

To look at me.

I stepped back a pace, staring at the grape-shaped lumps of flesh where eyes should have been, before telling myself to get a grip. He wasn't looking at me. He couldn't know I was here. It was random—

"It wasn't some shoplifting spell they ran into," Caleb said roughly. "It was one of the special orders Augustine has been doing for the Corps."

"Special orders?"

"Weapons, essentially."

I looked up at him. "Augustine designs *dresses*."

"And you've seen some of the mods he's put on your gowns. Think that's standard?"

I tried to process that for a second; then I pushed it away. I didn't care about explanations right now. "Just call him!"

"I already did. But he can't help us. The spell wasn't finished and he doesn't have a counter for it yet."

"He doesn't have—" I stared at him. "Then why the hell did he leave it lying around?"

"He didn't. It was in his private workroom, which was locked and warded and where no one has permission to go. And he was supposed to be the first one back tomorrow—"

I shook my head violently. I didn't care. "Caleb! Just reverse it!"

"That's what I'm trying to tell you; I can't."

"You—then what happens?" I demanded, gesturing at Jules.

Caleb's massive arms crossed. "You can try a necromancer, but the whole point of a war spell is that it be debilitating. If it was easy to undo, it wouldn't help us."

I didn't say anything. I couldn't. I just stared at Jules, and it felt like the bottom of my stomach fell out. I'd told him he would be okay. I'd told him it was no big deal. I'd told him—

There was a commotion behind me, and I turned to see the Valkyrie pushing her way through the ring of vampires. She walked over to Jules and bent down for a better look. She remained expressionless, but her lips all but disappeared.

"Nasty bit of work," she said, looking at Jasmine, who was kneeling on his other side.

Jasmine had been reaching out, as if she'd planned to touch him, but her hand stopped just short. "That is one word for it," she said softly.

"Can you break it?" I rasped.

They glanced at each other, and then at something behind me. I turned to see a rustle in the ring of vampires near the lounge, and then several jumped aside suddenly, possibly to avoid whacks from the stick the third little witch was using to clear herself a path.

"Why are you all so big?" she groused. "You're vampires. Size doesn't matter. Why do they never turn normal-sized men?"

Fred, who was standing across from me, started to say something, but then shut up. Maybe because she'd finally pushed through the forest of designer-clad legs and stopped by Jules. Who she proceeded to poke with her stick.

"What are you—"

"Hush," she told me, and swatted my hand.

The poking recommenced. And then she nodded. "Thought so. Clever boy. He's perverted a brownie spell, inverted it to harm rather than help."

"Fey magic," the Valkyrie explained, seeing my expression. "That's why the Circle pays Augustine to help them. He's part fey."

"Fey?"

She raised an eyebrow. "Couldn't you tell?"

I thought back to the ethereal creature I knew, tall, blond, and yes, elfin. It was sort of obvious, now that someone pointed it out.

"You've seen his gowns," Jasmine added. "No Arcane magic made those."

"It has better uses," Caleb muttered.

The Valkyrie sighed. "Yes, tell us again how much superior your magic is. But I don't see you solving the problem."

"I don't see you doing it, either."

"At least we could identify it."

"Identifying isn't reversing."

"We aren't finished yet."

"The covens have been finished for years," he snapped. And got whacked on the shin for his trouble.

"Slipped," the tiny witch said, unrepentant.

Caleb cursed. "If you want to keep him alive—or as

much as these things ever are—keep him away from them!" he told me.

Yeah. Only she was right; they'd known almost at once what they were dealing with. He hadn't.

"Can you remove it?" I asked the witches again.

Which led to another round of eye contact, but no one said anything. Until the small one piped up again. "I'm willing to have a go," she said cheerfully.

The other two looked less enthused. But finally, they nodded. "It *would* be in a city," Jasmine sighed.

"Why does that matter?" I asked—stupidly. Because it wasn't like I was going to understand the answer.

"It doesn't," Caleb said, sounding disgusted. "Magic is magic."

"We use a reserve of power to augment our own," Jasmine said, ignoring him. "As you do with the Pythian power. But ours is generated by the earth itself, the song of the sky, the land, the seas—"

"Bullshit!" Caleb said. "You're messing about with wild magic, and it's going to get you killed!"

Jasmine rolled her eyes. "You use talismans, do you not? They also gather the magic the earth gives off."

"Slowly, carefully, safely. What we do is like using electricity. You play around with lightning!"

"That's an exaggeration, as you well—"

"How many of your people have been fried, trying to channel wild magic?" Caleb demanded.

"And how many of yours have poisoned themselves playing about with alchemy?" the Valkyrie interjected. "Magic is inherently dangerous—"

"Not if you know what you're doing!"

"Ah, and there's the rub, isn't it?" she said, sneering. "Just because you can't do it—"

"Can't—" Caleb flushed. "We *choose* not to use something dangerously unstable and innately unreliable—"

"So unreliable we fought you to a standstill—"

"So unreliable you were all but destroyed!"

"After you betrayed us! Broke your promises and turned your back on honor—"

"As if a coven witch would know anything of honor!" Caleb spat.

And won himself another whack from the little witch's stick.

For a moment, everyone just glared at one another.

"I'm not sure I understand what you plan to do," I told Jasmine, who seemed to be keeping her cool better than the others.

"Druid is a combination of human magic—pre-Circle—and fey," she explained. "The combination allows us to borrow directly from the earth's natural well of power to augment our own, instead of using talismans to slowly gather it up. Being on earth requires altering the spells somewhat, which is why it is considered a distinct system from that of the fey. But it works quite well, I assure you."

"And that's different from what the Circle does?"

The three witches exchanged glances again.

"Theirs is based on ancient alchemy," Jasmine said slowly. "What we call hard magic, something that can be put into a test tube and experimented on. The Circle always wants something they can see and taste and touch, something they can control. The wilder, more flexible, more intuitive magic of nature eludes and confuses them. They cannot master it because they do not feel it."

"You see?" Caleb asked me. "This is exactly the sort of mumbo-jumbo you can expect from the covens. I can give you formulas, show you precisely how a potion or ward or spell works—and how to reverse it. And if Augustine was using the Arcane, he could, too—and we wouldn't be in this mess!"

"The Arcane is Circle magic?" I asked, for clarification. I'd heard the term before, but I wanted to be sure I understood what they meant. It was my responsibility to Jules to be sure.

The witches exchanged another look. Even Caleb appeared a little taken aback. And then he got whacked again.

"Witch!" he snarled. "If you hit me with that thing one more time—"

"Don't you take that tone with me," she told him. "And you deserve a good whipping. Why is the Pythia asking a question like that?"

"Like what?" I asked.

"You see? She doesn't even—" The little witch made another jab, but Caleb danced back out of the way.

To my surprise, though, he wasn't glaring at her. If anything, he looked a little shamefaced. "That wasn't my call."

"Then whose call was it?"

"She was brought up by the vampires. And the one she lived with didn't want her trained."

"At *all*?" the Valkyrie demanded, looking incredulous.

Caleb didn't say anything. But the truth was kind of obvious.

Jasmine just sat there, looking appalled. But the Valkyrie couldn't seem to quite grasp the concept. "You've received *nothing*?" she demanded.

"He's exaggerating," the little witch told her. "He has to be."

And then someone pinched the hell out of me.

I jumped and twisted around, but no one was close enough. Not that that meant anything with vampires, who could move like the wind. But I didn't think the ones by the door were too interested in pranking me. They hadn't taken their horrified eyes off Jules.

And then somebody did it again, and I damned well knew they hadn't moved that time. And anyway, it had been from behind me. And then from the left and the right and—

"Ow!" I said, whipping my head back and forth. "What the—"

"Cut it out," Caleb growled, but not at me. He was

looking at the tiny witch, and unlike his previous threat, his voice had gone flat, and his eyes were cold and blank. I'd seen that look on Pritkin's face a time or two, and it scared me a lot more than a few pinches.

"Caleb—" I said, reaching out.

"She doesn't have shields!" The tiny witch was beside herself.

"You don't, do you?" Jasmine asked, wonderingly. "You battled a Spartoi . . . unprotected?"

I didn't respond, because Caleb was starting to worry me. "Just relax," I told him as the pinching stopped.

"A war mage's first duty is to protect the Pythia," he said softly, his hand on the potion belt at his waist. A lot of the younger mages didn't use one, preferring spelled bullets that could go farther and hit more accurately. But like Pritkin, Caleb preferred to double up on his weaponry, and he used both.

And I did not want to find out what the vial he was currently fingering did.

"It's okay. It didn't hurt," I lied. Because I was going to be polka-dotted tomorrow.

"Assault is assault—"

"Oh, please!" the Valkyrie said. She looked at me. "Our apologies. But you can hardly blame us. The fact that the Pythia—the person on whom all our lives may depend—cannot even do a simple protection spell—" She threw up her hands. "It's enough to shock anyone!"

"Shock isn't the word I'd use," the tiny witch muttered, bending to look at my arm. And then waving a hand and muttering something—

Which she didn't get a chance to finish, because she was suddenly across the room, pinned to the wall. Jasmine was likewise out of commission, on the floor and trapped by the massive boot on her chest. And the Valkyrie and Caleb were facing off, he with the vial in the hand that wasn't outstretched, restraining her companion, and she with what looked alarmingly like a wand denting the skin of his throat.

"She's not the only one needs to work on her protection spells," she hissed.

"Go for it," he told her tightly. "And we'll see who needs protection."

"Don't tempt me, mage! After the hash the Circle has made of this, I might be doing us all a favor!"

"By restarting a civil war?" someone asked, from over by the door.

I looked up to find Jonas standing there, his magnificent mane an electrified halo about his head, crackling like a storm was blowing in. But his voice had been mild, and his touch was gentle as he helped the little witch off the wall. Or tried to.

"I can manage," she grumbled, hopping down as spry as someone my age. Although I didn't think I'd be as calm as she was under the circumstances. Hell, I hadn't moved, and I still wasn't calm.

"Did you call him?" I demanded, looking at Caleb. Who was starting to sweat. But he didn't drop the pose, even when his boss came up along one side. And gently pushed his subordinate's boot off Jasmine.

She was up in a liquid move worthy of a vamp, her beautiful face distorted. But she didn't do anything. She backed off, looking at the Valkyrie, who was still threatening Caleb.

For a moment, nobody moved.

Jonas cleared his throat. "No," he told me. "He did not."

It was mild, but Caleb swallowed.

"I came to see you. I had planned to in any case, but then that hotel manager called Central, demanding that someone come out to, er, de-chicken his security force?"

The Valkyrie's lips twitched.

I blinked, because I'd expected to hear a sermon about the battle on the drag. Had been expecting it since I got up, actually, only nobody had mentioned it. Which was a little weird, come to think of it.

But I sure wasn't going to be the first to bring it up.

"I thought that would just wear off," I said instead.

"Yes, well, that's what we told him. But it lasts rather longer on humans, you know, and he was insistent. And after calling up here . . ." He raised an eyebrow, his eyes going around the group.

"Caleb came at my request," I told him, "to reverse a hex. And the coven leaders are . . . uh. Helping him."

Unsurprisingly, it didn't look like he bought it, although the Valkyrie did lower her wand thing. I still didn't get a good look at it; it disappeared inside her coat faster than a cell phone in the hand of a teenager. Which didn't make me feel better, since she could obviously take it out again just as quick.

Caleb, on the other hand, looked visibly relieved.

At least until the little witch came back over, looking like she was spoiling for a fight. But despite the wall incident, he wasn't the target. "Jonas Marsden! Just the man."

"Beatrice," he said, sighing.

"I want to know what you think you're doing, letting this girl go untrained!"

"We *are* training her," Jonas said patiently. "But there are priorities—"

"Priorities? Like allowing her to go about completely defenseless?"

"She is hardly that. She has guards, as you can see. And wards. And normally a trusted member of my force is assigned to her, as well—"

"None of which kept us from breaking in here—"

"Yes, well, your skill set is somewhat greater than the norm—"

"—or taking the lobby apart! Where the girl was messing about, completely alone, and completely defenseless—"

"She isn't as defenseless as she appears, as I believe you discovered. And in any case, what would you have me do? Lock her up?"

"I would have you show some sense! You should

have called us in, long before this. Old rivalries are well
and good, but when lives are on the line—"

"You think I would deliberately endanger—"

"I think you *have* endangered—"

I stopped listening. I wasn't interested in hearing a
bunch of people debate my education or lack thereof.
Again. I wasn't interested in hearing them talk at all.

I was interested in Jules.

"Can you remove the hex or not?" I demanded.

The little witch had been glaring at Jonas. Now she
turned the glare on me. For a second, before her eyes
softened. "Yes, yes. Well, probably," she hedged. "But it's
hardly worth the effort—"

"Not worth the effort?" I stared at her.

The room grew suddenly quiet.

"She didn't mean it like that," Jasmine said, looking at
me with pity in her beautiful eyes.

"Then how exactly did she mean it?"

"You must understand, the spell has already done
most of the damage that it was designed to do. Removing it now will prevent more, yes, but . . ."

"But *what*?"

"But it cannot reverse that which has already been
done," she told me softly. "I am sorry, lady. I do not know
of anything that can."

Chapter Twenty-five

I don't know what happened then. I wasn't hearing them anymore. I was hearing Jules. *I took care of you. Take care of me.*

I knelt on the floor beside him.

The face was bad, but the body wasn't any better. He had been wearing a nice blue cotton button-down, starched and preppy like the man himself. Now it was almost like it was wearing him, with the fabric all tangled up in the too-smooth skin of his chest. It was as if his body had folded over on itself, like dough in a mixer, and taken pieces of the cotton with it. The area on his shoulders was still mostly intact, mostly normal. But the hands . . .

His beautiful hands were all but gone, just two lumps poking up from what had been his stomach, with a few ridges where knuckles had once been. I covered them with my own anyway. Somehow I didn't mind anymore, didn't find them alien or horrifying or gross. They were just part of him, part of Jules. That was enough.

I closed my eyes, mainly to shut out the ring of staring faces. And as soon as I did, that feeling of connection strengthened. Maybe it was just my imagination working overtime, but I could swear I felt it: his anger, his confusion, his almost desperate desire to move, to gasp for air he didn't need, to *see*—

But mostly, I felt his fear.

It was cold, overwhelming, debilitating, almost as much as what was happening to his body. The spell was cruel, it didn't bother to trap the mind. Maybe Augustine hadn't thought it necessary. After all, a human or fey would be dead by now.

But Jules was neither of those things.

And so he was left to drive himself mad on an endless loop of speculation: what if there was no way to reverse this? What if he was trapped like this forever? Hope gone, looks gone, just this piteous and pitied thing, unable to move, to speak, to do anything but scream into a darkness that would never end, and never answer back—

My hands tightened over his, and the torrent suddenly stopped. And then increased, a hundredfold, a wall of babbling, half-mad terror hitting me all at once. I gasped, and opened my eyes to find myself bent over him, sick and dizzy and quietly sobbing, my tears splashing down onto the ruined chest . . .

And changing.

Like a drop of rain falling into a lake, the eddies rippled outward, disturbing the flawless flow of the skin, revealing small blemishes in the instant they passed over: a hair, a freckle, a scar. I let go of his hands in surprise, and the skin retained the imprint of my hands for a second. And it, too, looked different, with the knuckles clearly visible in the instant before that eerie nonflesh washed over them again, erasing them as smoothly as footprints in the tide.

It was so quick it made me wonder if I'd imagined it. But no. I scowled at the too-perfect flesh, because I *had* seen it, if only for an instant. I had seen Jules, inside the body bag his flesh was busy crafting for him.

And somehow I had to find a way to get him *out*.

I vaguely registered Marco pulling everyone back to

the lounge—the witches, the Circle, everyone except for the vampires. This wasn't for outsiders, if they couldn't help. This was about family.

Someone dimmed the lights; I don't know why. Maybe to give the gawkers less to stare at; maybe because it just felt like the right thing to do. And vampire eyes didn't need the light. Mine didn't, either, with a diffuse beam leaking through from the lounge, illuminating Jules like a spotlight.

It was enough. It was more than enough. I pressed my hands against him, both of them, palms flat and fingers outstretched, gripping hard enough to make indentations in his skin.

And then I swiped down, revealing pink nipples, hard abs, a concave stomach, and the brief indentation of a naval. It looked like a plasterer had taken a trowel to a wall, scraping away the surface to reveal what lay beneath. And what lay beneath was Jules.

He was still in there, somewhere.

But a second later, the healthy skin had been washed away, replaced by the pale, poreless perfection I had already come to hate.

Someone put a hand on my shoulder, but I shrugged it off. And tried again, but it was the same. Wherever my hands rested, and for a small space around them, the skin looked normal, and the body was whole, straight, perfect. But as soon as I took them away, or tried to move onto another spot, it was as if whatever magic was there simply vanished.

And I didn't know how to make it stay.

"No," I said, helplessly. "No!"

"Cassie. Come away."

I looked up to see Marco staring at me, dark eyes troubled. "Come away? I'm trying to help him!"

"I know. But there's nothing you can do. We . . . we'll call someone—"

"Who?" I demanded. "We already tried Augustine,

and if the maker and a senior war mage can't remove it, do you really think—"

"What I think is that you're exhausting yourself for nothing. You need—"

"Nothing?" I stared at him. "Don't you *see* it?"

"Don't I see what?"

I looked back down, at where my balled fists were resting on the pink and perfect skin of Jules' stomach. It looked like some kind of modern art installation, where a white painted mannequin is punched only to reveal part of a living person beneath. Only Marco didn't see that person. Marco, I realized blankly, didn't see anything.

I blinked at him, confused. I'd thought maybe I'd inherited some of Roger's skill, that maybe that was why . . . but was I imagining things? Was this necromancy or just wishful thinking? Or something else entirely?

"Come on, girl," he told me gently. "You've got raccoon eyes. You need rest—"

No! Let her try!

God, Marco must be right; I must be tired, I thought, rubbing my eyes. Because that had sounded like Jules. A lot like, I realized, as the voice came again.

Please, Cassie, please! Oh God, you can't—don't leave me like this! I can't bear it. I can't! I can't! I—

I was hallucinating; I had to be.

You can hear me? He sounded almost as shocked as I was. *You heard that?*

"I—no. No."

"Don't lie!" And suddenly, the tiny sound at the back of my mind that I might have been imagining was a full-blown voice, and there was no question this time. It was Jules. And he was talking a mile a minute. "Nobody could hear me! I've been trapped in here, screaming and screaming, but there's only been silence and—oh God. Oh, Cassie, oh God!"

"This isn't possible," I told him numbly. I wasn't a

vampire; I couldn't mind-speak. Well, with anyone but
Billy Joe, and even he had to be in residence. When he
was outside my body, I had to talk to him like anyone
else.

"Well, you're doing it!" Jules said frantically. "And I
can't—I haven't been able to talk to anybody. I've been
calling and calling, but nobody answered. I didn't even
try you; I don't know why. I guess I didn't think you
could do it—"

"I *can't* do it."

"Then what do you call this?"

I had no idea.

"What's going on?" Marco demanded. "Who are you
talking to?"

I hadn't realized that I'd closed my eyes again, but I
opened them to see him frowning from a crouch beside
me, his bulk blocking out half the room.

"Jules. Can't you hear him?"

"No." Marco didn't look happy about that, and neither was I, because I'd learned the hard way that anything in magic I didn't understand could and probably
would come back to bite me. But there were more important things right now. Only I still didn't know what I
could—

And suddenly, it was all there, laid out in front of me.
Instead of the dim living room, and the ring of glowing,
vampire eyes, I saw something like an old book. Not
grimoire-old, but a flashy paperback, like one from the
thirties, with a lurid cover and boldface type. I didn't get
a chance to read the title, because a wind came up, and
the pages started ruffling. The book opened.

It was about Jules.

Days like sentences, months like paragraphs, years
like pages flipping in the wind, going back, back, back
through Jules' whole life. Like an autobiography written
in flesh.

"What—how are you—" Jules choked.

"I'm . . . not sure." But when I put out a hand, and

stopped a page, suddenly I wasn't seeing the book any-more. I was seeing him.

I saw a boy on a farm where no rain fell, but where billowing sheets of sand swept over the landscape, bury-ing the farmhouse up to the windows. I saw him bundled into an old jalopy by his parents, along with half a dozen siblings like little stair steps, with the mother's belly al-ready rounded with the next. I saw them flee their ru-ined home for a brighter future in a promised land. Which only led to a life of backbreaking labor when they could get it, hunger, scorn, and constant motion.

"But I had a talent," Jules said softly.

"Your face."

I saw it change as he grew, a random ordering of genet-ics that took his mother's thin features and his father's florid ones and crafted exquisite perfection. Enough to make people stop and stare at the ragged little boy with the angelic features. And suddenly, they all wanted to help.

Money, a place to spend the night, work for the fa-ther, new clothes . . . The family received assistance again and again from people who thought they were be-ing charitable, but who were really just charmed by a boy learning to use his greatest talent. It took him far—

"A little too far," Jules said quietly.

He wasn't exaggerating. Hollywood, parties, drinking binges, the pages flipped, and Jules changed. His father's floridity started to show up around the edges as the big roles, the meaty ones, the ones that would make his name and fortune, went elsewhere. Until the day he ended up on a ledge, looking down. And wondering how to fall to ensure that his perfect face survived the jump.

"Mircea talked you down," I said, seeing Mircea walk-ing along the ledge, looking exactly the same except for a twenties-era suit with too short lapels. He was as sure-footed as if he were strolling down a street, despite the fact that they were twelve stories up.

"Not exactly," Jules confessed. "I was too drunk to

see reason, and he tired of talking to a potential asset that seemed determined to destroy himself."

"What did he do?"

Jules laughed, a bright sound that seemed more than strange in the circumstances. "He threw me off."

And he had. The next instant, I saw him pick Jules up by the shirtfront and casually drop him over the side, all with a faint smirk on his face. And then use vampire speed to catch him before he hit the ground.

Just.

"He'd heard that a lot of the people who commit suicide regret it halfway down," Jules told me, with a catch in his voice. "He wanted to find out if it was true."

"Was it?"

Jules choked on a laugh. "I wet myself. And then I sobered up, and asked him how he did that. And he offered me a new sort of contract. An immortal one."

"But you don't sound happy." And he didn't. Bitter, with a side of world-weary and maybe an edge of hysteria thrown in there for good measure. But definitely not happy.

"Some days—" His voice broke, and he paused before continuing, stronger. "Some days, I wish Mircea had missed."

"What? Why?"

"Think about it, Cassie!" he said fiercely. "Eternity when you're a screwup is a very long time! I thought I would eventually get good at this, learn to be the suave, überconfident vampire, start to feel comfortable—but it never happened. I just learned new ways to be a failure. Mircea's vampires are either diplomats or soldiers, and I'm neither."

I didn't bother to point out that there were other jobs. Jules wasn't the type to be happy doing the laundry. He was talking about prestige positions, and yeah, that about summed it up.

"You could always ask for a transfer," I said instead. "Go to a different house—"

"And do *what*? Look good?" Jules laughed again, and this time, it was humorless. "A face like mine may make you a fortune in the human world, if you go about it right. But you know what it means in the vampire? When any third-rate glamourie can give you the same result?"

"You're more than just your looks, Jules."

"Am I? How many thespian vampires do you know? Or performers of any kind?"

"Vamps have . . . hobbies," I offered, a little lamely, but it was true. They did a variety of things in their spare time. Paint, sculpt, sing . . . I used to know one who took weird photos of people's worst features, a sort of beauty pageant in reverse.

"But not as a profession," Jules insisted. "Not as a way to leave a mark, to *count*. There are people who are good at this life, who take to it naturally, and then there's the rest of us. But there's no way to know which you'll be before you get in, and once you do, there's only one way out."

And yeah. The kind of contract vampires were offered didn't have an expiration date. It was something all those eager applicants often forgot.

"I'm sorry," I told him, and meant it.

"Don't be. Just promise—if this doesn't work—promise me you'll end it."

"Jules—"

"Or have Marco do it. I don't care, I just—I can't live like this. You understand? I *can't*—"

"Jules!" I said, sharply, because the hysteria was creeping back, big-time.

"I'm sorry, I'm sorry," he said, sounding a little calmer. "But I want your word."

"Listen to me," I said, striving for calm, because I wasn't doing so great myself. "I won't promise you—"

"Cassie—"

"No, listen!" I said, my voice shaking slightly. "I'm being straight with you, okay? No bullshit." Not this time; not ever again. Not with people I cared about.

What a way to learn a lesson.

"Okay."

"And I won't tell you that this is going to work. I'm not a witch; I can't undo a hex their way—"

"And it wouldn't help, even if you could."

Apparently, those missing ears still worked just fine. And yeah. That must have been fun, lying helpless, and listening to everybody sound his death knell.

"No," I confessed. "But I can try to take you back to before the damned thing was laid in the first place. Basically, I'm going to put you in a time bubble—"

Jules made a choking sound. "Spare me the details."

Yeah. I probably wouldn't want them in his place, either. He'd been through enough tonight already, but I couldn't leave well enough alone because he wasn't well enough. And he wasn't going to be if I didn't manage this.

And we both knew it.

I nodded, licked my lips, and tried to concentrate.

It was just as well that Jules hadn't wanted details, because he wouldn't have liked them anyway. Not only because I hadn't done something exactly like this before, but because I wasn't the best at precision timing. It was why I hardly ever got away with anything when I shifted. Agnes had been able to come back to her body at virtually the second she left it, so nobody ever knew she'd even been gone unless she chose to tell them. But she'd had either a gift or a heck of a lot more practice, because I usually missed by a mile. Fortunately, there was no chance of that the way I felt. I'd woken up tired and was fast approaching exhaustion, and I hadn't even done anything ye—

A bubble sprang up around Jules, small but perfectly formed.

I blinked at it, surprised, since I'd half expected to fail. But it was real. The light from the lounge shone off it in a swirl of iridescent colors. It looked like a soap bubble—and about as stable. I needed to hurry.

I concentrated on the mental biography Jules had shown me.

It was thick. Not only had Jules had a long life; he'd had a busy one. Luckily, we weren't covering a lot of time here, and I didn't need to worry about all those pages and pages. Just a few words back, maybe even a couple of letters ought to be—

The wind I'd felt before picked up again, fluttering the pages, and it was a lot stronger this time. I made a mental grasp for them, but they slipped through my fingers as if they were oiled. One, two, three pages back, and finally I managed to grab one, trying to tamp down my power enough to stop the gale without killing it— and the bubble—completely.

And it must have worked, because I heard a collective gasp. And glanced at Jules. And did a double take.

It looked like his face had been submerged in a vat of pale paint, and was now being raised up again. Eyes, nose, mouth were all becoming visible, as the slick, too-flawless surface sloughed away on every side. Pores emerged again, and eyebrows, and lashes and—

And I could barely breathe.

Because it was working.

His chest was harder to look at, doing strange things to my brain as it writhed and churned in a way flesh was never designed to. But the same process was happening there, with random bits of material coming together into a shirt once more. Like the body underneath, which was starting to look like a man again, and like the hands . . .

I'd barely had the thought when Jules' beautiful, graceful hands rose up from his stomach like two birds, still encased by the bubble, but no longer trapped.

Like the pages of the book, I realized. They suddenly fluttered out of my grasp, as if they had a mind of their own. A gust of that strange wind caught them, and they fell in a single, rippling cascade, decades passing like seconds.

Shit! I grabbed for them, but they had an almost frictionless surface, impossible to hold. Until I finally slammed myself down in desperation, trapping the still bucking and moving book under the full weight of my mental body.

And at last, it was enough.

"Cassie—" someone said, and I glanced at Jules. And then stared, transfixed, as color bloomed on once-pale cheeks, as blond hair lightened, as a beard sprouted and then retreated and then sprouted again—

"Cassie!"

Marco's voice rose in my ear, loud and panicked, as I slashed my hand through the bubble. It evaporated in a flash of light bright enough to make me close my eyes. And when I opened them, I saw Jules, still sprawled on the carpet but flexing two perfectly fine hands with a look of stunned wonder on his face.

And Marco, who was pale and tight-lipped. And Fred, who looked like he was about to faint. And Rico, the brunet member of the trio, a daredevil type who was famously unafraid of anything.

Except me, I thought, meeting eyes that held that unmistakable emotion, before quickly skittering away.

"What is it?" I asked, staring from them to Jules. Who was still flexing his hands—his pink and healthy and obviously perfectly fine hands.

"My God," Fred whispered.

"What?" I asked again, starting to worry. "It worked. He's back to normal—"

"Normal?" Marco asked fiercely. "You call that *normal*?"

I looked at Jules, who finally looked up. His eyes were a little different as they met mine, bluer maybe. And his skin looked different, too, almost . . . sun kissed. If anything, he looked better than before.

"Yes?" I said, growing more confused by the second. "What do you call it?"

Jules gripped my hand again, and this time, his was . . . different, weaker, warmer. And I could swear I felt a pulse in the wrist he held against mine. And there were fine freckles, which a moment before, had been glamoured away. And—

No. No, it couldn't be, I thought, staring at him in disbelief.

"Human," Jules said hoarsely.

Chapter Twenty-six

I went back to bed.

Not because I wanted to. But the room had started to telescope around me when I tried to get up, and Marco had put his foot down. And then threatened to drag me if I didn't go by myself.

I'd managed to avoid being carted off like a sack of potatoes, but only just. And now the ceiling of my bedroom seemed to be pulsing in and out, even with me flat on my back. It was kind of trippy, but it was also disturbing.

But not as much as what had just happened to Jules.

Oh God, what had I done?

It was a stupid question. I knew what I'd done. I'd stripped Jules of his master status, destroyed his position in the family, which was pretty much everything to a vampire, and reduced him to a servant at best, prey at worst.

I hadn't just ruined his life; I'd destroyed his death.

And okay. He'd just finished saying how much he longed for a do-over, but that was *Jules*. He should have been an actor, because he was a drama queen and everybody knew it. And he'd been facing a situation where even a normal human life had probably looked pretty damned good by comparison. But tomorrow? The next day? The day he looked at his beautiful, unchanging face in the mirror and saw the first wrinkle?

I tried to tell myself that it would be okay. Once the ceiling stopped waving around, I'd figure everything out. I'd sit down and take his hands in mine and . . . and do the opposite of whatever I'd just done.

Except that I didn't know what I'd just done.

It seemed like he should be just a slightly younger version of a vampire. But I hadn't been trying to shave off a little time; I'd been trying to lift a curse. And some people considered vampirism to fall under that category. So maybe my power, which frequently had a mind of its own, had misunderstood.

And decided to lift *all* the curses.

That would explain the imagery of the book, which had been so different from the less-than-creative calendar flip my brain usually showed me when I time-shifted. But a calendar wouldn't be appropriate if I was regressing Jules through his life rather than just through time. So it got clever and came up with a biography instead.

Okay, I could go with that.

But that still didn't explain how I'd done it.

Or how to fix it.

I put an arm over my face, trying to block out the room, trying to block out everything. But it didn't help. I still saw Jules' panicked face—his *human* face. Because whatever the reason, he was free of the disease that caused vampirism.

So if I aged him, wouldn't he age as a human? And what if I got another of those crazy power surges, like the one that had regressed him eighty years in a couple of seconds? He didn't have immortality on his side anymore. He could end up an old man.

Hell, he could end up *dead*.

Like me, when Mircea found out.

Because Mircea was going to *kill* me.

And it wasn't like he didn't have cause. Sure, he could

make Jules a vampire again, but he'd start out a new-born, wouldn't he? Just like everyone else. And there was no way to know if the delicate cocktail that made a master vamp would come together for him a second time. Part of the equation was desire, and the first time around, Jules had had it in spades. But now? When he knew he'd only go so far and no farther? When he'd had time to be disillusioned?

He might be lost to the family forever, thanks to me.

And that was . . . that was a very bad thing.

Jules hadn't just been a vampire; he'd been a master. And master vamps weren't exactly a dime a dozen. They were a precious part of any senior master's property, more valued than money or land or virtually anything else except power, because almost anything else was easier to get. Any master could make a vampire, but to make another master . . . That was tricky.

A huge number of things went into the process that led to some vampires transitioning to master level, but the power of the one who had turned them was a large part of the equation. It meant that low-on-the-totem-pole masters, like Fred or Rico or Jules himself, had only a very small chance of ever producing a master. So much so that most low-ranking masters preferred to remain with their families rather than to strike out on their own and form another family they might not be able to protect.

But even in cases like Mircea's, masters were still rare. Most vampires remained vampires, stuck as servants and errand runners, lackeys and paper pushers for all eternity. Having one transition to master status was a cause for celebration and a source of personal pride for his maker, and likely a status boost, as well.

When they spoke of wealth in the vampire world, they spoke in terms of how many masters you controlled.

And Mircea now had one less, thanks to me.

I stared at the phone gleaming ominously on my bedside, and wondered how long I had. It was late afternoon, so normally, Mircea wouldn't even be up yet. Of course, his usual schedule couldn't always be relied on these days.

The senate had lost a lot of its members in the war, which meant that every senator who remained had had to do the work of two. Plus, Mircea had been negotiating a treaty with the other senates, and doing some other stuff I wasn't clear on, but that had to do with finding new senators to help carry the burden. He'd said that would be over soon, maybe by the end of the week. But right now, he was really busy, and there were a lot of people who needed his time and —

And I was a coward who should just woman up and call him, already.

My hand actually stretched out to grab the phone, because that was the one useful thing I could do while flat on my back. But then it dropped. Because where did I *start*?

And where would it lead?

It was the same problem I'd had all week. I loved Mircea; I didn't *like* keeping things from him. But telling him anything was basically the same thing as telling the senate, like telling Jonas would have been like telling the Circle.

Only I wasn't dating Jonas.

Which actually made things easier sometimes. I didn't feel guilty that Marco had bum-rushed Jules into one of the spare bedrooms before Jonas had a chance to get curious. This was family business; it didn't have anything to do with him. And I didn't think Mircea would appreciate having the Circle learn that I could unmake masters now.

But, technically, the same argument could be made for the whole Pritkin thing, which didn't have anything to do with Mircea.

Yet I felt guilty for not telling him anyway.

And that was such bullshit! Mircea wasn't any better

at sharing than I was; in fact, he probably took the close-mouthed prize. From the vamp's perspective, I was *married* to the guy, yet I didn't know what his favorite color was. Or his favorite drink. Or what he did all the time when he wasn't here, which was most of the time lately.

I didn't really know that much about him at all, and it was maddening. But worse, I couldn't even complain. Because then he might—hell, he *would*—suggest an exchange of information, and there was so damned much I couldn't tell him. . . .

I stared at the phone.

It stared back.

I chewed my cheek for a while and then got disgusted with myself. I wasn't going to wait around like this for hours. I'd have a stomach full of ulcers by then to go with whatever was making me so exhausted. I was going to do it. I was going to call him. I was going to do what I should have days ago and just pick up the phone and—

Someone knocked on the door.

I looked up, my heart in my throat, sure it was Marco with a phone in his hand.

And then Fred pushed open the door with a foot, because his hands were full of beer, one of them wrapped in a paper towel because we're classy like that.

"Oh, thank God," I said as he handed it to me.

He looked a little surprised at the fervency of his welcome. "Figured you could use a drink," he said, and tossed my phone on a chair so he could sit down on the bed.

I drained half the bottle in one go and then flopped onto my back again. And stared at the ceiling some more, which looked slightly more friendly now that I had beer. But no more helpful.

"Is Jules all right?" I asked, after a minute.

"He's human," Fred said, with an odd lilt in his tone. Like he still couldn't quite believe it. "He's a little hysterical, sure, but otherwise, he's fine. I mean, maybe not

if he stays like this, you know, but for now . . . So there's
no need to go tearing yourself up over it, all right?"

Yeah. Unless I couldn't figure out how to reverse this.

"Did everybody go home?" I asked hopefully.

"Oh, hell no."

Of course not.

"Jonas and the witches are having it out. You know, I
used to think it was just an old fairy tale, but witches *really* don't like missing a party, do they?"

I couldn't help it. I laughed. "I guess not."

"I tried to eavesdrop for you, but they're in the kitchen
under a silence spell. And they closed the blinds." He
looked aggrieved. "All I got was that they think he's mo-
nopolizing you, and a bunch of arm waving."

I hoped that arm waving wasn't of the spell variety.
"Is Marco with them?"

"No, he's trying to get some sense out of that girl."

"What girl?"

"Rhea something; I didn't get a last name. You know,
the witches brought her."

"She's not another witch?"

"Yeah, but not a coven leader. Best I could gather,
she's one of your court."

"My—" It took me a second. "You mean the Pythian
Court?"

"You got two?"

"I wasn't sure I had one. It's not like they've bothered
to come by and say hi."

"Well, now they have."

Yeah, and I guess the outfit should have clued me in.
"What does she want?"

Fred sighed. "I don't know. But she keeps babbling
something about this being all her fault—"

"What is?"

"Jules. Oh, not the getting-cursed thing; that's all on
him. But the other. It seems like having one of your coven around increases your power or something—"

"Wait." This was going way too fast. "What coven?"

"Your coven."

"Fred," I said impatiently. "We've been through this. I'm not a witch. I don't have—"

"Well, according to her, you do. That's what the Pythian Court is—the Pythia's coven. And coven members give their leader a power boost. It's sort of the reason they exist," he added when I just looked at him. "For a bunch of magic workers to pool their power. You know?"

Yeah, I just hadn't known it applied to me. But that's the sort of information that might have been useful, oh, a few hundred times. I frowned.

"I don't feel like I've had a boost."

"Maybe not now. But I think she's saying that you wouldn't have, er, overshot the mark with Jules if she hadn't been here. And given you a lift you didn't expect."

I took a second to absorb that. "And she didn't bother to mention this before?"

"She said she thought you knew. And I think she was waiting for the witches to leave before talking to you. I got the impression they didn't get along that great."

"Why was she with them, then?"

Fred didn't say anything.

"Fred?"

"Maybe you want to wait and ask her—"

"I asked you."

He sighed again. "She said she fled to the covens for protection. Seems there's some kind of problem with your court. She wouldn't say what, won't talk to anybody but you, but she found out and went to the witches."

"And they decided to drop her on my doorstep."

"Pretty much. I got the idea they think she's a nut, but they wanted to get a look at you anyway, and she was a good excuse. And she's . . . well, maybe you'll have more luck with her."

Great. "Luck" in my life now meant finding out about some new problem I was going to have to deal with. When it already felt like I had plenty on my plate, thanks.

But one thing the whole situation with Mircea had taught me: putting stuff off rarely made it easier.

"Come on," I said, swinging my legs over the side of the bed, because at least the room had finally calmed down. "Let's go find out—"

Somebody started screaming.

I closed my eyes.

Of course.

It turned out to be Jules, standing in front of the balcony, a double shot of whiskey in hand, exercising his newly human vocal cords. But I didn't think the transformation was to blame. At least, not entirely.

"Get back in the bedroom until we deal with this!" Marco ordered, as soon as I came out of the hall.

I didn't answer, being too busy staring at the huge, gaping hole that had opened up in the far wall. The one with the fiery red edges and the disturbing sounds and the swirly black heart and the wind strong enough to flutter my hair. It looked like Casanova had been right, I thought blankly.

You knew it when you saw it.

"Cassie!" Marco snapped. "Get out of here!

"I can't."

"Why not?" he demanded.

"Because . . . I think that's for me."

He looked at me incredulously. "What?"

"I kind of have an appointment."

"With who? Lucifer?"

"Hope not," I muttered, and took a single step forward.

And stopped. Because, for the first time ever, I saw Marco do the unthinkable. And throw one of his highly illegal and ridiculously expensive Cohiba cigars in the trash.

"Get back. In the bedroom. Now."

I stood there for a second, debating. But not because I was intimidated. The worst Marco would do was to throw me over a burly shoulder and cart me off. And considering the state of my dignity these days, I didn't think another hit was going to matter.

"Is it always like this around here?" The Valkyrie had come out of the lounge, and was standing in front of the sliding doors, hands on her hips. And looking at the hell-mouth with disbelief.

"Pretty much," one of the vamps said lazily.

"Damn it, Cassie!" Marco looked pissed.

"We've talked about this," I reminded him. "You're not my jailer."

"Well, someone damned well should be!" he shot back, black hair whipping in the wind. "Running around all over creation, battling demons, *what you did to Jules*, and now *this*—"

"Battling demons?" I blinked, because I hadn't thought he knew about that.

It seemed absurd, like of course he would. But he hadn't mentioned it, and not even Marco was that tight-lipped. And this was Dante's, where loud, supernatural-themed shows took place every day. And that one had lasted all of what? Five or six minutes?

I wasn't sure, but I didn't think it could have been longer than that. And yeah, there had been a ton of witnesses, but those were either clueless tourists or guards under Casanova's control. Like the security cameras . . .

"You didn't know about that," I said, watching him.

"Bullshit. Everyone knew—"

"You *didn't*. Not half an hour ago."

Marco didn't say anything, but his face was enough. Because he was no more a diplomat than Jules. Mircea didn't send diplomats to me; they'd just be wasted anyway.

He sent tanks.

"How did you find out?" I demanded.

Marco crossed massive arms and tried staring me down. "I told you. Mircea knows what goes on around here—"

"Mircea? He called you?"

"That's not the—"

"When?"

"A few minutes ago, and we're not—"

"Mircea called you . . . and not me?" I asked, wanting to be sure.

"Maybe he thought he'd get further with me!"

Yeah, or maybe he was avoiding me.

And suddenly, it hit me like a ton of bricks. Mircea *was* avoiding me. I'd been so busy doing the same thing to him, I hadn't noticed. But of course he was.

He was busy, but he was also a first-level master. He could go without sleep for days if he needed to. There was a cost in power, sure, but he had it to burn. If he'd wanted to talk to me, he'd have talked to me. For as long as he liked and about whatever he wanted, and I doubted that my attempts at evasion would have worked for a second.

But they had.

"He's avoiding me, isn't he?" I asked Marco, in disbelief.

"Stop it! Stop it right now!" the Valkyrie demanded. We looked at her. She pointed at the portal. *"What the hell is that?"*

"Yes," Jonas said, coming up behind her. And regarding the hellmouth over his spectacles.

I looked back at Marco. "Tell me the truth. What's going on? Why doesn't he want to see me?"

Marco looked around, like he expected somebody to offer up a suggestion. But the vamps were clearly all suggestioned out. A couple of them were trying to talk Jules into going back down the hall, but hysteria feeds hysteria, and it didn't look like they were having much luck. A lot more were over by the bar, clearly feeling that tonight went into the above-and-beyond category and they'd had enough. And the rest—Jonas, the witches and the girl—were staring at the hellmouth, which had started spinning fast enough to flip the pages of a magazine on the coffee table.

Marco didn't find any help.

"Marco—"

"I don't know, all right?" he told me, exasperated. "I don't even know if he is."

"Did he ask to talk to me?"

"No. I—"

"Did you tell him I was unconscious or something?"

"No, he—"

"That I was in the shower?"

"No! Damn it, he didn't—" Marco stopped suddenly.

"He didn't what? He didn't *ask*?"

Marco just looked at me.

I stared back. "He called you up, informed you that I'd been seen battling demons on the drag, asked about the master vamp I just deprived him of, *and then he hung up*?"

"You need to ask him about this," he pointed out.

"How can I when he won't talk to me?"

Marco started to answer, but then Jules let out an especially shrill shriek. Maybe because the portal had started whirling around at something approaching warp speed. And unless I was mistaken, it was also getting smaller.

"Would somebody shut him the hell up?" Marco snarled.

But Jules didn't seem to like that idea. Jules appeared to have had about enough of us and our ideas. He gave another shriek and dove through the middle of his buddies, careened into some others, spun out of their hold like a football player heading for the goal line, and then ran all out for the door.

Marco went after him, but changed course halfway and lunged at me instead. Because I'd taken what was likely to be my only shot and dove for the rapidly closing portal. But then a second impossible thing happened, when the huge-but-graceful Marco suddenly tripped and went sprawling on the carpet, hitting down hard enough to rattle the windows and shake all the glasses in the bar.

I had a second to see what's-her-name, the initiate I'd spoken all of a few dozen words to, with her leg out. And judging by the angle, it hadn't been an accident. I looked at her and she looked at me, big-eyed and faintly horrified. And then I was through the flames and gone.

Chapter Twenty-seven

"Do you know who your mother *was*?" Pritkin demanded, scowling.

I scowled back, but not because of the attitude. I'd expected that. Actually, that was a lie. I'd expected worse.

He'd been bad enough when surprised and under fire at his father's court, or fighting for his life against the council's guards. But now he'd had time to *think* about it. And, apparently, to work up a massive attitude.

I seemed to have that effect on the men in my life, I thought darkly, and took another sip of something horrible.

We were in a bar in the hell known as the Shadowland, because the demon council didn't have anything like a normal jail. They had distant worlds where they marooned what they called the "Ancient Horrors," creatures I wasn't interested in knowing more about, thank you. And then, on the other end of the spectrum, they had . . . nothing.

I guess most people who pissed off the council didn't live long enough to need a holding cell.

But that meant, instead of visiting Pritkin in some dark, dank cell, I was visiting him in some dark, dank bar. On the whole, I'd have preferred the cell. I was sitting cross-legged in my chair to avoid the floor, which had passed nasty a year ago and was working on horrific.

Something squelched between my toes anyway, something I'd managed to step in on the way to the table.

I was trying not to think about what exactly it might be. I was trying hard.

"Bartender!" Casanova called hoarsely, and tried to snap his fingers. But he missed, and then kept on missing, frowning at his long, usually elegant digits as if he couldn't figure out what was wrong with them.

Unfortunately, the summons had included everyone who had trespassed on the council's good graces, i.e., had released a bunch of their former slaves into the ether. That included me and Caleb, as well as Pritkin. Along with one very sorry excuse for a casino manager, who was close to sliding under the table.

"Don't you think you've had enough?" I asked, even as the shambling hulk of a bartender set another bottle down on the sticky tabletop.

Casanova sent me a helpful gesture that indicated that, no, he did not feel that way.

I didn't return it, because I was busy trying not to be obvious about flinching away from the bartender. He had suspicious stains on his apron, and smelled like a slaughterhouse looks. He also kept squeezing Casanova's shoulder whenever he came over, as if trying to gauge how much meat was under the expensive material. It normally would have skeeved me out, but after today, I was all out of skeeve. And Casanova was too drunk to notice.

"Did you hear me?" Pritkin demanded.

I clutched my glass and resisted a strong urge to throw it at him. "Do I know who my mother is? Yes, yes, I do, Pritkin, thanks."

"I doubt that." He crossed his arms and leaned back in his seat.

"And you do, I suppose?"

"I've had a good deal of free time lately," he said grimly. "I used it to do some research. And let's just say, she is not remembered in the hells quite the same way as on earth."

"Is this relevant?" Caleb rumbled. "We got bigger problems, John."

He pointedly didn't look at the Rubik's cube of a city beyond the bar's dirty windows. I didn't, either, since I was facing directly away from it, but it was like the elephant in the room. It made its presence felt.

Behind my back, buildings folded up onto buildings, streets became avenues, became trails, became dead ends, cars appeared and disappeared, trees and planters and mailboxes strutted and fretted their brief moment upon the stage and then, poof, were replaced by a parking lot. And the light constantly changed, as lamps and streetlights and lit billboards winked in and out of existence, each flip, flip, flip of the scene causing the shadows in here to move and shift, like a club with a lousy DJ.

It was giving my migraine a migraine, which was ironic.

Since that was exactly what it had been designed not to do.

The spell that masked whatever the real city looked like had been intended to be comfortable, even homey. It was supposed to make the place look like your hometown, or at least an area you'd be familiar with, which I supposed made sense for a place that served as a giant crossroads for the hells. No one look was going to work for everyone, when "everyone" was a thousand different species with totally different senses. So the Shadowland's proprietors had said screw it and just given everybody what they wanted.

Or they'd tried. It never worked quite as planned, since it didn't cover the people, most of whom would have gotten a double take even on the Vegas Strip. But it also didn't normally look like the origami creation of a possibly insane artist.

But then, it didn't usually have a pissed-off demon lord messing with it, either.

At least, that's why I assumed that the street outside, which was supposed to lead to the council building, had suddenly acquired a severe case of ADHD. Rosier was clearly intent on me not being allowed to make my case. And so far, he was doing a damned fine job.

My power worked, to a limited degree, in the Shadowland, at least when I wasn't exhausted. But I couldn't shift when I didn't know where I was going. And when the road was changing even as I looked at it. And while dragging along a guy who apparently didn't want to go anyway.

"Yes, it's relevant!" Pritkin said. "I am trying to make Cassie understand why she needs to drop this and go home!"

"I'll be happy to," I told him evenly. "After we see the council—"

"We don't need the council—"

"We do when you can't go back to earth without them!"

"I'm not going back to earth." It sounded final.

Like hell it was final.

"I didn't come all this way, go through all that"—I waved an arm wildly, because I didn't have words for the last week—"just to go home without you!"

"Well, get used to the idea," Pritkin said curtly, and sloshed some more hell juice into his glass.

"What is this stuff?" Caleb asked, looking at his drink suspiciously. He had yet to touch it.

"Local specialty. They ferment it from berries that grow in the hills," Pritkin said curtly, knocking back the majority of his.

"Is it strong?"

Pritkin shrugged.

"If it gets a vamp drunk, it's strong," I warned.

Caleb raised an eyebrow and glanced at Casanova. But it was hard to tell if the vamp was actually sloshed or just overwrought. He'd been crying into his not-even-close-to-beer since we got here.

I guess Caleb must have decided he was just being his usual overly dramatic self, and took a healthy swig. And somehow kept it down. But under all that dirt, he turned about as white as a black guy can.

"Pritkin told me once that alcohol doesn't affect him much—something about what he was raised on," I told Caleb.

Caleb glared at his buddy. "What the fuck were you raised on?"

Pritkin held up his glass. "This."

"Figures," Caleb wheezed, and frantically gestured the bartender over to order some water.

I went back to glaring at Pritkin.

It was vaguely satisfying in a way I couldn't immediately define. Maybe because it was the only normal thing in my life right now. I glared at Pritkin all the time. It was what I did. I decided to do it up right and put some oomph behind it.

"You can look at me that way all you like. It doesn't change the facts," he snapped.

"And what facts are those?"

"That getting to the council, even assuming we could manage it, won't help. They hate me—"

"I bet they hate the gods more!"

"And that would be the point," he said viciously, and gulped the equivalent of paint thinner.

"Okay," I said, reaching tilt. "Okay. I've had kind of a bad week, and I'm not much for hints right now. So why don't you just cut to the chase, and tell me what is wrong with you? Do you *want* to go back to Rosier's? Do you want to sit around and wait for some assassin to get lucky? Or your dad to whore you out to the highest bidder? Is that really so much more appealing than coming back to earth with me and, I don't know, having a goddamned life? Well, *is it*?"

Something squelched between my toes again, and I

belatedly realized that I was on my feet and halfway across the table, and what I was doing couldn't really be called glaring anymore. If he'd had a shirt on, I'd have had my fists in it. As it was, they were flat on the table and I was about an inch from his nose and if looks could kill, we'd both be dead.

"Oh, sure," Casanova slurred. "I has how it starts. But then you give them the bes' centuries of your life, and wha' happens? They lie to you and stab you in the back and . . . and . . ." He seemed to lose his train of thought, assuming he'd ever had one to start with. He trailed off.

And Pritkin slapped the table, hard enough to make all the glasses jump. "This isn't about what I want," he told me fiercely. "It's never been about that!"

"Then what is it? Because you're not making sense!" I'd hoped that, once we got this far, I'd have an ally. Instead, I was having to fight both him and his father. And it sucked!

By the look of him, Caleb didn't get it, either. "If you got something to say, say it," he told him. "Then we need to figure out how to get you out of here."

"I'm not getting out. You are," Pritkin said, and there was a note in his voice this time, a note of fierce jealousy and hopeless longing. And damn it! Whatever he said, he did not want to go back there.

"Why?" I demanded.

Pritkin sloshed some more rotgut-and-everything-else in his glass and sat back. "Do you remember your mother's nickname on earth?"

"What?"

"Answer the question!"

"The Huntress," Caleb rumbled.

Pritkin glanced at him. "Yes. Care to guess what she hunted?"

I sat back down.

"There's a reason that the 'gods,' as they're known, liked earth," he told me. "Even though they couldn't feed there."

I didn't say anything. We were about to face the demon council, assuming we could find it, possibly about to be shivved in the back by one of our fellow patrons, and almost certainly being poisoned by the damned bartender. But Pritkin had dropped into lecture mode, and he didn't do that for no reason.

"Like what?" I asked, crossing my arms and sitting back against the sticky seat.

"Earth in the Scandinavian legends was known as Midgard, or Mittlegard in Old English," he told me. "It's where Tolkien got his idea for 'Middle Earth'; it's almost an exact translation. The Vikings called it that because of its position in the middle of their map of the cosmos, halfway between the heavens and the hells."

"Yes, so?"

"Have you read the sagas?" he demanded.

"They're on my list." Along with about a thousand other things.

"Well, if you had, you would know that they tell the story of beings, the 'gods,' who originated somewhere in the dimension known as the heavens. But like the Vikings, they became restless and went exploring. Among other worlds, they discovered Faerie, known as Alfheim, or the 'land of the elves,' to the Norse. It was fairly unremarkable, except for one thing: it was closer to the divide between dimensions than any other world they had encountered. And as such, it had connections that none of the others did—connections to a completely new universe the so-called gods knew nothing about."

"Faerie connects to earth," I said, wondering where he was going with this.

"Yes. Earth is the counterpart to Faerie on this side of the dimensional rift. And just as Faerie had connections to the rest of the heavens—"

"Earth has connections to the rest of the hells," Caleb murmured, looking like something had just clicked into place for him.

Well, that made one of us.

"Earth is technically in the hell dimension," Pritkin agreed. "But as the closest world to our side of the rift, it shares aspects of both dimensions, as does Faerie on the heavenly side. Together, they form a bridge—the only one known, and likely the only one that exists—between the two universes."

"The bifrost bridge," Caleb said softly.

Pritkin nodded. "The old legends—Greek as well as Norse—speak of a rainbow bridge allowing the gods to travel back and forth from earth to their home world. Presumably, they were referring to the ley lines running from here into Faerie, and the portals cut through them."

Caleb just sat there, looking stunned. And making me feel even dumber than usual, because I didn't see what difference any of this made. "So? We knew they came from somewhere else," I pointed out. "All the legends talk of them going back home, to Asgard or Olympus or wherever, on a regular basis. This isn't news."

"Then perhaps this is," Pritkin said, leaning forward. "The gods stayed on earth, even though they could not feed there. Why? Why was it so important to them? Why were they so enraged when your mother found a way to banish them? Why have they been working so hard, and for millennia, in order to get back?"

I frowned at him. Now that he put it like that, it didn't seem to make a lot of sense. "I don't know. Maybe they liked being worshipped?"

"Enough for everything we've seen them do? Enough to risk dying, for nothing more than an ego stroke, and from a people they treated as little better than animals?" He shook his head. "No."

"Okay, then, what's your theory?"

"It's not a theory. I've spent months on this, and it wasn't easy. The only beings who had the information I wanted were not keen to discuss the subject. But I managed to get a hint here, some confirmation there, and then another piece from—"

"Pritkin! Just tell me."

Green eyes met mine. "The gods weren't interested in earth for its own sake. They wanted it for its role as a . . . a watering hole . . . if you like, for their real prey."

"What prey?" I asked, starting to get a really bad feeling about this.

"The gods can't feed off human energy, not because they can't process it, but because it is so weak it does almost nothing for them. Your mother could have drained a city and been very little the better for it. But there were creatures on this side of the divide who lived far longer, gained energy much better, and stored it up far more efficiently—"

"Cows!" Casanova said, waving his glass. "Ever'body's jus' somebody's cow."

I frowned at him, not least because he'd just splattered hell juice all over my arm. But Pritkin nodded. "It's not a bad analogy."

"That we're *cows*?" I demanded, vainly looking around for something to mop up with.

But everything in here was already dirtier than I was.

"No, we're grass," Pritkin said. "The demons are the cows." He saw my expression. "Think of it this way, Cassie. Humans can eat grass, correct?"

"Yeah, I guess. Technically."

"But nobody does. Why is that?"

"I don't know . . . because it's *grass*."

"It's lacking in nutrition, in calories, in all the things we need for life, yes?"

I nodded.

"A human would starve on a diet of grass. But a cow . . . a cow does quite well on it. Gets fat, even. And then, if a human eats the cow—"

"Okay, wait," I said, my head spinning. "You're telling me . . . that the gods came to earth, found a bunch of fat demons chewing up all the human grass, and decided to have a barbecue?"

He nodded. "Something like that. Remember, demons live much longer lives than humans, and have the capacity to store up a great deal more energy. In some cases, from thousands of feedings over hundreds of years. And not merely from earth. But from all their home worlds, as well."

"But their home worlds don't yield as much," I said, recalling something Rian had said.

"No. Which is why earth was so prized when my father's people, and others, stumbled across it long before the gods ever did. And then started coming in droves, to feed off the humans who couldn't detect them and had virtually no defenses against them."

"But someone's always higher on the food chain," Caleb said, with a certain grim satisfaction.

Pritkin nodded. "And when the gods discovered the demons, they felt toward them the way the demons had felt toward the human population. Here was a huge source of energy, ripe for the plucking, who had almost no defenses against them. Yes, they could buck and kick a little, but does that stop a lion from taking down a gazelle? And only the greatest of them could even manage that much of a response."

"Then why didn't the demons just stop coming?" I demanded. "Once they knew the gods were here—"

"Do gazelles stop coming to the watering hole?" he shot back. "Even though they know the lions come there, too?"

"Yeah, but that's water. That's a necessity."

"As is energy in a world where power rules. Why do you think Rian betrayed Casanova? She's known him for centuries. They have a bond—"

Casanova huffed out a bitter laugh.

"It's true," Pritkin insisted. "You gave her a great gift. The greatest you can give a demon. You gave her power, more than any other host she could possibly have found. And power can give her . . . everything else."

"So she sold me out for power," Casanova said bitterly. "I suppose she thought a vampire would understand that."

"She sold you out for life," Pritkin said sharply. "Which

she might otherwise have lost in one of the power struggles that are epidemic at court—at *every* court. Rian was young and weak when she came to earth. Now, after gorging for centuries on as much energy as she could absorb, she goes home, not as a pawn to be used and possibly sacrificed to someone else's ambition, but as a power broker in her own right."

Casanova blinked at him, looking as thoughtful as a guy with that much hell juice in him could. But I just stared at the tabletop, where the flickering light turned the dust that had gathered in the sticky bits into a topographical map. A map of a universe that was suddenly far larger than I'd ever imagined.

"And at the time we're discussing, power was even more important than it is now," Pritkin added. "The ancient wars were ongoing, with the few demon races who stumbled across earth losing badly before its discovery. The power they gained from it helped renew their resources, gave them a fighting chance in battles on a scale humans can't imagine, battles that lasted hundreds of years and spread across countless worlds, battles that, if they had been lost, might have resulted in the destruction of their entire species. So yes, they came, no matter the risk. And the gods knew that they would."

There was silence at the table for a moment, as everyone struggled to grasp that. I didn't know how the rest of them felt, but I wasn't doing so hot. Pritkin was right; I couldn't imagine war on that scale. I couldn't imagine something else, either.

"I still don't see what this has to do with my mother, or with you," I said, after a moment.

"Artemis the Huntress," Caleb murmured, his eyes suddenly widening. As if maybe he did.

"Yes," Pritkin confirmed. "She was the most feared of the gods by demonkind. The most respected, and the most hated."

"Why? You said all the gods hunted demons!" I said hotly.

"Yes, but she didn't merely wait at the watering hole for them to come to her," Pritkin said quietly. "She could open the gates between worlds, a talent that allowed her to take the offensive far more easily than the rest of her kind."

"She hunted them here," Caleb said, as if he didn't quite believe it. "She hunted them in their own worlds."

"No," I said, but Pritkin was nodding.

"Every source I've managed to find says the same thing. She tore a bloody swath through a hundred worlds. Cassie—" He held up a hand, when I started to protest again. "I'm sorry, but it's true. You must have seen the souk in Zarr Alim?"

"Zarr Alim?"

"My father's capital city."

I nodded, confused and angry.

"Well, if you'd had time to look around, you might have come across small amulets being sold by old women in the marketplace, amulets with a familiar face on them. They are still used as wards against bad fortune by the local inhabitants, even though no one really remembers why anymore. Just that once, long ago, their ancestors wanted protection from the face on those coins."

"And what a pretty face it was, too," someone said as a hand stroked down the side of my hair before abruptly clenching in it.

A very familiar hand.

And *fuck*.

Chapter Twenty-eight

"Release her!" Caleb jumped to his feet and threw out a hand—and a spell. Which ricocheted off the demon lord at my side and exploded against the ceiling, leaving a big black mark among the dirt and smoke stains. None of the bar's regulars so much as flinched, except for the bartender, who hurried over with a bow and another glass.

Pritkin didn't react, except to pour another drink, so I didn't, either. We both knew Rosier couldn't hurt me. He'd sworn a vow, which apparently would kill him if he broke it, not to take my life.

Unfortunately, it hadn't said anything about not plaguing my existence.

"Sit, sit," Rosier told Caleb genially, who was looking in confusion from Pritkin to his father, maybe because he'd finally noticed that my assailant and his friend could have been twins.

I guess he'd kind of been too busy before.

Well, except that one twin had never had a chance to clean up after his joyride out of hell. As a result, Pritkin's bare chest was streaked with dirt, his hair shed little puffs of dust if he moved too fast, and he hadn't lost his shoes only because he hadn't had any on to begin with.

He had found some jeans somewhere to replace the ridiculous silky pants, but that was about the only improvement.

Rosier, in contrast, was wearing a plain dark gray suit, but the cut would have made Armani weep with envy. His shoes were polished to a high shine. His casual silk shirt was forest green, his son's favorite color.

Or maybe it was his, too, although probably not for the same reason.

At a guess, Pritkin liked it because it had reminded him of home while he was stuck in the middle of the desert. Rosier probably chose it deliberately, to bring out the vivid color of his eyes. The ones that were so much like his son's. The ones that were smiling at me as he took a seat.

I had to sit on my hands so I wouldn't try anything fun—like clawing them out.

"Don't stop there," Rosier said, glancing at Pritkin. "Tell her the rest."

Pritkin ignored him. Caleb remained standing, body tense and ready. The only one who moved was Casanova, slowly sliding under the table.

"Very well. I shall, then, yes?" Rosier glanced around at us, white teeth bared. "Let us see. I believe Emrys covered the part about—"

"His name is Pritkin," I said harshly, cutting the bastard off.

"That's even worse than the terrible 'John,'" Rosier reproached. "In any case, Emrys is a human name."

"But he doesn't *like* it."

More big white teeth. "In life, my dear, there is much we do not like but have to accept. It is part of growing up. Something *Emrys* is long overdue to learn."

I glared at him. He grinned back. The kind of reckless, insouciant grin I would have thought Pritkin incapable of, before I saw him windsurfing a rug through hell. "You really don't favor your mother, do you?" Rosier asked, searching my face. "Pity." He leaned back and a lit cigarette appeared in his hand. "Now, there was a beautiful woman."

"Too bad she thought of you as cattle," I snapped.

Rosier didn't look perturbed. "Yes, no doubt. And that is part of your problem, isn't it?"

I debated not answering, but I needed to know what he meant. I needed to know why Pritkin was just sitting there drinking, instead of yelling or conniving or . . . or doing *something* to try to get out of this mess. I needed to know why he looked like we'd already failed.

"What is?" I finally asked.

"You haven't put it together yet?" Rosier sighed out some smoke. "But then, you always were a little slow, weren't you?"

"Then make it simple," I grated out, wishing I had something, anything, that would work on this son of a bitch. But it's a little hard to age someone out of existence when that existence is measured in millennia.

"Very well," he said, suddenly brisk. "The so-called gods might have fed off us, but it seems they weren't much kinder to their human bait. Except for your mother, who decided that they were destroying the creatures to which she'd foolishly allowed herself to become attached. Or so she said." He let out a sigh and looked at me through the haze of smoke. "I've always found that excuse to be rather . . . paltry . . . for someone decidedly not steeped in sentiment."

I glared at him. "So? What does any of this have to do with—"

"Think about it, girl, assuming you have the capacity! She wants to protect her beloved humans, she determines that her fellow gods must go, and her gift—which was rather stronger than your little version, by the way—would allow her to banish them and slam the gates shut behind them. The trick, of course, was ensuring that they did not return."

"She used a spell," I said, wondering why my stomach had just dropped.

"Yes, a spell. Which she had to cast herself, and then maintain until her little Silver Band or what have you could grow strong enough to do it themselves. And there was sure to be opposition, sure to be a mass of forces battering the other side. By denying her fellow gods the free run of earth, she was also denying them their only way into the hells. No more fat . . . cows, was it? No more free meals. Without earth, they were restricted to the heavens, and if that wasn't enough, she cut them off from Faerie, as well! I suppose she had to; better to block the whole bridge than half, and she had so many faithful worshippers among the fey. . . ."

Rosier paused, but I didn't say anything this time. Because he was right—sometimes I didn't pick up on things as fast as Pritkin or Caleb. Sometimes this crazy new world I'd somehow stumbled into made my head hurt trying to comprehend it. Sometimes I'd bitched about wishing I had an instruction book, something to lay it all out, to make it simple.

Right now I was kind of glad I didn't.

Because right now my brain was coming up with answers I didn't like.

"Starting to make sense?" Rosier asked evilly. "A huge spell, a god-denying spell, and not just around one world, but encircling two. And then to hold it, against all comers? To reinforce it as needed, until the weak, pathetic humans could take over? Where did she get that kind of power, hmm? She was strong, yes, but not that strong! Not anything close. *So where do you think it came from?*"

I looked at Pritkin, but his eyes were on his father. He hadn't said anything, but one hand was flexing slightly. I didn't like that. I liked Pritkin loud and bitching, in other words, his normal state. I didn't like it when he got quiet.

Nobody else usually did, either.

"Where?" Rosier asked, and his hand hit the table, hard enough to make me flinch. "You can't be that dim-witted!"

"She hunted demons for it," I said, because he was right; it was obvious.

"Yes" came out as a hiss. "But not just any demons. She'd always gone after big prey in any case, preferring a challenge. Why should this be any different? And, really, small fry wouldn't help her. She needed so much power, only the biggest, juiciest prey would do. She hunted, oh yes—Artemis the huntress, Hel with her fiery hunting dogs, Diana with her bow! She hunted in whatever name they call her, whatever confused, tortured, muddled memory they have, the people in my world, in yours, across hundreds more, they may have forgotten much, but they remember that yes, she *hunted*."

There was no pretense of amiability now, no calm demeanor, no mask. Rosier was on his feet, backing me into the wall, the face that was usually so like his son's suddenly alien as it twisted in pain, in fury.

"Through thousands of years, across hundreds of generations, even your people could not forget the vague but persistent memory of the greatest hunt of them all! It's in your statues, on your vases, in virtually every depiction of her ever made. The memory of the methodical, the tactical, the relentless butchering—"

"No!"

"Yes! The *butchering* of the greatest among us. The Great Reaping of the demon lords." My back hit the wall, but he didn't stop coming. "Just where, my dear, do you suppose my father went? Why am I Lord of the Incubi, and not him? Did you never wonder what became of him? Never crossed your mind? No?"

I shook my head. This couldn't be true. Couldn't be. The demons . . . they could be terrifying, but they weren't . . . they couldn't have deserved . . . it wasn't true.

"She killed him on a whim. Happened across him one day when she was raiding elsewhere and followed him home. Might not have bothered to venture into our world otherwise, as her daughter would so recklessly and thoughtlessly do, for we incubi, we're not worth the effort. But when he fled for his life, in mortal peril, the instinct of the hunter—"

"I don't believe you! Why should I believe you?"

"You don't need to take my word for it. You wish to have your day in court? Please. Feel free. Go plead your case in front of the survivors of your mother's massacre, and see how far you get! But this one," Rosier said, grabbing the shoulder of the son who still hadn't moved. "The one you took from me, as your mother took my sire—no. No, little child of Artemis, no. Him you do not take!"

And suddenly, something came over me at the sight of Rosier's hand clenching on Pritkin, of his fingers digging into his flesh. Something wild and strange and unexpected. Something I didn't understand except as a trickle of that dark emotion I'd felt on seeing Pritkin again, trapped and coddled at his father's court, dressed in finery he had no use for, surrounded by sleek, sterile perfection instead of his usual cheerful mess, with none of the things he loved in sight, no potions, no books, no crazy weapons for fighting the creatures that were his jailers now.

Just a man lost and bitter and alone, in a world he hated. A man surrounded by the jealousies of a court who would happily see him dead. A man who was suffering for one reason, and one reason only.

Because he had dared to help me.

And suddenly, the trickle became a flood.

"I will *take him*," I said, knocking Rosier's hand away, "anywhere I damned well please, *demon*!"

"Ah, there it is," he hissed. "*There it is!* The arrogance of the goddess. Unfortunately, you are not your mother, girl. You do not have the power to back it up. You don't have the power to do *anything*. Why you're not dead yet, I will never understand, but I have the strong suspicion that it has a great deal to do with bewitching my son.

Somehow." He looked utterly baffled. "Somehow you managed to tie him to you, to drag him into your fights, to endanger his life again and again. But no more!"

"That's for the council to decide."

"It's not their concern!" Rosier snapped, and pulled on his son's arm. "Any more than it is yours. Come, Emrys."

Pritkin didn't move.

His father made a disgusted sound. "You know how this will end!"

"He doesn't know!" I said. "None of us do, until the council rules. And my mother said—"

"Your mother hasn't seen the council in thousands of years! She doesn't know anything about it! She was lying to you, girl, probably to get you to stop plaguing her life!"

I flinched, because I'd had a similar thought myself. But I didn't really believe it. And even if it was true, it wouldn't change anything.

What other choice did we have?

"I don't know what will happen if we go in front of the council," I told Pritkin honestly. "But I know what will happen if you go back there, back to that life. And so do you."

He didn't look at me—it was almost like he didn't even hear me—and Rosier smiled.

"Yes, he knows. He'll be the prince of a great house. You would have him a pauper. He'll rule a large court, and have influence in countless others. You would have him a servant, running your errands, cleaning up your endless debacles! I will give him a vast kingdom—what would you give him?"

I looked up, so angry I could hardly see. "His freedom!"

Rosier snorted out a laugh. "That hoary platitude. Sometimes I forget what a child you are."

"It isn't childish to want to choose your own life!"

"No, it's criminally naive. The only free person is the beggar in the gutter. And he's only free to be cuffed about by his betters. Everyone of any substance has obligations. It is time for Emrys to live up to his."

He pulled on his son's arm again, and this time, it worked. Pritkin got up. And I grabbed his other arm in both of mine, because this wasn't happening.

"Pritkin, *please*. Mother wouldn't have sent me here if she didn't think there was a chance!"

Nothing.

"Why won't you play for that chance?" I said, my voice rising in panic because I didn't understand this. I didn't understand any of this!

"You're better off if I don't," he told me, lifting his head.

"What?" I asked incredulously. Because he looked like he meant it.

"Finally, he comes to his senses," Rosier said, pulling his son away, only to have Caleb step in front of him. "Have a care, war mage! I have taken no oath to spare you!"

"Right back at you," Caleb said, eyes steady and feet planted.

"You're as foolhardy as she is," Rosier snapped. And then kept on talking, which he liked to do as much as his son didn't. But I wasn't listening.

"How can you say that?" I asked Pritkin. "How can you just give up?"

"I'm not giving up. I'm accepting reality."

"What reality? You *don't* want to go back there! And I need you—"

"You don't, as you've made clear these past few days. If you can break into my father's court, fight off the council's own guards, force a meeting . . ." He ran a hand through his hair. "You'll be all right, Cassie."

"No! I won't be! I need you—"

"Why? What can I give you that others can't?"

"What?"

Green eyes suddenly burned into mine. "It's a simple question. You said you need me. Why?"

"I—I told you. This job—"

"Which you're handling admirably."

"I am not! I couldn't even get to my parents without help!"

"There are other demon experts—Jonas for one."

"But I need you!"

And all of a sudden, Pritkin was backing me around the table. Not like his father had done, in a rush of anger, but slowly, relentlessly. To the point that I kept tripping over chairs.

"Then give me a reason."

"I . . . there's so many—"

"Name one."

"I can name a hundred—"

"I didn't ask for a hundred; I asked for one. And you can't give it to me."

"Yes, I can!"

"Then do it!"

"I . . ." I stared at him, because he looked like there was a lot riding on my answer. Maybe everything. And I didn't know what he wanted to hear, because I'd told him the truth. There were literally so many things that I didn't know where to start. How could he not see all the ways he'd changed my life? How could he not know—

But he didn't. It was in the way he turned his head away, when I just stood there. In the way he closed his eyes. In the small, self-mocking smile that played around his lips that I didn't understand but knew couldn't be good.

I had to say something, and it had to be the right thing, and I didn't know—

Pritkin's eyes opened, but I couldn't read his expression. For once, the face that was usually flowing with a thousand emotions was . . . blank. Resigned. He was already distancing himself, already leaving me in every way that mattered, before his body ever walked out that door.

And I didn't know what to do about it.

"You're right," I told him desperately. "I can get others to do what you do. They won't be as good, but . . . okay. It could work. But it doesn't matter because no matter how good they are, they can't replace you. They can't because I don't need you only for what you can do. I need you . . . for you."

I'd learned that the hard way, all week. I hadn't realized how much I'd relied on his scowls or his shrugs or his grudging looks of approval to help me figure something out—until they weren't there anymore. Or how I could talk to some people about a lot of things, but only to him about everything.

And how unbelievably valuable that was.

I stared into his eyes, wondering how to get through. I sucked at emotional stuff; I always had. It was easier to make a joke or some stupid quip than to try to put into words emotions I was never supposed to have. Emotions that were dangerous to have, because they left you vulnerable and I'd learned early that vulnerability was a *very bad thing*.

When I'd heard that my governess had been murdered by Tony, I hadn't cried. It had felt like someone had twisted a knife in my gut, but I still hadn't, because I knew she'd hate it. Knew she'd view it as weakness. "Tears are useless," she'd told me a hundred times. "Don't cry; act!"

And I'd tried. I'd tried. Because mostly I agreed with her. But now I didn't know what actions would help, and I didn't have the words.

I didn't have anything.

"You called me admirable," I told him miserably. "But I'm not. I mess up all the time, and not all of them are things I know how to fix. The Pythia is supposed to have all this power, but there's *plenty* I can't fix! And some days, most days lately, I just feel like . . . like I'm going to explode. And there's nobody around to tell me I'm being stupid or to bring me terrible coffee or to make me run a marathon until I'm too tired to worry about it anymore. Or just to *listen*—"

"To your unending babble?" Rosier snarled, turning away from Caleb. "If you want a confidant, buy a diary! My son is meant for better things!"

I met Pritkin's eyes. "Yes. You are. But you asked. And I don't know how to say it right; I don't know what you want. I just know I need you, I need *you*, I can't do this without you—" I was crying now, as I hadn't for Eugenie, as I hadn't for myself. But I couldn't help it because I was screwing this up, I was getting this all wrong, and he was going to leave—

"Oh, spare us," Rosier said, sounding disgusted, but I barely heard him. All I could see was Pritkin's face. All I could think was that this might be the last time I ever saw it.

And that was enough to do what an army of demons hadn't, and send me into a full-blown panic. "You can't go! You can't!"

Hard hands tightened over mine. "Cassie—"

"Just try. You just have to *try*."

"It isn't that simple. Even if—" He stopped.

"Even if *what*?"

"Cassie, the council . . . it isn't like a human court, with rules and procedures and some semblance of justice. They are arbitrary and capricious at best, and at worst . . . they're the definition of chaos."

I blinked at him. Because I'd heard that word before. "Mother said chaos is like jumping off a cliff, not knowing what's at the bottom," I told him. "But she didn't seem to think that was so bad. I didn't understand what she meant then, but I think . . . maybe I do now. Sometimes there are no guarantees. Sometimes, if you want something badly enough, you just have to *jump*."

Pritkin still didn't move, but something shifted in his face as he looked at me. I wasn't sure what it was, but his father didn't seem to like it. At all.

"Fine," Rosier said flatly. "We'll do this the hard way."

Chapter Twenty-nine

The hard way turned out to be pretty damned hard.

"Shit!" Caleb cursed as the door blew open and the bar was swarmed by a mass of familiar blue-robed guards. Who looked like they remembered us, too. And no way could the two of us take on that many.

But then Pritkin grabbed Rosier and threw him into the first wave. Who staggered back into a table full of the locals, sending mugs and arcs of hell juice flying. And knocking a bunch of dusty, gray-garbed patrons to the floor.

That didn't seem to bother the guards too much, who were busy thrashing back to their feet, more than one of them drawing those damned curved blades. Until a gnarly, lumpy, gray-green limb, less like a hand than a proboscis, snaked out from under one of the patrons' cloaks. And crumpled the nearest sword like tinfoil.

And okay, that works, I thought, right before guards and furniture started flying.

I had to hit the disgusting floor to avoid a chair, which splintered against the wall behind me in a hail of bits. But by then I was under the table, grabbing Casanova and the bottle he was still holding. "Give me that!"

"Getcherown," he slurred, and grabbed it back. And blinked around blearily, before focusing on the veiled guard who had just dove after me. Only Casanova apparently thought he was also after his precious hell juice.

So he bonked him on the head with it.

"Was' goin' on?" he demanded as the guard slumped over, leaving us with a view of struggling legs and flashing blades. And a gray-green fleshy lump that appeared to be eating a chair.

"Bar fight!"

"Oh. I haven't been in one of those in—" A curved sword cleaved the table clean in two. "And now I 'member why."

We scrambled back as the sides fell away, leaving us staring at a massive blue-robed warrior, his blade sheened with black blood. I stared at him and he stared back, and underneath the veil he wore, I saw him smile. Because we didn't have any weapons and Caleb and Pritkin had been jumped by half a platoon and the closest cover was a pillar a few yards behind him, which might as well have been on another *planet*—

And then the sword was slashing down and there was no time to scream, no time for anything except shifting or dying, and I couldn't shift and I *knew* I couldn't—

And I didn't.

At least, not us.

I knew that because a second later, we were still sitting in the same puddle of spilled hell juice, inside the same cleaved-in table, in front of the same murderous guard. But the pillar that had been over there . . .

Was now over here.

With a wicked-looking blade stuck halfway through the middle of it.

"What did you *do*?" Casanova screeched, his voice reaching into the falsetto. Maybe because the tip of the blade had stopped inches away from his crossed eyes.

I stared at the blade, and then out the window, which was still shuffling like a deck of cards. And thought maybe I knew. "This is the *Shadowland*," I hissed as the guard started trying to pull his blade out.

"So?"

I grabbed Casanova's head and turned it toward the window. "So you can think things how you want them!"

"But . . . but that's just about how it *looks*."

"You sure?" I said as the frustrated warrior gave a roar and punched the stubborn post.

Which promptly moved a foot backward and smashed into his face.

And punched him back.

"See what you mean," Casanova said as the guy fell on his ass, an imprint of the day's specials stamped onto his forehead.

And then several more guards rushed to their buddy's aid. And had the table halves slung at their heads by a rapidly sobering vampire. And then we were rolling and yelping and crawling along the filthy floor, trying to keep the bar's pillars between us and the guys trying to kill us.

But that's a little hard when you're rattling around between wildly shuffling pieces of wood, like a pinball in a particularly aggressive game.

Or make that impossible. A pillar suddenly appeared in the space right in front of me, causing me to almost break my nose. Casanova banged into another, fell back into a sprawl, and had a third slam into being between his legs.

An expression of mingled pain and fury came over his wine-flushed face. And then an unfortunate guard decided to hit a vamp while he was down, and lunged for him. And got batted back toward the door like a baseball when Casanova jumped up, grabbed a chair, and started swinging.

"Shift us!" he yelled.

"I can't!"

"What?"

"My power is acting up—"

"What?"

I jumped to the side to avoid a guard who came sliding by on his back. And then again to miss the creature chasing him. And then had a third start a weird dodging dance with me, his sword and the pillar I was somehow keeping in front of me as a shield.

Because it looked like Rosier's oath not to kill me didn't extend to his people.

And, okay, this was no time for an explanation of the difficulty of using my power outside earth. Or the fact that I was having problems with it even back home. Or the fact that I didn't understand what those problems were. There was only one thing that mattered right now, with Casanova staring daggers at me because I couldn't twitch my nose and get us out of every possible situation.

"I can't shift, damn it! Think of something else!"

But Casanova didn't want to think; he wanted to bitch at me. *"You came to hell with no way to get out? Are you insa—"*

He broke off as three guards jumped him, apparently mistaking constant whining for weakness.

But Casanova wasn't weak. He preferred to let other people to deal with his problems, preferably while he stood around and informed them about what they were doing wrong. But when it came down to it, he was perfectly capable of throwing down—and to the side, and through a window—as the guards quickly learned.

"Make for the bar," he yelled at me. *"The bar!"*

And yeah, the massive old looked-like-oak-but-probably-wasn't rectangle was the only cover available, except for flimsy tables that broke when you looked at them. But the bar seemed a long way away, and we were fast running out of pillars. And then I *was* out, as the one in front of me was finally hacked in two, and a blade came slicing at my jugular.

And missed.

Because the guy holding it lurched and staggered back, which made no sense.

Until I noticed that he was suddenly a lot shorter.

"Ha!" Casanova said, having just pulled the rug out from under him Shadowland-style, and wished away a large hunk of floor.

And then a customer was thrown into him and they staggered into me and we all went down. I hit a table and bounced off, only to get knocked to my knees by somebody's elbow. And then to the floor by somebody's knee. And then my chin hit down hard, and when I looked up, dazed and hurting—

It was to see a bloody and thrashing Pritkin being dragged toward the door.

He was surrounded by what had to be a dozen demons, while Rosier and half a dozen more fended off Caleb. And suddenly, I got it. The old adage about possession being nine-tenths of the law must hold true for the demon realms as well, because Rosier was going to take him.

And then defy the council to violate his sovereignty and come take him back.

Our eyes met for an instant across the bar, and triumph flashed across his. Because we both knew they weren't going to set a dangerous precedent for the daughter of an old enemy. Once Pritkin went back into his father's realm, he wasn't coming out again.

Pritkin must have realized that, too, because he was fighting hard. But he had no weapons and one of his arms was dangling uselessly at his side and the other had five guards hanging off it—who suddenly staggered back, screaming, when a fireball erupted around Pritkin's shielded arm and set their robes ablaze.

But a bunch of reinforcements were streaming inside, despite the fact that the odds were already ridiculous. Six of them grabbed tabletops to use as shields and jumped Pritkin and the rest ran to help Rosier. Which left him able to turn toward his son and lift a hand—

And the fire abruptly went out.

Pritkin still had his own shields up, at least for the moment, but it didn't matter. The guards had obviously had enough of trying to drag a reluctant demon lord anywhere, and with the extra numbers, they didn't have to. They just hoisted him up, off the floor, and there were too many for even him to fight, and he was almost out the door—

So I did the only thing I could.

And moved it.

Specifically, I moved it onto the ceiling, which was the only place I could think of that might help. But that appeared to have surprised the guards, who were still trying to use it to come in. And who ended up falling through the roof instead, and onto the ones surrounding Pritkin.

Bonus, I thought blankly as they kicked and thrashed and he sprang free, looking a little crazed.

But not as much as Rosier when he spun toward me, and screamed something in a language I didn't know. And every warrior in the place abruptly stopped. And looked up, too.

And then came rushing straight at us.

"Jodor," Casanova breathed.

I didn't say anything, because I was struggling to get on my feet—why, I don't know. It wasn't like I had time to do anything, or even to form a plan. But it didn't matter, because my legs weren't taking orders, and my eyes kept losing focus and then something hit me on the head.

But it wasn't a guard.

It was—

"Good one," Casanova breathed. And started rapid-firing bottles over the bar that we were somehow suddenly behind.

I grabbed my throbbing head, which had connected with the underside of the bar top, feeling dizzy and confused and really pretty unwell. And saw the bartender stooped in a crouched position over by the wall, looking equally bemused. Maybe because he suddenly had nothing to be crouched in back of.

Because we hadn't moved to the bar; the bar had

moved to us. But I hadn't done it. And then someone came sliding across it, and someone else jumped on top of him, and—

"Was that you?" I asked Pritkin, who was somehow over here now, on his back, his one good hand wrapped around his father's throat.

"The door," he said, half-strangled, because the same was true in reverse.

"No, *I* did the door," I said, and hit Rosier over the head with one of our dwindling stash of bottles.

"*That* door!" Pritkin rasped, his eyeballs rolling up.

Which I took for a bad sign until I looked up, too.

And was hit in the face by something hairy.

I pulled it off and found a coil of rope in my hands. Weird, I thought. And then Rosier was somehow gone and Pritkin was looping it around my waist.

I tried to help him, because his hand didn't seem to work right. But then, neither did mine. "Wer' we going?"

"Out."

"Oh, good."

"Come on!" I heard Caleb's voice and looked up again. And saw him hanging out of the bar's front door, which was now opening out of the ceiling above our heads.

And then I was being hauled on a fast ride up and out, onto the roof, where I landed on some nasty shingles that bruised my butt. And then froze it, because the Shadowland was always cold. But that was okay, because it cleared my head slightly.

Enough that I realized that Pritkin and Casanova were still down there.

I scrambled back to the edge of the door, where somebody else was on the rope, somebody heavy enough to cause Caleb to strain. I grabbed for the end of it, but before I could do anything, Casanova was climbing out of the opening.

"I saved one," he told me, looking a little disheveled.

"What?"

He hauled a bottle of hell juice out of the darkness and set it on the shingles. "Only one left."

The building shook as some kind of serious spell went off in the room below, and I grabbed his lapels. "Where's *Pritkin*?"

And then there he was, struggling to pull himself past the doorjamb with only one functional arm. But he managed, even before Caleb could help him, like he was in one hell of a damned hurry. And a second later I realized why.

When the section of roof I was kneeling on suddenly caved in.

I had a split second to see Rosier's evil face and a forest of shiny swords and the floor all rushing up at me—

And then my arm was almost snatched out of its socket when someone caught me.

I looked up to find Casanova staring at me, as if he couldn't believe he'd managed that, either. Especially one-handed, because the damned bottle was still clutched in the other. And then he was screaming and yanking me up and screaming again, because his feet were slipping on the widening edge.

And then Caleb jerked him back and Pritkin grabbed me. "Run!"

Which, yeah. But the cascade of old tiles and half-rotten ceiling beams and moldy plaster that had been the roof made it seem like we were running in place even as we pelted for the edge. Because the precipice was coming along with us, nipping at our heels.

And then consuming them, in a boiling mass of debris, just as Caleb grabbed me and swung me up, which seemed the wrong direction but I couldn't scream with a throat full of plaster dust. And then we were going down again, fast, but I couldn't figure out why until—

"Shiiiiiiit!" I screamed, finding dust no match for a zip-line ride down a sparking electric wire, dangling off

the bit of rope Caleb had thrown over the top and speeding fast, fast, too damn fast toward a one-story building
across the street.

Which we reached just as a bunch of indigo guards
burst out of the bar behind us, and took off like bats out
of hell. Or servants of one very pissed off demon lord,
anyway. And then I couldn't see them anymore because
we were running up some stairs, and then pelting across
the second building's flat roof and running to the edge
and no, no, *no*—

And then jumping across a too-wide cavern we almost didn't make, Casanova's feet slipping on the edge
and his arms spiraling wildly, and me grabbing him and
spinning around, and then Caleb grabbing me and all
three of us doing a strange, death-defying dance on a
two-inch ledge before Pritkin grabbed us and yanked us
back.

And then we were off again.

"Where's the council?" Caleb yelled as we pounded
across the roof.

"Less than a block," Pritkin said, which should have
been good news. Only he didn't sound like it.

It didn't look like Caleb thought so, either. "What's
the problem?" he demanded.

"That," Pritkin said as we ran up to the other side of
the roof.

And yeah.

This side had a fire escape going down, but it didn't
do us any good. Because the street below had suddenly
decided it didn't want to be a street anymore. And
turned into a culvert.

And then flip, a stone-walled garden. And hey presto,
a sewage tunnel. It was shifting so fast, it was making me
dizzy, and I wasn't even down there. I couldn't imagine
trying to navigate a yard through the middle of a landscape that was constantly changing, much less a block.

Only it didn't look like someone wanted us to have
even that tiny chance.

Because the building suddenly shook all around us, like the aftershock from an earthquake had hit it. Only the earthquake was coming, not going. And tossing us up—

And up and up and up some more, as the building sprang out of the ground, additional stories popping out of the earth like cars on a freight train heading straight into the sky.

"Oh, shit," Casanova said miserably. And then, "Fuck that!" as the bits of rope came out again.

And this time, I was siding with Casanova.

Because yeah, there *was* another electric line, attached to the side of the building. And yes, it *had* grown up along with the rest of this place. But the building was now a good fourteen stories up, making the line into an almost perpendicular plunge to a tiny pole way the hell down there.

Which might not even be there in a minute, the way things were going.

And then it wasn't, as Pritkin waved a hand and the pole went scooting down the street-that-was-a-street again for the moment, weaving in and out of the crazy landscape like a skier on a hill, only to stop at the entrance of a large edifice at the very end.

An edifice that looked like a municipal building, but probably wasn't.

"Oh *God*," I said, with feeling.

"Fuck *that*!" Casanova repeated, backing away.

"It's doable," Caleb said staunchly.

"In what universe?"

"You have a better plan?" Pritkin asked, throwing his very thin and not-at-all sturdy-looking piece of rope over the line.

"Yes! Anything that takes place on the ground!"

"Man up," Caleb advised.

"I'm a *vampire*—"

"Yet you're afraid of heights."

"Yes!" Casanova said hysterically. "They're one of

the few things that can kill me! I hate fire and I hate heights!"

"How do you feel about stakes?"

"Very funny! Very goddamned—" He broke off when a familiar streak of red lightning tore across the roof and exploded against the lip of the building.

"What are they *doing*?" he screamed.

"Trying to get a payday," Pritkin snarled. And I remembered what he'd said before, about having enemies, even at court. But damn it, Rosier was here—

Only he wasn't, I realized. There was no slick gray suit among the blue robes leaping from the other roof to ours. He must be down on the street, keeping the card flip going. And that meant—

"Oh, shit!"

And I guess Casanova agreed. Because he grabbed Caleb, who grabbed the other bit of rope. "No, Caleb takes Cassie!" Pritkin said. "You come with—"

I didn't hear the rest, if there was any, because I was being shoved brutally backward. I hit concrete hard, just as red lightning exploded where we'd all been standing, and part of the roof disintegrated into a mass of flying stone. I would have ducked and covered my head, but it was the part Caleb and Casanova had been standing on, and I was screaming and scrambling up and—

And watching them zoom away along the slender lifeline that Caleb had somehow managed to snag even as they dropped. An almost dizzying wash of relief flooded me. They were going to be all right; as long as the line held, they were going to be—

"Cassie!" There were spells going off everywhere, deafeningly loud, but I heard that and my head jerked around. To see Pritkin, lit for a second by unnatural spell light, and silhouetted against a massive ball of boiling energy coming this way. And then I was grabbing him because he couldn't grab me and the rope, too, assuming he was able to grab it at all when I couldn't even see it with all the weird jumping light—

And then we were jumping, too, and falling, and the roof was exploding and—

And there was a disorienting moment of free fall amid flying debris and hot, rushing air, and *no, no, no, no, NO*—

But then we caught—a barely perceptible jerk on a filament of line that hardly changed the feel of things at all because this was almost free fall, too—a crazy mix of whistling wind and abject terror and pant-wetting desperation. And that was just the initial descent. Then we hit the curve at the bottom, where the line dipped almost all the way down to the street and I felt loose pebbles in the roadbed roll under my filthy toes for a moment, a completely surreal experience that would have lifted my heart to my throat if it hadn't already taken up permanent residence there—

And then we took off, our momentum shooting us up and forward at the same time, on a mad slalom down a constantly changing street.

For a long moment, I couldn't see anything but a rush of neon on either side, colorful streamers like kites in the night, rising and falling as signs and buildings sprang in and out of existence and taxis honked and people shouted at us or ran to get out of the way.

But for some insane reason, I was *laughing* as we ran up a car's roof, pushed off, sprang over top of a bus, swooped down on the other side right in front of another madly honking car, and then bounced up onto a red, double-decker bus that caught us just as our improvised zip line gave up the ghost.

I hit the open aisle, still gasping on wild, insane, out-of-control laughter to match a crazy situation that couldn't possibly exist, but somehow did, and it took me a second to realize that Pritkin was laughing, too. And then we were running down the spiral stairs and jumping onto the sidewalk and crashing into Caleb and Casanova as they ran up to us on the street.

"Show-off," Caleb said breathlessly.

From there it was a short dash through the doors of the great building, and across a strangely normal-looking lobby, and down a not-so-normal looking hall, and then through a set of double doors—

Into a seemingly endless dark oval, slick and seamless, and littered with stars.

And a voice that crashed like thunder all around us. "Council is now in session."

Chapter Thirty

I don't know what I'd expected. Maybe a courtroom or a boardroom, something made to look comfortingly familiar to human eyes. But all that had ended at the door. I guess if you made it this far, you either weren't supposed to need comforting or weren't thought to deserve it.

I wondered which category we fit in as I gazed around, trying to get a grip.

It was a little hard, since there was nothing to grip *on*. It was like we'd stepped out of a spaceship into a star field, being suddenly confronted by a big, dark space and hundreds, maybe thousands, of versions of the light creature I'd seen on the drag. Some were small and dim, others large and brilliant, but I couldn't tell if that had to do with power or if some were just closer than others.

I couldn't tell much of anything else, either, since I literally couldn't see my hand in front of my face. There was plenty of light in here, but it didn't seem to reflect on anything. It was like the space between the stars, limitless and black, just a featureless void.

And creepy as hell.

It was also really inconvenient. Not only couldn't I see Pritkin's face, or Caleb's or even Casanova's despite the fact that he'd been right beside me a second ago, but the utter darkness was playing havoc with my sense of direction. I kept thinking I was about to fall over but couldn't seem to do that, either. Or maybe I already had. My brain kept sending me weird sensations, like maybe I wasn't entirely vertical anymore.

It sort of felt like we were floating, just random spirits washing along on the tide, me, the guys, a bunch of pissed-off demon lords . . .

"We all float down here," Caleb muttered, somewhere off to my left, as if he'd heard me. And yes, that's what I need right now, Caleb, I thought viciously, Stephen freaking King. But, for once, my brain didn't latch onto the prompt and start torturing me. Maybe because it already had that covered.

It was so unbelievably quiet. After that initial statement, nothing else was said. I didn't know if they were waiting for us, if we were supposed to do or say something, but nobody was. Including Pritkin, who had been here before, so presumably knew the drill. So I didn't, either, but it wasn't fun.

I'd read somewhere that the human brain doesn't do so well when deprived of the usual sources of input. Like when people go into those sound-deadening chambers that cut out normal background noise. It would seem like it should be restful, peaceful even, all that quiet . . .

But after a few minutes, their input-starved brains start to freak out, because they need that kind of stuff for navigation and balance and to not start imagining monsters in the corners.

Not that that was an issue here.

But only because this place didn't *have* corners.

No, it just had a crap-load of things that went bump in the night and who didn't like me much and who ate people anyway and who probably thought they were due some payback after everything Mom had put them through and—*shut up, Cassie.*

Yeah. Yeah, that would be good. Except that when I shut down my mental babble, I started having trouble with the auditory stuff, half-heard whispers and distant, not-found-on-earth sounds. And odd rustlings, like if I could see behind the collective light show, what was there wouldn't look entirely human. Or, you know, at all.

And okay, maybe I'd been wrong.

Maybe dark wasn't so bad.

And then it suddenly wasn't anymore.

Two things happened at once: my mother popped into the middle of the huge space, shedding a large halo of light around her, and a massive power drain hit, hard enough to send me staggering.

Not a normal I'm-so-tired drain, like the one I'd been experiencing lately . . . like ever since I visited her. And yeah, maybe I should have put that together before now. But this was worse, and also a lot more literal, as if all that power I hadn't been able to access for things like shifting and fighting and saving my life had been welling up, like a wall of bright water behind a dam. A dam that had just been breached.

And oh, *crap*.

I could almost see it, a sparkling river of power flowing from me to her, curling around her feet in a glistening stream. Or maybe a flood because this was way, way more power than I used for shifting or stopping time or . . . or anything. Way more than I'd ever channeled at once before in my life.

And that was despite the fact that she wasn't really here. I could see stars through her on the other side, although she wasn't a ghost. I knew ghosts. It was more like she was on an intertemporal version of Skype.

And the signal was running straight through me.

So it took me a moment to pull myself together, to pay attention to something besides the forceful complaints of my too-human body, and to notice—that she looked exactly the same.

Okay, maybe not exactly. There were a few changes;

the mane of bright hair was a copper flame in the darkness, the violet eyes were huge and luminous, the porcelain skin glowed like it had its own light source. But she was still dressed in simple white, she wasn't thirty feet tall or a mass of boiling energy like the last god I'd seen, and she wasn't carrying any of the props I suppose I'd subconsciously expected: bows, arrows, shield, crown. . . .

It wasn't that I was disappointed . . . exactly. It's just that, well, we could have used a little intimidation factor right now. Instead, she took a moment to survey the scene and then smiled, almost coquettishly. "It has been a long time, my lords. Miss me?"

Not cool, Mom, I thought a little desperately, as an unhappy rumble reverberated around the room.

But it didn't seem to bother her. Long eyelashes shadowed porcelain cheeks for a moment as a wry smile tugged at her lips. "No. I suppose not."

"We know you, oh, Ninmesarra."

One of the stars dropped from the sky, transforming into a pleasant-looking man in a dark business suit. He was blond, like Rosier, but the similarities ended there. His hair was thin and sleeked back, his face was round and not particularly memorable, except for a noticeable cleft in an otherwise unremarkable chin. He looked young, maybe my age, maybe a few years older, and his voice was mild, almost sweet.

I frowned at him.

He had no business being a demon.

"What we do not know is why you come before us," he added, stopping a few feet away from the glow Mother was shedding on—yes, there was a floor down there, I guess for the use of us corporeal types. I could see it when he walked, in the shadows shed by his body. Because Mother's light did throw them.

And it was amazing how much better I felt, just seeing those few square feet of normality. I picked my feet up, one at a time, and put them back down again, deliberately scraping them over the floor I could actually feel now. And the weird loop-de-loop my brain had been doing quieted down somewhat.

Too bad it didn't do anything about the power drain.

Mother glanced at me. "Communication using Seidr is difficult for humans, and my daughter must carry the burden alone. I will therefore be blunt, for my time here is brief. She has come to ask you for the life of one man. I . . . have not."

That did get a reaction, in the form of a dull blink, from me. And a mental replay of some of Pritkin's history lesson. Please tell me I haven't fucked this up, I thought blankly. Please, please, please . . .

"Then why are you here?" the man asked, frowning slightly. As if he wasn't any happier with her answer than I was.

"To grant you a boon, Adra. Or should I say, another?"

"When has the World Destroyer ever done us anything but harm?" It was a harsher voice this time, but I couldn't tell where it came from.

Until a shorter, stouter figure stomped onto the bit of floor Mother's light was illuminating.

And, okay, that was better. The first guy might have lulled me into a false sense of security, had I met him anywhere else, but that wasn't an issue with this one. Not that that meant a damn—for all I knew, the new guy was a pushover. I'd learned from dealing with vamps that it didn't do to judge on looks.

But that was kind of hard when the looks in question were so bizarre.

He— and I was guessing that solely based on voice— was pasty-pale and lumpy under a dark robe. And as far as I could tell, he had no facial features a human would recognize. He did have a head; at least I was assuming that was what the bulge on what I was also assuming were shoulders could be called, although it was a toss-up. But in place of eyes, nose, and mouth, he had a bunch of feelers or tentacles or, hell, I don't know, white waving things emerging from pustules on the lump like the strands on an anemone. They were surrounding a hole lined with what had to be at least a couple of hundred tiny, pointy teeth.

And okay, maybe that was the mouth. I didn't know, because I didn't want to get close enough to find out. And yeah, that was me being species-ist and bigoted and whatever, but . . .

I still didn't.

But Mother didn't look bothered. She lifted a single eyebrow, the way I'd never been able to do. Every time I tried it, both of mine went up, leaving me looking surprised instead of elegantly amused. But she nailed it.

"When, Asag? When I killed Ninurta, and set your people free from ten thousand years of bondage. When I slayed Pazuzu along with half his legions, and thus put an end to the war you could not. When the great Kamish fled from me, bleeding from a thousand wounds, and weak enough to allow you to hunt and exile him—"

"You did none of that for us! You were not trying to save us!" The voice was furious.

"Of course not. But the result of my actions was helpful, was it not? Or have you forgotten how they scourged you, the ones you now term 'Ancient Horrors,' but whom once you called lords and served humbly along with all your kin? Have you so quickly forgotten how they gloried in blood and war, while your people suffered in want and endless fear, waiting to be called up again and again, for no victory was ever enough, and no defeat deemed final . . . ?"

Mom kept talking, but I was having real trouble concentrating on her.

I was experiencing something like the electric frisson I'd felt with Mircea, only that was like saying a raindrop felt like a deluge. And okay, yeah, this might explain a few things. Like how I kept popping into other people's heads, or them into mine . . . or it might have if I knew what the crap was going on. But I didn't, and I couldn't focus with what felt like a few thousand volts running along every vein.

Help, I thought vaguely.

"They left you bleeding on the battlefield," Mother was saying. "Fodder for the carrion eaters. Or cowering behind your wards, alone on your little worlds, unable to grow or interact or explore, for fear of what prowled in the night—"

"You chief of all!" The demon sounded like he was choking.

"Oh, not chief, Asag, surely. Not for you. I only preyed on the powerful."

The room laughed, if slightly uncomfortably. It didn't do much to break the tension. I had a feeling nothing would.

"Whatever you may think of me," Mother continued, "the fact remains that the killing of the great ones allowed saner voices to prevail at many courts, helped to bring about the end of the ancient wars, and did much to usher in the current era of, if not peace, at least of more stability than you have ever known."

"And we should thank you for this?" the one she'd called Adra asked mildly.

"No, but you should, perhaps, thank me for thousands of years of freedom from my people's depredations. When I barred them from earth, it cut them off from your worlds as well. You may think I took a heavy toll on your numbers, but how many would they have taken? In more than four millennia, how many?"

"Do you hear?" Asag demanded. "She is our benefactor now!"

"It is difficult to hear anything," another voice interjected. "Over your chatter. Some of us would prefer to hear the Queen of Heaven."

"Heaven is where she should have stayed. Along with the rest of her kind!"

"But we did not stay. We will not stay," Mother said

sharply. "You asked me why I came; it was to tell you this. My people have become desperate. They feasted in the good years, and grew strong. But also far more numerous. And unlike you, they did not restrict their population. They come now because they must; our world cannot support so many, even at a basic level. And when they come, whatever the price, they will come for you. And they will not take merely the ancient ones and be done with it, as I did. They will take you all."

"Suddenly, they can return, after being barred for so long?" the one she called Adra asked. "Suddenly, your great protection fails?"

He sounded less crazed than the other guy, but I wasn't sure he was any less skeptical. I guess I couldn't blame him; it sounded like she'd played them pretty well in the past. But if she was going to bring them around now, she'd better hurry.

I'd passed tingly, traveled through fiery, said good-bye to scorching. And was starting to approach whatever it was called when one of those cartoon characters pushed a finger in a light socket and it lit him up, showing the skeleton through the skin. Even my hair felt crunchy. A human wasn't meant to channel this much raw power.

And this one wasn't going to be doing it for much longer.

"No, but as their hunger grows, so does their desperation," Mother said, more quickly. "They will now risk things they once would have scorned. And I am no longer here, to be a bulwark for the twin worlds, or for you."

"That sort of bulwark we can do without!" Asag said. "Do you not see what she is doing?" he asked his fellow demons. "Even from the grave she strikes at us! She uses her human child to speak to us, just as she would use her and the incubus' spawn to finish what she began. And destroy us all!"

"My son has nothing to do with this!" Rosier's voice rang out from somewhere. "I told you, it's that girl—"

"Be silent! If you had not opposed his execution years ago, we would not be facing this peril now!"

"The peril you face is not of their making, Asag," Mother said mildly. "Your paranoia is as strong as ever, and as ever it is misplaced."

The demon started to respond, but was cut off by the demon Mom had called Adra. "You may voice your concerns afterward, my lord. For now, let her speak."

"It is not Asag's ramblings that you need to fear," she said. "Or others like him. It is those too timid to speak now, but who, when I am gone, will cloak their fear in the voice of reason. We will do as we did before, they will say. We will take refuge behind our walls, behind our locked and barred gates, and wait. It saved us once; why not again? And from enemies who may never return, or who if they do will not have the same skill as She Who Controls the Paths. They did not dare to hunt us before, in our own lands. They will not dare now. We are safe...."

She trailed off, gentle mocking in her tone, and the room became deadly quiet.

"I come to tell you that you are not safe. You were only so before if you did not interest me. I could have taken any of you, anytime I pleased, and there are those now as powerful as I once was. They do not have my gift, no. But they have others. And they will use them."

"Lies!" Asag exploded. "Lies! Who is the only one who hunted us, who used us, for whom we swore eternal hatred? Have you so quickly forgotten?"

"We have forgotten nothing," Adra said. "And I have warned you once."

At least, I thought that's what he said. I could barely hear over my heartbeat anymore, I couldn't feel my legs, and my whole body was trembling like I had a fever. I felt someone's hand on my arm, clenching tight, but I couldn't tell whose. Someone who was trying to keep me upright, but I was past caring. I didn't need to be on my feet; I just needed this to be over. I just needed ...

To give her time to finish.

Mother's eyes swept the room, and there was no amusement in her voice now, no banter, no teasing. It was flat and uncompromising, the voice of an oracle in full control of her power. In spite of everything, it sent a wash of gooseflesh over my arms.

I wondered if anyone else realized; she wasn't just talking anymore.

She was prophesying.

"You are poised on a razor's edge. Join my daughter. Fight with her. Give her the incubus and whatever other help you can. For if you do not, there will come a time, very soon, when you will wish you had."

Chapter Thirty-one

Five minutes later, I was on a couch in the lobby, slightly steaming. If I was a cartoon, I'd have had a blackened face, hair standing straight on end, and wisps of steam floating out of my ears. And I wasn't the only one.

"Well, that could have gone better."

That was Caleb, mopping his face with an oversized handkerchief he'd pulled out of all that leather. His hair wasn't standing on end because he didn't have any, but his usually rich skin tone had an ashen cast, and his eyes were a little more open than technically necessary. If it had been anyone else, I'd have said he was flirting with a panic attack, only war mages didn't.

Of course, they didn't usually stand in front of a full session of the demon high council, either.

Not that we were anymore. I'd lost the connection, whatever it was, to Mom shortly after the room erupted in chaos. And not the good kind. The weird-vibrations-that-made-my-skin-feel-like-it-was-about-to-come-off-the-bone kind, like we were in a giant drum and somebody had suddenly decided to beat the hell out of it. And then there had been the noise, which probably hadn't been metallic shrieks and high-pitched squeals and elephant-like trumpets, but my brain had given up trying to make sense of this crap and had just started tossing random junk in there.

So yeah.

Could have gone better.

On the other hand, the vibrate-y, noisy stuff had caused me to retch and flop over. And collapsing into nothing, not even a floor because I still couldn't feel it properly, just *nothing*, was something I could live without ever experiencing again. But the good news was, it had gotten us kicked out on our collective asses.

The bad news was, Pritkin hadn't come with us.

I stared at the big double doors leading back into hell's inner sanctum and, despite everything, had a sudden urge to run back in there. And I guess more than an urge, because the next thing I knew, I was halfway to my feet and Caleb's arm was holding me back. "Not a chance," he grumbled.

"I just want to listen—"

"To what?" he demanded. "The shrieking?"

"They won't let you in anyway," Casanova reminded me. "They said no humans in the deliberations."

"Pritkin's in there—"

"He's the accused. That's different."

"That's what I'm afraid of!"

"Here." Casanova handed over his precious bottle of hell juice.

I blinked at him.

"You're white as a sheet," he said gruffly.

I took the bottle, a little gingerly. And okay, if I'd needed confirmation that things were bad, I'd just gotten it. Casanova was being nice to me.

We were so fucked.

I drank. People, or things, or things pretending to be people came and went, paying no attention to the three bums sprawled in the corner. Caleb kept glancing around, but not like he was tensing to fight. More like the bland familiarity of the lobby was reassuring to him.

It wasn't doing a lot for me.

Long minutes passed.

"Maybe it was intended as a negotiation tactic," Caleb suddenly blurted out.

I glanced over at him. He looked a little less freaked-out, but no happier. I knew the feeling.

Having time to think was a bitch.

"What?"

"You know," he told me. "All of that stuff about the gods . . ."

I passed over the bottle. "You think Mom was lying?"

Caleb took a swig, and made a face. "I'm not saying that. We've already had one god show up, and the punk-ass kids of another. But she could have been exaggerating. She was bargaining with them, and in a negotiation, you always ask for more than you hope to get. We want Pritkin, so your mother asks for—"

"An army?" Casanova said incredulously. "A demon *army*?"

Caleb scowled. "I thought you were the one who thought that was a good idea. You spent half the damned walk into Rosier's capital bitching about—"

"The fact that we could use some help with the war *we already have going*," Casanova said, snatching his bottle back. "Not being informed that there's an army of ravenous gods preparing to lay waste to the hells, and planning to use earth as a staging ground!"

He belted back a couple shots' worth, all at one go.

"Well, forgive me for hoping it's not true," Caleb retorted. "As someone who'll have to fight it!"

Casanova leaned over me to stare at him. "And the rest of us won't? You think the gods are going to wipe out the war mages and just leave everyone else—"

"The Corps is the obvious target, yes. We're the only ones with enough magic to oppose them—"

"Oh, please!" Casanova said fiercely. "If those things—did you see those things?—in there are shaking in their boots, what chance do you think you have?"

"Better than you think, or they're expecting. The Corps isn't the ragtag little group they remember—"

"Yes, which is why *the goddess who started your order* just said we're screwed without the demons! Face it—if the gods get past that damned spell, we're dead, we're *all*—"

"Stop it," I said, but no one was listening.

"Thus speaks the great military mind of a casino manager!" Caleb snapped.

"Who has lived long enough to have seen a few wars in his time," Casanova snapped back. "And it's never just the combatants who suffer—"

"I didn't say it was—"

"And we both know it's easier to run a staging ground if you don't have to worry about sabotage!"

"Stop it!" I told him. But he didn't.

"If I were them, I wouldn't want anyone anywhere near my only doorway to this universe, not after what happened last time. Easier to kill us, kill the fey, hell, kill the humans, too. It's not like they need them anymore if they're invading the hells anyway—"

"They'd need them to feed their precious herd," Caleb growled. "There's no way they would—"

"If they want to feed their cows, they can do it with creatures like we saw on Rosier's world. If even the incubi can control them, the gods'll never have to worry about rebellion. They'll never have to worry about any—" He broke off as I got up. Because it was either that or start screaming.

"Where are you going?" Casanova demanded.

"Somewhere else!"

"Cassie—"

"No," I told him as he grabbed for my wrist. And missed, because he was drunker than he'd been in the bar. "I can't, all right? I just—I *can't*."

"It's okay," Caleb told me. And then grimaced, because it wasn't and we both knew it. "Just . . . sit back down."

"I don't want to sit down!"

"It's not like you have a choice," Casanova pointed out. "Where else are you going to go?"

I didn't answer because I didn't know. I just knew I couldn't sit there and listen to them argue when there wasn't a damned thing I could do about any of it. I was staggering with exhaustion, but I couldn't sleep, either, not with Pritkin in there pleading for his life. And it didn't look like there was enough left in that bottle to get me drunk.

I didn't know what I wanted.

"I know how you feel," Caleb said, and took my hand.

He didn't grab it or yank on it or even trap it, which, in the state I was in, might have sent me over the edge. The fingers were slightly open, the hold loose. I could have pulled away at any time.

And so, perversely, I didn't want to.

"I feel the same way," he told me. "I've known John over fifteen years. He's saved my ass half a dozen times, and I've returned the favor maybe half that many—"

"I think you might have evened the score today," I said, a little unevenly.

"Maybe." *If this works out* remained unsaid. "But there's nothing I can do for him now. Except wait. They'll have a decision when they have a decision, and John's going to need us then. And we need to be here for him. All right?"

I nodded, because I suddenly couldn't say anything. And let Caleb pull me back down on the sofa, or whatever it really was. I didn't know, but it was comfortable, and then he pulled me onto his shoulder, which wasn't. But I didn't mind right then.

"Sorry," Casanova said, which might not have meant anything. But then he handed me the bottle again.

"It's okay," I told him, looking at it blearily. "I think I've had enough."

"No such thing," he muttered, glancing around. And upended it.

*   *   *

I woke up on something hard. I tried punching it, because this pillow had seen better days. But it didn't seem to help.

So I punched it again.

"Ow," someone said mildly.

My eyes opened, and I found myself looking at something that might have been a knee. I blinked, and it came more into focus. Yes, it was a knee. A very dirty, denim-covered knee that also appeared to have been drooled on.

I raised myself up slightly. And realized why my pillow had been so damned hard. My head had been resting on someone's thigh, and whoever it was hadn't skipped leg day.

I turned my head the other way and saw a stomach. I frowned at it, which wasn't fair, because it was a nice stomach. Flat and hard, and with the beginnings of the deep V of muscles sometimes called an Adonis belt above the loose top of the jeans.

But there was something wrong with it anyway. And that included the sculpted, lightly furred chest above. And the rocklike shoulders above that. And the face—

My body came upright abruptly. Maybe a little too abruptly, since the room did a lazy spin around me. But I didn't care, because I'd finally realized the problem: the body was right, but the skin was wrong. Instead of Caleb's rich mocha, it was pale and sun kissed and—

I grabbed one of those oversized shoulders and shook it as hard as I could, which meant I maybe jiggled it a little. "They released you?"

An eyebrow rose. And damn it! Everybody could do that but me.

"No," Pritkin told me. "They're in deliberations. They didn't seem to feel they needed me for that."

"Oh." I sat back, waking the rest of the way up. And checking him over.

He looked okay. Well, actually that was a lie. "Okay"

was a relative term considering where we were, and encompassed a lot of things. But he didn't look any more beat up.

Unfortunately, that was about the only plus.

He hadn't found any extra clothes to go with the dirty jeans, which were now also cut in several places, and scorched down one side, probably the result of the near miss on the rooftop. His hair, always terrible, was now extra Pritkin-y, meaning it would have put any self-respecting stylist on suicide watch. Although it matched his face, which was a stubbly mess, and his left eye, which was black and swollen, and his right arm, which was in a sling, and his ribs—

"You wouldn't even get in the door at Rosier's looking like that," I told him, after a minute.

His lips pursed. "Should I worry that you sound pleased?"

"I do not!" That was ridiculous. "And I meant you look terrible."

"Would you like a mirror?" he asked sweetly.

"No."

I glanced around. We were still on the sofa, only someone had added a rattan privacy screen on one side, shielding us from the view of the rest of the lobby. That seemed to happen to me a lot.

I guess even hell has some standards.

Although Caleb, at least, was doing earth proud. He was standing by a pillar, arms crossed, eyes watchful, face back to its usual fuck-with-me-and-die expression, maybe kicked up an extra notch or two because of where we were. His knee-length leather duster was likewise looking sharp. Of course, it was war mage issue, meaning that it was less a coat than self-healing armor, knitting up any little boo-boos almost as soon as they happened. I suspected it might be self-cleaning, too, because he was suspiciously lacking in dirt.

Casanova, on the other, other hand, was bringing our average back down again, although less because of looks than attitude. He was still sprawled on the couch on my other side, and he must have finished off the bottle he was still clutching. Because his handsome face was pasty and crumpled, like his once-nice suit. And his eyes kept darting around the lobby blearily, as if trying to see through the bland beige glamourie.

Altogether, we were a sorry lot, and then my stomach growled plaintively. "Have I been out long?" I asked, tucking a limp strand of hair behind my ear. And wincing, because even that hurt.

"A few hours," Pritkin told me. "You weren't unconscious, just exhausted. We thought it best to let you sleep. It'll likely be hours yet before we hear anything."

I digested that. And, unfortunately, nothing else. My stomach spoke up again, more forcefully.

"Does this place have a coffee shop?"

"No," he said, getting up, and grimacing. I guess I wasn't the only stiff one. "But there's a food cart next door. If I remember right, it's one of the safe ones."

"Safe?" Caleb frowned, like that word didn't compute around here. "Am I misremembering the bunch of guys who just tried to kill us?"

"That was before we reached the council," Pritkin said, and stretched, cracking his back. I tried that, too, because it sounded like it would feel awesome, but I was too bendy. I just flopped over. So I pretended to be touching my toes since I was already down there.

And, God, my toes. And the rest of my poor feet. Filthy, pedicure gone, cut and bruised and traces of hell gunk between the toes.

And after everything, the running and the fighting and the almost dying . . . that was what did it.

That was what finally had me tearing up.

Until a pair of honest-to-God flip-flops were dangled in front of my face.

I looked up. "How—"

"Shop around the corner," Pritkin told me, about the time that I noticed his nice, clean, flip-flop-clad feet.

"You got a bath!" I accused, staring at them.

"Sponge." He nodded at a discreet sign on a nearby wall. Which had an arrow pointing down a hall and a curly script that read *Bathrooms*.

And I realized that I had something else to take care of. "Be right back," I told him, grabbing the shoes.

"Wait." That was Caleb, staring at the sign suspiciously. "How do we know what's in there?"

"What?"

"There's a toilet in there," Pritkin told him, looking vaguely amused. "Many of the demon races have bodies, you know."

"And what if one of those bodies attacks her?" Caleb demanded. "Or some spirit does?" He glanced around unhappily. "This place is crawling with threats."

"Not for us. Once the trial started, we came under the council's protection. And I believe you remember their security staff?"

Caleb scowled, but he didn't seem satisfied. "I'm going with her," he announced forcefully.

"You are not," I told him, equally forcefully.

His eyes narrowed. "Then John goes. I don't care which of us it is, but you go nowhere by yourself. Not here."

"I just told you we're under protection," Pritkin said, looking at his friend impatiently.

"Yeah, the *council's* protection. Why doesn't that make me feel better?"

"It should. Nobody is going to test them, particularly not in their own building. Cassie will be perfectly safe."

Caleb hiked up one of the straps holding some of the eighty pounds or so of weapons he was carrying. "I know she will. Because she'll be with me."

"This is ridiculous," I told him.

"I'll stay outside the stall—"

"You'll stay here!"

"This is not up for discussion."

"I agree."

Caleb crossed his arms and glared at me. I glared back. Something squelched between my toes, which grossed me out and pissed me off in about equal measures, because I should be washing it away by now.

"This place isn't as dangerous as you seem to think," Pritkin told Caleb, trying again.

Caleb transferred the glare to him. "Did you get hit over the head?"

"Yes, several times—"

"Thought so."

"—but that doesn't change the facts. The Shadowland exists for trade. The proprietors have a vested interest in keeping some kind of order—"

"Yeah. I've felt really secure so far!"

"Most people are not being chased by an irate demon lord when they come here," Pritkin said dryly. "The council finds it a useful meeting place because of its being neutral ground. But they're a very small part of local life. I am not saying the place is without its dangers, but they can be navigated, even by humans. Mages come here fairly often to buy potion supplies, for example—"

"No sane ones!"

"Jonas gets most of his here—"

"You're not helping your case," Caleb muttered.

"—and Cassie is easily more powerful than him. If Jonas can navigate these streets on a semiregular basis, bargain for supplies, and get back out again safely, I think she can manage to go to the bathroom by herself!"

For some reason, Caleb was looking at him as if he'd lost his mind. His voice sounded like it, too. "Cassie is more powerful than Jonas," he repeated.

Pritkin frowned. "Of course. She's Pythia."

"She's—" Caleb seemed momentarily at a loss for words, so I seized the opportunity.

"I couldn't shift before, because Mother was rerouting most of my power for . . . well, whatever she did in there. But I feel better now—"

"Yeah, you look it!"

"I didn't say I'm a hundred percent," I told him impatiently. "But I can defend myself—"

"Good. But it's my job to see that you don't have to."

"If Agnes had told you to stay here, you'd stay here," I said angrily.

"Lady Phemonoe wouldn't be here! She'd be *at court*, surrounded by a crack security team! Meeting with dignitaries and mediating disputes and—and doing anything but running around almost getting herself blown up!"

"Did you ever *meet* Agnes?" I asked, but Caleb wasn't listening.

"Did you see her today?" he asked John. "Those witches were right; she doesn't even have *shields*, and I couldn't reach her and all she had for protection was a damned vampire—"

"Hey, fuc' you, too, buddy," Casanova slurred, from behind us.

"—and she almost got killed! I almost let her get—" Caleb broke off, fuming.

"You didn't let me do anything," I told him. "We got in trouble, but it wasn't your fault—"

"I can see me explaining that to the old man," Caleb snapped. "See, sir, she ended up incinerated, but it wasn't my fault!"

"It wasn't! I wanted to come here—"

"Yeah, and I should have had the sense to say no. Just like I should have the other day!"

"You should have said no?" I repeated. "I thought war mages did what the Pythia wanted."

"Pythias don't want this!" Caleb said, suddenly furious. "Pythias don't *do* this! They don't invade hell and fight demons and *battle gods*—"

"They also didn't live in these times," Pritkin said, cutting in. "They didn't have to face anything remotely like this. Do you think Lady Phemonoe could have done what Cassie did today? What she did yesterday? Do you think she would have *dared*?"

"I think she'd have found another way!" Caleb said,

like a man who had been standing by that pillar for the last two hours, thinking. And coming to the conclusion that maybe Casanova's drunken ramblings hadn't been so far off the mark. And panicking, after all, because he'd had all this dumped in his lap at one time, literally overnight. And he didn't know what to do with it.

And I didn't think he'd felt like that too often in his life.

"I had no idea—" He looked at me accusingly. "You made it sound like we were just going to sneak into some palace. Just grab John and hightail it out—"

"Which is what we did."

"That is not what we did! We—" Caleb stopped and stared around again, but the bland, beige lobby didn't seem to give him anything back. "This place, the hells, the *size*—" He broke off, staring from me to Pritkin, half in anger, half in wonder. "There's whole *worlds* down here."

Pritkin gazed at his friend, and his face changed. From exasperation working on pissed, to . . . understanding. Because maybe he'd felt like that once, too. Overwhelmed and inadequate, faced with a suddenly huge universe that he didn't understand at all.

"Yes," he said simply.

Caleb stared at him for a minute longer and then turned away abruptly, leather coat swinging.

And I finally got it.

I'd been dealing with stuff like this for more than three months now. And it had been hard. And scary. To the point that, most days, I'd felt like hiding under the bed, or just running and never stopping. And the truth was, if there'd been anybody else to stick with this job, I probably would have.

Like Caleb would probably love to run out of here. But he hadn't. And he wouldn't, because he was a decent guy. And because a lifetime of duty and discipline stood in the way. And because there was nowhere for him to go, either.

But right now he needed something to ground him.

Something familiar. Something he knew how to do. Even if it was just something stupid.

Even if it was just escorting me to the bathroom.

"Come on," I told him, sliding a hand on his shoulder. "If there's nobody else in there, I'll leave the door open."

Chapter Thirty-two

"Are you really going to eat here?" Caleb demanded, fifteen minutes later.

"Damned straight," I said, my mouth watering.

The restaurant wasn't a cart, although it was about the size of one. It was a small rectangle wedged between the courthouse and a bunch of shops. The shops appeared to be closed, although there were some across the street that were open. Cars passed on the still-busy highway, zipping along with headlights that blurred slightly in my tired vision and doubled in the mirrorlike sheen of the street.

I looked up, and some rain hit me in the face. That might have been an illusion, too, for all I knew, but it felt real. Everything did. Just a dark blue, rainy street, closer to winter than summer, with people bundled up and hurrying along their way.

And a brightly lit slab of Formica in front of me, with a two-page menu taped to the top. And a bunch of smells emanating from a griddle in back that had me ready to crawl over the counter. Hot damn, I thought in wonder, I was actually going to get dinner.

Maybe.

I glanced around furtively, waiting for the hammer to

drop. For someone or something to prevent me from getting any food. And it wasn't like there weren't plenty of candidates.

I couldn't tell what time of day it was, since it always seemed to be dark here. But there were plenty of people on the streets. And I knew where I was; I knew what they were, or most of them, anyway. But none looked all that sinister to me.

A mostly human-looking woman came by, with a shock of pale purple hair that could have come as easily from a trendy boutique as genetics. She was carrying a bag of groceries and talking on a cell phone with the preoccupied, slightly annoyed look of someone running late who is also getting rained on. She passed within a few feet of me and never gave me a second glance. She also didn't attack me.

I stared after her for a moment, faintly surprised. I knew from experience that the Shadowland had plenty of people who would try something, given half a chance. But then, that was true of most human cities, too, wasn't it? Was this really so different?

Okay, yeah, it was *different*, but—

"Are you going to order?" Pritkin asked, dragging my attention back to the menu. Where freaking everything looked good.

And then the short, squat guy in a grease-splattered apron handed Pritkin something in a paper boat that made my eyes bug out of my head. "They have *Phillies*?" I said, in something approaching awe.

"This street belongs to the potion sellers, and this cart has a fair amount of human traffic," he told me, taking the greasy bundle of awesomeness. "But elsewhere . . . you have to be careful. Not everything here is safe for human consumption."

"Yeah, but what's in it?" Caleb asked, peering suspiciously at the towering mound of meat and melty cheese and peppers and onions and mushrooms and—

"I'll have one of those," I told the cook quickly. Right now I didn't care what was in it.

"The usual." Pritkin shrugged. "You know how hard it is to glamourize food and get everything right: looks, smells, taste . . . It's easier and cheaper just to cook the real thing."

"You sure?" Caleb asked, looking longingly at his buddy's meal. "What about that old rule, eat in hell and you never leave?"

Pritkin arched an eyebrow. "I lived here for years. And I left."

"Yeah, but you keep coming back."

"Not by choice."

In the end, Caleb ordered a Philly, too. Casanova eyed up the demon cook, who shot him the bird, and then we all got beers. And leaned against the front of the diner to drink them, since there was nowhere to sit.

Pritkin snared a cheese-covered mushroom off the top of his sandwich, and my stomach gave off a roar that sounded like thunder.

His lips twitched, but he ate it anyway, the bastard. Watching me as I watched him in hopeless desperation. And then licked his fingers while I salivated.

And then he handed it over.

Oh God. So *good*. I practically dove in face-first, and for a while, I didn't know anything else.

When I came out of my food-induced stupor, it was to see that Pritkin had gotten what I guess was my order, and had eaten about half of it, while Caleb was just being handed his. "I'm gonna go sit on the bench," Caleb said, nodding at one alongside the courthouse where Casanova was already slumped with his beer. I guess he was trusting Pritkin to save me from everything but cholesterol.

Pritkin nodded. Caleb took off with his food and a handful of napkins. And we ate, in my case until I was so full I thought I might pop.

I thought about undoing the top button on my jeans, but when I surreptitiously glanced around, Pritkin was watching me. And I suddenly realized what he must be seeing—hair everywhere, mouth and probably half my face shiny with grease, T-shirt dirty and sweat-stained. I swallowed the last bite I'd taken, feeling suddenly self-conscious, the way I'd been too hungry and tired to be before. I licked my lips.

And his eyes followed the movement.

My own eyes widened slightly, and then looked away, because that was what I always did when something like that happened. Not that it did often. Other than for a few bits of metaphysical lifesaving, Pritkin mostly acted like I was a boy.

Which was good. Which was how I liked it. Which was how it should be.

I drank some beer. "So, uh, how do you think it went?"

Pritkin went back to his food. "Difficult to say. But they seemed to take your mother's warning seriously."

"That's good, right?" I asked. Because he had that particular crease between his eyes, the one that said he was puzzled about something.

"Perhaps. But then, they shouldn't have needed it."

"Come again?"

He made an unsatisfied sound, halfway between a grunt and a sigh. "The Circle might have managed to hide Apollo's brief return to the supernatural community as a whole, but do you really think the lords didn't know? When the battle took place at Dante's? Where half the damned payroll are demon-possessed?"

"Well, yeah, but those are incubi. And maybe Rosier didn't want them to say anything. Maybe he was afraid . . . I don't know . . . that it would help your case—"

"But I didn't have a case then," he pointed out. "I didn't until after you killed the Spartoi, which alone should have been enough to raise some eyebrows. It certainly caused me to start asking questions, when I woke up in my father's court. It could hardly have done less for the council, unless the Circle covered that up, too?"

"They never had the chance," I told him, grimacing at

the memory. "The vamps were broadcasting the coronation, and the whole damned thing was seen live by a few hundred thousand people. Not to mention however many saw the newspaper articles and the photos and—"

"Then they know. And likely more than was reported. They would have investigated even without the incident with Apollo. And with it—that's two major attempts to circumvent the ouroboros in as many months. They could not possibly have failed to notice. And yet the response to your mother's announcement . . . it almost sounded as if most of them had no idea."

I frowned. "Maybe the leaders are trying to keep from panicking everyone, until they can decide what to do."

"Cassie, the council *are* the leaders. There is no head; each member has a single vote. It was set up that way after the wars, when no one wanted more bloodshed over who would rule. That isn't to say that they have no factions, and of course some members' votes carry others. But we're not talking about a vote, we're talking about information they simply do not seem to have had."

I thought about that for a moment, and ate mushrooms. I was stuffed, but they had been browned on the griddle in butter, and then covered with melted cheese and crusty meat bits and, well. "But somebody has to decide what is brought up. I mean, they couldn't talk about *everything*—they'd never do anything else."

"That is what the Adramelech does."

"The what?"

"Your mother referred to him as Adra, for short. I am not sure why."

"I am," I said dryly. Mom hadn't exactly been on her best behavior in there. Or maybe she had.

At least she didn't kill anybody this time.

"She didn't seem pleased about the composition of the council," Pritkin agreed. "But while not, perhaps, polite, the term was not an insult. Adramelech is a title, not a personal name. He functions as the speaker or president of the council."

Damn. And he'd seemed like the nice one. "I thought you said the council doesn't have a head."

"It doesn't, if you mean someone with more power than anyone else. He is mainly there to maintain order."

"So he's the one who should have maybe got around to mentioning that the old gods were about to stage a comeback?"

"Not necessarily. The Adramelech only organizes matters to be discussed and attempts to keep the debate on topic. He doesn't usually propose topics himself."

"Then who does?"

"Whoever has the oversight of the region in question."

"And who has oversight of earth?" I asked, because Pritkin was sounding grim.

"You saw. That was the reason he was called forward. Asag of the Asakku."

Great. "So, what reason does this Asag guy have for just ignoring the return of one god and the kids of another?"

Pritkin shook his head. "I don't know. And I'm not likely to. I had difficulty even obtaining the basics on your mother. No one wants to talk about the ancient wars—or how they ended. Most go about trying to pretend they didn't happen."

"So they're about to let them happen again?" I asked, in disbelief. "They can't be that blind!"

"It's not a matter of being blind," Pritkin said, drinking beer. "It's . . . fear, terror even. You have to understand, Cassie, the demons who dared to face the gods once . . . they were ancient compared to the ones you saw, powerful beyond belief, and bloodthirsty to a fault. They gloried in battle, lived for it, reveled in it. And yet they fell, as one of the few who would talk to me about it said, like a sky full of falling stars. Those who survived believe they cannot fight—"

"They can't if they won't even try! Would they prefer to be slaughtered?"

"They'd prefer not to think about it at all. The ones who lived—remember, they were those who didn't interest your mother or the other gods. Who weren't powerful enough to be pursued, or who survived by hunkering down, by playing it safe, by being cautious—"

"You can be too cautious. You can die hiding under a bed or whatever the demon equivalent is, as much as on your feet, fighting."

Pritkin sent me an odd look.

"What?"

"When I met you, you preferred running, liked hiding. You told me several times it was what you were best at."

"Yes, but it made sense then, when all I had to worry about was Tony. But it won't help us now. Like it won't help them!"

If anything, it would help our enemies, if the council decided to hide its collective head in the sand until a hungry god came along and ripped it off. No wonder Mom had been pissed. She must have looked over the group and wondered what had happened to the kind she'd fought. Or maybe she'd wished she'd left a few of the scarier ones alive.

"You look furious," Pritkin said, watching me.

"I just—I can't understand not fighting for your life—for what you want. Just giving up—"

A corner of his mouth quirked. "No. You would not understand that. You never stop trying, do you?"

"What else is there?"

"Despair. Hopelessness. Anger. Depression."

"But those don't get you anywhere."

He huffed out something that might have been a laugh, only it didn't sound happy. "No. They don't."

I drank beer and didn't say anything. Because I got the impression that we suddenly weren't talking about the council anymore. But I wasn't sure, since I couldn't see his expression.

The proprietor had apparently not trusted scent to drum up enough business, and had draped strands of twinkly lights around the front of the shop. As a result, darkness shaded Pritkin's eyes, which were above the lights, but under the shade of the awning. But cheerful, incongruous colors splashed everywhere else—green over a cheekbone, amber along a toned arm, rose across his neck. It looked like he was swimming in rainbow water.

He ducked his head slightly, and his eyes caught the light when he moved, flashing brilliant emerald. "How do you do that?"

"Do what?"

"Stay so . . . hopeful. Optimistic. *Certain.* You grew up around some of the most cynical creatures outside of demons. You saw the way they view the world, always hungry, always scheming. How their every waking thought is about improving their position in some way—"

"They'd say that it also improves their families' position, and their allies'," I reminded him. "Vampires aren't selfless in the human sense, maybe, but they take care of their own. Sometimes better than humans, since it hurts their power base if they don't."

"Which is my point. It always comes back to them somehow. And you grew up in that, were steeped in it, and yet . . . you came for me."

"Yeah, well, you know. That wasn't entirely . . ."

"Wasn't entirely what?"

"I just meant, I got something out of it, too, so you can't say—"

"What did you get?"

"I—we covered that, remember?"

"No. No, I don't remember. I thought we decided that you could find many other people—"

"Not *many.* I don't know too many half-demon war mages."

"—others, then. To assist you in my place. Such as Caleb. Or Jonas."

"Yes, well . . . that's . . ."

"But no, that's not quite right, either, is it?" He tilted his head. "You said something else . . . something about needing me, for me. What did you mean?"

"I meant—I mean, well, we're friends—"

"Are we? Are we friends?"

"I—yes. What else would you, uh . . . "

"I am not sure what I would call it. I had never given it much thought until recently. There did not seem to be a point."

"Yes, yes, exactly. And there's no reason to suddenly—"

"But I suppose I shall have to now, if I am returned, that is. Won't I?"

"Um," I said, and stopped. Because I knew how Pritkin argued. I ought to; it was his favorite hobby. Which would have been fine, except that he was better at it than me. And right now he was going in for the kill.

I could tell because of the voice, which had gotten faster and sharper, but also because of the expression. He'd moved slightly, leaning toward me, with one elbow resting on the counter propping up the hand he'd tucked under his chin. It was his boyish look, which he got when he was pleased, and that usually meant that someone else was about to be in trouble. And there was only one someone else here.

Someone who was employing tactic number two hundred and fifteen in dealing with irascible war mages, and changing the subject.

"I was wondering about something you said earlier, too," I told him, after finishing off my beer. "You said you don't come here by choice. Does that mean you don't miss anything about it?"

Normally Pritkin got annoyed when I changed the subject on him—or when I tried. Because half the time, he called me on it. But he didn't this time, and he didn't seem upset. He even smiled slightly, a strange little half smile that I didn't like at all.

"What would I miss?"

"I don't know. Your father's court was . . . well, parts of it were beautiful—"

"Many things are beautiful. Few are also good." He moved a step closer.

"Yes, I . . . I guess," I said, backing up slightly. "But it must have been hard, turning your back on all that wealth and power and . . ."

"There are only masters and slaves there. I did not wish to be either." Another step.

"Well, no. But there must have been other things. I mean, he's a demon lord—"

"There is nothing I want that he can give me."

"But . . . but you could rule there. You could have anything you want—"

"Not anything," Pritkin said softly, and my back bumped Formica.

I appeared to have run out of room. And he was still looking at me. But I couldn't read his expression again, only this time, that wasn't due to the lighting. I just wasn't familiar with that particular—

He's probably thinking how crappy I look, I told myself hurriedly, and that I'm going to have to go back in front of the council like this, and that it isn't going to help our chances any, and damn, I wish I'd thought to grab one of those purloined Augustine dresses before heading out, not that it would probably have survived everything that happened in between, but you never know, and I wonder if any of these shops sell something that might be—

A thumb reached out and wiped away something at the corner of my mouth.

My thoughts froze.

I should laugh, I thought blankly. Grab a napkin, say what a mess I'd managed to make . . . only I couldn't. I couldn't seem to move.

And that was stupid, because clearly, he was just being nice. He was trying to make sure I didn't go back in there and embarrass myself more than I was probably already going to. He was just trying—

The thumb began to move along my lower lip, slowly tracing its fullness. And my breath sped up, even as it tried to catch. Which should have choked me, but somehow got tangled up in my chest instead. To the point that it hurt.

This wasn't—we didn't—not that he—

"I did have regrets these past six months," he told me quietly. "I found it a curse as much as a blessing, all that time to think. About the things I could have said, that I should have told you . . ."

"John!" The voice came from a distance. He ignored it.

"I thought I was sparing you, but I think I was really trying to spare myself. For a long time, I was almost grateful for my father's curse. As hard as it was, it made some things simpler. I didn't have to worry; I didn't have to *risk*—"

"John!" the voice came again.

Pritkin glanced up, grimaced, and then looked back down at me again. And his expression was fiercer than I'd seen it in a while. "But somewhere in the last six months, I realized that, after what happened to my wife, I returned to earth, yes. But I didn't return to *life*. I was as much a prisoner there as I was at court. Not just because of the curse, but because I wouldn't allow myself—"

"John!" The voice was closer now. It was Caleb's.

Pritkin said something under his breath and grabbed my arms. "Cassie, I don't know how this will turn out. With the council, there's no way to know. But whatever happens, I want you to know, I want you to remember, that I'm *glad* you came back for me. I'm glad I had a chance to know you. I'm glad—"

"John!" Caleb grabbed his arm. "We have to go—now. They're calling for you—they have a ruling!"

"Of course they do," Pritkin said. "Of course they bloody do!"

And, apparently, you don't keep the demon high

council waiting. We left the rest of the food and jogged back down the sidewalk, Pritkin and Caleb grim and silent, Casanova bleary-eyed and staggering, and me—I don't know what I looked like, but my head was spinning like a tornado.

Not because of what Pritkin had said; I couldn't think about that now. But because they had to let him go. They *had* to. After everything Mother had said, they couldn't just . . . could they?

I didn't know. They were like a million years old, but that only made it harder to guess. I had enough trouble figuring out how centuries-old vampires thought. I had zero chance of predicting the behavior of creatures who made them look like children. All I knew was that they *really* hadn't liked Mother, and as her child, I wasn't any more popular. As Pritkin was a repeat offender, as far as they were concerned. But like Mom had said, he was just one guy, and if they weren't going to cough up an army, the least they could do—

And then we were back, coming in the front doors at the same time that the double ones to the council chamber burst open. That was sort of a surprise—I'd thought they were the type to expect *us* to come to *them*, not the other way around. But the blond demon with the pleasant voice was coming toward us, and his hand was extended and there was a smile on his face. And that looked—dear God, it looked—Caleb said something, an expletive but there was a lungful of relief behind it. And I turned to him for a second, hugging his arm. Because we'd done it, finally, we'd *done* it—

And then someone was shoving me into Caleb, brutally hard, enough that we both went staggering. And there was a sound, new and deafeningly loud. And a cry, of such tortured anguish that it cut through the air, spinning me on my feet even as I fell, pulling my head up—

To see Pritkin, lit for a moment by harsh spell light, silhouetted against another explosion. But this time, there was no outrunning it.

His mouth was open, but it wasn't moving, and neither was the rest of him. For a second, he hung suspended in air, caught halfway through a jump, as if I'd managed to freeze time. But I hadn't; I knew I hadn't. I could still see dust motes turning lazily in the spell light behind him, golden yellow and burning like the sun —

And then it engulfed him and he fell, still motionless, to the floor, his father rushing to grab him, another of those keening cries coming from that usually cynical mouth.

Pandemonium was breaking out between guards and council members, and people were jostling and bumping and stepping on me as I pushed and shoved my way forward, and then I was kneeling by Pritkin, grabbing him, screaming at Rosier, "What happened? What *happened*?"

"What happened?" Green eyes blazed into mine, bright with grief and incandescent with hate. "What happened is that you killed my son!"

Chapter Thirty-three

Half an hour later, I was back in my hotel suite in Vegas, and staring at another scene of carnage. It felt unreal, like the one I'd just left. It felt impossible.

"It happened shortly after you left us," Jonas said. "We only managed to obtain the images a few moments ago."

I tried to look like I was paying attention as he said something else I didn't hear. His voice was fading in and out, like a distant loudspeaker in a high wind. And even when I could hear the words, they sometimes didn't make sense.

Like the scenes in my head.

I shoved Rosier away and grabbed the too-limp body. Pritkin's head dropped back, the short blond strands falling against my arm, soft, too soft without whatever product he usually used on them. Wrong. Like the body, so horribly still, or the face, lacking wit or anger or those weird flashes of humor—

Or anything.

"No." I felt my skin ice over.

"It was a bomb, obviously," Jonas said. "Likely a number of them. The wards had been tampered with. We're still searching for the exact cause."

Time rippled around us and Rosier stuttered, like a fig-ure on an old TV screen flooded with static. But my power didn't work right in the Shadowland; it never had. The time distortion fizzled out after only a few seconds, leav-ing Caleb and me staring at each other.

Jonas was looking at me, so I nodded. I'd seen the mansion that housed the Pythian Court once before. Mircea had taken me there to get a glimpse of my mother when she was still the heir. It had been a beauti-ful Georgian building, lit up for the party that had been taking place that night, the creamy white columns and elegant brick facade bathed in a warm golden glow.

It looked a little different now.

It was raining in London, which is where the images of the court were coming from, via some spell I didn't care about, but which had turned the French doors to my balcony into a strangely chopped-up movie screen. It didn't matter. The scene rippling across the beveled glass panes and luxe door pulls wasn't one I wanted to see any better.

Jonas was watching the salvage efforts, looking strangely calm. I didn't know if that was because he'd seen it all in his long decades with the Circle, and another crime scene just didn't faze him. Or if he was trying to shield me.

Either way, I wished I had his detachment.

But the rain-soaked, fire-gutted building was hard to take. Although not nearly as much as the body bags, so many and so small, laid out on the sidewalk. They were getting wet, rain beading and then running off the plastic coverings, although there wasn't any choice. There were too many of them to be taken away all at once, with more being drawn out of the wreckage all the time. It had been big, this court I'd never seen, these girls, sworn to my ser-vice, who I'd never even met. It had been . . . big . . .

"Help him!" I told Caleb, who was already muttering something that surged over both of us, making my skin crawl from the power behind it.

But that's all it did.

Caleb cursed, and jerked Pritkin away, shoving me back when I would have grabbed him again. He pushed him down to the floor and put a hand to Pritkin's chest, snarling something that made the too-still body shudder, almost like he was coming around. Until the magic faded and Pritkin fell back against the lobby's beige carpet again, unmoving.

"Turn it off," Marco said gruffly. He wasn't looking at the scene, although I doubted it affected him any more than it did Jonas. Marco had seen things through the years that would make a veteran war mage blanch; a bunch of anonymous bodies already zipped away in bags weren't likely to turn his stomach.

No, as usual, he was looking out for me. Or trying to. And I appreciated it, but I didn't want it.

I wanted to see this.

"Where did it start?" I asked hoarsely, trying to identify one part of the wreckage that looked worse than the others, something that might indicate an origin point. But the building was hardly a building anymore, with a blackened crater in the center that still steamed despite the gentle rain. There were pieces across the street, pieces stabbed through surrounding buildings, and so much broken glass in the road that the emergency vehicles had been forced to park well away, to avoid blowing out their tires.

The whole thing looked like the origin point.

No wonder nobody had gotten out.

A human word, savage and angry. Another incantation, strong enough to raise Pritkin's limp body half a foot off the floor, to outline it in pale blue fire. And then another expletive, because that hadn't worked, either.

"Caleb—" I breathed.

"A major curse," Casanova muttered. "I saw it land—"

"Caleb!"

"He isn't responding." Caleb looked up, eyes dark with the same emotions flooding through me.

"Then try something else!"

"I've already put enough magic through him to lift a dozen curses!"

"Cassie?"

I looked up, and realized I'd missed Jonas' answer. And based on his expression, whatever question he had asked after. "What?"

"Leave her alone! Can't you see she needs to rest?" Rhea, I thought vaguely, seemed to have come out of her shell. Her eyes were snapping at Jonas as she handed me some coffee. I guess she'd figured out how to use the pods. Not too surprising; she looked completely unlike the frightened girl I'd come across in the kitchen.

"She will," Jonas said calmly. "But first I must know."

"Know . . . what?" I asked. My lips felt numb.

They were bringing out smaller body bags now, ridiculously small. They couldn't have belonged to initiates. They looked like they'd barely fit a child of five.

"The nursery," Rhea snarled, and okay. Timid girl was definitely MIA. She was gripping the mug so tightly I was afraid she was going to break it and spill scalding coffee all over herself. It didn't look like she'd have cared. I didn't think I'd ever seen a purer form of hate on any face.

Well, maybe one.

"Where do you think you're taking him?"

"Away from you!" Rosier snarled, his face white with grief. If I'd ever wondered if he loved his son, I didn't now. *"Away from you, where he should have stayed!"*

"Cassie!" Jonas' voice had sharpened. "I really must know if you've seen anything, anything at all, that might help us."

"About this?" I shook my head. "No—"

"Not about this. About *Ares*."

"What?" I looked up, confused, and tried to remember what we'd been talking about. But it didn't matter, since the answer was the same. "I haven't had a vision about anything."

"Even in the tarot?"

"No. That is, the Star card showed up, but . . ."

"But . . . ?"

"It lied."

"How can this be the will of the council?" Caleb demanded. *"Did you hear nothing Artemis said?"*

But the council was already leaving, the guards holding us back. They did not explain themselves to mere mortals. They'd killed him, and they wouldn't even tell us why.

"Answer me!" Caleb said, because no one had ever said he lacked courage.

And then one hesitated, and slowly turned. The very last one I'd have expected. The one Mother had called Adra.

The one who had killed him.

"They heard," Adra said quietly. *"More than you, war mage."*

"Meaning what?"

The demon's eyes found mine. "They heard the final gambit in a great game."

"Goddamnit, Jonas!" That hadn't been Marco or the girl, but rather the tall witch with the short gray hair, whose name I'd forgotten.

At least, I had until Jonas looked up, frowning. "Do you know, Evelyn, I really do not need—"

"It's not your needs I'm interested in," she said, getting in Jonas' face. There was a war mage at his side, not Caleb, but someone I didn't know. Someone I didn't even remember arriving. But he made a small movement, and the witch bared her teeth at him. "Feeling lucky, sonny?"

"I don't need luck," he said, very low.

"No, but considering who you work for, I assume skill is too much to—"

I stopped listening.

"What are you talking about?" Caleb looked like he wanted to put a fist through Adra's face.

I didn't. I just wanted Pritkin to move. Wanted to see

the chest go up and down. Wanted to see him open those eyes and glare at me about something, anything . . .

"I am talking about the fact that the being you call Artemis had won an entire universe for herself by her treachery, for she was the only great power left. She had ensured that by hunting the greatest of my kind to extinction, and then by exiling her own people. But she made one miscalculation. She left herself too weak to capitalize on her victory."

"You lie!"

"Why? For telling you what you do not wish to hear?" Adra asked, unfazed. "The one you call Artemis may have founded your order, war mage, but make no mistake. It was to serve her needs, not yours."

Caleb turned away with a curse and Adra looked at me. "We don't know what went wrong. Perhaps the spell took more energy than she'd planned, perhaps her fellow gods fought harder than she'd expected. All we know is that the aftermath left her vulnerable, and she was forced into hiding. And she was good at it, for we sought her, those of us she had wronged. And while we did not find her, we ensured that she could not surface, could not risk feeding on our lower orders, could not regain her great strength. We might not be able to bring her to justice, but we could force her to fade into obscurity among the humans, to die alone and unsung, bitterly brooding over how close she came."

I'd been bending over Pritkin, but at that I looked up at Adra through a veil of tumbled hair. "You're twisting everything."

"But we were wrong about one thing," he told me steadily. "We underestimated, by far, how long that process of decline would take. Just when we were sure she must have died, just when we thought ourselves safe at last, she formed another plan. A plan involving a child."

"I want a word with the Pythia," the older witch said. It didn't sound like a request.

"If Cassie wishes to speak with you, she may, when

we are finished here," Jonas informed her. "Perhaps you can agree that stopping the return of an ancient menace is a little more important than whatever minor issue—"

"Yes, *minor*," she said. "Do let's worry about the politics before we concern ourselves with silly women's issues. But if I may remind you, it was a *woman* who brought you this information, *women* who assisted in getting her here, women who died tonight!"

"I am not going to do this with you, Evelyn. Really I'm not," Jonas said, little spots of color appearing on his fair cheeks. "This is not an example of misogyny despite your strange determination to make it one. This is—"

"—*ridiculous*," I said, looking at Adra in bewilderment.

"*Is it? A child who would be half human. A child who could feed here, on earth, as the gods could not. A child who could be hidden in the most unlikely of places until she grew up, until she came into her power*—"

"*No! That isn't what*—"

"*A child who could be groomed to succeed to the only power of the gods that remained on earth, and then use it to go back in time, to join forces with a mother who may have lost her strength through the centuries, but none of her cunning*—"

"*I've been fighting the gods*," I told him furiously. "*Not trying to bring one back!*"

"*Of course you have. They are rivals, threats that could challenge and overthrow you. They had to be fought off until you could find her, and bring her here*—"

"*I haven't brought her anywhere!*"

"*You brought her thoughts. You opened a connection in the council's own chamber. Do you have any idea how it felt, to see her again? Standing there, alive and amused—amused—at our consternation, at our shock and fear? To hear her give orders as if no time had passed, as if nothing had changed*—"

"*She was giving advice, not orders. And her thoughts are not* her—"

"But you are in touch with her. You can go back, can find her, whenever you like. You've proven that—"

"And yet she didn't bring her here." That was Caleb's angry voice. *"If Cassie was part of some elaborate scheme, that would have been the first thing she did on becoming Pythia. There's no getting around that!"*

Adra smiled slightly. *"Isn't there? It's clear you were not cut out for the political realm, war mage."*

"You let her go into *hell*," Evelyn said. "Yet you won't let her save her own coven? And when did it become a case of you *letting* the Pythia do anything?"

"We have an understanding with the council," Jonas told her. "And I know a council summons when I see one—just as I know a trap! There was no reason to kill those children, no reason at all, unless it was to force Cassie to come to a place and time of her enemy's choosing—"

"What if it was? Whatever the cause, those children are just as dead—"

"And that is a tragedy. But losing Cassie would be a greater one. And at any rate, one does not willy-nilly corrupt the timeline!"

"You and I corrupted it," I reminded him numbly. "We went back—"

"To save a world. Not a handful!"

So where do you draw the line? I wondered. At a million? A thousand? One?

Because right now one seemed a terrible loss to me.

"And what does that mean?" Caleb snapped.

"The council suspects that she is Artemis' daughter in more ways than one," Rosier said spitefully, answering before Adra could. *"That she decided, after meeting my son, after learning not only who he is but what, that she no longer needed her mother. That with his help, she could mine the demon lords for all the power necessary to fight off her rivals, to secure her control, to rule herself—"*

"I don't want to rule!" I choked. *"I didn't even want to be Pythia."*

"And you never should have been!"

"We were talking about the information Ms. Silvanus has brought us," Jonas said, looking at Rhea over his glasses.

"What information?" I asked, trying to force my attention back to the here and now, when all it wanted to do was go back. To find a solution. To make it right.

But some things don't have a solution.

"The incubus has been regressed," Adra told me. *"It is an old method of execution that sends the soul back through his or her lifetime, into previous versions of himself. When his soul reaches the beginning of its life journey, it will wink out of existence, and the body will die."*

"That's a bunch of bullsh—" Caleb began.

"It isn't," I said, thinking of Jules. And for a second, my heart sped up as I wondered if I could do the same thing for Pritkin. But there was a difference. Jules' body had been changed, but his soul hadn't. It had been in there, encased in a fleshy tomb, but present. Pritkin's wasn't. And it was his soul that had been cursed.

Adra had chosen his weapon perfectly.

Rhea was looking at me, her eyes huge and pained. She didn't say anything, but she didn't need to. I knew that expression. I'd seen it in the mirror once or twice. "You had a vision," I said.

Huge brown eyes met mine. "I never have visions," she whispered. "Well, almost never, and never about anything important. It's why I'm still a senior initiate and not an acolyte. I help—I helped—to train the children, the new initiates."

"But this time you saw something."

"I saw Ares," she said, looking off into the distance. "Towering over a field in front of a storm-racked sky. He was here, in this world, fighting our forces. And we were losing . . . badly."

"Was anyone else with him?" Jonas asked sharply.

"What?"

"Any other gods?"

She shook her head. "I only saw him. But it was so quick—just a flash. I was going upstairs with some cold medicine. One of the children had arrived with the sniffles and had given a nasty head cold to half the dorm, and it just . . . hit me. All of a sudden, I was somewhere else and seeing these terrible things, and there was lightning and thunder, and people were screaming and trees were crashing to the ground and the sky flooded red and . . . and I dropped the tray."

"I probably would have, too," I told her, because she was white and shaking again, her voice barely above a whisper.

"Yes, but the stairs are marble; everyone heard," she said, looking at me with so much pain in her eyes that I finally got it; I wasn't the only one feeling responsible for tonight. "And I was so upset . . . the adepts made me tell them, and at the time I didn't realize . . . I couldn't see any reason not to . . . until I saw. They were happy. They were *pleased* about it. Then they saw me looking at them, and changed their expressions. But I knew, I'd *seen*—"

"And so you came to tell me."

She swallowed. "No. I should have done, but there were such rumors about you, they were saying . . . It wasn't until the coronation that I realized—you couldn't be what they said. The power had gone to you, the Circle had accepted you, and then at the coronation, you killed the Spartoi. You killed him!"

And suddenly, I knew why she looked familiar. "You were there."

She nodded again. "I saw you, but I—it was obvious you were trying to be inconspicuous and I didn't—"

"But you knew who I was."

She looked surprised. "Of course."

"Even though someone else was pretending to be me?"

She blinked again, like I wasn't making much sense.

"Yes, but I knew that wasn't you. There was no power, no aura, no—" She waved it away. "It was obvious."

So much for my great disguise.

"But the others didn't see you, and by the time I got away from them, you had disappeared. And then when I saw you again—" She gave another graceful little hand flutter, maybe because she didn't know a polite way of saying "you were battling a Spartoi in your birthday suit and almost getting fried." "But then the vampires took you away, and I didn't know how to reach you—"

"So you went to the covens."

"Yes. My cousin—"

"And the covens brought you to me."

"Yes."

"So you could tell me what? What are they planning?"

She shook her head. "I don't know, I don't know! I tried following the adepts around, to let them think I agreed with them, hoping to find out more. . . . But I'm not an actress, and they'd seen my face that night. They didn't believe me!"

I didn't tell her it was okay, because it wouldn't have helped. She didn't look like a girl who needed platitudes. She looked like a girl who needed something to do.

I knew the feeling.

"I'll go back," I told Rosier. "I'll stop the spell from being laid—"

"You will be prevented," Adra said gently. "That is why it was done here, to preclude such a possibility."

"Then give me the counterspell! I'll go back in time, I'll find his soul—" He just looked at me. "Pritkin did nothing wrong! If you have to hurt someone, hurt me!"

"They won't hurt you. They need you," Rosier choked. "But my son . . ."

Adra didn't agree, but he didn't refute it, either. And the worst part was, there was no hate in his eyes, no malice. This had been a policy decision to him, nothing more. A threat had been identified; a threat had been removed. But to me . . .

It felt like the end of the world.

"How many acolytes are there at present?" Jonas asked.

"It varies," Rhea said, looking at me. "Most of the court is composed of junior initiates, who have just been brought in—young girls who have been identified with unusual promise. And senior initiates, that's most of us, who have training but carry none of the power. The adepts are only a small group, chosen from the most gifted of the senior initiates. After Myra's death, there were only five."

I just looked at her for a moment, sure the state of my head right now was messing with me. But no. I must be hearing things. "Come again?"

"Did I—was something not clear?" she asked, starting to look worried.

"I really hope so," I said tightly. "You said the senior initiates don't carry the Pythian power. So by implication . . . the adepts do?"

She nodded. "They have to, for training purposes. They all receive basic instruction in the Pythian arts, and the one who masters them the best is often selected as the heir. It also allows for circumstances when an heir dies or is deposed. There has to be someone else who can take over, who has been trained. They are also available to help the Pythia, in times of need."

"In times of need?" I looked at Jonas.

He didn't say anything, but he took off his glasses and polished them, despite the fact that he'd just done that thirty seconds ago.

"If a mission is more hazardous than she feels would be prudent to handle alone," Rhea explained.

I continued to look at Jonas.

"Yes, well," he said briskly. "We already knew there was a problem with the court, thanks to Ms. Silvanus' testimony—"

"Jonas."

"You had enough on your plate as it was, Cassie! There was no reason to add more—"

"There was no reason to tell me *there's a whole group of Myras running around*?"

"It is hardly that," he argued. "The acolytes only have a small fraction of the heir's power, barely enough for training—"

"Jonas."

"And Myra was a traitor. Until now, there has been no reason to believe the rest of the court was the same, much less that they would attack their own coven—"

"Jonas!" He stopped, and looked at me. And something on my face must have registered, because he stopped whatever it was he'd been about to say. "Never keep something like this from me again. Never."

I got up and shoved through the French doors, out onto the balcony. Jonas didn't follow me, which was fortunate. I honestly don't know what I'd have done if he had.

It had been this way my whole life: people keeping things from me. Sometimes for what they thought were good reasons, sometimes, most times, because knowledge was power, and the less I had of the former, the less I'd be able to challenge them for the latter. Tony, the Circle, the senate, Mircea . . . someone was always working to keep me in the dark.

But there were things in the dark that could bite you if you didn't know they were there. If you couldn't avoid them because you didn't even know they existed. Knowledge wasn't just about power; it was about survival, mine and that of everyone who depended on me.

And I was heartily sick of the dark.

Evelyn came out onto the balcony. She didn't say anything. But her wrist was resting on the railing, not far from where my hand was clenching on it convulsively. And in hers . . .

It *had* been a wand, I thought, watching her twirl it expertly, back and forth, between her fingers.

Our eyes met.

"I think it's time the girls and I were going," she said. And then she just looked at me, gray eyes into blue.

I licked my lips.

"I'll walk you out," I said hoarsely.

Chapter Thirty-four

The mansion was dark and quiet when we shifted in to the front hall of the Pythian Court. London is seven hours ahead of Vegas, which would make it somewhere around midnight, and I had jumped us back as far as I could. Which wasn't very damned far, because carrying five has a cost, and it is high.

I dropped to my knees, staggered at the power drain. "Lady—"

"I'm fine," I told Rhea, harshly enough that she jerked back her hand.

I stayed down for a moment, watching the marble tile of Agnes' front hall pulse in and out, wondering if my eyeballs were about to pop. And cursing inwardly, because my time sense had kicked in to tell me what I'd already suspected. I'd had to drop the time shift earlier than I'd wanted or risk rupturing something.

At most, we had fifteen minutes.

Which meant I didn't have time for this, I told myself severely, and got up.

The place looked about the same as the last time I'd been here. Shafts of what were probably streetlights, but which looked like silver moonbeams, slanted through high, neoclassical windows. There was lots of marble, some paneling that looked like it might be genuine mahogany, and a couple statues of Grecian-looking women holding jugs. A staircase, the one where Rhea had had her vision I assumed, ran up to a landing.

A chandelier tinkled softly overhead, blown about by the freshening wind through a transom. It sounded impossibly loud to my straining ears, like the world's most expensive wind chime. Nothing else moved.

I found that less than reassuring.

Rhea seemed to think the same. "There should be guards," she said worriedly. "The Circle—it keeps people here, all the time."

"They're here," Evelyn said grimly, from behind me. I turned around to see her over near the main doors, where a figure in a leather trench coat lay slumped behind a potted plant.

I'd been about to ask how he'd died, but then she rolled him over. And I didn't have to. The skin was gray and papery, and crumpled into unrecognizability, since the flesh underneath had mostly withered away. It pulled back the mouth into a silent scream, left the eyes sunken into the head and the bones brittle enough that several cracked just from the gentle movement.

A ring dropped off a wasted finger, to clatter against the floor, and Rhea made a small sound. "McClaren," she whispered. "One of his granddaughters . . . She's a new initiate. . . ."

"Adepts," Evelyn cursed. "I was hoping Marsden was wrong."

"Question is, are they still here?" Beatrice asked.

"They shouldn't be." That was Jasmine. "A bomb destroyed the building, not an attack. If the adepts had any sense, they fled after setting it."

I swallowed. Maybe cutting things close hadn't been such a bad idea. But Beatrice didn't seem convinced.

A streetlight was shining through a window, glinting off her chains and turning her Afro faintly blue. And highlighting the frown on her face. "Then why attack the Circle's men? The adepts were already inside and free to move about. Why involve the patrols?"

"If they were messing about with the wards, they might have been nervous," Jasmine offered. "Wanted them out of the way—"

"And speaking of wards, why didn't we set any off when we came in just now?"

"You're with me," Rhea said, but she sounded doubtful. "But that should only have kept the general alarm from sounding. There should still have been somebody here by now, to check. . . ."

"Hence the attacks on the corpsmen," Jasmine said.

"All of them?" Beatrice demanded. "And how did a group of untrained girls manage that, Pythian power or no?"

"Took 'em by surprise," Evelyn said, fingering her wand. "Must have."

"And again I say, all of them? You know what they're like: suspicious, jumpy buggers, every one. And yet—"

"Let's just get the kids out," I said, glancing around. My skin was crawling. "Where are they?"

I didn't have to ask twice. Rhea had been vibrating, just standing there, and now she took off for the stairs. "Wait!" Evelyn called, and put a hand on my arm.

"We have less than fifteen minutes," I told her.

But she didn't answer. "Beatrice."

The little witch already had her staff up. One of the little indentations that I'd mistaken for hollows in the wood was glowing with a pale blue light, like a flashlight. Which I didn't understand the point of, since we could already see—

Nothing, compared to when she brought it down on the floor, hard. And a pulse came out of the bottom, like a wave heading to the beach. Or maybe like a stone thrown into a pond, because this one was moving outward in all directions, highlighting mop marks on the floor, dust in the corners, cracks here and there in the grout between tiles. Like a black light at a crime scene, it showed everything hidden.

Including the feet of a bunch of men arrayed along the walls.

"I hate when I'm right," Evelyn muttered, and then shoved me at the door. "Go!"

I hit the floor instead as the paneling bulged outward in the shape of bodies, dozens of them. And then melted away entirely as the spell ran up their legs, stripping off the camouflage as it went. War mages, and not ours, I realized, as they peeled off the walls and started slinging spells that sparked off the shield Jasmine had thrown up, barely in time.

But one had gotten through, a split second before the shield snapped closed, strobing the room in poisonous green. It missed, thanks to a curse I hadn't even seen Evelyn hurl, which hit the thrower at almost the same moment he moved. But it took out the transom and most of the front door with it, showering us with glass.

And finally sent wards screaming through the house.

"Well, the kids are up," Beatrice said as Evelyn turned on me.

"Damn it, are you deaf?" she demanded.

"If I leave, and the adepts show up, you die," I said, fumbling with the dead war mage's coat. And trying not to breathe because it was covered in flaky white dust that flew up everywhere as I pushed and pulled and broke him to pieces trying to get it off. But I had to have it. The coats were spelled to resist assaults, and I was about to get assaulted unless I was way luckier than usual.

"You heard Zara," Evelyn said. "They're probably already gone!"

It took me a second to realize she meant the witch I'd been calling Jasmine. "And if they're not? You may be good—"

"We're better than good."

"But you can't fight someone who can manipulate time!"

She started to answer, but the shield shattered as a dozen spells hit it all at once. And then Beatrice brought up her staff again. A different hollow glowed this time, a dark, bloody red. And all the lights around the room suddenly shattered, showering the floor with sparks and sending flames running up the walls.

"Nice parlor trick, old woman," a mage said, grabbing her.

The staff came down again.

And lines of flame tore out of every light, carving a pentagram of fire in the air and spearing half a dozen mages through with flame.

"Glad you liked it," she told him as the man collapsed at her feet.

But while it cleared our general area, it didn't do much else. Because mages were running at us from all sides now, rushing into the room from where I guess they'd been hiding, not knowing where we'd come in. But they knew it now, and we had to—

Hit the floor again.

Zara muttered something low and vicious, and the witches jerked me down beside them just as the windows all blew out. The curtains billowed inward and then broke off to fly across the room, and what felt and sounded a lot like a hurricane roared through the house. Mirrors shattered, the chandelier whipped about like a crazed thing, statues toppled over. And half a dozen mages who hadn't gotten shields up in time went flying. But others just hunkered down, shield bubbles dotting the room, waiting it out.

Because yeah.

I didn't think she was going to be able to keep that up for long, either.

"If they planted the bombs, they're not here," Evelyn yelled, to be heard over the roar of the storm. "This was likely a trap. The old man was right—they're after you!"

"You were right, too," I panted, still struggling to free the coat. "They're willing to kill a few dozen children to get to me."

Evelyn swore. "I can't protect you and help the girls, and they can't take this many on their own!"

"Then don't protect me," I said as the wind died and the coat came free with a sickening crunch, both at the same moment.

Shields popped everywhere as mages surged back to their feet. We were about to get overrun, and the witches couldn't cast and shield at the same time, and letting a bunch of mages get to point-blank range wasn't smart. Of course, neither was this, I thought, grabbing them and shifting all four of us to where Rhea was flattened against the stairs, halfway up, the thin bubble of her shield rippling in the still-strong winds.

And then collapsing entirely as a bolt of purple flame hit it.

I threw myself on top of her, the coat covering both of us, but it wasn't enough. Another curse hit, and spelled or no, the coat had aged along with its occupant. I felt something lash my back, a thin line of fire along the weakened back seam, and screamed even as I shifted.

And landed in the middle of a bunch of mages at the top of the stairs, who were heading down now that the hurricane had tapered off to a tropical storm.

And then tripping and falling as we shifted into the middle of them.

Literally, in Rhea's case. She'd ended up welded to a mage through the skirt of her dress, which was now bisected by a heavy leather coat—and the leg behind it. She jerked away, and he screamed, which only made her jerk harder. And then she was grabbed by another mage and slung to the side—

And the man's leg came off at the thigh.

Because flesh and bone don't react well to being split by a swath of embroidered linen.

Blood spewed everywhere, coating surrounding mages and splattering me. And sending Rhea, who had obviously not had this as part of her training, into a frenzy. She tore away from her attacker, kicked another into the railing and fled up the remaining stairs, none of the mages trying to stop her since she already appeared mortally wounded.

Or maybe because they were lunging at me.

And there was nothing I could do, because I couldn't shift again, not right now, maybe not ever. But it didn't matter because triple bolts of something red and lethal tore past me, one bolt close enough to singe my hair. And ripped holes through the mages left above me.

And then I was being pulled up the stairs by three maniacs, who were cursing everything in sight. And getting cursed right back as the mages in the hall figured out we weren't there anymore, maybe because a bunch of their fellows had just fallen on their heads. But they were behind us, and the landing and a hallway were ahead, the one Rhea had just disappeared into.

Something hit the wall beside me, leaving a heavy scorched mark, and something else lashed my back, turning my arm numb even through the coat's protection. But then we were in the hall, and Jasmine—Zara—was throwing a shield over the end of it, like a plug.

Which sent three mages staggering back when they ran straight into it.

We pelted down the hall, where small people in white nightgowns were already spilling out of several rooms. Or maybe it was their day-wear, since who could tell the difference? But it looked like Rhea hadn't lost it as much as I'd thought, because she appeared at the door to a room down the hall, breathing a little funny, but with a child in each hand.

And screamed, "Behind you!"

Damn, that hadn't lasted long, I thought, and hit the floor, just as something blew out a light on the wall beside me. Glass scattered and children screamed, but to my amazement, they didn't run amok. Not when Rhea snapped out a command and started them moving in orderly lines down the hall, even as the witches cursed the shit out of everything behind them.

But the odds were ridiculous, and we were getting tired. The next time Zara tried a shield, it was popped almost immediately, under a barrage of spells so thick it looked like a miniature sun had gone off in the hallway. The only thing that saved us was the fact that this wasn't one of those made-to-look-old kinds of places, but the real deal. And the hall was narrow, not allowing us to be rushed by everyone at once.

But it let through enough, more than enough. Zara took a hit to the arm, screaming half in pain and half in fury. And something hit me, catching one side of my coat on fire that didn't go out. I had to shed my only protection or go up in flames with it, throwing it down the hall at the mages.

They batted it away, but it distracted the ones in front for half a second, which was long enough for Evelyn to throw a spell—not at them, but at the ceiling. And there was enough power behind it to bring half the hallway down, cracking it along the center and spilling a load of billowing plaster and falling debris on our pursuers. Along with a bunch of water pipes, dripping and then spewing on their heads, which didn't seem to bother them much.

Until Beatrice sent a plume of flame down the hall, and turned the water to blistering-hot steam.

And it seems that even dark mages have an aversion to being boiled to death. Some got up shields, but more panicked and tried to turn around, crashing into those behind them. Creating enough of a temporary bottleneck that we were able to get the last of the kids out of the dorm rooms, pushing them down the hall as fast as small legs could move.

I didn't know where we were going, but everyone else

seemed to, with the older kids helping the younger. Down the hall and around a bend, to a back stairway. Which would have been great, except that it was as narrow as the hall that fed into it.

I stared at it, not even needing to do any mental math. And the looks on the faces of the witches would have told me the truth, even if it hadn't been obvious. I didn't know how long it was going to take all those kids to get down all those stairs, but it worked out to more than we had.

A lot more.

And then the dark mages were coming again, around the bend, with shields initially, and then dropping them to fire when they realized the truth. A mass of spells like the one they'd done before, that had shattered Zara's shield, only this time, we didn't have a shield. But the spells stopped anyway.

Or, to be exact, they slowed to a crawl, because I didn't have enough power left to stop them completely.

"You have six minutes," I told them. "Get them as far away as you can."

Beatrice nodded, grasping Zara, who was panting and shaking and pale as a sheet, firmly by the arm. But Evelyn just looked at me. "And what are you going to do?"

"Buy you time," I choked, because talking was . . . hard right now.

"I'll stay with you," Evelyn said staunchly.

"That . . . wouldn't be a great idea."

"And why not?"

I was panting now, my vision blurring. And the stupid woman was still talking to me. "Because I won't . . . have enough . . . to shift you out."

"And you'll have enough to shift you?"

Okay, maybe not so dumb.

"I'll be okay."

"You'll be dead! And then the power will go to one of those miserable adepts—"

"No, it won't," Rhea said. She'd wisely sent the older children down first, and was now shepherding the smaller. But she paused for a second, to look back at me.

"And how do you know that?" Evelyn demanded. "They're next in line!"

"Because the power chooses the Pythia," Rhea said, fierce pride on her face as she looked at me. "It was what you needed to understand today, what I needed to remember these last weeks. It doesn't just go to the next in line, whoever people think is best. It goes to the actual best, the very best choice out there." She dropped another of those perfect curtsies. "Lady."

I stared at her, and for the first time, and I guessed the last time, I was proud, I was damned proud, that it had come to me.

And then they were gone, Evelyn still complaining, bringing up the rear as the last of the children faded into darkness in front of them. I went to my knees, because it was easier. And because it didn't matter anymore if I looked good, since there was no one to see me but a bunch of guys who were about to die with me.

Because I didn't think they'd be so enthusiastic if the adepts had mentioned what was about to happen to this place. But I had no way to tell them, and no strength to do it if I had. The corridor was dimming even as the spells sped up, noticeably moving now, about the pace a person could walk casually. And painting the floor and ceiling with lines of unnatural spell light.

I watched them come, and thought it was funny. Because they looked strangely familiar. Like the ones in the skies over Rosier's court. Dangerous, but so beautiful. Like the moon-flooded sands of an alien world, like the endless stars in the council chamber, like the flash of attraction in a pair of green eyes.

Pritkin, I thought, feeling gold spangled light on my face. And shut my eyes.

Epilogue

I opened them again in bed, with a blond demon sitting nearby.

I bolted upright and grabbed him, before my eyes focused on the three-piece gray business suit, the thin blond hair, and the cleft he'd added to the chin. The one distinguishing feature in a bland mask to make it easier to pretend that's what he really looked like. Adra, I thought, staring into calm gray eyes.

"So I ended up in hell, after all?" I croaked in disgust.

He smiled. And then apparently decided it deserved better, and laughed. "I think you're safe," he confided as I flopped back against the bed. "I don't know of too many that would volunteer to take you."

I swallowed, because my tongue felt fuzzy. And blinked around at what was either a damned fine illusion, right down to the pinkish stain on the carpet from a glass of wine I'd spilled a week ago, or was my room in Vegas. And I didn't know why anybody would waste an illusion that good on me.

"Why are you here?" I demanded. "Why am I here?"

"You are here due to us pulling you out at the moment your spell collapsed. It was quite close. For a moment, I did not think we were going to manage."

"You pulled me out," I repeated, because that didn't make a lot of sense.

He nodded.

"But . . ." I frowned, trying to think past a massive migraine. "How did you know . . ."

"That you needed assistance?" he asked, leaning back and crossing his legs. "That would have to do with the Seidr spell your mother cast."

"What?"

"The spell that she used to speak with us is one the gods used to communicate with each other. It creates an illusion that many minds can inhabit, similar to what you would term a conference call. Admittedly, I do not think it has been used to dial across time before, but then . . . she was always clever."

"Yes, so?" I asked harshly. Because I'd decided I didn't care.

"Well, it is a very old spell. A very rare spell, since the gods are now gone. Few people these days know how to cast it . . . or how to end it."

That took me a minute, but I got it. "You were spying on me."

"Essentially." At least he didn't try to sugarcoat it. "When you were in council chambers, we noticed the existence of several other Seidr links in your mind. Neither of which you seemed to be aware of, and neither of which you had bothered to close."

"Several—" I stopped, because suddenly a couple of things made sense. "Mircea and Jules."

"I do not know about the vampire. The first bond was tightly closed off; even we could not explore it without risking injury to you."

Mircea, I thought grimly. He had mental gifts he didn't talk about, but which were kind of hard not to notice. I wasn't sure how far they extended, but maybe . . . maybe they'd been enough for him to hang up on his own. Maybe that's also why he'd suddenly gone incommunicado. Finding out your girlfriend was half goddess would be bad enough, without having her suddenly start spying on your brain.

I freaked Mircea out, I thought dizzily.

"But the second," Adra was saying. "Yes, it is to a human named Jules. He has been having rather uncomfortable dreams, of late, thanks to you."

I bet. "So between the time my mother laid the first spell on me at her house, until I actually got to the council, there was a period when I was making other calls on my own, not knowing that's what I was doing?"

"So it would seem. I would wonder why your mother did not better inform you about the spell she planned to use, but . . . I think I know. In any case, we hardly thought someone would deliberately choose to keep open three distinct lines, when even one is somewhat debilitating. It therefore occurred to us that there was a chance you had not been taught about the workings of the spell, and that you would not know to close ours, either."

"But I felt it close. I felt relief—"

"From your mother and most of the council leaving. Only a few of us stayed 'online' with you. The burden was still there, but it was less with fewer minds communicating. After the power you had been forced to channel before, it seemed like relief."

I scowled at him. "So you hoped to do what? Discover what kind of revenge I was planning?"

He sighed. "Cassandra—may I call you Cassandra?"

"No!"

He sighed again. "We have, it would appear, gotten off on—the wrong foot? Is that the term?"

"The wrong—" I just stared at him.

"I'm sure that's right," he said, looking up as if referencing something. "Yes, yes, that is the phrase."

"That is *not* the—"

"But you have to understand our dilemma. Ares and the other gods are actively working to return to earth, something a few of us have been at pains to keep quiet, to avoid a general panic. But you not only made that impossible, but appeared before the entire council demanding an army."

"My mother wanted the—"

"Yes, and that was the point, was it not? Frankly, if our only choice is between Ares and Artemis, we would prefer the former. His skills are formidable, but his movements through the hells are restricted. His return would allow us time to consider . . . extreme measures. Your mother's would not."

"So you killed Pritkin."

"It seemed prudent. Whether you intended to return your mother to her former glory, or to rule in her stead, you would need the incubus. Few are able to transmit power as his line can, and Lord Rosier's antipathy for your mother is well known. I believe he would die before he would help her to regain her strength. But his son . . . we were not so sure of him. Or of you."

"So you spied on me."

"We wanted to know what you would do, once you were deprived of him. Some on the council were pushing for your death as well. But to others of us, that seemed . . . imprudent . . . with the gods attempting to return and your record of opposing them in the past. We required more information."

"Like *what*?"

"We wished to know what you would do without the incubus. Would you try to find another strong enough to replace him? Would you visit your mother again, and formulate a new plan with her? Would you go to some heretofore unknown accomplice and strategize? What would you do?"

"You know what I did!"

"Yes. We know. And, for the first time in more years than I can count, I admit to a feeling of . . . astonishment."

I didn't say anything. I just wished he'd go away. But apparently, ancient demons leave when they want to.

"At first, we did not understand," he told me, still sounding faintly surprised. "We thought you would shift out when the witches had gone. We thought you were . . . grandstanding? Is that the word?"

"Look it up," I told him harshly, and swung my legs out of bed.

"But then, when you did not . . . when we realized you would not, even to save yourself . . . it occurred to us that perhaps it is possible to be too cynical. To forget that not everyone thinks as we do."

And he couldn't have had that epiphany yesterday, I thought, pain twisting in my gut. I felt dizzy with it, aching. As if part of me had been carved out and left gasping on the floor. I wanted to scream, to rant, to throw things. I wanted to cry and never stop. I wanted him gone so I could curl around my hurt.

"You said several reasons?" I rasped.

"Yes. I wished, we wished, to give you this," he said, taking out what looked like an eel-skin wallet, but probably wasn't. And handing me something from inside.

It was a piece of paper. A lined bit of notebook paper, which seemed kind of chintzy for an ancient demon, but I didn't care. Because all it had on it were a bunch of meaningless squiggles.

"What is this?" I demanded, thinking about tearing it up.

"The counterspell."

I looked at it blankly for a moment, and then up at him. I don't know what was on my face, but he searched it for a long time. And then smiled slightly.

"That is what I meant. This is what I had . . . forgotten."

That meant exactly nothing to me. "Why . . ." I cleared my throat. "Why are you doing this?"

"The council believes that it is unlikely that someone who aspired to world-altering power would so easily give up not only her quest, but her life," he told me gently. "And for creatures who could be of no use to her."

"Then . . . this is real." I looked back down at it, my heart starting to beat.

"Yes, it is real. If you can find him before the curse concludes, you can save him. But I warn you—it will not be easy. The spell we used was specifically designed to thwart your power. His soul will pass through each year of his life only once and then never again. Afterward, you can use your abilities to return to the same moment again and again, but you will not find it there."

I clutched the paper in one fist, hearing it crinkle. "But . . . I can't read this."

"It is an ancient tongue; there are few who can. Fortunately, one of them is pleased to accompany you."

"Pleased is not the word I would use," came a scathing voice. Right before something hit me in the solar plexus.

It was a backpack. And holding an identical one was—

"Oh, shit."

"My feelings exactly," Rosier hissed. "Now get dressed. We're running out of time."

"Are there clothes in here?" I demanded.

"Yes—"

"Then I'll dress when we get there. When are we going?"

"Eighteen eighty. And you'd better damned well hope we catch him there."

"Why there?"

"The curse gets progressively faster as it goes on, girl! And I've no desire to go larking around some barbaric era with the likes of—"

Yeah, I thought. He still liked to talk. This was going to be hell.

So why was a smile breaking out over my face?

I clutched the spell in one hand, threw the pack over my back, and grabbed Rosier.

"Shut up," I told him.

And I shifted.

FROM *NEW YORK TIMES* BESTSELLING AUTHOR

Karen Chance

EMBRACE THE NIGHT

Cassandra Palmer may be the world's chief clairvoyant, but she's still magically bound to a master vampire. Only an ancient book called the Codex Merlini possesses the incantation to free Cassie—but harnessing its limitless power could endanger the world...

CURSE THE DAWN

Most of the supernatural power players don't want the independent minded Cassandra Palmer as chief clairvoyant—and they'll stop at nothing to see her six feet under.

The Vampire Senate supports Cassie but their protection comes with a price. And even the vampires will have trouble keeping Cassie alive now that the self-styled god Apollo, the source of the Pythia's power, has it in for her in a big way. To save her life—and the world—Cassie's going to have to face down her creator...

Available wherever books are sold or at
penguin.com

New York Times and *USA Today*
bestselling author

Karen Chance

FURY'S KISS
A Midnight's Daughter Novel

Dorina Basarab is a dhampir—half-human, half-vampire.
Subject to uncontrollable rages, Dory has managed to
maintain her sanity by unleashing her anger on those demons
and vampires who deserve killing.

Together with sexy master vampire Louis-Cesare, Dory will
have to face off with zombie vampires, fallen angels, and the
maddest of mad scientists—if she's going to get to the bottom
of a deadly smuggling ring and somehow stay alive...

"Karen Chance takes her place along with
Laurell K. Hamilton, Charlaine Harris,
MaryJanice Davidson, and J. D. Robb."
—SF Revu

Available wherever books are sold or at
penguin.com

facebook.com/projectparanormalbooks